Gray Riders II

By Ernest Francis Schanilec

Also by Ernest Francis Schanilec

Blue Darkness
The Towers
Danger in the Keys
Purgatory Curve
Gray Riders
Sleep Six
Night Out In Fargo
Ice Lord
Rio Grande Identity

GRAY RIDERS II

Copyright © 2007 by Ernest Francis Schanilec
Second Printing July 2012

All rights reserved.

No part of this book may be reproduced or transmitted in any form or by any means electronic or mechanical, including photocopying, recording, or by any information storage and retrieval system, without permission in writing from the copyright owner.

This book is a work of fiction. Names, characters, places and incidents either are the product of the author's imagination or are used fictitiously, and any resemblance to any actual persons, living or dead, events, or locales is entirely coincidental.

Author - Ernest Francis Schanilec
Publisher - J&M Printing, 407 Hwy 13 East, Gwinner, ND 58040, 1-800-437-1033

International Standard Book Number: 978-1-931914-50-5

Printed in the United States of America

DEDICATIONS

I feel proud to dedicate this novel to all the men and women of the armed services, especially those serving in Iraq. Their sacrifices make us safer from international criminals and terrorists. Thanks, guys and gals, you're doin' great work. Keep it up.

ACKNOWLEDGMENTS

Thanks to my reader-critiques: Joanne Leinen, Grace Schanilec, and Vern and Faye Schanilec. My granddaughter Grace is a high school junior at Northfield, Minnesota.

My son Clayton did the copy-edit, and as usual did a great job. A special thanks to my former high school classmate, Elsie Klitz, from Mansfield Center, Connecticut for proofing Gray Riders II.

Ya' all did a great job.

THE FAMILIES

WALKERS:

George and Angie: Moved off their farm by Order 11.

Sons:

Will, age 21: Killed at Battle of Wilson's Creek.

Carr, age 14: Killed in Tarrytown schoolhouse during skirmish.

Daughters:

Helen, age 21: Living with parents.

Jessica, age 18: Living with parents.

Their land encompassed Tarrytown to the north and the west.

KINGSLEYS:

Martin and Beth: Moved off their farm by Order 11.

Son:

Abel, age 21: Member of Gray Riders.

Daughter:

Sarah, age 16: Living with parents.

Their land bordered the Walker's to the west.

JACKSONS:

Priam and Virgilia

Sons:

Jordon, age 19: Killed during Battle of Hemp Bales.

Elkanah, age 21: Protecting their farm and the Kingsley herd.

Baskhall, age 19: Protecting their farm and the Kingsley herd.

Daughters:

Elisha, age 18: Living on their farm.

Brittany, age 15: Living on their farm.

They lived on a forty acre plot in the northeast corner of the Kingsley land.

HAGGARDS:

Ben and Anna: Killed by hostiles in 1863.

Sons:
Justin, age 20: Member of the Gray Riders.
Jubal, age 15: Member of the Gray Riders.
Daughter:
Clarissa, age 24: Living with husband in Jefferson City.
Their land bordered the Kingsley's.

HASTINGS:
Henry and Emma: Moved to Independence as a result of Order 11
Sons:
Grady, age 22: Leader of the Gray Riders.
Thomas, age 16: Joined the Gray Riders.
Daughter:
Genevieve, age 21: Living with parents.
Their land was on the south side of Tarrytown Road and bordered MacTurley's Woods.

MORTONS:
Samuel and Tullaby: Left the area.
Son:
Sammy, age 22: Left the area.

SUNNERLANDS:
John and Mary: Killed by hostiles in 1861.
Sons:
Lafe, age 25: Riding with the Riders.
Jesse, age 22: Riding with the Riders.
Their land adjoined the Hastings's and was traversed by Bear Creek.

MCGREGORS:
Orly, a widower
Sons:
Mitchell, age 23: Riding with the Riders.
Paul, age 19: Died from wounds suffered at Battle of Hemp Bales.
James, age 16: Riding with the Riders.
Daughter:
Jennifer, age 18: Living with parents.
Their land bordered the Sunnerland's.

1

GRADY HASTINGS CREPT UP THE GRASSY DRAW, peering over tops of waist-high bushes. He turned his head and placed his fore-finger on his lips. Abel Kingsley drew abreast. "What do ya see?" he whispered.

"Looks like redlegs to me," Grady said, handing his glass to Abel. He waved at Mitch McGregor who was making his way to the top of the hill. Close behind Mitch, Thomas Hastings plodded along, holding his carbine with the barrel pointing toward the sky.

Thomas's mother had vehemently opposed his leaving their temporary home in Independence and joining the Gray Riders. He had reached the age of sixteen and argued that Frank James's younger brother Jesse had seen battle at age fifteen. "Kilt hisself a Union general, he did."

She refused to step outside the house and watch her son ride off. Emma's expression remained stoic as she actively worked the rocking chair in the kitchen. Henry firmly grasped the hand of his son. "God speed," he said to Thomas. Just before Thomas's horse disappeared around a copse of trees, he raised his arm and saluted his family on that day in May of 1864.

Grady grabbed the glass again. "What do ya think, Mitch?"

"Ah'm for chasin' them the hell out of 'ere. Kill 'em if they don't go."

Grady nodded. "Thomas, go back and tell Jubal and the boys to get mounted. Then, bring our horses forward. We'll attack as soon as we're ready."

"Yes, sir," Thomas said and hurriedly scampered down the hill.

He was almost as tall as his brother...but lighter complexion and rounded face...clear blue eyes as opposed to Grady's green. His long arms dangled from his wide shoulders, grasping a carbine.

— —

GRADY SIGNALLED WITH HIS ARM and the Riders formed a line on each side of him. He raised his right arm. "Hee! Ya!"

Abel Kingsley, as he had done so many times in the past, spearheaded the charge. The Riders ferociously galloped down the slope, each rider brandishing a hand gun. The jayhawkers dropped to their stomachs, waving carbines and revolvers. They begin firing.

"Jaysus, they're bait!" Grady yelled. "Go Back!" He almost got thrown from the saddle as he jerked on the reins with all his might. Grady had realized in an instant that he had led his Riders into a trap. Quickly, he retreated along with the rest of the Riders.

The sound of thundering hoof beats filled the air as several horsemen appeared from two different directions. Grady led his Riders to the top of the hill from which they came. He stopped and assessed the situation. "This way, men!" he yelled. Grady led the Riders through a shallow draw, heading upward toward the mountain.

Grady yelled, "Ya all know what to do! Pass the word!" Suddenly, the Riders dismounted and spread out along a half-moon shaped ridge. The thick stand of trees to their rear would prevent them from being surrounded.

"Jaysus, there must be about thirty of 'em," Jubal Haggard yelled at Thomas, who lined up next to him. Lafe Sunnerland lay prone next to Thomas. The attackers continued at full gallop toward them.

"Hold yar fire, boys. Be ready!" Grady exclaimed. "Pass the word!"

Moments later, massive gunfire broke out after Grady pulled the trigger. Several of the men galloping toward them fell off their horses, getting shot by the intense gunfire. Smoke and the arid odor of gun powder saturated the air.

"Bring the horses!" Grady yelled.

Hurriedly, the Riders remounted. Some of them pointed their sabers as they galloped after the enemy down the slope. Others kept one hand on the reins and fired a revolver. Most of their original attackers lay on the ground, some dead, some moaning.

Lafe Sunnerland waved a saber high over his head, his bunchy, blond hair bouncing on the top of his shoulders. "This is for pa and ma," he yelled in a high-pitched tone, viciously striking one of the mounted enemy across the shoulders. The man spewed blood as he fell to the grassy soil below.

The last men standing threw down their weapons and raised their arms into the air. Grady signaled the Riders to stop firing. "All right, boys, let's get some rope and tie 'em up." He added, "Thomas, get the shovels out."

Thomas dismounted and removed the short-handled shovel from back of his saddle. He walked over to a victim and stared at the face. The man's eyes were slightly open, dark slits between the eyelids. His long hair was caked with mud, the reddish hole in the man's chest exposing some of the heart.

Thomas grasped the shovel and began to dig, his arms moving swiftly. The sooner we get this man in the ground, the better, he thought. It took four hours for the prisoners and the Riders to dig graves.

"Good job, Thomas, and all the rest of ya. Let's head back to camp." Grady led the Riders back to their mountain camp with six captured men and several horses.

2

THOMAS RODE NEXT TO MITCH MCGREGOR. The Gray Riders had been patrolling the area in and around Tarrytown all summer. Late September had arrived bringing with it the relief from intense heat and insects. Mitch led the Riders along the peak of a ridge on the northern slope of Bear Mountain. In the distance, faint outlines of the buildings of Thomas's home became visible, disappearing at times as they rode through the trees.

His mind drifted to thoughts about his father. Thomas visualized him pacing the grounds in front of his farm house, a long dark cigar protruding from his mouth. Thomas had witnessed his father's reaction as a Union cavalry unit rode by. He feared that Pa would yell something the Bluecoats wouldn't like.

Mitch's light-reddish colored hair stuck out in all directions as he signaled a halt. He turned, his large blue eyes narrowing. "Keep an eye out yonder, boys, we're ridin' down to the road." Mitch's bushy, red sideburns and beard nearly matched the color of his horse's hide.

As the Riders descended the slope, Thomas recognized their split-rail fence that lined the eastern edge of their property. It had several breaches in its alignment...some sections totally missing. Pa wouldn't like that, he thought. He'd have a fit.

They reached the Tarrytown Road. Mitch raised an arm. It extended from his extraordinarily, wide shoulders like a fence post. The group halted and scanned the area in all directions. "Looks all clear. Let's head for town," Mitch yelled.

Thomas always felt nervous passing along that edge of MacTurley's Woods. So many tragedies had occurred in that area. The Sunnerland parents had been murdered right over there. He pointed and remembered them lying dead in the grass, next to an overturned wagon.

Mitch halted the group again after reaching the corner of the woods, the school house and cemetery in plain view. Thomas felt as if a hundred years had gone by since he attended. It's actually only two years ago, he said to himself...two extremely long years.

Mitch picked up the pace and they hastily rode by the church, then the Smith Building. It's now a ghost town, Thomas thought. He felt amazed at the lack of destruction. The spirits up there must be protecting our town. They're keeping it intact waiting for the good people to return.

The Riders reached the outlying edge of town. Mitch pulled on the reins of his horse, stopping it in front of the livery. "We'll rest the horses," he said and dismounted.

The Riders rode northward along the fence, toward the railroad tracks. They reached the northeast corner of the Walker property and headed west along the tracks. Jaysus, there hasn't been a train through here in a long time, Thomas thought.

Later that night, Thomas lay on his bunk, glad that the Riders had all returned safely from their scouting expedition. He thought about his family, safe and sound in Independence. I'll be glad when this war is over and my parents return to the farm, he thought. He rolled over and instantly fell asleep.

— —

"RIDER COMIN'," JUSTIN HAGGARD said. Grady Hastings turned his head.

Justin sat tall in the saddle, watching a lone horseman approaching at a gallop along the split-rail fence dividing the McGregor and Sunnerland property. The stump remains of his right leg protruded high above the stirrup. He lost the limb after getting wounded in the Battle of Lone Jack.

Justin spent a short time in a Union prison in southern Illinois. He rode homeward on horseback, his physical condition in precarious condition. Later, he learned that his wife and parents had all been murdered by marauding redlegs. He thought of them as a self-serving, righteous bunch out of Kansas who forced their beliefs on them.

Thomas Hastings spotted Justin slumped on his horse as the mount walked through Main Street. He summoned the doctor, likely saving the brave man's life. After seven days of death-threatening fever, he miraculously recovered.

"Let's ride down and meet 'em," Grady said and dragged a spur lightly across his horse's hide.

The rider coming up the slope slowed his horse and reined it to a stop, awaiting Grady and Mitch. The horse's nostrils widened, breathing in extra oxygen. It's hide steamed with perspiration.

"Ah'm lookin' for Hastings," he said. "Ah got a message from Sergeant York."

"Ah'm Hastings," Grady said.

The rider handed him a paper.

Grady read for a few moments and turned toward Justin. "The sergeant wants us to join General Price whose forces are moving westward along the big river."

"Does it give a date?" Justin asked.

"'Bout two weeks hence," Grady said.

"What do ya think?" Justin asked.

"It's been quiet around. Ah think we could spare some of the boys."

"Ah'd like to go," Justin said.

Grady grimaced. "Naw, ah don't think so. What if we git into one of those dismounting predicaments? You'd be at too big a handicap."

"Ah heck, Grady, ah can take care of myself."

"Ya best stay and take charge of the camp while we're gone," Grady said and turned his head.

Justin narrowed his eyes and stared at his friend. Grady looked back at Justin. A smile broke out on his face and he nodded.

3

AT DAWN ON OCTOBER 19TH, the Gray Riders, led by Grady Hastings and Justin Haggard, rode out of camp. They lined up in a column of two. Behind Hastings rode Mitch McGregor and Lafe Sunnerland. They were followed by Abel Kingsley and Jesse Sunnerland. Next, Jubal Haggard flanked Thomas Hastings; James McGregor directly behind them. Mitch, Grady, Lafe and Abel wore official confederate jackets.

Grady led the thirty-six horsemen down the mountain slope toward the Tarrytown Road. He signaled a halt next to Bear Creek, all eyes surveying the surroundings. They crossed the road and headed for the railroad tracks. Their destination: the Missouri River.

"Do ya think we'll be in a battle?" Thomas asked.

Jubal smiled. "Ah hope so. We need some action. It's been too quiet 'round here lately."

Thomas's eyes widened. "Did ya ever kill a man, Jubal?"

"'Bout a dozen or so."

Thomas stared at his close friend. "Did ya see 'em die? I mean right after ya shot 'em."

"Naw, ah just kept on shootin' 'till my revolvers were empty."

"What happened then?"

Jubal eyeballs rolled upward. "What happened then? I hate to say this, Thomas, but ah turned tail—ran like hell."

"Where was your horse?"

"Back a ways. We snuck up on this camp on foot."

"Jaysus, how many of the Riders were with you?"

"Half a dozen or so. The redlegs were thicker than fiddlers in hell."

"Anyone get hurt?"

"Yup."

Thomas waited for an answer. "Yup, who?"

"Sorley took one in the shoulder." Jubal's chin dropped. "He bled to death 'afore we could get him back to camp."

— —

THE GRAY RIDERS STOPPED AT THE END OF A FIELD of hemp, dust billowing and forming a cluster of clouds. Grady grabbed his field glasses from its case behind his saddle. He studied the rolling hills ahead and handed it to Justin. "Thar's some riders watching us—see 'em at the top of one of them hills?" Grady said.

"Too far away to tell for sure—maybe they're Bluecoats and maybe they ain't," Justin said and handed the glass back. "How far do ya think we're from the big river?"

Grady looked westward at the lowering sun. "'Bout half a days ride. Ah hope to get there by noon tomorra."

Justin nodded and cleared his throat. "Do ya think we should keep goin' straight ahead? We're gonna run right smack into them riders—whoever they are."

Grady pointed. "Ah'd like to get as far as that ridge line up there to spend the night—first we're gonna have to stop at the creek below for the horses."

He broke his horse into a trot. As they approached the slope, suddenly Grady stopped. A lone rider, watching them, sat on his horse between them and the creek. Grady reached back for his glass. The rider disappeared.

"Ah didn't see any blue," Justin said.

Grady nodded. He turned his head. "Check yar guns, boys." Pulling his colt revolver from its holster, he set his horse into a gallop, descending toward the creek. He jerked the reins sharply after reaching the bottom. His horse neighed loudly, its legs straining to move its mouth closer to the water.

Grady pointed, signaling the other riders to water their horses. The men dismounted.

After the horses' thirst had been satisfied, Grady mounted. "Come on, let's follow the creek." The Riders rode their steeds slowly, scanning the slopes and hills ahead.

"Wonder what happened to that rider?" Mitch McGregor asked from behind.

"Dun-no, but he sure ain't 'roun 'ere no more."

Grady and Justin surveyed the high ground, searching for a place to spend the night. They headed for a grove of trees on a hillside that overlooked the creek. Stopping at the top of the ridge, Grady said, "Alright, boys—" He turned his head. "Set up camp and git yar horse grazin'."

— —

THE 20TH DAY OF OCTOBER DAWNED. Gray clouds, pushed by a cool, damp wind, drifted westward. Thomas shivered chewing on a dried chunk of beef. His right hand trembled slightly raising a tin of coffee to his lips. Them clouds are mighty low this mornin', he thought. Bet we'll be wearin' them dusters today.

"Saddle up boys!" he heard.

"Mitch's voice sounds a little gruff this mornin'," he said to Jubal.

Jubal smiled. "Whiskey—one too many, perhaps."

Thomas coughed and wiped his lips with his hand. He chuckled. "He'll be sharp as a nail by the time we get goin'."

Thomas gave the girth an extra pull and gently tapped his black roan on the side of its neck. "Ya look ready to go." He mounted and eyed his carbine. "Today, Nellie, we find General Price."

He rode next to Jubal Haggard, second from the last in the column. His brother and Justin led the column along a ridgeline northward, eventually crossing the creek as it angled toward the Little Blue River to the west. Narrow streaks of blue appeared in the gray sky above, the clouds rising substantially with each passing hour.

His brother raised his hand and the column halted. Four riders approached them from the north. "Them's us," he said to Jubal.

Thomas's insides bubbled with excitement. Justin had raised the Rider's flag. The blue banner furled in the breeze.

"Yup...look et them gray jackets."

The approaching riders halted next to Grady and Justin. They talked for a bit, then Grady signaled and the column advanced, veering slightly toward the northwest, following the four horsemen.

"Well ah'll be!" Jubal exclaimed, his lanky frame towering over some of the others.

"Must be two-three thousand of 'em," Thomas said.

Confederate cavalry soldiers, riding in disorganized columns, stretched as far as Thomas's eyes could see. Hundreds of wagons filled gaps between them, followed by thousands of cows. The mixing moos, squeaky wagon wheels and horses hooves stunned Thomas's ears. Cavalry units protected their rear.

He felt uneasy because many of the soldiers did not have rifles or carbines. They marched with their heads tilted down. This army looks like a herd of cattle, he thought. Thomas shrugged his shoulders and glanced at Jubal.

"Now ya know why they need us," his friend said.

4

THE BRIDGE SPANNING THE LITTLE BLUE RIVER, eight miles east of Independence, swelled with Confederates as they crossed to the west bank. Grady halted his column and they watched as hundreds of horses and men moved in unison. "Looks like they're gonna stay close to the west bank the rest of the day," he said to Justin.

"Gee willikers, those wagons and cattle are staggerin' around like a blind horse in a punkin patch," Justin said.

"Hey there, Corporal Hastings," Sergeant York said after halting his horse next to the front of the column.

Grady nodded. "Top of the day to ya, York. What do ya want us to do?"

"General Fagan wants more men in the rear—guard our behinds, he said. We need fresh horses back there."

The Riders reversed their direction and rode toward the rear of the massive contingency of General Price's Army of Missouri. After crossing the two rivers, the army's direction of travel would change to southward. The past few months, the general's army was in constant retreat, attempting to find safety in a section of Missouri that had less Union presence.

The sound of gunfire reached the Rider's ears. Grady drew out a revolver. He raised it into the air and galloped toward the intensifying sounds. The column broke and the riders spread out, ambitious Abel Kingsley in the lead. "Hy-eee! Hy-eee!" he screamed and fired his pistol at a cluster of union cavalrymen.

— —

THOMAS SHOT AT A HUMAN BEING for the very first time in his life. His innards felt like they crept upwards towards his mouth, after seeing a Bluecoat fall off his horse, blood spurting from his neck. Sorrow changed to anger when a bullet grazed his shirt.

His revolver clicked on an empty cylinder. Thomas jammed it into the holster and drew out a second revolver from his belt. His horse neighed as its front legs soared into the air, dumping Thomas on the ground. "Yar horse got hit!" Jubal yelled. "Git up behind me—quick!"

Thomas's horse desperately attempted to rise, but it lay on its side and became still, an occasional snort emitting from its inflated nostrils. Thomas grabbed his carbine from the scabbard and leaped up behind Jubal. He wrapped one arm around his friend's waist, grasping the carbine with the other.

"We best git the hell otta here," Jubal stammered and pulled on the reins to change directions. After galloping away from the skirmish, Jubal halted his horse next to a rider-less mount. "Thar ya go, Thomas. Git that one."

Thomas slid off and slowly walked over to the grazing animal. He grabbed the reins and stuck his carbine into the empty scabbard. Thomas mounted and adjusted to the gold-rimmed saddle.

"Yar one of the big boys now," Jubal said, chuckling. "That's a Union officer's saddle."

Minutes later, Grady and the rest of the riders returned. "Are ya alright, Thomas?"

"Yup, just lost my horse."

"Ah see ya got a fancy new 'un."

Thomas smiled. "Gotta new name—*General*."

"Come on, boys, we're headin' for the bridge," Grady said, dragging a spur across his horse's underside.

The Riders galloped toward the river and crossed at a walk. General Fagan's division remained on the east bank, protecting the Confederate rear, including the wagons and cattle.

They dismounted, allowing their horses to water at the edge of the Little Blue. Mitch and some of the others lay down in the tall grass and stretched out their arms.

Fighting and shooting had temporarily ceased, allowing Prices' forces to haul their wagons across the bridge. The cattle forded across half a mile to the south. General Fagan's rear guard had successfully held off the Union's Major General Alfred Pleasanton's provisional cavalry division, pushing them back farther from the river.

— —

GRADY AND JUSTIN ATTENDED A MEETING THAT EVENING in General Marmaduke's tent, one of General Prices's assistants. They heard the officers decide to make an attempt to cross the Big Blue River at Byram's Ford. After succeeding, they would proceed southward toward the Little Sante Fe and hopefully a safe distance from the concentration of Union forces.

The orders for the Gray Riders: patrol the west bank of the Little Blue River for a distance of approximately ten miles; engage the enemy if they appear; slow their progress; and with vigor send a galloping rider back to headquarters with a report.

The two men returned to their camp, feeling the warmth of a substantial pit fire situated in the middle of a circle of over thirty tents. They dismounted. Justin leaned heavily on his crutch and stood close to the flames.

Thomas slumped down in the tall grass next to his tent, listening to the sorrowful sounds of a harmonica. According to his markings in a small notebook that he kept in his pocket, October 20th would become history at midnight.

"Thanks, Jube," he said to his friend and lifted a bottle of whiskey to his lips. Thomas coughed and cleared his throat, handing the bottle back to Jubal.

"Time for me to get some shuteye," Thomas said and crawled into his tent.

— —

BREAKFAST CONSISTED OF SLICES of dried beef and chunks of hardened bread, plus a steaming cup of coffee. Thomas rolled up his tent and attached it to the back of his saddle. His newly acquired steed appeared a little frisky. I'll have to teach him to settle down, he thought. His great speed could come in handy.

A short time later, all the Riders had mounted. The top rim of the sun made its brilliant appearance above the ridge of a hill east of the Little Blue River. Ah wonder what the day has in store for me today, Thomas thought. Ah just hope no one gets hurt.

He rode next to Jubal in the middle of the 32-man column. The air was still and felt crisp on his cheeks. Less dust rose when they reached the tall grass near the river.

They moved slowly for a few miles and halted at the base of a hill. Grady and Justin left the column and rode to the top. Thomas watched anxiously as the two riders neared the crest. He felt relieved seeing an arm waving, signaling them to follow. Beyond the hill, a copse of short trees and large bushes marked a creek bed that drained the land to the west.

The column moved along the creek and crossed where the clusters of bushes and trees thinned. They rode to the top of another hill and followed its crest back toward the river. Several shots rang out, coming from a bushy area. Thomas's steed reared. He grabbed the saddle horn, struggling to remain mounted. Another rear! Another hang-on! Thomas struggled to get the steed under control.

After succeeding, he became confused. The gunfire had increased dramatically. The Riders had formed a circle of sort, firing upon enemy that didn't appear to exist. Thomas rode his horse into the middle trying to get his bearings.

"Back!" he heard his brother yell.

"James is down!" someone yelled.

Mitch McGregor leaped off his horse, picked up his fallen brother and draped him over his saddle. He quickly got back on the saddle and yelled, "Hee-Ya!"

Thomas leaned forward and low, galloping his anxious horse northward. The gunfire ceased after they all rode hard for a short period of time. He pulled up next to Lafe Sunnerland. "What happened?"

"Ah don't know—ain't got any idear how many riflemen were perched on the ridge. Damn it, anyhow, James got hit."

Just then, Grady fell off his horse, blood dripping from the saddle. Thomas dismounted quickly and ran to his brother. "Where did ya get hit?"

Grady moaned, "The shoulder." He pointed with his right hand.

"Justin! Mitch! Hep me get him up into the saddle. I'll follow Mitch. He's headin' back to Marmaduke's unit. They got many Doctor Wagons, I hear."

The three men gently helped Grady back on his horse. Thomas remounted and Mitch handed him Grady's reins. They made sure that Grady was secure in his saddle, and Thomas nudged his horse.

Thomas led the column back toward Price's army. He kept his horse at a fast walk but still took two agonizing hours to reach the wagons.

— —

THE DOCTOR, A BLOODY APRON covering his midsection and chest, came out from the back of a wagon. He glanced at Grady's wound and assisted Thomas in getting Grady inside. The curtain closed and Thomas sat down in the grass. He pulled a flask out of his back pocket and lifted it to his lips. "This is gonna hurt," he whispered and took another swig.

The minutes crawled by. Thomas hadn't heard a sound and that didn't surprise him. Grady's got a strong backbone, he said to himself. He's never one to complain. At last the curtain opened and Thomas watched with anxiety as two men helped his brother down.

"Ya don't want to bounce around any, young man," the doctor said. "That means no ridin' for a couple of days. Understand?"

Grady grumbled words that Thomas didn't understand. The doctor pointed. "Take 'em over to that wagon. He can lie down inside."

Thomas's guts tightened as Mitch McGregor rode up. He brought two saddled horses with him, including Thomas's.

"How did it go with Grady?" Mitch asked.

"Got the darn bullet out," Grady grumbled.

"Yah and he's not supposed to ride for a couple of days," Thomas added.

Mitch lowered his head. "Ah've got bad news....James is dead."

Thomas felt moisture building in his eyes. He lowered his chin and took several deep breaths.

"Ah'm sorry, Mitch," Grady said, his mouth quivering.

Mitch nodded, a far-away look on his face. "Let's get goin'."

Grady's facial expression showed the strain from his pain as he walked alongside Mitch and Thomas on their way toward the wagon.

5

THE RIDERS, NOW LED BY MITCH MCGREGOR, rode along the south flank of the massive army as they headed toward the Big Blue River and Byram's Ford on October 22, 1864. The church spires of Independence appeared in the distance. Thomas knew what he needed to do: get Grady to his Pa and Ma's home.

Thomas strayed from his column and rode toward the front. He pulled up next to Justin. "Ah'm gonna take Grady to our parent's home. Should get better doctorin' there."

Justin nodded. "Not that far, is it?"

Thomas tightened his lips together. "Nope."

Grady worked his way to a front seat on the wagon he had been placed into. He had left definitive instructions with Thomas to keep his horse nearby. Grady heard a pair of galloping hoof beats. He turned and saw his brother and a rider-less horse.

Thomas pulled up alongside. "Grady, Ah'm takin' ya to Pa's house. Justin's orders!"

The wagon stopped. Thomas dismounted and helped his brother mount. He grabbed Grady's reins and led both horses on foot northward away from the wagons.

After they'd advanced a mile. Thomas asked, "How's the

shoulder?"

"Hurts like hell. Git on your horse and lets get there as fast as we can."

Thomas saw his brother cringe as he set his horse into a gallop, holding Grady's reins alongside.

— —

EMMA STOOD IN THE DOORWAY, her eyes narrowed, creases expanding across her forehead. Grady fell into Thomas's arms as their father, Henry, hurried over to help. "Easy does it," Henry said as his arm draped around Grady's waist.

Minutes later, Grady lay on a bed. "Your pa is high-tailin' it to the doctor's office," Thomas said and left the room. He sat down on the porch and lit one of his father's cigars. Ah hope Pa and the neighbor get back with the doctor—and soon.

Thomas heard the front door open as his mother stepped out. "He's burnin', Thomas....But the bleedin's stopped."

Thomas stood, his eyes anxiously searching the landscape for signs of his father's carriage and the doctor. "There they come, Ma!"

Emma entered the house. Thomas watched as the black-clothed man wearing a derby hat stepped out of the carriage. He reached back and grasped a black bag. The doctor followed Henry as they stepped onto the porch and entered.

Thomas patiently waited on the porch. An hour later, the doctor came through the door. He cleared his throat. "Your brother has lost a lot of blood. Your parents should be able to control the fever with cold water packs—the well water should do." The doctor nodded. "He should be all right, young man."

Thomas breathed a sigh of relief. "Thanks, Doc."

— —

THE SUN HAD JUST SET IN THE WEST on October 23rd. Thomas mounted his anxious steed and trotted down the street southward. He pulled on the reins and looked back. His mother stood on the porch.

Her hands were clasped in front. Thomas raised an arm. She didn't move. I may never see her again, he thought. A tear escaped his eye as he prodded the animal and it broke into a gallop.

Thomas rode hard for the next hour, anxious to return to the Riders. His thoughts drifted to Sarah Kingsley, his school friend who lived with her parents in the Kansas City area. He stopped. The encampment that he saw ahead was occupied by Bluecoats. Thomas didn't waste any time directing his horse westward, hoping to find a way around them.

He heard a yell behind him. Four riders came over the top of a ridge. "He-YAH!" Thomas dragged his spur across his steed's belly. He felt astounded with the speed of his new addition—a Union Officer's horse at that.

In a matter of minutes he had outrun his pursuers, pulling on the reins to give his horse a rest. Thomas felt the dampness of the horse's perspiration inside his trouser legs.

Finally, he arrived at the Big Blue River. He felt relieved seeing a section of Price's Army—the rear guard. Reason told Thomas that the Riders would be on the west bank, probably near the river. He stopped and talked to a lieutenant. The officer pointed. Thomas nodded and galloped off.

He crossed the ford and arrived at the Rider's camp just before dark. "Got yar tent set up for ya," Jubal said.

Justin struggled with his crutch as he hastened toward where Thomas had dismounted. "How's Grady doin'?"

Thomas smiled. "Gonna make it, the doc said."

Justin smiled. "He's a mighty tough one. It would take more than a Bluecoat bullet to take him down."

Thomas took down a couple slugs of whiskey and spread out on his blanket. The exhausted Rider found sleep immediately.

— —

GENERAL PRICE'S ARMY, pursued and attacked every day, headed toward Fort Scott in Kansas. His supply train had great difficulty after crossing the Big Blue River. They engaged in battle at

Mine Creek on October 24. The next day they had more problems crossing at the Marmiton River Ford. The Union forces kept the pressure on but, because of their own exhaustion, could not defeat Price.

On the 25th, the Gray Riders left the Price Army and headed toward their homeland. Thomas thought about his brother most of each day. He knew that it might be a long time before he saw him again...or never.

They re-crossed the Blue River and rode southeastward for most of the day, not engaging any hostile forces. Thomas felt the cold breeze on his cheeks and tightened the collar of his duster. The feel of winter is in the air, he thought as they set up camp near a creek, close to Jackson County.

Thomas unbuckled his saddle bags and set them down on the ground. He released the girth straps and pulled off the saddle. Thomas led *General* toward the grazing horses. He returned to set up his tent. Satisfied, he sat down on his saddle and opened one of the bags to look at the books his mother had given him.

He walked over to Mitch McGregor who sat on a log next to the fire, a bottle of whiskey in his hands. "How ya doin', Mitch?"

"Depressed."

"I would expect."

Mitch nodded. "Ah hope Grady gets better."

"Thanks. Ya know how me and my family feel about James."

"Yup."

"Ah see you brought his remains back with you."

Mitch grimaced. "Couldn't stand the idea of buryin' him in the ground out there."

Thomas swallowed and cleared his throat. "We'll take him up to the cemetery in Tarrytown and give him a decent burial."

"That's what ah want," Mitch said.

Thomas walked away slowly. He turned. "We'll be gettin' back to camp tomorrow. I'll take some of the boys the next day and we'll dig the—get the ground ready."

"Thanks."

6

FORTY TWO RIDERS STOOD AT ATTENTION at Tarrytown Cemetery as Lafe Sunnerland read a passage from a bible. "Dust to dust...."

The men stood around in small clusters as the sounds of clods of dirt hit the wooden coffin. Thomas finished the project by pounding the top of a small wooden cross into the ground. He stood back, his lower lip covering his upper.

James was a quiet fella, he said to himself, never caused a bit of trouble for anybody. Thomas didn't dare turn his head until the wetness in his eyes had dried.

Thomas's memory drifted to three years ago. He was standing alongside his parents when the preacher read over Paul McGregor's coffin. Paul was James's older brother and he died as a result of a wound suffered at the Battle of the Hemp Bales in Lexington.

Thomas's thoughts switched to his brother. He could remember only one Rider who survived a wound—Justin Haggard. Everyone else had died. Thomas feared that he would never see his brother again. He swept a glove over his eyes and walked stiffly back to his horse.

After the ceremony, the Riders rode silently back to their camp. Thomas shuddered thinking about the cold winter coming up. The gray clouds in the west had a dreary look to them as the sun's penetrating rays retreated beyond the horizon.

— —

THOMAS WATCHED THE SUN RISE on a March morning. The ground had been covered with a blanket of snow for the past two weeks. The millions of icicles hanging down from low hanging branches of spruce trees sparkled like diamonds.

The latest news regarding the war didn't help his mood. The Confederacy appeared to be a lost cause. General Lee's army was in perpetual retreat—same as Price's. His men, short of supplies such as boots and weapons, valiantly fought for their survival. Thomas had heard recently from a rider near Tarrytown that Lee and his depleted troops were somewhere in western Virginia.

Every single day, Thomas thought about his brother. Mitch McGregor took command of the Gray Riders and he sent some of the boys out on scouting expeditions. The last time Thomas had gone, they rode through Tarrytown. They hadn't seen any signs of redlegs or jayhawkers for over a month. The buildings in town were all boarded up and hadn't been disturbed.

Thomas felt nostalgic whenever the Hastings farm building came into view. The remains of the barn consisted of partially charred walls. He felt glad that his father wasn't around to see what he saw. Someday, he said to himself, we'll build a new barn. At least Pa and I will.

Mitch had told him and the others a few days ago that no Union forces passed along the Tarrytown road since last fall before the first snowfall.

Thomas raised the tin cup to his lips and enjoyed a sip of the hot coffee. His close friend, Jubal Haggard, stomped out the door of their shelter. "Ya goin' with us today, Thomas?"

"Yup, sure am."

Thomas gazed northward past a thick stand of woods and he saw movement in a field. He watched the figure, thinking it may be a deer. "Somethin' is moving toward us from the big field below."

"Ah'll get the glass," Jubal said.

Thomas nodded and waited. When Jubal returned, he took the glass and focused on a moving object. "It's not a deer, Thomas. A lone rider but can't tell who 'tis."

"Probably someone from Sergeant York's squad," Thomas said. "Ah'll go in and tell Mitch and Justin."

Five minutes later, Jubal, Thomas, Mitch and Justin had mounted. Mitch set his horse to a trot and led the four riders down the steep slope. They entered the woods at the beginning of one of many trails that traversed the woods on the slopes of the mountains.

A short time later, they approached the first clearing at the edge of the trees. Mitch slowed his horse and brought it to a stop. "Thar he comes," he said. "He's headin' straight for us."

Thomas watched with mixed feelings, fully expecting a messenger from General Price's army. Suddenly, he gasped and held his breath. "It's Grady! He's come back!" Thomas exclaimed, raising a fist into the air and setting his horse to a gallop.

Mitch turned his head toward the other Riders. He muttered, "Leave 'em go, boys. We're gonna have a great day today."

— —

GRADY HASTINGS'S RETURN BROUGHT WITH IT a new wave of confidence to the Riders. He brought in his belongings and lay them down on his original bunk. The boys gathered around as he unpacked his saddlebags, mostly using one hand, and handed out several copies of newspapers with news of the war.

Even though his shoulder had totally healed, Grady's posture changed. His shoulders stooped slightly—the right drooped lower than the left. It angled downward to an arm that hung limp. Thomas knew that his brother would never fight again—never lead the Riders in a charge.

Thomas spent the next few hours reading about reports of General Price's retreat southward, and the declining effectiveness of General Lee's army in Virginia. "The war is going to end soon," he muttered to Jubal.

That night, two whiskey bottles made their way around the one end of the bunk house. "Ah toast you, Grady Hastings," Justin Haggard said. Everyone laughed when whiskey streamed down the front of his throat.

Thomas got very drowsy shortly after midnight. He felt immensely relieved that his brother had not died. He lay down on his bunk and fell asleep with his boots on.

— —

THE EMOTIONAL UPLIFT FOR THOMAS felt great, but he yearned for the end to the war and the return of his family to the farm. Each time he rode by his Pa's damaged buildings, he experienced a sinking feeling in his stomach. Thomas stepped outside, tin cup of coffee in hand. He took a sip and coughed lightly. Suddenly, someone yelled, "Smoke!"

Abel Kingsley came running out of the building. He exclaimed, "It's at the Jackson's! Elkanah said he was gonna signal us if they had any trouble. Saddle up, boys! Hurry!"

A short time later, several horses had been readied. Thomas mounted his *General* and moved into position behind Abel. Mitch McGregor and Justin Haggard followed them. The rear was brought up by Lafe and Jesse Sunderland. Thomas glanced back at the shack and saw Grady standing beside the door. He felt great sadness for his brother. Grady will never fight again, he said to himself again.

Abel set his horse to a fast trot and he led the column onto a trail in the woods. They descended down a steep slope, eventually spreading out onto a grassy field at the Sunnerland and McGregor property line. After crossing Bear Creek, Able led them directly to the Tarrytown Road.

Abel held up his arm. "What do ya think, Mitch? Should we spread out and attack?"

Mitch nodded.

Able turned his head. "You swing out to the right. Ah'll take Thomas and some of the others to the left."

Abel prodded his horse into a gallop. Thomas followed on General. He felt the energy of his horse, knowing that it wanted to gallop wide open. They passed the burned-out Haggard buildings and the Jackson house came into view. The smoke appeared to be coming from behind the buildings, a short distance away.

Several men on foot scurried toward their horses that grazed next to a group of oak trees. Thomas had his Colt revolver in his right hand, holding the reins with the other. "Jaysus, Abel, they've got the Jackson's all tied up, down on the ground. Abel galloped toward the men who panicked, attempting to mount. He opened fire.

Gunfire erupted, coming from all the Riders as they rode at the intruders. Thomas saw two of the redlegs drop to the ground. From around the other side of the house, he saw Mitch and his followers flank the enemy.

Massive gunfire continued until the last of the intruders lay dead on the ground. Lafe leaped off his horse next to the Jackson brothers, Elkanah and Bashhall. He knifed through the roping that bound their arms and legs. Others did the same with Virgilia and her two daughters.

Thomas dismounted next to Priam who lay still. He knelt down by the fallen man. "Thank ya, sah," the elderly man whispered. "Come closer," he added.

Thomas positioned his ear close to Priam's mouth. "Take care of my family, Abel."

Thomas's heart dropped into his stomach as the elderly man's head drooped. Jaysus, he's dead, he thought. Thomas removed his hat and anxiously turned his head. He saw that Elkanah and Baskhall had rid themselves of the last of their bindings. Thomas led his horse toward Abel, lowering his chin and slowly shaking his head.

7

Lee's Surrender at Appomattox

RICHMOND, VIRGINIA FELL TO General Grant's troops on April 3, 1865. General Lee's army headed westward with very little hope they would have further success. On April 7, General Grant initiated a series of written communications delivered to General Lee. The confederate leader responded and asked for terms of surrender.

The next day on the 8th Grant responded. He mentioned only one condition. "Men and officers surrendered shall be disqualified for taking up arms against the Government of the United States."

General Lee responded later in the day, stating that, "My intention is not to surrender the Army of North Virginia." However, he added that he would like to meet and discuss the restoration of peace.

General Grant replied: "The meeting proposed for 10:00 a.m. today could lead to no good. I will state, however, that I am equally anxious for peace with your army."

Later in the day, following more message exchanges, the two men agreed to meet at the home of Wilmer McClean. General Lee arrived first and he entered the first floor drawing room alone. Minutes later, General Grant did the same.

After the staff members of both generals were allowed to enter, Grant and Lee discussed their common endeavor in the Mexican War. Lee requested that Grant write out the terms of surrender. After he finished, his eyes fell on the handsome sword that hung at Lee's side. Grant decided not to require the officers to surrender their swords nor their horses.

The clock readied to strike 4 o'clock when the two generals shook hands. Lee bowed to the other officers and left the room. All the officers outside who surrounded him, Union and Confederate alike, appreciated his sadness.

Lee mounted as Grant appeared on the porch. He raised his hat in salute. All the other officers did the same. Lee raised his hat respectively and slowly rode off to break the sad news to his men.

— —

PRIAM JACKSON'S GRAVE HAD BEEN DUG next to that of his son, Jordon, who was killed at the Battle of the Hemp Bales two years previous. The grating voice of Lafe Sunnerland penetrated the stillness as he read from the Bible. The Riders stood at attention, hats held against their chests.

The big book thumped shut. Virgilia sobbed where she stood with her two daughters. Baskhall and Elkanah assisted their mother and their two sisters onto the wagon seat. Their older sister flicked the reins and the wagon begin its trek down the hill, followed by the two sons on horseback.

After reaching the road, the wagon paused. The passengers turned their heads and waved. The mounted Riders responded by raising their hats high.

Abel Kingsley put his hat back on. "They should be safe. Ah'm headed to Stillman Mills and find out about the war. Who's comin'?"

Abel trotted his horse onto the road and headed toward Tarrytown. All the other Riders followed.

Thomas cringed when riding past the schoolhouse. The door was still boarded up and he wondered if it would ever be used again. I had some good days there, he thought. Except for the day my friend Carr Walker got shot and killed.

They continued on past the black cross that marked the place where victims of the Battle of Tarrytown had been buried. The buildings in the town of Stillman Mills came into view.

Suddenly, jubilant yells and shouts caught their ears. Abel increased the pace and minutes later they entered Main Street. Men were shooting their pistols into the air and passing whiskey bottles around. "It's over! The war is over!"

— —

THE RIDERS DISMOUNTED and tied their horses to a rail near the saloon. Abel pushed open the swinging doors and they entered. He dropped a coin on the bar. Four blue-clad men sitting at a table a short distance away turned their heads. The biggest one stood. His jacket exposed a bulky midline. The salt-pepper whiskers on his face jutted out wildly.

Sergeant stripes ordained the standing man's jacket. He pushed away his chair and strode over to the Riders. He pointed a finger at Abel. "You boys are goin' to 'ave to give up them guns."

Abel wiped his lower lip with his hand. He glared at the bluecoat. "Yar gonna have to take 'em away from me, mister." Abel stood and lowered his right hand until the fingers touched the handle of his revolver. The other Riders spread out and lowered their hands.

The sergeant glanced around anxiously. He raised his hand. "Well now, fellas, tell ya what. You have a drink on me and we'll talk about it another day."

"We'll buy our own whiskey. Now you git back to yar table and be quick about it!" Abel exclaimed.

The sergeant left. Thomas laughed and slapped Abel's back. "Ah was wonderin' who won the war. Now ah know."

The others laughed.

Some time later, the Riders banged their way out through the swinging doors. Jubal had his arm around Thomas's shoulder. "So ya think we won the war, huh?"

"We're still here, aren't we?" Thomas said.

The Riders mounted and left town, hoof beats clattering on the hardened ground. The moon shone brightly as they passed through Tarrytown. "Look, Jubal, the bell in the church is all lit up," Thomas said.

"Yup, sure is—just like you are."

Thomas laughed.

They followed Abel after he turned off the Tarrytown Road on the Hastings's side of Bear Creek. He led the Riders up toward Bear Mountain. Thomas cringed when he saw the outline of his family's buildings silhouetted by the moon. Suddenly, his spirits lifted. He would talk to Grady about returning to the farm. We can do it tomorrow, he said to himself.

"Tomorrow, Jubal."

"Tomorrow what?"

"We go home."

BOOK TWO

TEN YEARS LATER: 1875

1

THE *OCEANIC* SWAYED SMOOTHLY TO the water undulations in Liverpool Harbor. Gleeful passengers walked in groups over the bridge that connected the ocean steamer to the dock. The sun shone brightly on an early August morning. Departure was scheduled to take place in one hour.

Conor McGearney walked slowly, stumbling slightly as he stepped onto the planking. The weight of a shoulder bag and a cube shaped suitcase caused him to buckle at the knees. He recovered and set his luggage down on the planking. Inhaling deeply, Conor picked up his belongings and trudged on.

"Mornin' to you, Air," a shipmate at the ship's gate said. "Set your luggage down 'ar there. I'll see to it that it gets placed in yar compartment."

Conor rotated an elbow back and forth and set the bag down. "Thank ye. I'm all a bit daft about the upcoming voyage."

He rubbed his chewed off fingernails against his chin, moving his shoulders up and down, attempting to loosen up chronic stiffness. His flattop tweed cap, perched on top of a thick head of dark black hair, tilted to one side. He straightened it and walked over to the rail.

Conor hadn't shaved for two days, his whiskered, darkened face enhanced by a strong chin line. Conor's heavy, scraggly, black eyebrows trespassed slightly upward onto his flat forehead. A woman passenger who had just boarded gave him a second glance. He glanced at her and she quickly strode away.

Four massive masts towered above the boarding passengers, the sails neatly secured near their bases. Conor had read the liner's measurement before boarding. The *Oceanic* was 420 by 40 feet in size. It was fit to hold 3,707 tons of supplies. The massive vessel had space for over 1,100 passengers. The single propeller was powered by a 2x2 cylinder-type engine.

Conor glanced at his ticket and followed a group of people down a metal stairway. He moved his way along a corridor, twice brushing against the side of another passenger. Grabbing the handle of 204, he turned it and pushed it open. The double berth almost completely filled the small, postage stamp-sized room. Conor entered and sat down on a chair. He heard a gentle tap on the door and turned his head. The rest of his luggage had arrived.

The aide set his bags down by the bunks and turned to leave. "Aye, got somethin' for ye," Conor said and placed a coin into the man's palm. Conor closed the door behind him. He walked to the small port window and peered out. The dredge loading supplies from a flat-surfaced boat anchored next to the *Oceanic,* rolled gently with the waves.

Conor lay down on the lower bunk and closed his eyes. Half an hour later, the booming sound of a foghorn stirred him from his malaise. He rose and picked up the key from the small cabinet top in the corner of the room. Carefully, locking his door, he strode up the stairway and joined others at the rail on the deck.

He experienced a surge of heartsickness as the cruiser slowly moved away from its mooring to begin its voyage. Conor watched with amazement as deck hands climbed up the masts and released the sails. He knew that the *Oceanic* didn't rely totally on sails, and felt reassured hearing the rumble of the engines down below—the ship does over 14 knots, he had read.

— —

SHOUTS FROM THE CLUSTERS OF PEOPLE waving on the dock began to fade into space as Conor stood silent with both hands on the rail. He sadly watched the shores of his homeland dwindling to dark shadows. On the western horizon, streaks of horizontal, jagged, white clouds emerged as if to weld the water to the sky.

An hour later, he could no longer see the land mass in the east. His stomach churned as the ocean waves intensified. The deck began to weave and bob. Conor debated returning to his room. Taking a series of deep breaths successfully calmed the threatening, turbulent gyrations in his stomach and he decided to remain on the deck.

Conor thought about his father. He visualized him, Mathew McGearney, lying in his hospital bed. Conor and his two brothers, Patrick and Timothy, crowded around the pallet. His father forced a smile. Then Conor glanced at his eldest brother, Patrick, and looked away quickly after noticing a wide, bulging tear streaming down his cheek.

"You lads have made me very happy. I'm proud of ye all," the old man had said, his voice reduced to a whisper. "I've not only been blessed with a fine family, but also times of plenty. I owe it all to the Lord."

Conor had felt a twinge of fear when the surgeon walked into the room—the expression on his face appearing strained. The white-cloaked doctor sat down and cleared his throat. "Mr. McGearney, I have bad news."

The senior McGearney had placed a hand over his mouth. "What is it? What is it, doctor?"

Patrick had emitted a strained gasp and sat down. Timothy and Conor remained standing, their face muscles tight and quivering.

The doctor ran the tip of his tongue across his upper lip. "Your shortness of breath is due to malfunctioning lungs. Your heart is seriously lacking oxygen. Ah don't wish to say this, but you don't have long to live—it is time for you to make settlements."

The doctor cleared his throat. "Sorry, lads, but I thought you would want to know the truth."

Mathew's mouth remained agape—he appeared too shocked to speak. Conor hadn't seen him look like this since their mother died, over five years ago. His father placed the fingers of his right hand over his heart. "Aye, but couldn't you be wrong? I have no pain."

"Perhaps the Lord will spare you. It is out of my hands."

Mathew shook his head slowly. The doctor stood and reached out a hand. "Peace be with you, McGearney. I wish you a good day."

The doctor left the room, resulting in dead silence. The three brothers ages, 32, 35 and 38, all stared at the floor.

— —

FIVE DAYS INTO THE VOYAGE, Conor McGearney's stomach had returned to normal. He had spent the first four days sick to his stomach in bed, tossing...tossing....

He pulled on a heavy sweater and ventured onto the deck. The waves looked more gentle than usual. He grasped the rope rail and inhaled deeply several times. Peering to his left, he saw a woman sitting alone on a bench. She wore a light green shawl and had her hands clasped tightly together in front of her breasts. Conor left the rail and stopped directly in front of her.

"Splendid day, ma'am."

"The only thing splendid will be when we get to New York. I hate traveling like this. First, people with the vomit—then an infinite sea—sky and water everywhere."

"My name is Conor McGearney. May I ask yours?"

She raised her knuckles against her chin. Forcing a smile, she said, "Blanche...Blanche Perkins."

"Where do ye hail from, Blanche?"

"Wales."

"I'm from Ireland, meself. My family all gone—the famine wreckin' my business—America was my only choice."

"Would you care to sit, mister...?"

He smiled. "McGearney," he repeated. "Conor McGearney."

Conor sat down on the far end of the bench. "Have ye been ill like I has been?"

Her greenish, watery eyes narrowed following a wisp of wind that blew across the deck. She feathered strands of reddish hair from her face. "All this wind and salt—at times I can hardly see, but ill—no, Mister McGearney, I've not been ill. Have you?"

"Four bloody days, lass—I thought I was gonna die. One morning when I awoke, I thought that I did die. I saw an angel through the portal."

Blanche laughed. "That could've been a seagull, but we're too far out at sea."

Conor and Blanche exchanged pleasantries for the next half an hour. Blanche stood. "I've got to get back to my quarters. I enjoyed talking to you, Mr. McGearney."

"Conor—you may call me Conor."

"All right then, Conor," Blanche said and slowly walked toward her room.

Conor watched her until she disappeared from view. Now, that's a fine shape to carry around. He walked around the entire deck, stopping on the north side to stare at a glistening horizon. He felt a touch of nervousness—what am I seeing? He asked himself. Is that ice?

During the days that followed, Conor and his new friend Blanche met at the same bench, and he sat down next to her. Seven days had passed since leaving Liverpool. He cleared his throat and pulled his collar tight against his neck. "I overheard one of the mates say barring bad weather, we should reach land in two days."

Blanche smiled widely. Her face beamed.

"Ah thought you would like the news," Conor said, placing an arm around her shoulder.

She nodded and wet her lips with her tongue. "At last, this torture is about to end."

They remained quiet for the next few minutes.

Conor's new friend gasped and pointed aft. "Those are icebergs over there!"

"Aye was hopin' you wouldn't see them."

"Are you afraid, Conor?"

"Not a bit, I tell ya—not a bit," he lied.

— —

"LAND HO! LAND HO!"

The fear of the liner smashing into an iceberg had dissipated for Conor. The very next day, after viewing the glistening ice with Blanche, it had disappeared from view. His heart beat rapidly as he stared at the shadowy looking land mass to the west.

Conor and Blanche spent the entire day walking, sitting and watching the eastern coastline of America growing in size with each passing hour. The deck became crowded as the *Oceanic* steamed toward New York Harbor.

Conor and Blanche stood side by side as they passed by a group of islands. "Aye, Blanche, there 'tis—New York Harbor—the East River Pier, it says here in our brochure."

Grasping one of her hands, he extended it upwards. "America the beautiful! Look!" he exclaimed, pointing a finger.

The skyline of New York City came into view. They stood silently next to the rail watching the boating activity in the harbor. Conor grabbed Blanche by the waist when the liner lurched and veered sharply to correct its approach.

Masses of waving people milled around on the huge wooden platform below. "Someone told me it takes over an hour to ready a boarding platform. We may as well enjoy the scenes from up here."

"Conor, I really have enjoyed your company."

She buried her face in his shoulder. "I shall likely never see you again."

Conor extended his arms around her shoulders and lowered his lips to meet hers.

She responded by kissing him and grasping him tightly.

"We're home, Blanche—our new home," Conor said. "We shall meet again."

Ocean Liners and Immigration

THE OCEANIC STEAM NAVIGATION COMPANY formed in 1869 as a merger between the White Star Line and Nelson, Ismay & Co. They hired the shipbuilding company, Harland & Wolff to build all their ships. Their first vessel, the Oceanic, *departed on August 27, 1870.*

New to shipbuilding liners were the rails which replaced the old style bulwarks. They featured large dining saloons, which allowed every passenger to have their own chair. The Oceanic's *length measured 420.3 feet, its beam, 40.85 feet wide.*

The Oceanic's *maiden voyage began in Liverpool on March 2, 1871. The numbers listed a surprising low total of only 64 paying passengers. The voyage became tainted when the liner developed engine problems only hours out of Liverpool, forcing the liner to return.*

On March 16, the maiden voyage of the Oceanic *resumed. Weeks later it finally reached New York, initiating a wild celebration of approximately 50,000 people.*

Oceanic *was modified considerably over the years, creating a successful, very seaworthy, speedy vessel. The White Star Lines eventually replaced the* Oceanic *with updated liners. After her final Liverpool to New York voyage, the liner was chartered by the Occidental & Oriental S.S. Co. for a San Francisco-Yokohama- Hong Kong service. In December of 1876, the* Oceanic *made a speed record crossing between Yokohama and San Francisco.*

In 1889, the Oceanic *made its last record breaking voyage, doing the same route in 13 days, 14 hours and 5 minutes. Six years later, the liner was returned to White Star management. Attempts to refurbish the liner were abandoned, and on 1896, the classic liner left Belfast for the last time—towed by a Dutch tug.*

From 1840 until World War I, approximately 37 million immigrants arrived in the United States. The first thirty years brought to America about 10.5 million people, mostly from Germany, The British Isles and Ireland. In later years, immigrant numbers increased for people from Southern and Eastern Europe.

The main reasons for the massive immigration were religious persecution, industrialization and poverty. They were caused by famines and mechanization of farming in rural areas, and overcrowding and unemployment in cities. Ellis Island, in New York Harbor (actually located in New Jersey), didn't become an immigration station until 1890. Until that time, the passengers were processed at a place known as Castle Garden in the Battery on the tip of Long Island.

The Dutch first settled the spot in 1623, and they named it New Amsterdam. In 1664, they surrendered it to the British who renamed it Fort James. The point of land changed hands several times over the years, and in 1689 a "Halfe Moone" military battery was built on the site.

By 1756, the battery consisted of 92 guns. The Americans eventually took over the property and turned it into a fortification, referred to as the West Battery during the War of 1812. In 1815, the site was renamed Castle Clinton and became headquarters for the Third Military District. Eight years later, the site was ceded to New York City.

One year later, it was renamed Castle Garden and leased to the New York State Commissioners of Emigration. More than 8,000,000 new Americans were processed there until 1890, at which time immigration processing was transferred to Ellis Island.

2

COLLIN AND BLANCHE STOOD in a long line of people waiting for immigration processing at Castle Garden, a former military fortress built on the tip of Manhattan Island. Two hours had passed and Blanche could hardly stand. He put his arms around her waist to keep her from falling. "Only one more and we are next."

"Name please?"

"Collin McBride."

"Destination?"

"Heaven."

The immigration agent looked up from his table. "All right—no jokes—destination!"

"Missouri."

The agent asked several questions, filling a form as he did. Looking up at Collin, he nodded and pressed a rubber stamp down on one form and then another. He handed one of them to Collin and said, "Next."

Collin grabbed the paper and turned toward where he expected Blanche to be standing. He didn't see her and anxiously looked in all directions. Collin surveyed all the people standing in line and others who sat on benches or lay in clusters on the ground—no Blanche. He felt sickened with the thought that he would never see her again.

He walked outside the Castle, laden with two pieces of luggage, one extremely heavy. His back felt like a concrete slab. Collin succeeded in hiring a horse drawn wagon to haul him to the train station. Collin felt the sharp breeze on his face as the wagon rumbled through the streets. He continued to look for Blanche amongst the many people walking in and around the streets. His back stiffened and his torso felt exhausted as he got off the wagon. Collin paid the driver and lugged his pieces into the station. He studied the lines at the ticket counters, calculating where he could set his larger piece of luggage while standing in line.

He decided to take both pieces with him and move them along as he got closer to the ticket seller. After nudging his luggage along for close to an hour, he finally stood in front of the small window.

"Name, sir?"

"Con—ah, Collin McBride, 'tis."

Collin felt perspiration spreading on his forehead. He felt the flush of his cheeks. I am no longer Conor McGearney. Henceforward, my name is Collin McBride, he said to himself.

"Sign here, Mr. McBride. Welcome to America."

— —

COLLIN MCBRIDE JOSTLED HIMSELF AWAKE. "Where are we?" he asked the man across the aisle.

The tall, lean, black-clothed man turned his head slightly, the pupils of his narrow black eyes shining from the light in the window. "Harrisburg, Pennsylvania."

Collin shrugged his shoulders. "How far is that from New York?"

"Depends where ya headin'?"

"Missouri."

"Then, it ain't very far that we've gone." The tall man stretched out his legs and pulled the brim of his hat down over his nose.

Collin stood and twisted his frame back and forth. "I'm mighty stiff, aye tell ya."

The tall man didn't respond.

Collin sat down. The ever-changing landscape lulled him into a lethargic daze. He closed his eyes and thought about the past.

It was a damp, drizzly day when Collin went for a walk that evening back home in Ireland. The air smelled of the sea. With a smoke pipe in his backpack, he set out to his favorite place, just beyond the glen—a sheltered area. Many times previous when feeling the need to think deeply, he had gone there.

The moisture in the air gravitated between a mist and areas of rolling fog. Collin was just a bit short of reaching his destination when he heard two people quarrelling. He stood silently, straining his eyes to identify them. Collin saw his brother Patrick who was shouting at a second person. It looked like Timothy, his other brother.

Tension built in his stomach as he watched his brothers yelling at each other. Collin snuggled tightly to a tree, hidden. The quarreling continued. Collin couldn't hear exactly what the argument entailed, but he didn't have to. He bloody well knew—Paddy's decision to pass his estate to Patrick—all of it—only to him. His brother Timothy had gotten himself into an awful twist about it.

Suddenly, Patrick turned and began to walk away. Collin held his breath watching Timothy raise a long object and strike Patrick over the head—he fell. The club went up and down several more times.

Collin felt stunned, his hands shaking, and fearful of moving. Timothy stood over his brother for a time, his head bowed. Then, he quickly walked away, disappearing in the fog, taking the club with him.

Collin remembered breathing in short, jerky gasps. He truly didn't know what to do. How could he ever forget what he saw after walking over to his brother Patrick? The head had been beaten to a bloody pulp. Peering into the fog where his killer had disappeared, Collin made a decision—do nothing—say nothing. He didn't like Patrick anyhow and losing him didn't sadden him.

Conor had returned to his father's house and went directly to his room. He lay on the bed with his face in the pillow for what seemed hours. The sharp knock on the door jolted him to reality.

"Conor, have you seen your brother?" Patrick's wife asked from behind the door.

"Nay, I have not," Conor lied.

"Can I come in?"

"Aye."

Mary opened the door. She stood in the doorway, a worried look on her face. "Would you and Timothy help me look for him? Patrick went for a walk but that was two hours ago. He should've been back long ago. This is so unlike him."

Conor, Timothy and Mary spread out and walked toward the glen. Conor noticed that Timothy, too, evaded the area where Patrick lay dead. The inevitable scream came. "Ahhhh!" Mary's frame spread out over her husband's body.

Timothy knelt down by her. "Heavens Almighty, what's happened here?"

Conor's memory of what happened next remained vague at best. He remembered his father, Mathew, sending a messenger by horseback to neighboring Galway to fetch authorities. Hours later, a constable, along with a Guard Investigator arrived. They concluded Patrick had been bludgeoned to death.

Even though there wasn't conclusive evidence as to who perpetrated the crime, Timothy became the Guard's only suspect. Family and neighbors had also come to the same conclusion. Timothy didn't have an alibi during the time period when the crime occurred. He, too, had gone for a walk that evening.

There were never any formal charges filed against Timothy, but his father refused to honor him as his heir, strongly suspecting that Timothy had killed his own brother. Instead, Mathew allotted the total inheritance to his youngest son, Conor.

Mathew's heart failed before he had the opportunity to finalize the legalities, and Timothy successfully used the courts to divide up the estate equally between himself, his younger brother Conor and Mary, his sister-in-law.

Severe bitterness arose between the two brothers. As time passed, the animosity between them grew into intolerable proportions. Timothy made a decision. He sold all his assets in Ireland and acquired property in America—an established farmstead and land in western Missouri. It was the Sunnerland property that belonged to two brothers, Lafe and Jesse, who had chosen to sell their farm after the Civil War ended.

3

THICK, BLACK SMOKE BILLOWED FROM SMOKE STACKS in the countryside. The smell and appearance of that type of smoke are rife across much of England and Ireland. Collin scratched the top of his right shoulder. He had studied the map earlier in the day and knew the town coming up was Pittsburg, Pennsylvania.

An hour later, the railcar couplings banged on each other as the train moved slowly westward. He heard the car door open. The conductor entered, moving slowly down the aisle, occasionally muttering to passengers and looking at their tickets.

"Did you have a good night, Mr. McBride?"

"I'll tell ya straight out, it was a long night—mighty long night." Collins's elbows jutted outward. He yawned as the conductor passed.

Later the train crossed a wide river. He stood and moved into the aisle to stretch his legs. Collin stood next to a tall man sitting across from him. He reached out his hand. "I'm Collin McBride—who do I have the pleasure of meeting?"

"Mantraux. Pierre Mantraux."

"Glad to meet you, lad. I'm goin' for me walk."

"Cincinnati! Cincinnati! Ten minutes," the conductor cried as he wobbled down the aisle.

— —

A HERD OF DEER FED in a field as the train crossed the border into Kentucky. Collin saw more horses in a span of about ten miles than he had ever seen in Ireland during his entire lifetime.

Three hours later, the train arrived in Louisville. They re-crossed the Ohio River and headed west. His mind grew weary as they chugged by endless miles of rolling hills and forests.

The conductor strolled by and said they would be in St. Louis by dawn. Fatigued, Collin fell asleep. Several hours later, he opened one eye slightly and faced the bright rim of the rising sun. He became alarmed looking down, seeing nothing but water. He had heard the Missouri River was wide.

More time passed. The conductor, a different man, skinny with a warbling voice, came through. He sang out, "Jefferson City next—Jefferson City."

Collin's stomach rumbled with hunger. He reached in his bag and brought out the last of his vittles. I better wait with that, he said to himself, still a long way to go.

The tall, dark-clothed man who earlier had introduced himself as Pierre Mantraux stood in the aisle. "How much farther is it to Stillman Mills?" Collin asked.

"Five hours—give or take—depends on whether the James gang will pay us a visit or not."

"The James gang! Will yeh tell me who they are—the James gang?"

"Robbers—they rob stagecoaches and trains. Nuthin' ta worry about unless ya got a lot of cash on ya."

Collin sat up straight. He grabbed his smaller bag and placed it on his lap.

Mantraux narrowed his eyes, staring at Collin. "Then, ya do 'ave somethin' to worry about."

Collin forced a smile and set the bag back down on the floor. He took periodic glances out the window, hoping not to see the James gang. He became considerably more relaxed as the hours passed.

Mantraux leaned forward and pointed toward Collin's window. "See that big tree way up that hill? That's a lone jack oak. We're passin' through the town of Lone Jack. There was a big battle near that tree during the Civil War."

— —

PIERRE MANTRAUX CLOSED HIS EYES, his mind drifting to the past—his experiences during the Civil War. The smell of bacon and coffee reached the sergeant's nostrils as he sat in front of a vat of water, washing his face and hands. He heard the usual grunts and groans coming from his fellow soldiers who didn't appreciate the beginning of a new day on a potential battlefield.

Pierre hailed from a small town in central Illinois. His father and mother had migrated from France in 1841 when he was only one year old. At age 19, he volunteered to join the Illinois State Guard.

During training, many of his sidekicks talked about how President Lincoln had grown up in Illinois. Some of them agreed and others didn't that the Union needed to be preserved regardless of the cost. Pierre felt all along that the president was going to plunge the country into a civil war.

Other than a skirmish with a handful of Rebs the previous evening, Pierre had never seen action in a battle. Lieutenant Farnsworth had talked to his group at last light the previous day. He said that the enemy was not very far away, and advised the men to be prepared for action at any given moment.

A strange looking tree stood alone on the landscape of a pronounced hill—lone jack oak, someone called it yesterday evening, he remembered. General Foster, his commander, had ridden over to the tree earlier. His officers gathered around the trunk and ate their dinners. Some of his aides set up his headquarters in a tent near a two-story building a short distance away to the northwest.

"Coffee, Sergeant?" a soldier asked, carrying a large metal pot.

"Yes, I certainly would like some."

Pierre took his first sip, savoring the taste as it flowed down his throat.

A gunshot split the air and Pierre leaped to his feet. He looked out across the grassland to the west and saw the tops of hats and shoulders weaving their way through a grassy field as they approached the hill.

He remembered the next three hours of the battle as filled with smoke and screams. A herd of horses totally out of control had galloped right through the firing line, many of them falling.

Three times he and his group retreated to the cornfield behind them. During the fourth charge of the day he remembered shooting at and hitting a Reb in the tall grass. He saw the rifle fly into the air and the soldier fall down. Moments later, he was forced to retreat, not being able to reload in time to defend against two saber-yielding black men.

The battle ended shortly after the noon hour, mainly because both sides suffered from exhaustion. Pierre remembered his sadness seeing a wagon full of raggedy-looking Reb prisoners. They're a sorry looking lot, he said to himself. Then he saw the face...he knew instantly it belonged to the Confederate who he had shot in the tall, grassy field earlier.

Pierre never forgot the painful look on the soldier's face. He asked Lieutenant Farnsworth, one of his officers, where the wagon was headed—the prison in Butler.

Two weeks later, Pierre furloughed back to his home in central Illinois. During his trip, he stopped at the prison and couldn't believe it when he saw that face again.

Later he learned the soldiers name—Justin Haggard.

4

COLLIN, PARTIALLY ASLEEP, HEARD HIMSELF SNORING. Gunshots startled him. His upper body jerked and he sat up, alarmed.

"Where—what!" he exclaimed.

The conductor came hurrying up the aisle. "Any of you fellas got money belts? Best give 'em to me now. We're about to get held up!"

Collin felt his heart thumping as he anxiously watched out the window. Suddenly, a horse and rider appeared abreast of his window, smoke emitting from a long-barreled pistol. Quickly reaching into his bag, he grabbed a metal box. "Conductor, my life depends on this."

The Conductor placed the box into a canvas container and hurried down the aisle, adding items from other passengers. Soon as the conductor vanished, the train began to slow. Collin heard the wheels screech on the metal rails. Several jerks later, the train came to a dead stop. The inside of the passenger car became very still.

Suddenly, the rear door snapped open. Two men entered. One of them waved a pair of pistols. "All right, ladies and gentleman—nothing to worry about. Just place your watches, your money and your rings into this bag."

"Hey, look at this, Jesse—a diamond," one of the bandits said.

The well dressed, good looking woman in the seat behind Mantraux exclaimed loudly, "How dare you! How dare you take my ring? You are a coward."

The bandit held up the ring for everyone to see. "Ah can use this for me, honey," he said, sneering and then smiling.

Mantraux leaned toward Collin. He whispered, "Sit still,

McBride—don't say a thing or try to be a hero. The shorter, dark-haired bandit is Jesse James. The taller one is Cole Younger."

Suddenly, the man who Pierre referred to as Jesse turned away from the woman and looked at Collin. "Ah'll take your money now, mister."

Collin dropped a fist full of bills into the bandit's bag.

"Thank ye, sir. Much obliged."

Collin felt relieved when the bandit turned away from him and approached Pierre Mantraux across the aisle. "Thanks much, mister."

Collin tensed when he saw the portly man in the seat ahead of Mantraux holding a small pistol in his fist. He held his breath as the bandit advanced two steps toward him. The man chose to hide the pistol and remove a gold watch from his vest. He dropped it into the bag. That was close, Collin thought.

He heard the rear door open again. Another bandit entered. He heard Mantraux whisper loudly, "That's Bob Younger comin' up the aisle. Stay still."

Collin's stomach tightened again as the third bandit approached.

"Good day, ma'am," the bandit said to the woman sitting behind Mantraux.

She began sobbing hysterically, struggling to talk. "Mister, they took my diamond ring. It's the only item of remembrance I have of my dead husband. He died fighting for the cause—the Confederacy."

The bandit paused, his face expressing sorrow. "Hey, Jesse—hold up a bit!" the bandit yelled.

Younger hastened up the aisle. Momentarily later, he returned. The tips of his fingers clutched a diamond ring. "Here ya are, ma'am. Good as new."

"Oh, thank ye—ah—Mr.?"

"Younger, ma'am—Bob Younger."

Collin's mouth gaped open as the bandit stooped over and kissed the woman on the forehead. He held his breath as she reached up an arm and grasped the robber around the neck, pulled his head down and kissed him on the lips.

Younger paused for a moment looking down at her, a wide smile on his face. He stepped away. "Sorry for the interruption, folks. Enjoy your trip," he said and hurried toward the front door.

Half an hour later, the train started up again. Collin felt immensely relieved when the conductor brought back his box. He clutched it to his chest. Taking a couple of deep breaths, he placed the box back into his case.

He felt even better a few minutes later when the conductor came by and said. "Stillman Mills, next."

— —

COLLIN MCBRIDE SAT UP STRAIGHT AS THE TRAIN slowed. Short chugging gasps from the engine spurted charcoal-colored puffs of smoke from the top edges of the black-stained smokestack. The conveyance, which he boarded in New York nearly a month ago, at long last approached Stillman Mills in western Missouri. His trip originated in Ireland and neared its end. Final destination: Tarrytown, Missouri.

The passenger cars jerked and clattered before coming to a screeching stop. The woman perched on the edge of her seat just back of Pierre Mantraux glanced at him and smiled. Collin's coal-dark eyes came alive, looking beyond other passengers who shuffled with their belongings in the aisle. He had built up strong feelings for the woman.

Miss Rosemary Pikes, who boarded in St. Louis, reduced Collin's drudgery of travel during the final leg of his train journey from St. Louis. They spent many hours talking about their life's experiences. Collin inhaled and held his breath for a moment, enjoying the aroma of her perfume as she hastened to tidy up before disembarking.

I'll tell ya straight out, me man, he said to himself, aye could go for that lass. She's a bit too much of a charmer, though. Reminds me a bit of my cousin's mate back in Dublin. The train robber must've got his fill of the perfume.

His tweed flattop hat with a bit of green in the mix matched his baggy-kneed trousers. The light-brown waistcoat bulged because of his watch and chain tucked in a breast pocket. If I hadn't hid it, the bandits would have gotten my ticker—my only remembrance of my grandfather, he said to himself. Collin stood and scratched his unshaven chin. He picked up his coat that lay on the seat next to him.

"Aye there, Miss Pikes. May I be of any assistance to you?" Collin asked wistfully. "I'm glad that you got your ring back."

"I do appreciate your concern, Mr. McBride, but the trainman is sending someone to carry my luggage and things out onto the platform. From there, they will wheel it to the stagecoach office, wherever that is."

"Aye, Miss. That's where my loot is all going. Are ye then going to take a ride west on the same conveyance as I am—pitiful steeped wagon that it may be?"

Rosemary ran a hand over her three-tiered hoop skirt of muslin printed in a paisley pattern of light blue and white. She repeated the process several times to remove the wrinkles. "Yes, Mister McBride. I only hope that we have arrived in time to catch your previously mentioned, pitifully-wheeled transport, or find some alternative way. I dare not trust my safety to a stranger."

The Irishman nodded, running his bitten-off fingernails over his shaggy eyebrows. He padded some of the hairs down with the tips of his finger. "Aye, I wouldn't mind having a go at loaning a horse and buggy. Would ye be interested at all, Miss Rosemary?"

Rosemary rounded her deep red lips and quickly stepped into the aisle. "No, thanks. I think it would be safer on the stagecoach." She wrapped her fingers around the handle of a large brown bag that lay next to her. She groaned slightly as she dragged it across the seat and stood in the aisle.

"'Twas a privilege meetin' you, mister," Rosemary said and began her trek toward the front of the train car where the line of debarking passengers had shortened.

Collin watched the woman as she moved along, her right shoulder drooping, strained by the weight of a large bag. The stagecoach—as much as I've heard horrid stories about it, I'm going to give it a go, he said to himself.

— —

COLLIN STOOD ON THE WOODEN PLATFORM at the railroad station and watched in amazement as horse drawn wagons of all shapes and sizes paraded in front of him.

A dray loaded with trunks and baggage finally began to move. Its wheels squeaked much like chimpanzees did entertaining a crowd of people at the zoo in Dublin. He felt the soft, moist soil underneath his boots as he walked off the platform and followed.

Farther down, he saw many people milling about. They stood on planked boardwalks next to the muddy road. Gads, the street is thrice the width of the one in my village of Minen, he thought.

Saloon—he read the sign across the street where saloon doors continually swung open pushed by cowboys passing through. Cowboys are known as *horsemen* in my country, he said to himself—their infamous saloon is known as a *pub*.

Horses tied to hitching posts along the boardwalk stood lazily and quietly, an occasional head drooping down to nibble at grasses growing wildly where the street met the walkway. He stopped and looked into the face of a black stallion, its face appearing to be all eyes and teeth.

He saw it for the first time—the stagecoach. Not what I expected, he thought. It was colored a scarlet-red—magnificent, beyond anything he had ever dreamed of. The two back wheels were extraordinarily large—close to twice the size of the front ones. Six heavily harnessed horses, teamed in pairs, stood stoically, patiently waiting for a command.

Collin entered the stage depot office. He felt delighted to see his new acquaintance, Miss Pikes, sitting on a bench next to a window. Aye, she is staring at me, he thought, watching her long red hair beneath her bonnet dance on her shoulders. He nudged by a group of people and reached a barred window. The ticket master, a round-faced, bald man sat on a stool, his glasses propped down on his nose.

Collin's jaw stretched back and forth. "Aye! 'Tis Collin McBride that I am. I have a reserved ticket on the stage to Tarrytown."

"It's all in order, Mr. McBride. The boys are loading your baggage on the stage as we speak. Two dollars will take care of your end of the finances, mister."

Collin handed the man two coins and reached for his ticket.

"Ya give this to Lafe Sunnerland. He's the big 'un out there loadin' bags and gear."

Sunnerland—where 'ave ah heard that name before? He asked himself, frowning. He wrenched an elbow and flicked a thumb over the tip of his chin. *Sunnerland*—it's a bit of a shemozzle, but that's the name of the people who my brother bought his land from—the reason for me being here, 'tis true.

The Stage Coach

WELLS FARGO ORIGINATED IN CALIFORNIA ON MARCH 18, 1852, as a subsidiary of American Express Company. By 1863, they purchased the Pioneer Overland Stage Line. The original purpose of the company was to deliver mail.

By the end of 1863, the company had 180 depots throughout the West. The Overland Stage Line purchased its stage coaches from a company in Concord, New Hampshire. They built large coaches usually painted red except for a yellow underbelly. Wells Fargo ordered 30 of the nine passenger variety, mainly to service the men who were building the Transcontinental Railroad. Some of the coaches had a seating capacity of 12.

Holdups of stagecoaches by bandits such as the legendary Black Bart and Rattlesnake Dick occurred frequently. There were 313 holdups recorded during the '60s. Wells Fargo hired private detectives, which led to the convictions of 240 outlaws and the prevention of 34 holdups.

As the 19th century came to a close, Wells Fargo had over 2,800 branch offices and had close to 38,000 miles of Overland Stage. In 1918, Wells Fargo and American Express Company merged into the American Railroad Express Company. In 1923, Wells Fargo merged with the Union Trust Company and became known as Wells Fargo Bank and Union Trust Company.

See References in the back of the book.

— —

COLLIN WALKED OUTSIDE TO MAKE CERTAIN his luggage had been hoisted to the top of the coach. "Thank ye, Mr. Sunnerland. How much time will it be?"

"About half an hour," the stocky, barrel-chested man said, his voice sounding like the loud chirp of a bird. Collin nodded and smiled, looking into the man's light gray eyes. The man had a thin blond mustache, the same color as the long hair draped over his shoulders.

Collin walked back into the depot and took a seat on the long bench next to the wall. His thoughts drifted to his paddy, Mathew. and when he went by the name of Conor. He would never forget when the barrister showed up in their house one day. Paddy and their visitor met for more than an hour alone. Conor had overheard some of their conversation. They discussed the distribution of his father's wealth.

Patrick, the eldest, as family tradition dictated, would take his father's position and assume control of all the land and properties. He heard Paddy say, "Conor and Timothy can comfortably continue to live within the framework of Patrick's operations—they will marry, have families, and own their own houses."

After the barrister left, Mathew called Timothy, his second eldest, into his study. Paddy informed his son about his failing health, and winced watching his face. He saw deep sadness. When Timothy dropped his chin to his chest, Mathew rose from his chair and walked to a window. He gazed at the rolling hills that slanted out to the sea. Taking a deep breath, he walked back to where his son sat.

"Timothy, when I'm gone, you'll have a place here at the Lourgha. However, your elder brother will inherit all my property—it is a tradition that goes back for centuries."

Conor studied the expression on his brother's face. Looking away quickly, he feared at what he had just witnessed—a quick reddening. Timothy appeared shocked and disappointed.

Conor heard Timothy vigorously plead with his father. He insisted that he and his two brothers share the estate equally.

"My decision is final, son," his father said. Conor watched

Timothy throw up his arms in disgust and stomp toward the doorway. The door slammed shut.

Collin had no doubt that Timothy was angry enough to kill. Yet, he understood his pain.

5

"ARE YOU COMIN' WITH US, THOMAS?" Bob Younger asked.

"No, I'm afraid not. The farm needs my attention. Besides, ah can't leave Sarah alone. She's with child."

"I understand. Good luck."

"Where are ya headin'?" Thomas asked.

"Up north—Jesse and Frank want to settle a score with a scoundrel who Frank met during the war—now a banker in Minnesota—a place called Northfield."

Thomas Hastings sat in his saddle as he watched Bob Younger prod his knees into his horse and ride off. His friend's horse leaped over a small creek and galloped to the peak of a hill where other riders had been waiting. Thomas had an uneasy feeling as several arms waved. They trotted their horses toward a grove of timber. Thomas watched until they reached the trees. He saw one of them raise his hat. That's gotta be Bob, Thomas thought and took off his own hat, holding it high.

Moments later, the riders disappeared from view. Minnesota is one heck of a long way from here, he said to himself. The James's must have a very deep-seated reason to go that far. It's mainly to gain revenge, I've heard. The war ended eleven years ago. I can understand some of their thinking. Jesse's step-father was hung right in front of his own eyes by Union soldiers—didn't die though. The Younger boys had reasons for revenge also. Their father was murdered by Bluecoats while he was delivering mail for the U.S. Postal Department.

Thomas flicked his reins and his horse trotted eastward. He had been visiting his parents and sister in Independence. His father, Henry, had been experiencing ill health. Emma, his mother, enjoyed city living so much that Thomas knew she would never return to the farm.

Genevieve, his sister, had married an attorney from Kansas City. She traveled by stage to Independence to see Thomas when he visited his parents. She had two daughters whom Thomas had never seen. Genevieve had promised they would visit the farm the very next summer.

Thomas sat medium-tall in the saddle. The early growth spurt that had occurred during his teenage years slowed down. He stopped growing at just under six feet. Thomas's long, narrow arms hung from wide shoulders. His once ruddy, round face had darkened and narrowed. His bright blue eyes had not changed one bit.

Thomas thought about his wife, Sarah, and the child they expected in December. They got married in 1872 after most post-war hostilities ceased.

The war-related conflicts due to gangs of bushwhackers, redlegs and jayhawkers had inflicted severe damage to the Hastings' buildings. The barn was burned to the ground and the house survived, but it was heavily damaged. With his neighbors help, he repaired the house and built a new barn.

Thomas's brother, Grady, married Helen Walker. They lived on the Walker farm north of the Tarrytown Road. Grady, the leader of the latent band of Gray Riders, had survived the war, but the wound he got fighting at the Battle of the Little Blue River, left one of his arms limply hanging. Both of Grady's shoulders tilted forward slightly.

Thomas thought about his other neighbors: Lafe and Jesse Sunnerland; Jubal and Justin Haggard; Mitch and James McGregor; and Abel Kingsley. He knew that he would admire their bravery to his grave. They had all ridden and fought with the Gray Riders.

Thomas rode for hours before he could see the bluish shadows of Bear Mountain. He dismounted to rest his frame and eat the remaining food in his knapsack. He sat down with his back supported by the trunk of a tree. Thomas studied the high range of hills as he ate. They extended fifteen miles in an east-west direction, towering over his farm and that of his neighbors. He got back up on his horse and set it into a trot, excited that he would reach his home and loving wife within an hour.

— —

SARAH HASTINGS PEERED OUT THE WINDOW of the door that accessed the north porch. She anxiously awaited the return of her husband. The fingers of her hand pressed against the ever-enlarging bulge in her midriff. She felt movement and smiled. Her brother, Abel Kingsley, had visited earlier in the day. He helped her pass the time by getting her to laugh, deflating her feelings of emptiness.

The chairs on the porch sat vacant for yet another day. Her loneliness grew as she stared at the one Thomas sat on almost every evening. She thought about her husband and how he almost always had a long, dark cigar protruding from his mouth. She walked out onto the porch and anxiously eyed the Tarrytown Road, hoping to see Thomas and his horse approaching. She saw no one.

The buildings a good distance beyond the road belonged to her brother who had just visited. He had tripled the size of her father's Angus herd. Most of the cattle had amazingly survived the war—thanks mostly to his neighbors, Priam Jackson and his family.

The Jackson family, former slaves, had been released from servitude and deeded forty acres by Abel's father before the war began. Sarah thought about how her father's generosity proved to be a very good decision. They successfully protected the herds during the entire war. They suffered one tragedy. Their eldest son had been killed fighting with the Gray Riders and the Missouri State Militia against the Union at the Battle of the Hemp Bales in Lexington.

She remembered all the Jackson boys and their bravery during the war, even though she was only a young girl. A tear came to her eye when she thought about Jordon and his funeral. Later, Elkanah and Baskhall also rode with the Gray Riders. She remembered their heroics fighting off an attack by invading redlegs at the Haggard's farm. She visualized the perpetual-smiling Priam Jackson and his wife Virgilia. They were both alive and healthy, continuing to live in their original house. Their two daughters both got married—Elisha to Sammy Morton, and Brittany to Abraham Eagan from Stillman Mills.

Sarah wished that Abel would marry his girlfriend, Mary, currently employed at the mercantile store in Tarrytown. She liked her and admired her vivacious personality.

She heard men's voices yelling out near the barn. She walked out the front door and stood on the stoop. The torso of one of the hired men bobbed up and down ferociously as a young horse in the corral attempted to buck him off. Luke, the foreman, sat on a corral rail and waved his arms and shouted encouragement as the young rider struggled to remain on the bucking steed.

Sarah smiled and reentered the house. Her blonde hair was shortened considerably since her school years. Some of the reddish freckles that ordained her cheeks remained but had darkened. Sarah had unusual eye color—basically hazel with attractive streaks of blue. Her full ruby lips, slightly parted, exposed a set of white teeth.

She walked to the other side of the house and stepped onto the front porch so she could watch the Tarrytown Road. Sarah sat down with hope and watched the western countryside—still no Thomas. She shook her head.

An hour later, a single rider approached. She felt a surge of excitement. "It's Thomas! He's comin' home!" Sarah blurted and danced around on the wooden floor.

— —

THOMAS PULLED ON THE REINS abreast of Haggard's land. A cluster of deer ran along one of their fields. They turned and leaped across the Tarrytown Road, continuing to run toward a patch of brush west of the McGregor barn. Thomas waved to tall Orly McGregor, the elderly father, who sat on a chair on the porch in front of his house. His sons, Mitch and James, Thomas's friends, had recently taken over the running of the farm.

Thomas passed by the McGregor buildings and approached Jubal Haggard's on the other side of the road. Thomas and Jubal had been close friends since school days. The attractive house was built after the war, the original structure destroyed in a fire started by marauding hostiles.

Jubal married Jessica Walker, a sister of Helen Walker who became the wife of Grady Hastings. Jubal and Jessica brought into the world a son, currently age eight and a daughter age six. Directly behind the house, a white painted barn towered over a one-story bunkhouse that Jubal's brother Justin called home.

Thomas remembered Justin losing his leg after getting wounded and taken prisoner at the Battle of Lone Jack. He heard many versions of Justin's capture and escape from whisky-talking cowboys at the saloon in Tarrytown. I'll never forget the day Justin came riding into town, Thomas thought. He was close to a dead man in the saddle. It took seven days of miracle doctoring for him to survive and live to see this day.

He rode past the Haggard's property line. Timothy McGearney's farm loomed ahead. They were the last farm buildings he would see before arriving home. Lafe and Jesse Sunnerland sold their property a couple of years after the war to McGearney, who migrated to Missouri from Ireland after the war. The silver painted barn back of the house had survived the conflict and stood tall and straight. Thomas remembered helping to build the barn in 1863, doing his part by supplying the volunteer builders with nails.

Thomas approached Bear Creek, a deep, rugged gorge draining streams of water from Bear Mountain. It traversed the McGearney land from southwest to northeast, cutting across part of Thomas's land before angling across the Kingsley farm. Thomas approached the wooden planked bridge that allowed the water coming down the creek to flow uninhibited.

Flowering dogwood shrubs dominated the fauna near the road. The main creek, heavily populated with undergrowth and copses of oak and Lombardy poplar trees, looked rather dry, he thought. An occasional gray-greenish Russian olive tree stood in the midst of reddish-maroon kousa dogwood bushes. He halted his horse and admired the view—the area surrounding the creek, and the slope leading up to the mountain.

The clop-clop of his horse's hooves on the plank-surfaced bridge echoed across the valley. Thomas turned his horse onto his roadway and saw someone waving from the front porch, his feelings warming with each passing moment. "It's Sarah!" he exclaimed loudly and directed his horse into a gallop.

Thomas tied his horse to a rail next to the house and dashed over to Sarah, her face locked into a wide smile. Thomas kissed his wife on the lips and arched his back as he gently embraced her. "I missed you while I was gone. And how might you be feeling, dear?"

Sarah's face gleamed. "I know nothing but happiness at the moment, Thomas. I feel so good that you've returned safely. It gets so lonely—so lonely."

"Tomorrow I'll take you into Tarrytown and we'll pay Doctor Blake a visit."

"Oh, Thomas, do I have to?"

"Yes, my love, you do," Thomas replied firmly.

— —

ANNABELLE SMILED AND NODDED. Sarah's goin' to do just fine, she said to herself as she stood on her toes to put the last of the dinner dishes into the cupboard.

She wore a black dress sprinkled with clusters of hand-stitched flowers. Her round face, perpetually smiling, and gray hair pulled back into a bun, blended into rounded shoulders, a generous bosom and waist.

Annabelle's brother, Samuel Morton had been a slave of the Hastings's, prior to the Civil War. Annabelle remained behind instead of migrating to Pittsburg with her family to find work with a coal company.

She hummed a tune as she gathered crumbs and bits of debris from the floor around the kitchen table. She swept the small pile into a pan and stepped outside, flinging the debris onto the ground. Annabelle removed her slightly stained white apron and shook it out before reentering the house.

Thomas and Sarah Hastings had employed Annabelle as their housemaid for the past five years. They had an addition built onto the house so that she could live in privacy. Annabelle walked through the door leading to the front porch. "Goodness sakes, Thomas, you must be thirsty after that long ride."

Thomas turned. He smiled broadly at her. "Yar absolutely right, Annabelle. Would ya bring me a bottle of whiskey and two glasses?"

"What's the second glass fer, Thomas? Ya know Sarah can't drink."

"Ah, yes, Annabelle, I forgot. Bring some water please."

— —

PEDRO ORTIZ SMILED AS HE APPROACHED the Hastings's house. He had nothing but good feelings about his employer, Thomas Hastings. My boss treats my family and me proper, he thought. Pedro's family consisted of a wife, three daughters and two sons.

"Mistah Thomas—Misses Thomas. Good evenin' to you both," the short, stocky round-faced man said.

"Pedro, is there something ya need?"

"Si, we're almost out of sugar and coffee. Flour, too."

Thomas's smile died. He frowned. "I'll get ya what ya need when ah go into town."

"Si, senor."

The Ortiz family lived in the former Hastings's slave quarters. The buildings had been totally refurbished. Thomas paid his workers well, needing more and more help for his ever-increasing acreage of hemp and other crops and animals.

Sarah watched Mr. Ortiz as he walked away. She thought of him and his family in a special way, and volunteered to help them at every turn.

"Thomas!" she exclaimed.

"What is it, honey?"

"I think that we need to build the Ortiz's a whole new house. It's been so long."

Thomas nodded and thought about his father, Henry. He wouldn't have understood, but then again, times had changed. Maybe Sarah has a point, he thought.

6

ROSEMARY PIKES FOUND THE IRISHMAN to be amusing and entertaining during the long train ride from St. Louis, but she didn't feel interested in him—at least for now. His tale of discourse and failure in his native Ireland sounded a bit farfetched, she thought. I've got enough problems of my own and don't need to listen to someone else's.

She looked forward to seeing Constance again. Their families had been friends in St. Louis, and the two girls had gone to school together. Through a mutual friend, Rosemary had contacted Constance and was offered a very good position in the Frontier Saloon. "Lady Constance" is what the cowboys called her over there.

Her long eyelashes fluttered as she glanced out the window. A short, stocky man lifted one of her pieces upward to a man perched on top of the colorful coach. She had previously heard mention of a conveyance that people called a *stagecoach*. Rosemary didn't really know what to expect. There it is, she thought—wheels and horses, and that strange looking red-painted fairy tail carriage.

Perhaps leaving St. Louis after my husband died was not the best thing to do, she thought. Ever since we left, the atmosphere westward has looked more and more belligerent. Then things changed. I loved the train robbery. She thought about the sweet kiss that she had gotten from one of the bandits. He recovered her diamond ring that Jesse James took from her.

The canvas bag she clutched contained most of her valuable jewelry. Jesse James or whatever someone called him didn't get it, she said to herself. Mr. Mantraux and the conductor pulled off a fast one, probably because they had been robbed so many times before.

Rosemary closed her eyes. Her thoughts lazily drifted back to St. Louis. She had been exiled from her home by her late husband's family. Her brother-in-law threatened legal civil action against her—the brute claimed she was responsible for her husband's death. "Take what money you got and git," the man had said. Ha, she thought, little did the bastard know that my secret bank account was bulging with assets that have been accumulating for years. She chuckled. "Git, I did," she whispered, smiling, then laughing loudly.

She snapped her eyes open to the sound of shuffling feet. Rosemary looked around the waiting room and saw people leaving.

"Time to board," the squeaky-voiced, round-faced man behind the barred window said, looking at her.

Rosemary hurriedly got up and walked outside, stopping near the stagecoach door.

"After you, lass," she heard the Irishman say.

One of the stagecoach drivers supported her right shoulder with one of his massive hands. "Up ya go, ma'am,"

She took two steps into the coach interior and quizzically inspected the seats available. A gentleman, dressed in black, took off his hat and stood. "Madam, take my seat by that window." He pointed.

The man was extremely well-dressed and possessed well-defined, even features. A slender wrist and hand emerged from his sleeve as he reached out to her. She cautiously grasped the tips of his fingers and accepted his offer for a seat with a view. "Thank you very much, Mr.?"

"Pierre Mantraux at your service, madam."

Rosemary sat down and set her traveling bag on her lap. She watched as Mr. Mantraux reached out a hand to assist a young lady. "Watch your step, madam," he said, his French accent attractively amusing, she thought.

The young lady spoke, her voice timid, almost trembling, "Thank you, sir." She accepted his guiding hand, her long blonde hair splashing against her shoulder blades, as she sat down next to Rosemary Pikes.

"Hello. I'm Rosemary. Make yourself comfortable."

The pale-faced young lady said, "Why, thank you. I'm Cosette Barnard." The dimple in the middle of her chin deepened. Her tight-lipped smile exposed light blue eyes that glittered from the light filtering through a window.

Rosemary looked at her white poplin dress that featured a carter's frock. She nodded approval of the white stripped sateen underskirt. Rosemary cocked her head upward and eyed the lace choker, tightly snuggled under the high collar. Hmm, she sure has good taste in clothing, including the straw skimmer, Rosemary thought as she placed a hand on the young lady's arm. "Where're you headin'?"

"I'm going to be the new school teacher in Tarrytown."

Rosemary smiled wide and focused on the new people coming in the door.

A portly man dressed in a gray suit and wearing a black bowler hat took a seat in the forward section. Rosemary heard the coach's frame creak when he sat down. That gentleman is a detective, she had heard. He's here to capture the James-Younger gang. What a laugh, she thought.

Rosemary then watched the Irishman enter the coach and look around. His eyes locked on hers—a wide smile followed. Collin took a seat directly across from her. The talk we had on the train passed the time nicely, she thought. He's a handsome man. She turned away for a moment, then glanced back, capturing Collin's stare.

Rosemary quickly turned away again. A man across the street pushed through the swinging saloon doors. He staggered out onto the boardwalk, almost falling before regaining his footage. She grimaced with disgust when the man took off his hat and grinned. I've never seen an uglier face in my life, she thought to herself.

A bulky-shaped young man, wearing wide red suspenders and a bowler hat, too small for his head, took a seat next to the Irishman, directly across from Miss Barnard, the schoolteacher. Rosemary thought he must be a foreigner. He smiled a lot and apparently had a vocabulary of only one word, "Yah!"

Pierre Mantraux sat down by the other window, next to Miss Barnard. He placed a metal box under his seat. Rosemary heard the door slam shut. She counted four people sitting on the seats of the other section, near the front of the coach. Rosemary heard the stationmaster say the coach has space for nine passengers inside the coach and more on top the roof.

Suddenly, the door opened again and a panting young man entered. The brawny-framed, wide-eyed man took a quick look around and grabbed the final seat, next to the suspender-clad person. "Sorry, but I was held up at the train station."

He grinned at the school teacher, his thin, dark mustache stretching under a slightly flattened nose and soft brown eyes. His long slender fingers scratched the tip of his narrow, unshaven chin. He wore light brown duck trousers and a brown-plaid shirt, sleeves rolled up. That young man is brimming with energy, Rosemary thought.

"He-YAH!" someone above them yelled and on a late mid-August afternoon, the coach jerked forward.

— —

PIERRE MANTRAUX TAPPED THE HEAVY METAL BOX under his seat with the edge of his boot heel. He forced a grin, stroking his narrow, black mustache with his fingers. The gold had survived a bank robbery—the James-Younger gang, most famous of all bandits, he mused.

He had the experienced conductor to thank, using a concealment routine for valuables before the bandits came aboard. Pierre had been hired by Wells Fargo—a one time deal—to deliver the gold to the bank in Tarrytown. He agreed that transporting the gold in the usual area atop the stagecoach would invite disaster. Pierre felt the James-Younger gang would not waste their time on passengers who they had already robbed, if they chose to stop this stage.

The smiling Irishman, sitting across from him, had saved his metal box, too. I wonder what he has in his, he thought. There 'tis, right under his seat. If there is a robbery attempt between here and Tarrytown, we should be able to hold 'em off. There's a good man riding shotgun above; plus, the Pinkerton Detective sitting in the forward section, neither of whom will go down without a fight.

Pierre knew that he could never fall asleep riding in the bouncing coach. He relished the thoughts of finally arriving at Tarrytown, where his temporary employment by Wells Fargo of the gold delivery would end. Pierre felt very good with his decision to visit Missouri.

He didn't want to spend the rest of his life without meeting the brave confederate soldier he had shot at Lone Jack—and had seen as a prisoner in a wagon as well as Butler Prison.

Pierre planned on eventually taking the stagecoach west of Tarrytown, and hooking up with a passenger train. His final destination was California where his sister lived. She and her husband operated a fruit farm. He looked forward to putting his guns away, and perhaps finding a woman.

— —

A STAND OF TALL ASPEN TREES blocked the rays of the late afternoon sun, casting long shadows cross the roadway. The six horses, pulling the red-painted stagecoach, began a light trot westward. Buildings in Stillman Mills gradually faded into the distance.

Lafe Sunnerland skillfully worked the reins. "He-YAH!" he yelled again and set the steeds into a light gallop, his ears tuned to the familiar sounds of jingling harness, and the clopping, rhythmic clattering of the horses' hooves on the damp road surface. The gray mare behind his lead stallion appeared to be favoring her right-rear leg. Needs a shoe job when we get to the station, he thought.

Lafe looked forward to spending a night in his hometown of Tarrytown. His brother, Jesse, would take over the reins when the stagecoach departed the next morning.

He thought about his favorite room at the Grand Hotel and Mama's Kitchen where he would surely feast on a hot meal. Lafe smiled thinking about Lady Constance and her immaculate staff of women employees. He and his brother had joined Overland Stage shortly after the Civil War ended. As time went by, Overland was bought out by Wells Fargo, his current employer.

"Aeee," his partner, Morgan Taylor, yelled, dodging a clod of mud rocketing by his head—set into motion by the hooves of one of the horses. Morgan had been riding shotgun on the stagecoach for

Wells Fargo for the past two years. His skill at handling and shooting a rifle was well known. Morgan wore two long barreled Colt revolvers on his belt. A double-barreled shotgun and three lever action carbines were ready for use—the stocks protruding from four scabbards attached to his side of the stagecoach seat.

Lafe's barrel-chested upper body had grown in size considerably since he rode with the Gray Riders during the Civil War. Years of inhaling dust toned down his normally squeaky voice. The wide brim of Lafe's white Stetson hat succumbed to the wind, bending flat against his forehead. His sinewy arms bulged ahead of his rolled-up red-checkered shirt sleeves. Extended strands of rawhide held the flaps of his weathered, dark brown, vest together.

Lafe felt a nudge from Morgan's elbow. "Look o'er there, Lafe. Looks like the same riders as last time."

Lafe's stomach tightened as he fixed his light gray eyes on five mounted horsemen snaking down from Bear Mountain. Word was out that Black Bart and his band robbed a stage north of the river recently. They made off with a shipment of gold bullion and murdered two of the passengers. Just how the outlaws knew in advance about the gold shipment remained a mystery.

Even though his stagecoach wasn't carrying any gold on this run, he worried. His supervisor in Jefferson City whispered in his ear just before he stepped up onto the stagecoach seat. "Next time—next run—ya may be carryin' gold."

Morgan Taylor originally hailed from Harrisonville, hiring out to Wells Fargo after working for a lumber company in Jefferson City. He stood several inches taller than Lafe, his broad shoulders holding up a pair of wide, black suspenders. Morgan's thick black hair contrasted the long blond strands of Lafe's. A bulging mustache, covering the upper half of his mouth, drooped down to a trimmed beard. His black hat, trimmed with a red sash, matched his bandana and suspenders.

Flicking the reins, he felt the speed of the coach increase. "Only four miles to Tarrytown," Lafe yelled, attempting to make his voice heard above the noises of the moving stagecoach.

Morgan nodded.

— —

ROSEMARY RESPECTED THE UNEASINESS of the school teacher sitting next to her. The young lady shifted in her seat continually. Her face contorted at times, showing fear in her darting, light blue eyes. "Are you all right?" Rosemary asked.

Cosette Barnard turned her face and forced a smile. "Why yes, I'm fine, thank you."

Rosemary nodded. She noticed the Irishman spent most of his time staring at either her or the teacher. It's an uncomfortable stare, she thought. Why doesn't he look somewhere else? She smacked her lips together, drawing the attention of the Swede sitting next to the Irishman. Rosemary looked up into a wide-faced grin. She turned her head.

Everyone jolted upward a little when a back wheel struck an obstruction. Cosette locked her hands tightly together. The Swede opened his mouth slightly and nodded at her. He smiled, exposing large, crowded front teeth.

Collin McBride continued to stare at the teacher. Mr. Mantraux's long legs bounced each time the wheels engaged a bump in the road. His black boots crossed over each other, one of the heels almost touching the door. The front rim of the wide-brimmed black hat totally covered his face.

Rosemary felt the teacher jerk slightly in response to a dull, thudding sound.

"What was that?" Cosette asked.

Rosemary turned her head toward her. "Perhaps only a small rock—nothing to fear."

She noticed Mr. Mantraux sit up straight suddenly. He set his hat on straight and faced the window.

A bullet zinged past the window. Another cracked against the wall.

Rosemary looked around the coach. She saw the Irishmen lean forward and stare out the window toward the mountain. Cosette's hand grabbed her arm. Rosemary glanced at the Swede. His smile hadn't gone away.

Pierre said calmly, "Please stay calm and in your seats. We may be having some visitors."

Mantraux pulled a long-barreled pistol from a holster hidden under his coat. Oh, she thought hopefully, it could be the gentleman from the train out there, Mr. Younger. She feared to look between the curtains of the window, afraid of what she would see. Rosemary found the courage to look—she saw five riders galloping their horses, a distance away, but parallel to the stagecoach.

— —

MASON JOHN MILLER felt the Irishman's frame tighten after hearing the sound of gunshots. He knew they came from the south, the direction of the mountain. Mason John looked across and saw the school teacher turn pale and place a hand to her mouth.

He saw the woman next to the window and the Irishman looking out the window. "What's out there?" he asked anxiously.

Rosemary turned her head. "Five riders, but they're staying away—can't be the Younger-James gang."

He saw Mantraux, across from him, pull something long and black from underneath his coat. Mason John slid his hand down to his own holster, feeling the top of his revolver. He glanced at Mantraux again, noticing that the man didn't look concerned. Mason looked at Miss Pikes, who forced a smile and settled back in her seat, pulling the curtain over part of the window.

— —

LAFE STRAIGHTENED HIS BODY AND FLICKED THE REINS. "He-YAH!"

Morgan removed one of his carbines from its scabbard and pulled up on the riders. He aligned his eyes along the barrel, taking aim. Morgan lifted his head. "They've stopped comin', Lafe."

"Damn good thing. I bet it's them Erlocks," Lafe said. "They like to play games and scare the hell out of the passengers."

"Now look at that, they're laughin' at us," Morgan said.

Lafe looked over at his shotgun rider, forcing a grin. "They also know that yar a damn good shot. Why don't ya send 'em a message?"

Morgan looked at Lafe and grinned. He leveled his rifle again, aimed toward the riders, and pulled the trigger.

Lafe laughed loudly and turned his head. "Well look at that, they've pulled up. They're afraid of ye, Morgan."

Morgan placed his rifle back into the scabbard. Lafe slowed down the horses for the final two miles before arriving at Tarrytown. He thought about the cool beer waiting for him at the saloon.

Lafe glanced toward Bear Mountain and saw the lonely giant cross not very far from the road. As long as ah live, ah'll never forget that day, he said to himself. He was a member of the Gray Riders who had lined up on the east side of town to defend against Union Cavalry.

He had ridden next to his brother Jesse after hearing the '*Charge*' yell from Grady Hastings. We rode like hell bent for leather against them Bluecoats. We were lucky that day and lost only six men, he thought. The cross marked the spot where they buried their dead after the Battle of Tarrytown in 1863.

Lafe never admitted it out loud to anyone, but he knew that if Quantrill and his band hadn't showed up, it could have been different. Ah might not be sitting up here right now, he said to himself. The sight of that black flag that day was....Lafe shook his head.

I wonder how them passengers are doin' back there. A couple of them ladies were probably scared to death when they saw them riders comin', he thought. I bet that school teacher passed out.

Lafe saw the livery building and he slowed the horses to a trot, directing them toward the stagecoach station. "Yipee!" he yelled a minute later. "We made it."

My beer awaits just across the street, he said to himself.

— —

MASON FELT LIKE YELLING. The threat from the five mysterious riders had vanished. He got excited. Mason knew Tarrytown lay just ahead, and he looked forward to seeing his Uncle Seth. He had been promised a job in his Mercantile Goods & Services store. Mason looked forward to the adventures that he would experience in the west. He had heard that the people in Missouri stood tall and strong during the Civil War. I want to be among people like that, he thought.

Mason John had been working for a metal works factory in St. Louis. He came west because he didn't wish to spend the rest of life in the factory making just enough money to survive. He needed adventure—this is it, he thought, catching Rosemary Pike's wide smile.

7

GRADY HASTINGS RAN HIS FINGERS OVER HIS BROW, rubbing away beads of perspiration. The temperature had risen sharply after a cooling rain the previous day. He had just loaded the last bag of supplies into his wagon, the team of blacks tied securely to a hitching post.

Grady glanced at his two children, who sat on the front bench seat. Tyler, age seven, pushed his sister in the shoulder. Clarissa, age four, shoved back. "Hey, Tyler, watch it," Grady said authoritatively, shaking his head thinking how his son resembled Will Walker, deposed brother of his wife Helen.

His thoughts flashed back to the Civil War. I was disappointed but respected Will's decision to join the Union, he said to himself. It was a sad day for me and the other Riders. We rode off to war in different directions. Grady stiffened thinking about the day he found Will Walker dying by a tree in the final minutes of the Battle of Wilson's Creek in 1862.

Will had been my best friend, Grady said to himself. Ah don't know how ah managed to break the news to the Walkers. Riding out to their farm was one of the most difficult things that I 'ave ever done. War is God awful to begin with...much worse when neighbors fight on different sides.

Grady smiled. His wife Helen approached, coming from the mercantile store. Her whitish Swiss muslin dress fits her so well, he thought. The pink satin bows in her dark brown hair matched the trim of white lace ruffles on her dress. Her face beamed, lighting up her dark brown eyes. The dimple in her narrow chin deepened as she waved. She is the most beautiful woman in the world.

Grady had celebrated his thirty-sixth birthday in July of 1876. His dark brown hair didn't show a speck of gray. It matched his natural dark complexion. Because of the insistence by his wife Helen, he shaved his face daily, carefully trimming his long narrow sideburns that extended to his lower jaw line.

Grady's emerald green eyes widened, hearing a familiar unmistakable sound. He turned his head toward Stillman Mills and in the distance saw it—the stagecoach. Helen had also reacted to the noise. Her shoulders turned on her spindle-shaped waist to face the thudding, rattling and rumbling sound.

He walked stiffly to the wagon seat and brought down his two children. "Come on, youngins', let's go get yar Ma and watch the stagecoach come into town."

Grady's shoulder wound he got at the Battle of Little Blue resulted in stooped shoulders, dropping one lower then the other.

Grady picked up his daughter and held her against his chest. He grabbed Tyler's hand and walked toward his wife. They met on the boardwalk, Tyler pointing toward the stagecoach. Helen grasped her skirt, lifting the hem slightly, just enough to clear the ground as the four of them crossed the street.

— —

CHAIRS SCRAPED AGAINST THE WOODEN FLOOR as several men stood and headed for the door. Jubal Haggard and Abel Kingsley, neighbors and friends of Grady, led the way out of the saloon and onto the boardwalk.

Jubal Haggard patted Tyler on the head after catching up with them. "Hey there, big man."

Jubal and Justin, the Haggard brothers, had ridden with Grady and the Gray Riders during the Civil War. Justin got married before riding off to the Battle of Lone Jack—he never saw his wife again. Their father, mother, and Justin's wife were murdered by a band of redlegs.

Justin lost a leg after getting wounded during the battle. He returned later from a Union prison in Butler, Illinois to a burned down house—his wife and parents gone. He and his brother had since taken over the Haggard farm.

The door to the marshal's office opened and Ben Buford walked out onto the boardwalk. The tall and brawny officer moved to Tarrytown in 1869. The marshal replaced Constable Muldoon as the area's central law enforcement authority.

Buford had been appointed United States Marshal by the U.S. Attorney General in 1868. After serving in the Jefferson City district for four years, he was reassigned to a new office in Tarrytown and Jackson County in 1872.

He folded his arms and glanced up and down Main Street. He had piercing blue eyes, a prominent, lower jaw slightly moved off center. The marshal ran the long fingers from his right hand over his narrow, cleanly shaven, dark-skinned face. He dressed in his usual tan duck trousers, pumpkin-colored shirt, and brown leather vest.

His deputy, Lance Milburn, joined him minutes later and the two men strolled toward the stage office. "Hey, there, big fella," Lance said to Tyler Hastings, his whiny voice drawing a smile from the young lad. The heavily whiskered deputy patted the top of the youngster's head.

Tyler twisted and turned to escape the slim deputy's grasp. Lance laughed, let go of the lad and did a little boot dance on the planks.

Grady laughed, reached down and grabbed his son's hand. "Come on, Tyler, let's go see who gets off the stage."

— —

LAFE SUNNERLAND HELD ONTO THE REINS as Morgan tied the lead horses to a hitching post. He stepped down and hurriedly walked around to the stage door that had already opened. Pierre Mantraux stood inside, offering a hand to a woman. The pale-faced Cosette Barnard cautiously stepped down.

"Mama, there's my new teacher!" Tyler said loudly, drawing a few laughs from the people on the boardwalk.

Cosette's face reddened. She forced a smile and glanced slyly at Tyler.

Blaise Harrington, the town mayor, advanced quickly and shook Cosette's hand. "Welcome to Tarrytown," the tall, well-dressed man said, drawing her aside to allow space for the next passenger.

Rosemary Pikes appeared in the coach doorway next. She smiled widely and waved to the onlookers, accepting the hand of Mantraux to support her stepping down. Lafe reached up and grabbed her other hand. She thanked the two men and moved aside.

Mantraux came down and accepted a handshake from the banker, Douglas Herron. He leaned against the steps and reached under the seat, pulling out a black metal box.

"Look, Pa, that man looks just like our neighbor," Tyler said as Collin McBride stepped down.

"Welcome, sir," the mayor said. "How was your trip?"

Collin took a deep breath. He looked around and accepted the mayor's hand. "Aye, but it's good to be standing on solid ground. Is this Tarrytown?"

"Yup, sure is. How are ya feeling?"

"Fit as a fiddle."

Hjalmar Johannssen, the round-faced young man who had come all the way from Sweden came down next. "Good trip?" the mayor asked.

Hjalmar nodded, smiling wide. "Yah!"

Mason John Miller bounced down the steps, landing firmly on the planks. He pointed at his uncle, Seth Miller, wearing a stained white apron. The store owner walked forward, grinning from ear to ear. "Welcome, nephew. Ah been afraid you wouldn't make it." Seth grasped Mason John by his shoulders. "You've grown up."

Lafe assisted a portly gentleman who had been waiting in the forward section. The man stopped on the step and said to the driver,

"Hello, I'm J.P. Weatherby. I thank you for getting us here safely—so many bandits out there."

Lafe smiled and pointed at Morgan who had climbed onto the top of the stagecoach. "That man made certain that we got in safely. Even Black Bart doesn't mess with this stage when Morgan is up there with his rifles."

Weatherby planted both of his boots on the planks and looked around, pausing for a moment to catch his breath. He wore a gray tweed jacket, its open front exposing a dark gray vest, matching his trousers. A gold chain looped across a generous midriff.

He touched the tip of his gray bowler hat and looked at Jubal Haggard and Abel Kingsley. "I'm J.P. Weatherby, boys. Would you two lend me a hand with my luggage? I'll make it worth your while."

Jubal nudged Abel and stepped forward. "'Tis a grand hat you 'ave, sir," Jubal said, noticing the wide black band around the base. "Yes, sir. Where're ya headin?" he added.

"The hotel—I hear you have a splendid one."

Jubal nodded and reached up to grab a piece of luggage that Morgan held over the edge of the top of the stage. He set it down and grabbed a second one. "It's the best in the territory, sir."

Abel stepped up and did the same with two more, the second one slipping a bit and banging onto a plank.

"Whoa there, lads. Take it easy on that case—there's personals that could break in there." Weatherby reached into his pocket. "Much obliged. This'll take care of you two young men," he said and dropped two coins into Jubal's palm.

Jubal grinned and handed one to Abel. "Come on, Abel, let's git this luggage to the hotel." They picked up the four pieces and headed across the street, Weatherby waddling behind them.

Jubal waited in the lobby as the gentleman settled his business with Robert Packard, the hotel clerk. Jubal studied the curved stairway leading to the guest suites. "Gonna be a heavy carry," he said to Abel, picking up two large pieces of luggage.

Jubal and Abel each carried two pieces up the stairs and into Weatherby's room. "I thank you, boys," the newly arrived guest said, smiling.

The man's coat opened a bit wider, exposing a shiny, silver-handled pistol tucked into a fancy leather holster. "I wonder what this guy is doin' here," he said to Abel. "Did ya see that fancy gun he's got?"

"Yeah, he's got an air about 'em," Abel said. "Maybe that school teacher needs some help. Let's get back out there."

"Ah, you go ahead, I'll head over to the saloon. Justin said he's comin' over."

— —

MARSHAL BUFORD WATCHED PIERRE MANTRAUX and Douglas Herron walk across the street and enter the bank. "Hey, Lance, look at that. Betcha there's gold in that there black box. See how excited Herron is? His face is lit up like a full moon on a cloudless night."

Lance took off his tall, high-crowned, white hat and ran fingers through his scraggly hair. "Yeah, it looks darn heavy, the way he's carryin' it. Good thing Jesse James didn't know about that."

The Marshal sneered. "Ah'm mighty interested in knowin' who that Mantraux fella is. Doesn't seem to bother Herron any, though."

"Who do ya think that other feller is, the one wearin' the tweed jacket?" Lance asked.

"I'd be willin' to bet that he's a Pinkerton Detective. I got a wire the other day—from the marshal in Harrisonville. He mentioned somethin' about bein' on the lookout for one of 'em."

Lance nodded. "He'll probably have dinner at Mamma's Kitchen this evenin'. Are you comin' over?"

"Yeah, I probably will. We can have a talk with the gentleman then."

The final piece of luggage got handed down to Lafe. "Well, Lafe, I suppose yar headin' over to the saloon," Lance said.

"Sure am, soon as Toby shows up." Lafe looked toward the corral. "Ah, there he comes now."

The marshal grinned watching Lafe and Morgan crossing the street, heading for the saloon. He stood until Toby Miller and Billy led the team and stagecoach toward the corral. "Sure a lot of passengers today, but the one who looks the most interestin' is that Irish fella. There's somethin' mighty familiar lookin' about him."

Lance walked over to the bench in front of the depot. He saw one of the passengers sitting there and a wooden case setting on the planks. "Howdy, mister. Anything ah can do to hep?"

The Swede shrugged. "Yah." He pointed at his mouth and raised up the palm of his hand to support his cheek.

The deputy turned. "Hey, Ben. This one can't speak English. He needs some help."

The marshal walked over. "Lance, take him over to see Belle. He needs somethin' to eat and a bed." Ben reached in his pocket and handed the deputy a coin.

8

ABEL KINGSLEY STOOD ON THE BOARDWALK after returning from the hotel. He heard that a new school teacher was expected. He didn't know she would be so pretty. His heart fluttered and his legs felt like tree trunks when he walked over to the young woman.

Abel took off his hat. He stuttered, "May I help you?"

The woman looked up. He felt himself melting while looking into her pale blue eyes. Abel tripped slightly, brushing his boot against the edge of her wide-hoop skirt. "Excuse me, ma'am," Abel said, stepping back quickly.

She smiled, her long blonde hair tousled from a slight breeze on her shoulder blades. "Thank you, sir, but the marshal has already graciously volunteered his services." She pointed.

The school teacher appeared to be amused by the disappointed expression on Abel's face. She curtsied and said softly, "Perhaps another time."

"Abel. Abel Kingsley." Abel put his hat back on, smiled and said, "Good day."

He walked closer to the stagecoach that was in the process of being moved. The other lady must be the one who is going to replace Madeline, he thought, watching Lady Constance walk out of the saloon and move in his direction.

The tall, dark, slim man with the narrow black mustache, who arrived on the stage, made his way across the street. He had gone to the bank with Mr. Herron earlier. Sure looks like a gunslinger, he thought, frowning, but then why would he be delivering gold to the bank? There isn't much doubt that the black box contained gold. Abel watched the man pick up his luggage and head for the hotel.

Abel's deep-set hazel eyes glanced toward Toby's Corral and saw a flash of red as the back end of the stagecoach disappeared around the corner of the building. He envied Lafe and Jesse Sunnerland who worked for the Overland Stage Company, driving and riding shotgun. They're seeing the country, he often thought, and experiencing adventure.

Abel watched the Irishman struggle as he crossed the street, walking toward the hotel. He carried two pieces of luggage, one of them large and clumsy. The man looks and walks like my new neighbor, Timothy McGearney, he thought. Abel didn't totally trust the Irishman who had purchased the Sunnerland farm. Do we have another McGearney? he asked himself.

He turned and saw the new school teacher being escorted to the Smith apartment building by Lance Milburn, the deputy sheriff. She doesn't look so good right now, he thought, but I bet she'll be pretty as a lark tomorrow.

Justin Haggard entered the saloon across the street with his brother Jubal. Abel waved to them, his neighbors. Both rode with him and the other Gray Riders during the Civil War.

After the war, Jubal married Jessica Walker, but Justin remained unmarried. He occasionally rode shotgun on the stagecoach.

Abel inherited the farm from his father, Matt, five years ago. His sister, Sarah, married his neighbor, Thomas Hastings, who farmed directly across the Tarrytown road. Abel admired his father for introducing Aberdeen Angus cattle—virtually unheard of in Missouri—into the area about the time the Civil War broke out.

He hung around on the boardwalk until everyone else had left. Abel had hoped that the school teacher would return—she didn't. He heard the sound of hoof beats and turned his head. Abel saw five riders coming from the direction of Stillman Mills. They slowed to a trot after passing the corral.

Abel anxiously watched the two lead riders as they continued up the middle of Tarrytown Road. He spotted the whitish, smooth, hairless face of one of the leaders—the short legs and elongated chest—Erlock! he said to himself, dropping his right hand and feeling the hammer of his Colt with his finger. They've joined up with those ugly Lassitors...that means trouble for sure...that's Bertran ridin' next to Bone Erlock, the albino.

Abel's distrust of the kinky-haired Erlock had not lessened over the past ten years. The tyrant's wide, narrow, glaring pink eyes darted back and forth. Able felt distaste watching the man's crooked smile as his head turned to watch both sides of the street like a snake looking for a victim.

Ah better let Justin know, he said to himself, watching intently as the riders continued on through town.

— —

ABEL PUSHED THROUGH THE SALOON DOOR and walked over to the bar. Jubal Haggard lowered his mug, wiping his lips with a wagging tongue. "Hello, neighbor."

"Howdy."

"What'll it be, Kingsley?" Brett the bartender asked.

"A beer."

Abel heard the clunking sound of a crutch on the wooden floor and he turned to see Justin Haggard approaching. "Hey, Justin, I hear you're ridin' shotgun tomorra."

"Yup—sure am."

"Who's yar driver?"

"Jesse."

"How are you boys doin?" Lady Constance said, strolling over, holding hands with the lady next to her.

Abel nodded.

"I want you all to meet Rosemary. She comes to us from St. Louis, and I'm happy to say that she will be working with me."

The men tipped their hats and clinked their glasses.

Abel took a long draw from his mug. He looked at Justin and said, "Guess who just rode through town?"

The six-foot-five tall Justin set his mug down and leaned on one of his crutches. "Who?"

"Bone Erlock!"

Abel set his mug down. "The albino had his two brothers with 'em—and the two Lassitors."

Justin sat down on a stool, his lips tightened, his thin black mustache stretched out beneath a Roman nose. "Bet it was them outlaws that threatened the stage between Mills and here."

Abel frowned. "Ah didn't hear about that. What happened?"

"Lafe told me that on each of the last two runs from Stillman Mill, five riders came down from Bear Mountain and followed the stage for a bit. Today, they fired a couple of shots."

Abel nodded. "That was probably them that I just saw ride through town."

"They're gettin' more gutsy than ever," Justin said and took another swill of beer.

Abel looked around the room. He saw Lafe and Jesse Sunnerland approaching from the other end of the bar. "Here come our stage drivers now."

Justin's silver-gray eyes widened. He said softly, "Lafe's worried plenty about the possible whereabouts of Black Bart and his outlaw band. Word around these parts is that bunch seems to always know when the stage is carryin' gold."

"Howdy, boys," Lafe squeaked, his barrel-chest bumping against the bar.

"Abel—Justin—Jubal," Jesse Sunnerland said, his large, dark eyes darting around the room.

Abel smiled, lifting a mug to his mouth. He set it down and wiped his lips with his tongue. “Ah hear that the Erlocks paid you a visit between here and Mills today.”

Lafe held up two fingers for the bartender. “Yeah, them—and those no-good Lassitors rode at our speed for a piece. They had the guts to fire a couple of shots.”

He rubbed his chin and laughed. “Morgan sent ’em a message. Ah saw one of their hats fly off.” He laughed some more.

Justin raised an arm and held his mug up, tilting the brim toward his lips. A sliver of beer flowed onto his chin as he swallowed the rest. The mug banged heavily on the counter as he set it down.

Brett, the apron-wearing bartender, glanced at the empty mug. “Need another, Justin?”

“Yup, sure do.” Justin wiped his lips with his fingers and took a deep breath.

Jesse Sunnerland stood at least four inches taller than his brother, his long, dark sideburns ending in a point, close to the angle of his jaw. “Lafe says next trip, they may be haulin’ gold all the way from Jefferson City. He gets cavalry escort as far as Stillman, then the soldier boys head north.”

Jubal Haggard flicked up the brim of his brown hat. His thick black hair bunched up at the top of his forehead. He lit a cigar and stared at Jesse with his small, dark penetrating eyes. “Maybe we should talk the marshal into gettin’ an escort together for the ride from Mills to Tarrytown.”

“Sure wouldn’t hurt, little brother,” Justin said.

Lafe gritted his teeth together. “Well, one thing we don’t have to worry about is the James boys or the Youngers. They’re only after the trains and stages who stole from ’em during the war. They’ll never bother us here.”

Jubal blew a puff of smoke out of his mouth, “According to Thomas, the Youngers and James brothers are headin’ north. He talked to Bob just the other day.”

Justin rubbed two fingers over his nose. “Ah think that the only worry we have ’round ’ere is them Erlocks and Lassitors. They’ve been gettin’ mighty cocky lately.”

Abel cleared his throat. “We should’ve hung them blowhards all when ah had chance back then, during the war. Remember when we rode up there with Lafe and Jesse?"

"Ah sure as hell do," Justin replied. "At least we hung one of 'em," he added.

The doors swung open. Marshal Ben Buford and Morgan Taylor entered.

The marshal walked over to the bar where Justin, Jubal, Abel and the two Sunnerland's had gathered. He drawled, "Boys, Morgan tells me that the Erlocks and Lassitors did their little act again today."

Abel looked up into the marshal's blue eyes. "Yeah, and all five of 'em rode through town headin' west not more than an hour ago."

"'Tain't no law against ridin' through town, Abel," the marshal said, keeping his long, narrow bony jaw slightly ajar.

Abel nodded.

The marshal looked at Justin. "Better be sure you have enough rifles up in that seat tomorrow. Morgan carries about four."

Justin nodded.

9

VICTOR ERLOCK THRUST A HANDFUL of bread into his mouth. His three sons, Bone, Mutt and Grit watched him anxiously from their chairs across the table. The father slammed his fist down, causing two glasses to tip over, rust-colored liquids spilling onto the wooden floor. A crumb of bread squeezed out of the corner of his mouth. His face reddened. "What are ya, a bunch of dummies? Gold! It got away from ya bums."

Bone Erlock gritted his teeth. His whitish-pink face reddened. "Pa! There was a professional gunfighter inside—Ah've seen him work before. He'd a' picked us off one at a time. Besides, that Morgan feller up on the seat can throw out plenty of lead, too."

Grit leaned over, reached down to the floor and picked up his hat.

"Yeah, take a look at this." He pointed toward the hole in his hat.

Mutt's lips moved—no words came out—he hadn't spoken a word since birth—but the expression on his face and the nodding of his head silenced his father.

The elder Erlock stood, his dwarf-like physique stooped slightly. "Ya boys are hopeless." Victor stormed out of the house, slamming the door behind him. He gasped, bringing both hands to his chest. Moments later, he lay on the ground—dead.

— —

THE MOON'S RAYS CAUGHT THE WHISKERLESS face of Bone Erlock as he put down his shovel. Heavy beads of perspiration streaked down his forehead, his pink eyes burning. He swiped a dirty hand over his face, wiping away the sweat. Bone closed both eyes tightly and waited for the irritation to leave, listening to the thudding sound of dirt clumps landing in the hole.

Bone sighed deeply after opening his eyes, uttering a string of profanities. He kicked a clod of dirt with the toe of his boot, sending specks of soil flying, some of them landing next to one of his brothers.

Grit stopped working and raised up his shovel. "Hey, watch it!"

Bone picked up his tool again and rapidly threw in several fills of dirt. The dirty old man taught me most everything I know, he thought. Bone smirked. We're all better off with that old bastard down there—under the dirt. That's where he belongs. Bone spit into the hole.

The three men grunted and groaned, spades stabbing into the loose earth for another few minutes.

"That does it," Bone said and began walking back toward the house. His brothers followed.

They threw the implements down by the house and entered. Bone removed his hat and lay down on the floor. "Ah'm beat, brothers. We'll talk tomorra—ah want to see more of them sheep and dogs."

— —

THE ERLOCK BROTHERS RODE SILENTLY toward the Hastings's property line, crossed it, and followed the south side of the tributary near the bottom. Bone raised his arm and they dismounted after reaching Bear Creek close to the middle of the McGearney land. Tying their horses to tree trunks, they crossed it on foot.

Bone and his brothers needed an outlet to deal with their father's death. Violence was all they were ever taught.

"Oh, lookee!" Grit exclaimed. A large number of sheep, some lying down, others standing, grazed not far from the creek. He brought his carbine up to eye level.

Bone swiped his arm over the top of the barrel, driving it down. "Not now, ya fool. Look ova' there."

Farther down the creek, still on the McGearney land near the McGregor property line, another flock of sheep grazed and lolled, even closer to the creek. Bone led the three back to their horses. They rode in silence until Bone raised his hand and dismounted.

Bone removed a rifle from his scabbard and led his brothers down the gradual slope, stopping at the narrow stream and signaling Grit and Mutt to halt. He leaped deliberately across the narrow stream, landing next to a Russian olive tree. He felt the pain from a thorn that had stabbed his arm. He jerked it away, bringing it up to his eyes, noticing blood.

He cussed under his breath, and waved to his brothers, signaling them to follow. The three brothers stood next to each other behind waist high bushes, a short distance from the flock. Bone raised his rifle. A dog barked. He set it down.

"See that big fat ewe? That's our dinner tonight."

Bone took careful aim. He pulled the trigger and the ewe dropped. He chuckled and muttered, "Pa would've been proud of me."

"Awe heck, Bone, that ain't fair. Ah need one, too," Grit said and raised his rifle.

"Don't, you fool! One's enough!" Bone exclaimed.

He put a hand to his ear as Grit began firing, the smell of acrid gunpowder reaching his nostrils.

"This is fun," Grit said, laughing loudly. "Come on, Mutt. Hep me out."

After Grit and Mutt finally ceased firing, ten sheep and one collie lay dead on the hillside.

Bone halted his horse and raised his arm after riding some of the distance across the Hastings's property. He saw the buildings in the distance. One of these days, he thought. I'm gonna get even with that Hastings. I 'ad me eye on that pretty Sarah long 'fore 'e did. Anger built rapidly in his mind.

His horse neighed in pain as he dug the spurs of both his boots into the horse's flank. The Erlock's galloped their horses the rest of the way home.

10

TARRYTOWN SURVIVED THE CIVIL WAR without losing a single building. On the north side of Main Street, the livery, owned by Toby Miller, had been renamed *Toby's Corral.*

His friend Charley Stubbins built a blacksmith shop on the west side of his building, naming it *Charley's Smithy*. Between the marshal's office and the blacksmith, Wells Fargo Company had built a stagecoach depot. They rented part of it to Western Union for a telegraph office.

The constable's building had been rebuilt to house a U.S. marshal office, two jail cells, and a meeting room that also served as a courtroom. Marshal Ben Buford had moved to Tarrytown after being appointed by the Justice Department. He lived in a suite in the Smith Building and rumors around town partnered him romantically with Lady Constance, who owned the Frontier Saloon.

Digger Phillips, the undertaker, survived the war, and remained in business at his previous site, between the marshal's office and Shol Clarity's barbershop.

The Smith Building needed some remodeling after the war, but remained functional, housing several residential apartments plus the office of young Dr. Blake, who replaced the elderly Dr. Wells in the medical suite of the Smith Building.

Beyond a grassy area next to the Smith Building, the community church sported a glistening new paint job. The appearance of its pastor, Zack Wilson, had not changed during the past twelve years, but his demeanor had after losing over half of his parishioners. His bible-thumping style became one of smiles and mellowness.

On the southern side of the street, Seth Miller had remodeled the General Store and changed its name to Mercantile Goods & Services. The bank hadn't modified much of anything, except for adding one employee—Douglas Herron's son, John.

The Grand Hotel Building continued to be a home for the Frontier Saloon, still owned and managed by Lady Constance. She lost her main waitress, Madeline, who married immigrant Timothy McGearney and moved out to his farm. Constance added an old school chum to her staff, Rosemary Pikes from St. Louis.

Belle Streeter continued to own and manage Mama's Kitchen. Robert Packard still managed the Grand Hotel.

The people in charge of the one room school house had high expectations of Cosette Barnard. She was hired to teach the upcoming season. The building stood alone, about half the distance between MacTurley's Woods and the Grand Hotel.

Mayor Blaise Harrington was elected town mayor after the death of Owen Pritchard. He brought with him his wife, Jackie, from Jefferson City. They purchased and lived in a house on the slope of Bear Mountain behind the mercantile store. Blaise worked for Wells Fargo, maintaining a permanent office in the stagecoach depot. He conducted the town business in the marshal's office.

Toby Miller purchased six gas lanterns for the town. They mounted the lights onto wooden poles, three on each side of the street. Newcomer Hjalmar Johannssen was hired by the mayor to light the lamps at dusk and put them out at daybreak.

A telegraph line had been built by Western Union along the north side of the Tarrytown road. The poles stretched out for miles west of town, branching into a line leading to Kansas City, and another to Harrisonville.

Ivan Kamrowsky, employed by Western Union, managed and operated the telegraph office. He had been moved from Philadelphia to Tarrytown by the firm. Ivan didn't have any family and kept to himself most of the time. He usually had an early dinner at Mama's Kitchen and spent his evenings in his suite at the Smith Building.

The Telegraph

THE FIRST TELEGRAPH LINE IN AMERICA was built in 1844. One of the core physical units of the telegraph was an instrument called a relay, which consisted of magnets, wound with no. 16 copper wire; the other main unit featured a set of brass keys and was called a register. Together, along with other parts, they were referred to as "The Telegrapher." The entire apparatus weighed nearly two hundred pounds.

The electromagnet used in the relays was also used by Thomas Edison in his inventing career. He partnered with Franklin L. Pope, a pioneer telegraph engineer.

In later years, the cumbersome relays and registers were replaced with more efficient technology. James Clark of Philadelphia and G.M. Phillips pioneered the growth of the industry.

Hundreds of miles of telegraph lines built by Western Union sprung up across the nation. The wire was kept aloft with wooden posts approximately a hundred feet apart. They varied in height, most of them reachable by anyone mounted on a saddle.

See References in the back of the book.

11

TIMOTHY MCGEARNEY MOUNTED his horse. He glanced around at his buildings. Aye, but 'tis a grand barn, he said to himself. 'Tis my favorite building on me farm. Thomas Hastings told me that he was part of the men who built the structure. 'Twas during the Civil War, he had said. Timothy visualized the huge flame Thomas described after marauding invaders torched the original—redlegs and jayhawkers, Thomas Hastings called them.

The stirrups of his saddle were adjusted upward to accommodate his short, stocky legs. Timothy's blocky-shaped frame slouched slightly in the saddle. He turned and looked back toward the house, his disheveled, dark, bushy eyebrows and narrow sideburns showed a touch of gray, partially framing a flat forehead. Two days growth of his black whiskers further darkened his facial complexion.

He saw his wife, Madeline, standing on the front porch and waving. Timothy felt warm inside, deeply loving his wife of two years. He had met her at the Frontier Saloon in Tarrytown shortly after moving from Ireland. He remembered spending evenings at the saloon and languishing in his ale, all the same time keeping an eye on his now betrothed.

He had a difficult time talking her into accepting his religious background—Catholicism. After four years of courtship, their marriage took place in a small wood-framed Catholic church in Stillman Mills. His heart had almost ceased to beat when her attendant lifted her veil—the beauty of her thin face and greenish-hazel eyes gripped him.

He yelled, "Goodbye, Madie!" and waved his arm around and

around before urging his steed forward. He rode southward from his buildings toward Bear Creek, a deep rugged gorge that traversed across his land, a common runoff for the water flowing down from Bear Mountain. He approached the nearest section of the waterway, right next to Thomas Hastings's land.

His flocks of sheep normally remained close to the creek at this time of the day, so he started his inspection at the border and followed the creek southwestward. "Whoa," he said loudly and pulled on the reins near a cluster of stubby, dark, red-berried bushes. Timothy appreciated birds and became fascinated with their attraction to specific plants.

Timothy kept his horse at a walking gait as he continued along the creek, watching for the first sign of his sheep. He smiled seeing two brown and white collies running to greet him. He took pride in his pack of ten collies—they meant as much to him as his entire flock of sheep. Two of them had come by boat all the way from Ireland. He reached down from the saddle and gave them each a pat on the top of their heads.

A little farther down the creek, he nodded happily to see the hillside speckled with his sheep. His entire property north of the creek had been sectioned off with split rail fences long before he bought it. "Another week, woolies, and we're going to have to move ye to a fresh patch. This one 'tis 'bout gnawed to the gravel," he muttered.

Timothy had reached the top of a small ridge and stared in disbelief at the dead carcasses of some of his sheep, and one of his collies. He spurred his horse into a gallop, dismounting next to the first one.

One of the Almighty's poor creatures, he thought, looking down at a dead animal. He stared at a small, red-stained, round hole in the animal's head, feeling ire building in his mind and heat on his forehead. "Damn—that poor ram didn't fall to the wolf," he muttered.

He grimaced looking at an ugly bullet exit hole in the neck of a second ram. Kneeling down, he looked around. Timothy removed his rifle from the scabbard and walked over to a third fallen animal—it too had been shot dead.

Timothy inspected every one of the fallen sheep. All dead, he said to himself...all shot. Several of the carcasses were already visited by the predators. He felt frustrated listening to a flock of crows squawking their disapproval of him as they perched in the high branches of tall trees at the bottom of the creek.

His gray eyes squinted at the mid-morning sun. The days in the month of August had almost completed their run, September being two days ahead. Timothy preferred to ride in the morning hours to escape the afternoon's heat during the summer months, even though the past few days had been cool.

Timothy grabbed his horse's reins and led it down to the creek. Walking along slowly, he looked for signs. A small beam of sunlight filtering through the tree branches lit up an object lying on the ground. He reached down and picked up an empty cartridge casing.

Within minutes, he had placed seven casings into his pocket. He saw several boot tracks next to an olive tree. Timothy tied his horse to a tree branch and crossed the creek on foot. Just off to his left, partially washed by the stream, lay the innards of one of his sheep.

Timothy stood and stared at the remains, almost feeling better that someone had killed one of his sheep for food. Ah can handle that, he said to himself, but, to wantonly kill for sport, or whatever. The murderers!

He walked around and found the place where horses had recently stood, their excretions marking the spot.

Remaining on foot, he followed hoof tracks leading eastward. Three or four of them, he thought. He gazed at the mountain—damn them Erlocks. None of my neighbors would do such a thing, he thought.

Timothy crossed back to the other side of the creek and mounted his horse. He galloped it toward his home, angrier with each plod.

— —

THE CLERK ASSIGNED COLLIN MCBRIDE A ROOM and handed him a key. He tucked the metal box under his arm and headed up the stairway. Collin carried one of his luggage pieces and walked along the hallway, slowly eyeing the numbers on the doors.

He glanced in both directions before turning the key in the latch.

Collin entered and laid the bag down on the bed, immediately shoving the metal box underneath. He locked the room before returning back downstairs to get the rest of his luggage.

Collin finished putting the last of his belongings away, impressed by the magnificent furniture and accommodations. His wrinkled clothes hung from a rod next to the door. The rest of his things tucked nicely into the six drawers of the enormous dresser, a Victorian style piece made of mahogany wood. The frame of the mirror had a jagged frame that surrounded a sea of glass. He stood in front of it reminding himself that he needed a shave.

An ornate metallic lamp sat on a mahogany decorative table next to the bed. It had a large, pleated, white, glass-shade that narrowed in the middle but then widened at the top.

He lay down on the bed that had a backboard extending beyond the width of the pillows. It, too, had roadways of mahogany wood, but they surrounded empty spaces rather than glass.

He closed his eyes, visualizing the vaguely visible countryside out the window of the train and stagecoach. I stared out those windows near onto two weeks, he said to himself. Aye, but on the coach, I had two lasses to look at. Miss Pikes is a good-looker all right, but that school teacher, Miss Barnard—she is the sweetest looking creature on this earth.

I wonder why two fine persons as those lasses would want to come out to this godforsaken place to live, he said to himself. But then, what am I doin' 'ere? Aye, but 'tis my brother that caused me to travel all this way.

His stomach boiled thinking about his brother and what he saw him do back in Ireland. 'Twas him that murdered my older brother Patrick, but Timothy had been treated miserably by both Patrick and my father. I need to make my peace with Timothy, for better or for worse.

Collin got up off the bed and walked to the window. 'Tis not the same bit of view that I had in Ireland, but it'll have to do, he said to himself, watching a wagon roll out of town. He recognized the family of four whom he saw near the stagecoach earlier.

His need for sleep competed with those of hunger and thirst.

Pausing momentarily at the door and looking back at the bed, he made his decision. Collin took full advantage of the pitcher full of water and washed himself as best as he could. His boots thumped on the wooden stairway as he made his way down the stairway.

Collin heard the wall clock in the hotel lobby clang eight times. He paused, stared at the round-faced bald clerk, and smiled. I woke the poor man, he said to himself. Collin smiled, watching the clerk adjust his round-rimmed glasses.

The clerk said, "Good evening, sir."

Collin nodded and continued on through the lobby and into the corridor. He looked up and saw a sign that read *Mama's Kitchen*. He ran fingers over his dark whisker-laden chin, sorely in need of a shave, he thought. Aye, I'll have a bath and shave later, but first, I need food and drink.

— —

COLLIN ENTERED THE RESTAURANT and looked for an empty table. He saw none, but did see the portly gentleman sitting by himself near a window. Aye, that's the gentleman that rode on the coach with me, he said to himself. Collin walked over. "Pardon me, sir. You're Weatherby?"

The detective slowly turned his head. He said sternly, "You came on the stagecoach with me, didn't you?"

"Best of the evenin' to ye, sir. Aye, ah did come on the coach. Mind if I sit?"

"Please join me—your name?"

Collin glanced at a table by the window. Miss Barnard, the school teacher, sat alone. He wished that he had not made such a hasty decision. Besides, he didn't care for Weatherby. The detective, he thought, has an air 'bout 'em that ah don't like. I'd much rather be havin' vittles with the young lady, he said to himself.

"Excuse me, Mr. Weatherby. My mind drifted there for a moment. Collin McBride is my name."

"That's quite the accent you have—Irish, is it not?"

The Irishman pointed eastward. "Ye have it right. I sailed across the ocean on an ocean liner all the way from Liverpool. I think you boarded the train in St. Louis."

"That's right, ah did."

A round-faced woman with large blue eyes approached their table. "Gentlemen, would you like some dinner?"

Weatherby turned his head. "I certainly would. What's your specialty?"

"Angus steak and mashed potatoes with gravy."

He nodded. "I'll try that."

"What about you, sir?"

Collin smiled wide. "Ah'll have the same." He stared as the generous proportions of her body swayed side-to-side as she walked away.

Collin cleared his throat. "'Twas absolutely amazin' how those gentlemen bandits stopped the train and robbed us of our money."

"Gentlemen? Ah don't think so. They're wanted by the law all over Missoura."

"They didn't harm anyone."

"They took your money, didn't they?"

"Well, a bit of it—but, the conductor hid most of it for me. I didn't lose much."

"You were fortunate. The three bandits who robbed us were no other than the notorious Jesse James, Cole Younger and Bob Younger. They stripped some of the passengers clean as a baby after a bath. I and others have been hired by the United States government to gather a force together to put an end to their banditry. The James and Younger brothers all belong in prison."

Collin whistled. "Aye, but they didn't shoot at us—like them tyrants who rode down from the hill."

"This is dangerous territory, Mr. McBride. Ah wonder if you did the right thing by comin' out 'ere. Ya may have been better served remaining in New York."

"I've got business to attend to. It cannot wait."

"Business, what kind of business?"

"Best it remain private, Mr. Weatherby."

Weatherby leaned across the table. "Did ya see what one of those bandits did with the lady across from ya—the one by the window?"

"Aye, but he got her diamond ring back. This may sound a bit daft, but if the bandit would 'ave brought my money back, I would have kissed him, too."

Weatherby forced a smile. "Mr. McBride—you were a witness to the train robbery. Could I call on you when we catch those bandits? Mind you—we will catch them."

"That you could. I wouldn't mind getting my money back, too."

"How much did they take from ya?"

"Not sure—ah gave them what I had in me pocket—a few shillings. The conductor hid me money box—most of everything ah own. The trainman saved me."

They stopped talking when Belle Streeter brought over their dinners. She set the two plates down and bowed. "Enjoy your dinners, gentlemen."

Collin ate rapidly. In a matter of minutes, he said, "I thank you for the information. My supper is done. It's time for me to retire—I am really tired. What will ye do if you catch the bandits, may I ask?"

"Ah would like to see 'em hang. There're reward posters out reading, *Dead or Alive*. Sooner or later they will get caught," the detective said, his eyes glaring.

Collin brought a coffee cup to his lips, watching Weatherby closely.

"The firm out east which I work for, the Pinkerton Agency, they pay well. Would you be interested?"

"Not as we speak. I have other agendas," Collin said.

"All right then. I bid you a good day." Weatherby removed his napkin from his chest and placed it on the table. Getting up, he strode for the stairway.

Pinkerton...now that's a name, Collin said to himself. He toted up his supper purchases and dropped a coin on the table. Collin looked toward the windowed wall and saw that Miss Barnard had left.

12

RAIN DROPS SPLATTERED AGAINST THE WINDOW of Collins's hotel room. He watched them streak down the pane and disappear beneath the frame. Each droplet was replaced by another, and another. At least the room isn't bobbing around, he thought. My memory of the stormy weather in the Atlantic isn't goin' away easily.

Later, Collin staggered out of his bed and rubbed his eyes. He walked over to the window of his second story room. The rays of the sun splashed across the bright red side of the stagecoach. Six horses stood lazily as passengers stepped up into the coach. He saw a one-legged man hoist himself onto the seat next to the driver.

A tall man wearing a badge stood by one of the lead horses, one of his hands clasped on a bridle. The shorter man, holding onto the bridle of the other lead horse, wore long boots almost touching the knees. Collin pushed upward and opened the window. He heard the passenger door of the stagecoach slam shut.

"She's ready to go," a man yelled and backed away from the coach. Collin saw a badge pinned to the smaller man's shirt as well.

"He-YAH!" the driver yelled and the horses broke into a trot. Collin watched with awe as the stagecoach rumbled down Main Street. When it came abreast of a church, the one-legged man who rode next to the driver turned his head and waved his hat. Collin heard shouts coming from people down below on the boardwalk.

Collin's eyes followed the stagecoach until it disappeared from sight. He then got down on his knees and reached under the bed. Aye, he said to himself. The metal box lay right where he had placed it the night before. He set the box on the dresser and released the latch. He fingered the neatly stacked bills. They hadn't been touched since he left Ireland.

Collin had inquired the previous evening and learned that the hotel maintained a safe. He didn't feel that he could have faith in the clerk, so he chose to keep the money in his room. Collin also didn't trust bankers. He sat down on the bed and rubbed the thick whiskers on his chin. Me thinks I should visit the banker before deciding if he and the establishment are trustworthy, he thought.

The Irishman returned the box to its hiding place under the bed. He closed his door, put on his gray bowler hat, and traipsed down the stairs. Collin smiled and tipped his hat at Belle Streeter who stood by the window in the lobby, looking out onto the street. She puts out mighty good vittles over there, he said to himself while crossing the lobby to the front door.

Collin stood out on the boardwalk and looked around. A rugged pair of black horses plodded by, pulling a wagon full of supplies, heading westward. A back-bent elderly man, sitting on a bench in front of the barbershop, whittled on a stick of wood, a pyramid of fresh cuttings accumulating on the planks.

Collin walked past three horses tied to the rail in front of the Frontier Saloon. He hadn't been in there yet, but hoped to do so soon, and visit with Rosemary Pikes. He remembered her mentioning during the stagecoach ride that she would be employed there.

He strolled onward, stopping to look up at letters chiseled into the bricks of a building. "This must be the bank," he muttered. A white masonry facade perched above the entire width like the crown on a king's head. Collin glanced across the street and saw a man dressed in black standing in front of a doorway. That would be the undertaker, Collin thought. Digger Phelps was the name I heard mentioned.

Collin pulled the door open and entered the bank. Looking over the L-shaped, half-walled counter, he saw a bald gentleman sitting at a table with his back to him, studying a massive ledger book. The man sitting behind a barred teller window looked up and peered at him over the rims of metal-framed glasses.

"Top of the day ta ya," Collin said, smiling wide.

The teller, wearing a gray vest over a white shirt and black tie, looked up at him. "Can ah help ya?"

"Aye, I'm Collin McBride just arrived from Ireland. I need a safe place to keep me money."

The teller smiled and pointed toward the wall-high black-surfaced safe behind him. "Not even Jesse James can git into that one."

"Can I talk to the manager?" Collin asked.

"I shall see," the teller said and turned his head. "Mr. Herron, would you talk to this gentleman?"

Collin walked around the end of the counter and extended his hand to a short man standing next to a desk. He saw an over-sized stomach threatening the black buttons of the man's striped waist coat.

The man's ears nested in a forest of thick, curly black hair that extended down to his collar. The skin of his hairless top mirrored the glare of a lamp attached to the wall above.

"Ah'm Douglas Herron, owner of this bank. What can ah do for ya?"

"Collin McBride here, sir. Would me money be safe here?"

"As safe as anywhere, Mr. McBride. The safe which you saw in the corner has a time lock, and can only be opened at a certain time of the day—safe as any around these parts."

Collin nodded. "Very well, sir. I will be back in a bit." He shook hands with the banker and walked away, whistling as he walked out the door.

— —

COLLIN LOCKED THE DOOR BEHIND HIM and reached under the bed. He brought out his metal box and carefully transferred the stacks of bills into a small carpet bag. Collin walked over to the window and gazed up and down the street. It looks safe enough, he thought.

The banker smiled from ear to ear as he counted the bills stacked on his desk. Collin stood next to him, anxiously wishing to get the money into the safe. In a few minutes, Collin walked out of the bank, feeling satisfied. He kept a few of the bills, placing some into his money belt and the rest into his inside coat pocket.

A wagon, full of lumber moving westward, rolled by on Main Street. Collin listened to the loud squeaking sounds as the conveyance lurched forward on the bumpy road. He turned away and walked toward the large building, farthest in that direction.

He nodded reading the large sign high up on the flat-topped facade of the wooden structure, *Mercantile Goods & Services*. Collin walked in and recognized the face of Mason John Miller. He remembered the tall, brawny, young man who he had sat beside during the stagecoach run from Stillman Mills to Tarrytown.

"Top of the day to ye, Mason John," Collin said.

Seth Miller's nephew wore his usual brown-checkered shirt and light-brown duck trousers held up with wide red suspenders. Mason John smiled, his gawky frame bent slightly at the shoulders as he got up from kneeling next to an array of boxes near the door.

"Can ah help you find somethin', McBride?"

"I'll look around—need some riding clothes."

Collin walked along a wall of men's clothing. From the displays, he selected a white hat, red bandana, black duck riding pants, and a red-checkered shirt.

He laid them down on the counter. The clerk asked. "Will ya be needin' a pair of boots, too, sir?"

"The idea of wearin' boots has been niggin' at me, lad. Ah'll try some on."

He selected the dark brown pair and pointed at the gun rack. "Ah want to look at one of those."

"Ya mean a carbine?"

"Aye—a carbine—is that what ye call it?"

"If ya plan on doin' any ridin', you'll need one of these scabbards, too," the clerk said.

Half an hour later, Collin paid for his new purchases and the newly-hired clerk, Mason John bunched everything into a bag, except the rifle. Collin slung the bag over his shoulder, picked up his new rifle and left the store.

As his new boots clattered across the lobby floor, clerk Robert

Packard's eyes watched his every step. Collin paused and pointed at his boot before heading up the stairway.

Collin changed into his new riding clothes and stood in front of a mirror. Now I look like the rest of 'em, he thought. I'm regally attired.

— —

COLLIN HELD HIS CHIN HIGH as he walked across the lobby floor, glancing back at Packard before going out the door. He paused on the boardwalk, looking up and down Main Street. My God, this is small, not exactly a New York, he thought. Collin stepped carefully across the muddy street, not wanting to get his new boots overly dirty.

He saw a hoop-skirted woman come out of the Smith Building. It's the school teacher, he said to himself, the pinks of her cheeks catching the glow of the morning sun. Collin remembered the paleness of her face during the stagecoach ride. She's changed to the best, he said to himself, smiling.

He tipped his new white, high-crowned hat and bowed after stepping onto the planks. "Good day to ye, Miss Barnard."

"Why Mr. McBride, don't you look handsome in your new clothes?"

Collin's face darkened as a chill slithered up and down his spine. The woman has changed, he thought, watching her with eyes as keen as a cougar's. She's beautiful...nothing like that pallid, frightened face in the coach. "Are ya walkin' me way? I'm headin' to the corral."

"That I am for a spell," she said, Collin catching the star-like gleam in her eyes.

His legs felt like two clumsy, wooden poles, welded to his hips, as they strolled side by side. They drew the gaze of heavily whiskered Deputy Milburn, leaning against the outside wall of the marshal's office.

"Good mornin', ma'am," the deputy said, totally ignoring Collin.

Collin paused and looked into the window, seeing vertical iron bars lit up from the light coming through a small opening. "Is that what you call a jail around 'ere?"

"That 'tis," the deputy snapped in a high, whiney voice. "Ya keep yar nose clean and ya'll never see the inside."

Cosette laughed. "Are you talking to me or the gentleman, Deputy?"

Lance Milburn jerked his frame straight and tipped his hat. "'Twasn't you ah was talkin' to, ma'am."

"I'm going to cross here," Cosette Barnard said, pausing abreast of the stage depot. "I hear that the mercantile store has stacks of materials—and I can't wait to get over there and see them and buy some."

"Now, let me help you across," Collin said, pinching the end of her sleeve.

Collin felt his breath catch in his throat escorting the woman across the muddy street and to the door of the Mercantile Goods & Services store. She released the folds in her skirt, ignoring the muddiness of her boots. He bowed slightly and tipped his hat, his heart beating as she turned her head and smiled before passing through the door.

He paused on the boardwalk for a moment before turning and striding back across. His eyes gazed through a space between the stagecoach depot and corral, seeing several horses grazing within a fenced area.

He paused at an open doorway, coughing at the odor of forged metal. Rubbing his chin, he looked up and read: *Charley's Smithy.*

The sign over the next door read: *Toby's Corral.*

Collin entered and saw a rough-hewed, young-looking man pitching hay into a horse stall. "Now, don't trouble yourself, lad, but who do I see about buying meself a horse and saddle?"

The young man paused between tosses. "That would be Toby. He's out back."

"Thank ya, lad. Top of the day to ya."

Collin walked past several stables and continued on through a rear door into a harness room. He saw a small, narrow-faced man, wearing a high, narrow-crowned, dirty gray hat. He recoiled at the ugly, jagged stains above the brim.

"I'm looking to buy a horse, mister. Can ya help me?"

"How far are ya headin'?"

"Not far—just down the road westward. Do ya know where Timothy McGearney lives?"

Toby spat out a wad of tobacco juice, barely missing Collin's boots. "Sure 'nuf—jest past the Hastings's place. You'll see the buildin's when you get past the corner of the woods—MacTurley's Woods. McGearney is the next place beyond."

Collin nodded.

"Would ya happen to be a relative of McGearney's?" Toby asked, his eyes working up and down Collin's frame.

"Aye, all Irish are related."

"Hey, Billy, saddle up Nellie," Toby yelled. "Ah'll let you try the mare out before you decide to buy a horse," he said to Collin.

"I'll tell ye straight out, Mister Miller, ah haven't ridden horses much. Would ye give me a few pointers?"

Collin spent the next hour out back in the corral riding the mare under the watchful eye of Toby's hand, Billy.

"I think I got the feeling of it, lad," Collin said to Billy and trotted the horse twice around the corral as Toby watched.

The corral owner smiled and shook his head. "Ah've seen my share of dudes. Nothin' could top this 'un," he muttered.

"I'm off, then, Mr. Miller. I thank ye. Be back later today to make a deal."

13

THOMAS HASTINGS HELPED HIS WIFE UP into the carriage. "There, that'll do ya," he said, gently patting her enlarged midriff. He got up into his seat, untied the reins, and the pair of grays trotted toward the roadway.

"Look, Thomas, the stagecoach is coming. Isn't it just as beautiful as could be?"

Thomas pulled on the reins as their carriage approached the Tarrytown Road. He brought them to a stop and they watched the magnificent, red stagecoach approaching, coming from the direction of Tarrytown.

He could feel Sarah's heart beating fast as a white cloth appeared in a window near the rear. Someone held it out and moved it slowly back and forth, the wind stretching it to its full length. "They're wavin' to you, Sarah," Thomas said and took his hat off, holding it high. "Glory be, Sarah, that's Justin and Jesse up there. I wonder what's happened to Morgan?"

Thomas and Sarah heard hooves clopping, harness jingling, and wheels swooshing. They continued to wave as the coach clattered by. Suddenly, they heard Justin let out a whoop. Thomas held the horses at bay as he watched the stage fade away into the distance. After it crossed the bridge over Bear Creek, Thomas flicked the reins and steered his horses onto the Tarrytown road.

"They're off to Blue Springs—next stop," Thomas said, reaching over and clutching his wife's shoulder after he set the grays into a trot. "It's going to be all right today, honey."

She looked up into his blue eyes. "I know it will, Thomas. I know it will."

— —

THOMAS LISTENED INTENTLY AS DR. BLAKE SPOKE. "Yar wife is just fine. She should have a normal child."

"I'm much obliged, Doc," Thomas said and put an arm around Sarah's shoulder.

The tall, blond-haired young doctor wore a long white laboratory coat. His small, metal-framed glasses distorted the size of his eyes—making them look dark and large. "Have a good day, the two of ya," he said after escorting Sarah to the door.

Thomas assisted Sarah through the outside door and stepped onto the boardwalk.

"Hey there, Hastings, nice lookin' woman you got."

Thomas turned abruptly. Three rugged looking horsemen looked down at him and his wife. "The Erlocks!" Thomas gasped, tightening his hold on Sarah.

"How about a kiss, lady?" sneered the albino with the crooked smile.

"You three move along!" Thomas retorted loudly, dropping his right hand down to his holster. "I've got no quarrel with ya."

One of the men grinned widely, his eyes wide and black as a round coal. "Ah wouldn't do that if ah was ya, mister. Hey, brother, why don't you get down there and take that gun away?"

Thomas could feel his wife shaking. "Go back inside, Sarah."

"No, Thomas, I am staying with you. These cowardly men must move on," she said, her voice trembling.

A wave of rough laughter followed. One of the men dismounted. Thomas grasped the handle of his Colt with his right hand fingers. He heard the door leading to the doctor's office open.

"Move on, ya bullies!" Thomas heard the doctor yell.

Thomas turned and saw Dr. Blake pointing a double-barrel shotgun at the Erlocks. He had one of the hammers pulled back.

"Now, Doc, don't get so excited. We're only havin' some fun," the white-faced man said, sneering.

"Git! Now!" the doctor exclaimed, his finger tightening on the trigger.

"All right, boys, let's head over to the saloon. Doesn't seem like we're welcome here."

"Ya damn right you're not welcome here," the doctor said firmly.

The three men rode off toward the saloon.

"I'm gonna report this to the marshal," the doctor said and lowered his shotgun.

"Thank ya, Doc. Maybe ya should've pulled that trigger. Ya would've got at least two of 'em. I would have gotten the third. We would've been rid of those rascals for good," Thomas said.

"Best you get Sarah up into that buggy and head on home," the doctor said, walking toward his door, anxiously watching the three Erlocks tying up their horses in front of the saloon.

— —

THOMAS ASSISTED SARAH INTO THE CARRIAGE. He turned it around and anxiously looked up the street, relieved that the Erlock horses remained tied to the rail. He flicked the reins and rolled the wagon toward the mercantile store.

He grabbed his wife by the waist and gently set her down on the boardwalk. They entered the store and shopped for goods and supplies, including some for the Ortiz family. Thomas and Sarah met the broad-shouldered nephew of Seth's for the first time—Mason John Miller.

"Welcome to Tarrytown," Sarah said.

The young man smiled. "Ah like it 'ere—all the folks are nice to me."

Thomas placed a bag into the box. "That should do it," he said after watching Mason John toss in the last bag.

Thomas guided the team westward and had just passed the school. "Look, Thomas, looks like Grady comin'," Sarah said anxiously.

He nodded, glad that his brother approached, just having turned off the Walker roadway on horseback. When they came abreast, Thomas pulled on the reins to stop his team.

"Hey, Sarah—Thomas—how's things goin'?"

Thomas smiled at Sarah. "The doc says they're goin' fine, Grady."

"Glad to 'ear it."

"Grady, we had an in with the Erlocks over in front of the doc's office. If it wasn't for the doctor and his shotgun, who knows what would have happened," Thomas said.

"Why those dirty low-down cowards!" Grady exclaimed. "When will they ever learn? One of these days, ah'm gonna get the boys together and we're gonna get rid of 'em for good."

Sarah's reddish freckles flushed as she tightened her lips together. "Oh, Thomas, they didn't really mean anything. We don't need any trouble."

Thomas rubbed his chin. "Let's head on home, Sarah. See ya later, Grady."

He flicked the reins and his horses darted forward. Grady tipped his hat and galloped his horse toward Tarrytown.

14

COLLIN WALKED HIS HORSE up Main Street and tied it to the rail in front of the hotel. He had been in town close to a week, spending much of his time at the corral learning how to ride the horse he had purchased from Toby.

He strode up to his hotel room and brought down his newly acquired lever-action carbine. Placing it into a scabbard attached to the saddle, he mounted. "Here goes nuthin'," he whispered to the gray.

The insides of his stomach felt as if they were being tossed about like a bouncing ball by the time he got abreast of the church. Wearing no spurs, forgetting to buy a pair, he boot-healed the horse, back of the stirrup, and it broke into a gallop. "Whoa! Who-a! Whoa...."

Holding on tightly to the saddle horn, he held his breath until the horse slowed. What seemed like a long time to him—actually less than 45 seconds—the horse halted.

A farm house and other buildings dotted the landscape to his back and right. That's where Grady Hastings lives, Collin thought, remembering what Seth Miller had explained to him regarding the locations of the farms along the Tarrytown Road.

That must be the Kingsley's next, he said to himself. Nudging the horse's flank with his boot, the horse began to walk. The heavy wooded area to his left ended and he saw the barb wire with the white-faced cows enclosed within. The roadway leading to a farm loomed just ahead. "Thomas Hastings lives there," he whispered.

Collin coaxed himself, generating a new wave of courage, and he successfully got the horse to trot. Finally after relaxing a little, his innards adjusted to the annoying bounce. Crossing the small bridge over Bear Creek, he pulled on the reins. "There it is—that's where Timothy lives!" he exclaimed.

Collin dismounted. His knees buckled and he almost fell, dropping to one knee. Timothy uses barbed wire, too, he said to himself. The tall, rich green grass within the confines of the fence looked healthy. Farther down, within a separate fenced area, he could see a herd of sheep grazing. His stomach knotted—a man emerged from the house and walked toward the barn. "That's him! Me brother Timothy!" he exclaimed again.

— —

COLLIN STOOD NEXT TO HIS HORSE, gradually recovering from the shock of seeing Timothy again. He wondered if he had made a good decision coming here. Then he thought of the famine in Ireland. Where else could I've gone? he asked himself.

The murder of his older brother, Patrick, flashed through his mind. Was it really Timothy who I saw that foggy evening? He asked himself, yet he was tormented with the inevitable truth. What if it wasn't Timothy in the glen that night? It could have been someone else. Patrick didn't have too many friends. He got into scuffles at the pub many times.

Yet, there was no evidence of anyone else. The Suffolk police investigators didn't come up with a single suspect—well, except for Timothy. But then, they didn't have any evidence against him either.

I'm short of knowing what to do, he said to himself. Collin remounted and walked his horse eastward, the lowering sun's rays elongating his shadow ahead of him. He crossed the bridge and came abreast of the Hastings roadway.

15

THOMAS HASTINGS SWEPT A MATCH ACROSS HIS BREECHES. He lit his cigar and gazed northward toward Bear Creek and the Tarrytown Road. He had taken a seat on the bench of their north porch after eating supper and helping Sarah with the dishes.

He gazed across the flatland directly in front of him. A small herd of Herefords grazed on grasses that had been allowed to grow tall the past couple of months. Luke, his foreman, had moved the cattle from points south only a week ago. Some of the cows lay down in the grass. Easy life for them until they get slaughtered, he said to himself.

A few days had passed since he had taken Sarah to the doctor in Tarrytown. Fresh in his mind was the threatening encounter that he and his wife had experienced with the Erlocks. She had an appointment scheduled with Dr. Blake the next day. He worried that they would accost him and Sarah again. His hired hands were busy and he didn't wish to use up their time to ride guard.

The intensity of the bad blood that existed between the farmers along the Tarrytown road and the Erlocks had intensified. The Sunnerland brothers had lost their parents to murderers. There was strong evidence at that time that the Erlocks were responsible for their death. The Sunnerland boys and some of their neighbors hung the one who they thought led the raid on the victims.

"Grand evening, Thomas," Sarah said softly as she came through the door. She inhaled deeply and smiled at her husband.

Thomas stood. He strode over to Sarah and held her gently. He assisted her to the padded bench where he had been sitting. How ya feelin' this evenin', dear?" he asked.

"Just fine, thank you. I've fixed you a brandy. It's on the kitchen table if you don't mind fetchin' it."

"Sure will—thank ye, darlin'."

Thomas entered the house and returned with a steaming brown mug. He took a seat next to his wife and raised his mug in a toast. "Best of luck on tomarra's visit. The time is getting close."

"I can't wait for the birthin' to be over with. I'm prayin' and hopin' for a healthy child for us," Sarah said softly, touching Thomas's arm.

After Sarah had returned into the house, Thomas rubbed the ashes off his cigar. He lit a match and drew the flames through, blowing out a puff of smoke. His eyes settled on a lone rider coming up the Tarrytown Road on his side of the creek. He became more interested when the rider turned onto his roadway.

He doesn't look familiar at all, Thomas thought. Quickly going inside, he returned with a carbine. Setting it in his lap, he continued to watch the rider. He's too well taken care of to be an Erlock.

The rider turned toward the house. Thomas watched his every move. Looks like a dude, he said to himself. The horse stopped. The man waved and clumsily dismounted.

"Aye, Mr. Hastings, I presume."

"Yes. Who are ya?"

"Ah'm Collin McBride—arrived in Tarrytown a couple of weeks ago. Was wonderin' if ye could use another hand? Ah could use the work."

"Where do ya hail from, McBride?"

"Ireland."

"Ireland! Seems that's where my neighbor came from—Timothy McGearney. Do ya know 'em?"

"No, ah don't."

"Tell ya what, McBride. Ride out to the bunkhouse next to the barn. Talk to Luke. He does the hir'n. We could probably use another hand until winter sets in."

"Thank ye, Mr. Hastings. Ah'll do that."

Thomas watched the visitor mount his horse and walk it away. He's a horse tenderfoot for sure, he thought, smiling.

— —

THE NEXT DAY, THOMAS LEFT THE BREAKFAST TABLE after kissing his wife. He walked to the corral and saw his hired hands branding calves.

"Howdy, Luke, how's it goin' this mornin'?"

"Got about a dozen left. Hey, ya really sent me a dude yesterday, but ah hired 'em anyhow."

Thomas frowned, his patience challenged waiting for Luke's slow, deliberate, well-chosen words to came out of his mouth.

"Good, he seemed like a nice chap. He'll take some breakin' in, though."

"The dude has already been broke in."

"What da ya mean by that?" Thomas asked, grinning.

Luke chuckled. "The boys gave the Irishman a lasso and put 'em on Pride." Luke cleared his throat. "They let a steer loose in the corral and the dude went to work."

"And?"

"Well—" Luke wiped an eye with his finger. "He took a couple of spills—finally grabbed the steer by the neck and dragged it down. Ah've never heard the boys laugh so hard."

"Did he get hurt?"

"If 'e did, he didn't show it. When he finally got to his feet, the boys gave him a tremendous round of applause."

"How did McBride react?"

"He bowed—that he did. 'e weren't walkin' so straight when he headed back out the gate."

"Think he'll come back?"

"Yup, today sometime. That's what he said. The boys can use some hep roundin' up the calves for brandin'. The dude's gonna stay at the bunkhouse this week and learn from the boys. After that he'll be livin' in town."

Thomas nodded and smiled. "Now, Luke, don't be too tough on 'em. We all had to start somehow."

Luke stood three inches taller than Thomas. Long, bony fingers extended down from slender arms. He always wore a gray, high, crease-crowned hat.

"Would ya saddle up King, Luke? Ah'm goin' out to see to the western herd."

"Sure thing, boss."

While he waited, he ran his fingers over the barbs of his newly purchased wire. Pa is really gonna be interested, he thought to himself. Not a single Hereford has strayed since we rebuilt the fences using the new type of wire.

Barbed Wire

JOSEPH F. GLIDDEN OF DEKALB, ILLINOIS was one of two men given credit for inventing barbed wire. He had fashioned barbs on an improvised coffee bean grinder, placed them at intervals along a smooth wire, and twisted another wire around the first to hold the barbs in position

His successful invention resulted in a creative frenzy that eventually produced over 570 barbed wire patents. It also set the stage for a three-year legal battle over the rights to those patents.

"The Devil's Rope," a term coined by religious groups who opposed the development of barbed wire, occurred as a result of injuries to the cattle caused by the pointed barbs.

Barbed wire fence growth stalled because free-range cattle producers opposed the fences that restricted and threatened their futures. Fence cuttings led to deaths and uncountable financial losses.

Destiny won as Texas ranchers began fencing their boundaries. One of them, John Gates, became the largest stockholder in the American Steel & Wire Company.

Joseph Glidden, the original inventor, was born in New York where he lived until 1842. He moved to Illinois in 1843 and bought a farm. At 38 years of age, he was elected sheriff. He was 60 years of age when he invented barbed wire.

Jacob Haish, born in Germany on March 9, 1826 came to America in 1835. He moved to Illinois in 1845. In 1873, he, too, invented a barbed wire, receiving the first patent issued by the patent office.

Glidden and Haish became involved in a patent infringement suit, which was settled by the Supreme Court in 1892. Both men became wealthy and prominent in their communities. Farmers and ranchers benefited forever.

See References in the back of the book.

16

WILLIAM FARNSWORTH SAT IN THE SADDLE, his horse standing near Grady Hastings's. They waited on the Tarrytown Road next to MacTurley's Woods, about half the distance from where the woods ended.

Grady Hastings heard the former Union cavalry officer's deep-throated declaration, "Look like a gig comin'." Grady looked into his cold, steel gray eyes and watched him eyeing the road westward.

Grady nodded. "That should be Thomas and Sarah."

A stiff breeze from the west rippled the yellowing leaves of a cluster of quaking aspen, some of them *fluttering* to the grassy surface below. Varied colors of patches of wild flowers signaled the beginning of the fall season. Large billowing popcorn clouds floated steadily eastward.

Grady's eyes narrowed, scanning the stretch of trees in both directions. He perpetually watched for hostile horsemen, especially after the incident between the Erlocks and Thomas on their last visit to see Dr. Blake.

Grady said firmly, "Yup, that's Thomas and his missus. Ah'm gonna make sure that those Erlock's don't bother 'em this trip."

William had spent most of the past summer at the Walker farm, where Grady Hastings and his wife Helen lived. He had reached the rank of colonel in the Union cavalry during the Civil War and had the privilege of being present during General Lee's surrender at Appomattox in 1865.

William sat straight in the saddle, a couple of inches taller than Grady. His black Stetson matched his pepper colored, well-trimmed hair. William's coarse skin had darkened during the war after spending days and nights outdoors in camps. His face narrowed to a pointed chin, partially covered with a short beard.

Grady had managed the Walker farm during the past six years after marrying Helen Walker. Her parents, George and Angie, did not come back to the Tarrytown area after they were forced off their land by the infamous Order No. 11 in 1863. A Union general had ordered all residents in Cass and Clay County to leave unless they lived within a specific number of miles from a Union base.

Helen's parents both returned for Grady and Helen's wedding. They warmly participated and showed their support for the newlyweds. However, they also exhibited sadness over the loss of their two sons, Will and Carr, as a result of the war.

The two riders waited for the gig to arrive, nudging their horses off to the side of the road as it approached. Thomas pulled on the reins to slow his team.

"Hello there, brother, Sarah. We'll follow ya into town," Grady said enthusiastically.

"Much obliged," Thomas replied. "Hello, Colonel Farnsworth. How are ya today?"

Farnsworth smiled widely. "I'm good, young man."

Thomas flicked the reins and the carriage continued up the road toward Tarrytown. Grady and William trotted their horses, remaining a few lengths behind. Grady saw Thomas scrutinize the grassy area between the schoolhouse and MacTurley's woods as he approached the church area. The notorious Erlocks often used a trail that emerged from the woods south of the cemetery.

"No Erlocks today—yet," he whispered. "Ya never know when those gorillas will come ridin' out of that mountain."

Grady and William slowed their horses to a walk as they watched Thomas bring the carriage to a stop at the boardwalk in front of the doctor's office.

"We'll keep an eye out on your gig from a windah in Mama's Kitchen, Thomas," Grady said. "Give a holler if there's any problem," he added.

The two men dismounted in front of Mama's Kitchen. Grady looked across the street and saw the Swede come out of the smithy. "Look there, Will. Ah hear that Charley's hired Jal, and put 'em up in the back,,gotta bunk room there."

"Who's Jal?"

"He's Tarrytown's first Swede, and he came on the stage when all them others did—Mantraux, the Pinkerton Detective and the like."

— —

BELLE STREETER SMILED AT THE TWO MEN when they came through the door of the restaurant. "Howdy, boys," she said, her smile showing off her pearl-white teeth between her full, ruby-red lips.

"What's the special today, Belle?" Grady asked, removing his gray hat.

She blinked her large blue eyes and smiled widely, exaggerating the roundness of her face. "Dumplins', boys. Ah know you both love 'em to death."

"Mind if we sit over by that winder?" Grady asked, recognizing two men sitting at a table.

"Sure, boys, help yourselves," Belle said, winding her way back toward the kitchen.

The two men already seated next to a window turned to look as they approached. Thin-faced Abel Kingsley smiled. "Howdy, Grady—Will."

"Have a chair, boys," Justin Haggard said.

Grady nodded and sat down. "How's that black herd of yars, Abel?"

Abel smiled, his hazel eyes squinting. He tilted his head upward exposing his black, thick hair cut even with his earlobes. "Ah must admit that they've never looked better. Don't know what ah would've done without Elkanah and Baskhall Jackson. They each do the work of at least two men. Will—good to see you agin'."

Farnsworth nodded.

Abel ran his fingers through his hair. "Ah hear Thomas is havin' some rustlin' goin' on o'er thar, Grady."

"Yup, he sure is. It's them Erlocks, sure as shootin'."

"Glad to 'ere that your herd is doin' good, Abel. Hey, how's that stagecoach rider doin'?"

Justin Haggard smiled, his silver-gray eyes reflecting a beam of light coming from the window. "Ah'm still alive."

"When did ya get back from yar western run?"

"A couple of days ago."

"How did it go? Any action between here and Blue Springs?"

"None—went smooth as silk. Jesse drove them horses 'bout as good as one could. Nobody could 'ave stopped us if they 'ad tried."

Grady and William ordered a beer and food. Grady heard heavy footsteps approaching and turned his head.

"Farnsworth—Grady, how ya all doin'?" Mitch McGregor asked, throwing his hand out. He gave Grady's a big squeeze and then accepted the hand of Will Farnsworth. Mitch's long reddish-colored hair stuck out in all directions from underneath his black flattop hat.

Grady looked up at the bulky Scotchman. Still got that red mustache and neatly trimmed beard, he thought. His shoulders are at least as wide as his father's. A bit heavier, though, since he rode with the Gray Riders. Grady locked his fingers together. "Goin' good. How about you, Mitch?"

"Damn those bloody sheep—don't know what we're gonna do. Does Thomas 'ave any problems with 'em?"

"Yeah, he sure does, but his boys seem to be handling it all right."

"Ah wish that Irishman would take his muttons and go back to Ireland. We spend more time drivin' them blinkity-blankity sheep back across the line then we do on our own herds."

"Sorry to 'ear that, Mitch. How's yer pa?"

"Don't get out ridin' much any more. His back is botherin' 'em something awful. Well, ah best be gettin'. See ya boys."

William Farnsworth drawled, "Give my best to your pa, Mitch."

"Shall do."

Grady glanced out the window at Thomas's rig across the street.

"Dumplin's have arrived, boys—talk to ya later." Abel turned and gathered his arms around the steaming dish.

— —

GRADY FINISHED THE LAST FORKFULL of his food. "It's good to see some of the boys again," he said to William.

"You should all be proud. The Gray Riders became a legend in this part of the state during the second half of the Civil War," William said.

"Ah heard an officer talking about the Gray Riders at Appomattox. He said that this area was one of the few places where any buildings stood, come the end of hostilities.

Grady tightened his lips together. "William, none of us will ever forget the day ya brought your column through town when we were in the process of having the Haggard's funeral. My spine tingles when I think of it."

Grady's mind went back to the solemn day when the pastor led a wagon full with three caskets across the road. Grady had joined his family for the walk up the hill. The other Riders melted into the procession, slowly making their way toward the cemetery. The officer, leading the Union cavalry, raised an arm and the entire column came to a halt short of the procession.

Feelings of compassion spread through Grady's body when the officer removed his wide-brimmed, black hat and signaled the rider next to him. Grady saw the second Bluecoat's hat go down. Turning in the saddle, the rider next to the officer signaled to those in back of him. Like dominoes, all the Bluecoats in the entire column removed their hats.

As the long funeral procession stretched all the way from the church to the large cross in the middle of the cemetery, the Union Cavalry did not move. After the last of the mourners had passed and a trailing dog crossed the road, Grady had heard an officer yell, "For...ward!"

William puckered his lips and interrupted Grady's deep thoughts. "Ya were a brave bunch of lads to load those caskets onto that wagon when a quarter-mile long enemy column approached."

Grady smiled and looked out the window. "Jaysus, William, Thomas's rig is gone! We best get goin'."

17

PIERRE MANTRAUX RODE WESTWARD past the church and the school. He mused contentedly about a battle he'd survived. Pierre watched the black mare's head bob anxiously as he set it to a trot. Toby had said the mare might be a little frisky because she hadn't been out for some time. The corral owner had explained to him where Justin Haggard lived. *It's the first place on your right after you cross the bridge.*

Today he would meet the man whom he had shot during the war, face-to-face for the first time. It was time to deal with the regrets that still remained after all the killing over ten years ago. Pierre saw the first signs of color in and next to the trees—MacTurley's Woods, they called it.

He smiled passing by the first roadway. That would be Grady Hastings's place. The man will likely never know that he shot at me and missed at the Battle of Lone Jack. Pierre didn't remember the name of the other three Bluecoats who he had run into the field with to surround a Reb who had gotten ahead of the rest. That's what brought Justin to the front, to save the Reb, his neighbor, Abel Kingsley.

Pierre's thoughts deepened. I shot Justin...my three fellow Bluecoats shot at but missed Abel Kingsley. Suddenly, two black Rebs appeared out of nowhere, attacking us with sabers before we could reload. My three partners fell. I dropped my weapon and ran.

Pierre reached up and touched his left ear. I'll never forget the screaming, vibrating sound of the shot as it nicked my left ear. He shook his head muttering, "I got back to my line and dropped to the ground exhausted."

Pierre had learned from Lieutenant Farnsworth years later that the two black men who killed his comrades lived near Tarrytown. He stopped his horse and saw a roadway, two wheel tracks and a grassy island in between leading straight north down into a valley. Pierre saw the outline of a set of buildings. Elkanah and Baskhall Jackson live there, he thought. They're the ones who came after us with the sabers. Pierre shuddered.

He saw large herds of Black Angus cattle grazing within a barbed wire fence on the north side of the road. That has to be the home of Abel Kingsley, he thought.

Pierre rode across a small bridge spanning a deep creek. He saw more Angus, many more. Then he felt it—sharp stabs in the pit of his stomach as the Haggard buildings came into view.

He saw two horsemen in the Haggard field not far from the buildings when he turned the mare onto the roadway. Pierre felt certain that they would intercept him, so he kept his horse walking, not wanting to appear to be a threat.

"Who are ya—and what do ya want?" one of them asked after they had galloped over to the roadway and halted their horses in front of him.

"I'm here to see Justin Haggard," Pierre told the horsemen "I fought in one of the same battles with Justin and would like to talk to him."

"Ya can move ahead, but first give up your guns."

Pierre removed his belt and handed it over. One of the men took it and nodded. "Ah need the carbine, too."

Pierre pulled it out of the scabbard then turned it over. One of the two men grabbed the carbine and they moved their horses off the roadway.

— —

PIERRE SAW A TALL MAN ON CRUTCHES standing in front of the door of a small building. He walked his horse slowly, stopping three horse-lengths away. That has to be him, Pierre thought, choking on the pulsations rising from his stomach.

The two men stared at each other for a few moments without

saying a word. After what seemed like eternity to Pierre, he finally dismounted. He let the reins of his horse drop to the ground and slowly walked toward Justin.

"Howdy, you've got to be Justin Haggard," Pierre said.

Justin nodded. "I've seen you somewhere before, haven't I?"

Pierre smiled. "Yes, at Butler Prison in Illinois—maybe in Tarrytown, too."

Justin frowned, appearing confused. "That's a long time ago. Which side were you on?"

Pierre bit his lower lip. "I was a Union sergeant."

"Did you work at the prison?"

"No, I didn't—I actually stopped there to look you up."

Justin moved his head slowly from side to side. "Look me up?"

"Yup, I fought against you at the Battle of Lone Jack."

Justin scratched his chin and said laughingly, "The memory of that battle left me years ago." He pointed at the space underneath his leg stump.

Pierre looked up at the sky. "Mr. Haggard, it's taken me a long time to build up the courage to do this." Pierre tightened his lips together and looked into Justin's eyes. "I was—"

Justin's eyes narrowed.

Pierre had choked on his words. He cleared his throat. "I was the one who shot you."

Justin's stood there in silence and stared at his visitor. Then he opened up his arms. Pierre stepped forward and they embraced. Justin released him and smiled. "Good thing ya missed up here." He pointed at his head.

Justin pointed toward a bench. "Sit down. Ah'll bring out a bottle."

Pierre found it impossible to hold back tears when Justin told him about his homecoming—his wife and parents all gone with the wind. He put a hand on Justin's shoulder. "War is ugly enough, Justin—what those renegades did to your family was much worse."

Justin lifted up the glass and emptied it into his mouth. "Ah feel better now, Mantraux, not because ah'm gettin' drunk, but because you came—this took courage. I salute you." Justin refilled his glass.

18

THOMAS AND SARAH WALKED OUTSIDE after the doctor visit ended. She placed a hand over her eyes, shielding them from the bright sun. "Isn't this a grand day, Thomas?" she said, her freckles standing out like blossoms on a cherry bush.

Thomas's wide smile stretched from ear to ear. "Yeah, especially with what the doctor said to us. You're gonna have a healthy baby."

Thomas helped Sarah onto her seat. Walking around the other side, he got up on the seat and flicked the reins.

Sarah's expression tightened. "Aren't you going to wait for Grady and William?"

Thomas pulled on the reins. He hesitated. "Sarah, I'm anxious to git home. They'll see us leave, bet they're watching us right now."

He turned the team, sending them into a trot westward. Smiling, he glanced at Sarah. "Naw, them Erlocks won't bother us any more, especially with so many of the Riders in town."

They passed by the church. Thomas glanced to his left where he spent six years learning in a one room school house. He smiled, thinking about the benefits. Then he frowned, thinking about his friend, Carr Walker, who was killed during a skirmish between the Gray Riders and Union cavalry.

During a recent visit to the mercantile store, he had met the new school teacher, Cosette Barnard. "Two extra grades this year, Sarah. Remember when we had only six?"

Sarah laughed loudly. "Yes, you big lug. I remember well. You were always flirting with me. You're lucky that I didn't tell my pappa."

— —

PIERRE AND JUSTIN SAT ON A BENCH SEAT on the small porch in front of the house. They had talked for two hours, Justin going into the house for two cups of coffee to reduce the effects of the whiskey.

Pierre explained where he was brought up—not too far from Springfield, the home of President Lincoln.

Pierre took a sip of coffee. "Just like you, I've had a lot of time to do a lot of thinking about the war. I've changed my opinion about the president. Where ever I go, people talk about what a great president Lincoln was. I for one do not agree. Our president succumbed to the wishes of radical groups. He approved strong and unreasonable economic sanctions against the south."

Pierre tightened his lips. "He was a lousy leader—as exampled by his generals."

Justin nodded.

"You know, Justin, slavery would have ended eventually regardless. Wouldn't it have been a lot more prudent to end it gradually over a period of time, such as ten years? The Emancipation Proclamation sent forth over a million blacks into a tunnel of desperation: no jobs, no homes, no money, virtually no help—no hope."

Justin pointed. "Our neighbor Kingsley had already released his slaves. My father talked about it a lot and had planned to do so, but not without offering them a place to live and a place to work. Your views are most welcome, Pierre."

Pierre stood. "You just don't know how much better I feel now that I've met you face-to-face."

Justin narrowed his eyes. "The war wasn't your fault, Pierre. You were only doing your job. Ah didn't like killing anyone during the war, but ah didn't have any choice."

"I see that you ride shotgun for Wells Fargo now and then," Pierre said.

"Yup, ah've got another assignment next week—heading west."

"I might just be on that stage. I'm headed for California to live with my sister." He looked Justin in the eye. "You'll never know how much this meeting means to me...no one ever could." He narrowed his eyes and reached out his hand. Justin grabbed it—they hugged momentarily. Pierre stood. "Ah've got to go, Justin. We'll see each other again." He walked away slowly.

Pierre mounted his horse and walked it to the roadway. He turned and saw that Justin had stood. Pierre waved, feeling a troubling burden slip away.

He spurred the mare and trotted it toward the Tarrytown Road, stopping for only a moment to retrieve his guns.

Pierre had crossed the bridge again and approached the corner of MacTurley's Woods. He heard gunfire.

— —

THOMAS GLANCED UP THE SLOPE TOWARD BEAR MOUNTAIN. A large white cross towered over the gravestones dotting a small hill. As they neared the beginning of MacTurley's woods, he got edgy. He watched three riders coming down from the trail back of the cemetery.

"Gidup thar!" Thomas yelled.

The team of grays broke into a gallop. "Whoa," he said to give the horses a momentary break after passing the midway point of MacTurley's Woods.

His heart leaped up his throat. The three riders were coming hard towards them. He feared the worst, especially when getting a glimpse of white hair. It's the albino Erlock. "Gidup!" he yelled again.

The grays exploded into a gallop. Glancing back, Thomas could see the gap between him and them narrowing. He looked at Sarah and grimaced at the look of concern on her face. They won't dare follow me once I get past the corner of the woods, he said to himself, anxiously.

"Uheee! Uheee!"

Thomas could hear the hooves of the galloping horses behind him. He switched the reins to his left hand and pulled out his Colt revolver.

"Oh, Thomas, I'm so afraid...."

"Uheee! Uheee!" Their pursuers continued to yell.

A shot rang out. One of the gray mares veered sharply. The right front wheel hit a rock on the edge of the road, and the buggy spun out of control. It remained airborne for a moment before landing on its side. Thomas heard Sarah scream just before they both got thrown out.

His revolver flew from his hand as he rolled in the tall grass next to the road. Thomas landed on his shoulder, jolting his diaphragm, forcing all the air out of his lungs.

Gasping and panting, attempting to recover his breath, he saw a face of one of the Erlocks—grinning from ear to ear. It was the ugliest face that he had ever seen, he thought to himself, still gasping for air. "Sarah! Sarah! Where are you?" he exclaimed.

"Won't do ya no good, Hastings. Ah got ya this time."

Thomas thought of his family. He thought about Mr. and Mrs. Sunnerland. Suddenly, he heard a bullet whistle by, followed by two quick gunshots. Catching a hint of movement out of the corner of his left eye, he saw a horse approaching from the west at a gallop, the rider's silhouette pure black against a blue sky.

One of the Erlocks yelled, "Come on boys, lets git!"

Thomas heard the slap of leather and quickening hoof beats as the Erlocks galloped back towards their trail. He heard another bullet speed by over his head. The Erlock's riders left the road, heading for the woods. He saw a spike of dirt kick up next to one of their departing horses.

Getting up on one knee, his shoulder throbbing, Thomas saw the rider continue to fire at the departing Erlocks. After the Erlocks had turned off the road and disappeared into MacTurley's Woods, he saw two other horses galloping towards them, coming from Tarrytown.

Thomas heard the hooves of a horse dig into the soil as it halted. He looked up and saw a stranger, a black-clothed man with a long, narrow, black mustache. "Hey, mister, can ye help us?" Thomas yelled.

The man nodded and dismounted, placing his gun back into his holster. He walked over to where Thomas held onto Sarah, the smell of acrid gun powder reaching Thomas's nostrils.

The man stood there. “Is she hurt bad?” he asked.

Thomas nodded. “She’s out cold, but she is breathing.”

“We gotta get her to the doctor!” the man exclaimed.

“My brother will be here any second. Would ya see to the horses and wagon?”

Thomas continued to hold Sarah, tears in his eyes. Shaking his head violently, he knew that he would never forgive himself for not waiting for his brother at the doctor’s office. Thomas glanced up, appreciating the look of concern in the stranger’s dark eyes. If that man hadn’t showed up when he did, Sarah and I’d both be dead, he thought. Thomas thought about Grady and William. I should have waited! I should have waited! he exclaimed to himself, feeling terrible.

Moments later, Thomas heard heavy hoof beats approaching. Grady and William will be here in moments, he said to himself. Thomas glanced eastward and saw two horses galloping toward him. He rubbed fingers over his forehead, anxious for their arrival so he could get his wife to the doctor, yet he dreaded the look in his brother’s eyes that he would witness in moments.

Grady leaped off his horse. “Good God! What ’ave they done to ya and Sarah?”

“I’m all right, Grady, but Sarah ain’t so good. She needs a doctor bad,” Thomas said. “That gentleman saved our lives.” He pointed at the stranger who had moved away, tending to the two mares.

Grady’s eyes darted from Sarah to the buggy—back to the stranger holding onto the horses. “Come on, Will, lets get the buggy up. We gotta get Sarah to the doctor—right now!”

Grady dashed over to the man working on the horses. “Yar Mantraux, aren’t ya. I saw you get off the stage.”

Mantraux nodded.

Grady fought to control his trembling hands. His voice quivered. “Would ya hep us?”

Mantraux said, “I’ll help you get this buggy up-righted.”

Grady looked at William. “For Chris sake, Will, let’s get this buggy rolling.”

The wheels of the buggy dug into the soft soil momentarily before righting. Pierre brought the team back and with William’s help, they hitched them up. Pierre led the horses and buggy back onto the road and stopped them next to the place where Thomas held Sarah.

"Git up there, Thomas. We'll lift 'er up to ya," William said. "Would ya hold onto the team, Mantraux?"

Thomas looked down at the limp form of his wife, feeling moisture building in his eyes. Grady and William gently picked Sarah up and hoisted her up to Thomas who straddled the seat. Struggling to maintain control, Thomas set her down on his lap.

Looking into her eyes, Thomas feared the worst. He could feel an occasional movement in her chest, but there wasn't any movement in the rest of her body He held her close as Grady leaped onto the driver's seat.

"Gee-dap!" Grady yelled.

The team galloped toward Tarrytown, followed by William and Mantraux on horseback, Grady's horse trailing behind.

Grady slowed the team as they passed by the church. William galloped his horse ahead, passed the buggy and pulled up in front of the doctor's office. He quickly dismounted and hurriedly pounded on the door.

Curious people who had been standing on the boardwalk next to the saloon began crossing the street. Grady leaped off the seat. He and William gently took Sarah down. Thomas quickly jumped off and ran to the doctor's door.

— —

WITHIN A MINUTE, SARAH LAY on a bed in the doctor's office. Grady shook his head. "Come on, Will, let's go outside. Ah'd rather wait out there."

He saw Mantraux standing next to his horse. Grady extended his hand. "Ah'm Grady Hastings. The woman who was injured is my sister-in-law. You've saved my brother and his wife's lives. We'll always be obliged to ya."

Mantraux nodded, his dark eyes narrowed, the wrinkles at the outer corners of his eyes tightened.

They stood out on the boardwalk. Grady nervously paced back

and forth in front of the door. A bystander said, “What’s happened, Hastings?”

“Rather not talk about it now, fella,” Grady replied.

William raised his arms and took two steps forward. “Best ya all go home.”

Grady turned and walked to the doctor’s door. He continued to pace back and forth, then he heard footsteps. He looked up and saw the lanky Marshal Ben Buford approaching. Grady respected the man but he had reservations about the law the man represented. He thought the new law didn’t go fast enough or far enough, especially in cases such as this.

Knowing who committed the atrocious crime against his brother and wife, Grady knew that he and his neighbors wouldn’t sit around and wait. Yet, he appreciated the look of concern in the blue eyes of the marshal.

Grady nodded his greeting.

The marshal usually talked slowly, choosing his words carefully. He didn’t smile much, often twisting his lower jaw when awaiting an answer. His blue eyes looked friendly enough—one of the few faces that didn’t show a mustache or beard. Grady grimaced and waited for the marshal to speak. “What happened, boys?”

With words never heard in a church, Grady explained the attack by the Erlocks.

“If it hadn’t been for Pierre Mantraux, both my brother and his wife would be dead.”

“They’re a bad lot. Are ya sure ’twas the Erlocks, Grady?”

“That’s what Thomas said. He saw ’em.”

“Ah’ll talk to him when he comes out.”

“Tell ya one thing, marshal, with due respect for the law, ah’m takin’ some of the boys up there. We’re gonna finish those tyrants off, once and for all—ah mean it, Marshal.”

“Now hold on, Hastings. The war’s over. No more hangin’s and such. Ah’m hired to enforce the law, and by darn, that’s what ah’m fully intendin’ on doin’. Do ya get that, Hastings?”

Grady didn’t speak. His head turned toward the door, which opened slowly. Thomas appeared, his shoulders hunched and his chin down on his chest.

Grady walked over to him and grabbed him by the shoulders. "How is she, Thomas?"

The blood had drained from Thomas's face. His eyes were partially open and wet. "We lost the baby—maybe Sarah, too. Doc said it's too early to tell," his voice tailed off.

Grady rapped a fist into his palm, moisture gathering in his eyes. "Thomas, the Erlocks won't git away with it! Ah promise ya!"

The marshal scratched his forehead. "Grady, would ya round up some of yar Riders and bring 'em over to my office?"

Grady nodded.

19

U.S. MARSHAL BEN BUFORD GOT UP FROM BEHIND HIS DESK. "Boys, Riders. Any of you that are available, ah'm takin' a posse up into the mountain first thing tomorra' to hunt down the Erlocks. There is no doubt, according to Thomas Hastings, three of 'em killed the Hastings's child, possibly even Sarah—heaven help her. Bone is the only albino man living in this whole territory. It was them all right."

Lafe Sunnerland kicked his toe against the wall. "Count me in. We should've taken care of all of 'em 13 years ago when they killed my parents."

"How's that shoulder o' yarn, Lafe? Ah heard ya got it hurt on the last run," the marshal said.

Lafe rubbed his fingers across his left shoulder. "Ah can shoot with this one." He pointed a finger ahead of him.

The marshal's eyes fixed on Justin Haggard. "Justin?"

The six-foot-five Justin Haggard was sitting in a chair, his crutch laid across his lap. He stumbled on his words. Clearing his throat, he said, "Ya can rely on me, Marshal. Ah can't wait to set them bastards in my sights."

Grady nodded. "Marshal, ah'm not lettin' Thomas go. He needs to stay near his wife. But, some of his hands may be available."

The lank marshal nodded. "We can use as many men as we can git. Do ya think Farnsworth will come, Grady?"

"Yup, ya darn tootin' he will."

Wide shouldered, Mitch McGregor leaned against a wall on the far side of the room. His already large blue eyes got bigger and his cheeks reddened. He removed his white hat and brushed a tuft of reddish-colored hair from his face. "Me 'en James is both goin'."

"Abel? Elkanah?"

Abel Kingsley blinked his eyes and grimaced. "You bet, Marshal."

Elkanah Jackson glared at the Marshal, his eyes dark as coal. In a calm, soft-spoken manner, he said, "Baskhall and I will both ride with ya."

"Fine, boys. Ah'll meet ya all here in front of the jail at dawn tomorra mornin'."

— —

THE FIRST STREAKS OF DAYLIGHT EMERGED on the upper branches of the treetops of Bear Mountain in Tarrytown, Missouri on September 20, 1875. Craggy cries of crows signaled the beginning of the new day.

Riders, some alone, some in pairs and some in small groups filtered out of the morning shadows onto Main Street. The clopping sounds of their horse's hooves echoed off the buildings. They all had a common destination—the marshal's office.

Tall and lanky Ben Buford approached on foot from the direction of Toby's Corral, leading his two-tone brown gelding. He dressed in his usual tan duck trousers, a pumpkin colored shirt and a tan-colored leather vest. His bony, protruding jaw jutted off center as he surveyed the men in front of the jailhouse—his office.

Other than a few grunts and murmurs, there were very few words exchanged amongst the men. The marshal mounted. He spurred the rear of his horse and led the way up the middle of Main Street, heading west.

Grady Hastings followed behind the marshal. He looked up and saw the faces of two people watching from two separate hotel windows: the lady, Rosemary Pikes, held a curtain back with one of her lily-white hands; the round face of the Pinkerton detective resembled a portrait within the frame of the second window.

Quietly, the single file of ten riders moved past the church as the top rim of the rising sun emerged above the tree line of Bear Mountain. Justin Haggard's horse snorted, alarmed by a gopher that scurried across the road. He jerked on the reins to maintain control. Mitch McGregor, who rode directly ahead turned, sneering at the gopher.

Abel Kingsley followed Mitch. Behind him were his two farming partners, Elkanah and Baskhall Jackson. The bulky physique of Lafe Sunnerland blocked the view of James McGregor, who rode in ninth position. William Farnsworth, the former colonel in the Union cavalry, brought up the rear.

As they approached MacTurley's Woods, the sun exploded its full diameter above the mountain. The column continued on until they reached the corner of the woods. The marshal raised his hand and guided his horse into the field of shrubs and undergrowth at the eastern end of Thomas Hastings's boundary.

Grady glanced at Thomas's house. Ah wonder if he's at the doc's tendin' to Sarah, he asked himself. He saddened deeply thinking about what the doctor had said—only a 50-50 chance to survive the brutal attack by the Erlock's.

The marshal led the column deeper into the woods for another half an hour. The going got a little tougher as the horses climbed a rocky slope. When they reached first sight of the Erlock buildings, the marshal raised an arm. He turned. "Ah want you boys to spread out, at least four horse-widths between each of ya. Ah'm goin' up to the door. If any shootin' starts, git off yar horses, git behind a tree and start shootin'."

Grady's stomach began to flutter as he watched the marshal dismount and check his revolver. Grady nudged his horse onward, stopping it at the end of a partial clearing. Looking back over his shoulder, he made sure there was space between each of the riders.

Reaching down to his holster, he pulled out his Colt revolver and laid it on his lap. He had checked the load of both his revolver and Remington carbine before leaving home.

"Erlocks! Ah want ya to come on out!" the marshal yelled.

Moments went by—nothing happened. Then, Grady saw a shadow appear in a window. The outside light reflected off something metal—a gun barrel, Grady thought.

"Victor! If ya don't come out, we're gonna come and git ya! I have witnesses that say that three of your boys kilt an unborn baby!"

The marshal paused. "Ah've come to bring them back to town! They need to stand trial—a civilized, fair trial."

"There are women and children in 'ere, marshal!" a feminine voice screamed.

"Ah know that—that's why ah want yar three boys to come on out. They know who they are."

"The boys ain't home, marshal."

"Can we come in and 'ave a look?"

Except for an occasional squeak of leather, the air became deadly quiet.

Grady heard Mitch's heavy breathing nearby. The big Scotchman held his carbine with one hand, the hammer cocked. Grady felt certain that everyone was ready for the Erlocks.

The front door of the house flung open. The stooped figure of a woman emerged, holding her stubby hands high over her head. Two younger women and four children followed. Abel and James stepped forward, directing the small group into the shelter of a stand of trees.

The marshal looked back and signaled everyone to dismount. He moved forward, a long barreled Colt pointed at the door. Grady had tied his horse to a branch. He pulled his pistol out of his holster and walked toward the marshal.

The Riders all gathered around the marshal who said, "Abel, take Baskhall and Elkanah around to that side of the house. Keep an eye out on the trees. Mitch, you, Lafe and James take the other side. Grady, William, come on in with me."

The marshal burst into the house. He crouched in the middle of the room, moving his revolver quickly, seeking a target. Grady and

William flanked him to his left and right. The opposite door sprang open and Mitch McGregor burst into the room. Minutes later, they all realized that the Erlock woman hadn't lied. The three brothers were gone.

On their way back to the horses, the marshal stopped next to the three women and children. "Where's Victor?"

The elder woman looked up at him, showing no expression. "He's dead and buried. Is that good enough for ya, mister?"

"Who are you?" the marshal asked crisply.

"I'm Victor's sister." She pointed. "These are my nieces and their children."

"You git them back in the house." The marshal had a withered look about himself and walked toward his posse. Some of them had already mounted and were waiting for him to return. Frustrated, Ben mounted and waved for everyone to follow. He led the deputies to the southeast corner of the beginning of a trail that continued upward and eastward. He dismounted and studied the ground. "No fresh tracks here, boys," he said and remounted.

He walked his horse along the eastern edge of the clearing stopping at the beginning of a second trail—one that the Erlocks used a lot. It led down a steep rocky slope of Bear Mountain and eventually ended at a clearing near the cemetery.

The marshal felt disappointed that they hadn't found and arrested the three renegade Erlocks. Ah would've taken 'em dead or alive, he said to himself. There will be no peace for anyone in and around Tarrytown until the renegades are either behind bars or dead.

"Someone must have tipped 'em off that we were comin'," Grady said to the marshal as they stopped in the clearing above the cemetery.

The marshal tightened his lips together. He looked at Grady. "Ah think we've put 'em on notice, though. They shouldn't bother your brother any more."

Grady sighed. He looked up at a hawk drifting over the grassy area between the cemetery and the woods. "Depends on the whiskey, marshal. When they get liquored up, they git mean—real mean."

"If they show up in town, ah'll arrest 'em like ah promised ya," the marshal said.

The ten riders filed into Mama's Kitchen after tying up their horses out front.

20

GRADY MET MITCH MCGREGOR AND LAFE SUNNERLAND at the Frontier Saloon the day after the visit to the Erlock's home.

"We might've predicted that the three of 'em would've vamoosed," Mitch said.

Lafe set his beer down. He cleared his throat. "Yeah, yar right. But, they'll be back—and when they do come back, we'll catch 'em."

Mitch lifted the mug to his lips. He swept a sleeve across his lips. "Ah been wonderin', what brought the gunslinger Pierre Mantraux to Tarrytown?"

Grady rubbed his right cheek with his thumb. "Word is that he's workin' for Wells Fargo." He stared at the ceiling. "If he hadn't showed up when he did—Thomas and Sarah would both be dead."

Mitch whistled. "The whole town is talkin'. Mantraux shows up on the same stage the detective Pinkerton did. Wonder if they're workin' together. Ah heard the detective is after the James boys—and the Younger's."

"That's what ah heard, too," Grady drawled. "That was quite the load of new people ya dropped off in town that day, Lafe," he added.

"Yup, 'twas the most passengers ever come on the stage from Mills."

"When you drivin' again?"

"The next stage that comes from the west, I'll take it all the way to Jefferson City."

"Is Morgan goin' with ya?"

"Yup, he'll be ready."

Grady narrowed his emerald green eyes. "Did ya hear why this

Irishman, McBride, settled here? He was out at Thomas's last week looking for work."

Mitch asked, "Did he hire 'em? He looks like a total tenderfoot."

"Yeah, he did, but more or less to do 'em a favor. McBride spent a few days out there and learned how to ride. Thomas says he can use more help before the snow comes."

Mitch rubbed the red whiskers on his chin. "Somthin' ah'm puzzled about, though."

"What's that?"

"That McBride feller sure looks a lot like Timothy McGearney, he talks like 'em, too."

Grady brought up a beer mug up to his lips. "Maybe all Irishmen talk alike." He heard the loud voice of a woman and turned his head. Grady looked at the other end of the room and smiled. "Well look at that, Mitch. Rosemary Pikes was yellin' at that detective and now she's pointin' a finger at 'em."

Mitch laughed. "Weatherby must have said somethin' he shouldn't have. Ah don't' like that man. He acts so high and mighty. If he runs up against the James boys agin', he'll likely turn tail like he did on the train."

Grady watched Weatherby leave the saloon through the door that led to the hotel lobby. A few minutes later, the man returned with a sheet of paper. He plunked it down on the table in front of Rosemary. She picked it up and crumpled it with her fingers and threw it at him. Weatherby threw up his arms and left again.

"What's the Pikes woman here fer anyhow?" Lafe asked.

Grady ran his tongue over his lips. "Maybe she's lookin' for a man, Lafe? She's a mighty good looker, that one. Ya best watch yar comin's and goin's." Grady laughed. "Actually, boys, she's here to hep out Lady Constance."

Mitch cleared his throat. "Yeah, Lafe, she might just be the one for ya."

— —

PIERRE MANTRAUX WATCHED WITH SPECIAL INTEREST as he peeked through his hotel window and saw the marshal and posse leave town. They're gonna bring in the Erlocks and hang 'em, he thought. He smiled and remembered the fear that he saw in the albino's eyes when he rode full tilt toward him. They're a pack of bullies and cowards.

How low can you git? Attacking a woman with child, he said to himself, banging a fist into his palm. In a few days, the stage will stop here, coming from the west, and I should be on it. But now, I've found some new friends. It will be difficult to leave them. Perhaps, I will delay my departure.

He sat down at the small table and brought a sheet of paper and envelope out of the drawer. He began to write. *Dear Sister. I plan on remaining in Tarrytown for the time being. I have made conciliation with some of the confederate soldiers whom I fought against during the Civil War....*

Pierre sealed the envelope and got dressed. He headed down the stairs and out the door, knowing that he would not reserve a place on the next stage heading west.

21

THOMAS WALKED OUT THE FRONT DOOR OF HIS HOUSE after breakfast. He looked back and thanked Annabelle who had stepped outside onto the small stoop with a broom in her hands. "Ya say hello to Miss Sarah, now—do that, Mr. Thomas?"

He smiled and nodded his head. Thomas walked to the corral where Luke had his horse ready. "Ah'm goin' with ya today, Thomas."

Thomas shook his head and hoisted himself up into the saddle. He looked down into the anxious eyes of his employee. Patting the mane of his stallion, he said, "Luke, King can outrun the Erlocks any time. Besides, ah don't think they'll be hangin' 'round much with the marshal lookin' for 'em."

"All right, boss. It's yar funeral."

Thomas walked his horse up the roadway. Minutes later, he turned onto the Tarrytown Road and rode toward town. As Thomas approached the Kingsley roadway, he noticed a buggy heading his way.

He moved to the side of the road as the buggy stormed past. Thomas saw the portly man flailing a black mare with a whip. There's a man moving with passion, he said to himself—it's that Pinkerton detective.

When he reached the corner of MacTurley's Woods, Thomas anxiously looked up beyond the cemetery, toward the mountain. The last time he had ridden by, he planted a small wooden cross at the foot of his unborn child's grave.

As he approached the doctor's office, Thomas felt the usual anxiety and worrisome feelings about Sarah. Yesterday, she appeared improved, he thought. She didn't have that deadly depressed look and her face had some color. Then, too, her voice had gotten better—not so raspy. I need to get her out of there and back to the farm where she can spend some time in the sun.

He watched a pair of red-tailed hawks hover high over the schoolhouse. One of them swooped down to the grass below. Another bunny gone, he said to himself. The Erlock's are gonna get what that rabbit just did, sooner or later.

Thomas sent his horse into a gallop after passing the church. He slid off and quickly tied the reins to a rail, picturing the albino Erlock in his mind. Sarah will never be the same, he thought. They murdered my unborn child...they will pay.

He looked across the street at the horses tied up in front of the hotel and saloon. Satisfied that they didn't belong to the Erlocks, he entered the doctor's office

— —

THOMAS FELT ELATED seeing Sarah sitting up in her bed. That's the first real smile she's showed me since getting hurt, he thought.

Rushing to her bedside, he kissed her and reached his arm around her shoulder. Pulling it tight, he said, "Sarah, you look splendid—so sweet and loving."

"I feel good, Thomas. Thank you so much for coming. It's been such a long day. How's Annabelle? How's Luke?"

"They're keepin' our home comfortable and safe, Sarah. Both of 'em ask about ya. They're anxious for you to come home, and so am I."

Sarah continued to smile. "I'm gonna ask the doctor if I can leave here soon—hopefully by the end of the week."

Thomas felt excited, and gladdened that Sarah didn't ask about the Erlocks and the attempts the marshal and the Riders made to bring them in. Rubbing a fingernail across his chin, his thoughts wandered to the challenges of the future. Ah'm gonna need an escort when Sarah is along—no taking any chances, especially if the Erlocks haven't been caught. Ah can't expect to have Grady and William hang around the Tarrytown Road all the time.

He thought about his new employee, Collin McBride, whom he could ask to ride along. The Irishman's a greenhorn right now, Thomas mused, but he's practicing shooting and his riding skills are getting better each day. Thomas shook his head. Right now, he'd be no match for the Erlocks. Jaysus, ah can't even take Sarah to church alone, he said to himself.

22

ROSEMARY PIKES WATCHED OUT HER HOTEL WINDOW as Thomas Hastings left the doctor's office. She thought about her experience with Bob Younger during the train robbery. She met with Bob secretly the day after seeing him on the train and learned that Thomas and he were friends.

She shuddered remembering the warm feelings in the pit of

her stomach during her visit with Mr. Younger. That happened way back in August, but she hadn't heard from the man since.

I haven't experienced feelings like that since meeting my husband. They had lived in St. Louis where Barry managed a manufacturing plant. The business had been handed down to him by his grandfather. He took over at a very early age, and financial success followed. Then hell hit us, she mused. Just like his father, his heart failed—made me a widow.

Shaking her head, she thought about being forced to leave St. Louis by an arrogant brother-in-law. I need some new friends, and what I've seen in the town so far, it looks as if I'll have many of them.

Rosemary watched as Thomas led his horse toward the mercantile store. She hastened down the stairway and felt relieved not seeing Mr. Weatherby. She had overheard him talking about the James-Younger gang. She came to hate the portly well-dressed man when he said, "My job is to put them boys in jail for good."

She walked out onto the boardwalk. Thomas had tied his horse to the rail in front of the Mercantile Goods & Services store. She walked hurriedly and passed through the door shortly after he did. Hastings stood next to the wall where several saddles hung. Rosemary approached him, pretended to be interested in items stacked on the middle aisle. "Oh, excuse me, sir. You're Thomas Hastings, aren't you?"

Thomas laughed. "Yes, ah am, ma'am. Whom do ah have the privilege of meeting?"

"I'm Rosemary Pikes."

"You're new around these parts, ain't ya?"

"Yes, I am. I did hear that your wife was severely injured. Is there anything that I could do?"

Thomas shook his head. "Ah appreciate your concern, Miss Pikes. Perhaps when Sarah returns home, she would appreciate a visit. I know she would."

"I shall do that. Have you seen Bob Younger lately?"

"No, not since ah returned from my parent's home in Independence. Ah saw Bob and his brothers right after you met him on the train."

She held her hand up. "See this ring, Mr. Hastings? If it wasn't for Bob, it would have been taken from me during the train robbery."

Thomas smiled. "The Youngers and James may have a rotten reputation, but there's a good reason. Their lives and properties had been disrupted for over ten years through no fault of their own. They're still fighting back."

"Thank you, Thomas. I so enjoyed meeting you," Rosemary said. She placed a hand on his arm. "I must leave now," she added.

— —

THOMAS LEFT THE MERCANTILE STORE and stomped over to the Frontier Saloon. Looking around, he didn't see any of his friends, but he did see Marshall Buford talking to Pierre Mantraux. The marshal stood next to a table watching Mantraux shuffling a deck of cards.

Thomas owed the dark-featured man his life. If he hadn't come along, guns blazing, who knows what would have happened to me and Sarah, he said to himself. We'd likely be lying up in the cemetery along with our unborn child.

He didn't feel like interrupting the two men so he walked over to the bar. "Ah'll have a beer, Brett."

The pock-faced bartender smiled. "Good to see ya, Thomas." He filled a mug and clunked it down on the bar.

Thomas lifted the mug to his lips and took two big swallows. He set it down, enjoying the feeling of the brew as it flowed into his stomach. Thomas felt a tap on his shoulder. He turned.

Marshal Buford stood there, a look of concern on his face. "Thomas, ah need to talk to ya."

"Sure, Marshal. What's on your mind besides the Erlocks? Grady told me ya took a bunch of the Riders out to their place and didn't find the culprits."

"That's true, Thomas. Ah promise ya, we're gonna catch those menacing murderers. Shouldn't have any problems gettin' a conviction and sendin' 'em to the penitentiary."

Thomas took another swig of beer.

"Thar's somethin' else, Thomas."

"What's that?"

"Yar neighbor, Timothy McGearney came in earlier today. Someone slaughtered ten of his sheep. Know anythin' 'bout that?"

Thomas scratched his head above the right ear. He shook his head. "No, Marshall, ah don't." His head lowered. "But, ah'd put my money on the Erlock's."

The marshal nodded, a look of concern on his face. "How's Sarah, Thomas?"

"Ah've got good news, Marshal. She's a lot better today—had me really worried there for a bit."

"Glad to 'ear that. Ah might mention that as long as the Erlocks are on the loose, it ain't safe for you to use the buggy without an escort. If ya let me know in advance, I could have Lance ride out to meet ya."

"Thanks. Ah just might take ya up on that."

The marshal walked to the door. He paused, allowing a man to step in before leaving. Thomas recognized his neighbor, Timothy McGearney.

"Aye there, Thomas, top of the day to ye."

"Timothy, would ya like a beer?"

"Aye, an ale would gratify me thirst. How's yer wife?"

"She's gettin' better, much better."

"'Tis good to 'ear, lad."

Thomas swallowed the last drop of beer from his mug. He looked up at Timothy and saw the man's face turn pale, his eyes enlarging. Thomas lowered his mug and looked across the room. He saw that Collin McBride had entered from the lobby corridor and stood next to the door.

"Is somethin' wrong, Timothy? Looks like you've seen a ghost."

"Ah think ah 'ave. It's me brother who ah haven't seen since moving from Ireland."

Thomas felt uncertain, debating with himself whether he should tell Timothy that his brother came looking for a job and got one. Collin no longer stood by the door. Thomas looked about the room—

no Collin.

Thomas studied Timothy's facial expression. Jaysus, he thought, the guy looks troubled—somethin's wrong. "I need another beer, Brett."

Thomas took a long drag. He nudged Timothy's elbow. "Hey, neighbor, anything you'd like to talk about? I mean—is something wrong?"

Timothy ignored Thomas and drank the rest of his beer from his half-full mug in one lift. He plunked it down, his face as tight as a drum. "Time to go home," he said, his lips pursed.

Thomas nodded. Concerned, he watched his neighbor go out the door.

23

THOMAS STOPPED TO VISIT WITH SARAH before heading for his home. He kissed her goodbye and walked toward the door, meeting the doctor on the way.

"Could I see you for a moment, Thomas?"

"Yup, be right back, Sarah."

"Sit down, please."

"No thanks, I've got to get back home. What is it, doctor?"

"Thomas! I'm not positive, but it appears to me as if Sarah may never walk again. Now—I could be wrong."

"Not walk again! What does that mean?"

"There appears to be a certain amount of spinal cord injury—to what extent, I do not know. Time will tell. However, next time you come into town, she can go home."

"Then it's not life threatening."

"No—it's not."

"Thank you, doctor."

Doctor Blake nodded and left the room.

"Sarah, I've gotta go now. Be back tomorra."

"Thomas, what did the doctor tell you?"

"That you're gonna be fine."

Sarah smiled. "Good evening, Thomas. I love you."

— —

THOMAS STOOD ON THE BOARDWALK. He saw Timothy McGearney across the street staggering to his horse in front of the saloon. Thomas watched with amusement as the Irishman failed to mount after three attempts. The fourth attempt was successful. The horse reared sharply after Timothy applied a sharp whip. Barely staying in the saddle, he regained position and galloped out of town.

Thomas thought about Collin and what he had learned from Timothy...brothers! So why didn't he look for a job at his brother's farm? he asked himself. There's somethin' goin' on between them two that I don't know about.

But then my neighbors are not my main problem—it's Sarah. He grasped his cheeks tightly with the fingers of his right hand. I can't imagine her not bouncing around the kitchen, he said to himself. She looks like a school girl running out to the barn to tell me dinner's ready. It can't be—her never walking again.

Thomas refused to believe what the doctor had told him. Why, Sarah looked happy. She was smiling. If the doctor told me the truth, surely Sarah would know. He sat down on a bench and watched Timothy and his horse fade into the distance.

Thomas mounted his horse, his thoughts confused, not looking forward to spending another lonely night in bed. He dismounted and stood by his horse, his legs feeling weak from lack of regular activity. Thomas lowered his head and led his horse across the street. He tied it to a post and entered the saloon.

"Back for another, Thomas?" bartender Brett asked.

Thomas didn't answer. He found himself staring at Collin McBride sitting at a table with Rosemary Pikes. "Ah'll have a whiskey," he said. "Leave the bottle."

He coughed lightly and felt the first drop of whiskey slide down into his stomach, burning sensitive walls on its way. Once his insides returned to normal, he took a larger gulp. Now I feel better, he said to himself.

Thomas refilled the glass, and downed another. Burping loudly, he grabbed the glass and bottle and staggered to the table where Collin and Rosemary sat.

"Mind if ah jin you two?" he asked.

"Aye, Thomas. Ah heard your missus is getting much better."

Thomas slammed the bottle down on the table. Rosemary flinched.

"My man, what's the problem?" Collin asked.

"It's Sarah." Thomas hiccupped. "The doc say she's never gonna walk again." Thomas slumped into a chair.

Rosemary reached up and wrapped her fingers around Thomas's wrist. "Oh, I'm so sorry. Sit down, please, Thomas." Thomas looked at her, his blue eyes moist. "Anything I can do?" Rosemary asked.

"There's nuthin' nobody can do. Unless yar good at shootin' Erlocks."

Thomas grasped his bottle and poured another glassful for himself. "Need 'nother, Collin?"

"Ah've had enough, lad. Time for me to go up."

"Never thought I'd see the day that I would out-drink an Irishman," Thomas said.

Collin laughed. He stood, yawned and left.

Thomas glanced at Rosemary.

"Thomas, come on up to my room. You can use the couch for tonight. 'Tis no way you're ridin' home in your condition."

Thomas reached for his glass. He bumped it, knocking it over, the glass smashing when it landed. The remaining whiskey on the table dripped over the edge and onto the floor.

Lady Constance approached. "Well, Mr. Hastings, I see you've had enough—but then, I know what's troublin' ya, and there is no blame. You go up with Rosemary and she'll get you into bed—you need a good night's sleep."

— —

THOMAS AWOKE AFTER FALLING OFF THE COUCH. He rubbed his eyes and placed a hand on his forehead. "Uhhh—where am I?"

"Mornin', Mr. Hastings. Collin and I brought you up here last night. You got drunk." Rosemary laughed.

Thomas groaned again. He put his other hand on his forehead. "That I did. Damn, ah hope Sarah doesn't find out."

Rosemary snickered. "Even if she did, she'd understand. There are times in life when a man deserves to get drunk—this was one of them. Here, drink this coffee."

Thomas sat and sipped on coffee for a few minutes. "Rosemary, ah thank you and Collin. It's time I head on home."

Rosemary nodded. Thomas slipped his boots on and wavered on his way to the door.

"The fresh air outside will right you. Say, Thomas, your horse is over at the corral. Brett had one of his boys take it over there last night."

Thomas stepped lightly going down the stairway. He didn't look at the clerk, Robert Packard, as he hastened across the lobby to the door. Outside, he meekly and quickly walked up the boardwalk, angling across the street toward Toby's Corral.

He pulled the brim of his hat down low over his eyes as he trotted his horse westward. After reaching MacTurley's Woods, he set his stallion to a gallop.

24

TIMOTHY MCGEARNEY CLEANED THE LAST OF THE EGG from his plate. "Madie, you're the greatest cook in the world."

Madeline's greenish-hazel eyes glowed. She reached across the table and accepted her husband's hand, her tight-lipped smile creating a small dimple in her narrow chin. "I love to make my husband happy," she said softly.

He sat at the table watching his wife clean up the breakfast dishes.

Ah'm a lucky lad, he said to himself, watching Madeline stretch to place a plate into the cupboard.

Timothy thought again about his brother at the Frontier Saloon, his mind clouding. Am ah going mad? Did I really see my brother, or was it someone who looks like him? he asked himself.

Shaking his head to clear his mind and his doubts, he knew his brother had arrived in Tarrytown—but why? His breakfast began to do battle in his stomach. Timothy retched and placed a hand over his mouth to contain it.

Madeline turned to look at him, no longer smiling. "Tim, what concerns you? You look like you've seen a ghost."

"Ah have seen one, ah think. Yesterday at the Frontier Saloon in Tarrytown, ah saw a man. Ah know it's completely daft, but he looked so much like my brother, Conor."

Madeline spread her lips slightly. "Did you talk to him?"

"No, ah didn't. Ah was talkin' to Thomas Hastings at the time and suddenly ah felt my chest tighten. Ah needed time to think—ah could hardly breath. If it was Conor, what would he be doing here? Was he looking for me?"

"Why would he do that—come here all the way from Ireland and look for you?"

"There's been a famine in his part of Ireland the past five years. It wouldn't shock me one bit if he had lost his land. Ah haven't seen or heard from Conor since I left—hmm, some five-six years ago."

"If he is your brother, why don't you invite him over to our home?"

Timothy stood and replaced his chair. He walked over to his wife and put an arm around her shoulder. "Madie, there's something you need to know."

Madeline's forehead creased, her mouth opened partially and she held her breath.

"Conor murdered my brother, Patrick! Ah saw it!—that evening in the glen. True, it was misty and foggy, but the profile of the murderer was—"

Timothy's feelings warmed watching the concern cloud Madeline's face. She turned toward the sink. He gave her a hug from behind. Then he walked into the next room and stretched out on an easy chair.

— —

TIMOTHY FOUND IT IMPOSSIBLE TO CONCENTRATE ON HIS SHEEP as he rode southward in his fields. He realized that during the previous evening in the saloon he had had too much whiskey. Why would Conor follow me to Missouri if he did indeed murder Patrick in the glen? he asked himself. Maybe ah was imagining things, he thought. It could have been someone else out in the glen who looked like Conor.

The dilapidated slave buildings caught his eye. He got a chill at the thought of people actually living in those shacks. The cattle around those parts lived better then that, he thought.

Timothy set his horse into a gallop, then slowed to a walk at Bear Creek. My problem with the outlaw Erlocks is nothing compared to my brother showing up, he thought. Ah love this land.

Timothy stopped his horse next to an olive tree and dismounted. He led it to the south side of the creek and looked at the place where he had seen the innards of one of the sheep. Nature had swept everything clean with not even a bone remaining. He thought about his older brother Patrick. Ah never liked him, he thought—gone just like the remains of the sheep.

Timothy gazed up at the slope that blended into Bear Mountain. He watched waves of grass bend from the wisps of wind sweeping intermittently across the plain.

Timothy felt guilty as he angrily remounted, spurred his horse and demanded that it gallop wildly into the grassy uplands. The wrenching sounds coming from his steed's mouth signaled him to pull on the reins. He heard his horse's nostrils flutter and snort as it attempted to inhale more air. The mountain begins here, he said to himself, looking back toward his building.

As he had done so many times since leaving Ireland, Timothy appreciatively looked across the valley and recognized the beauty of his new land. He thought about Madeline and a future of love and happiness. He thought about his father and brothers—only Conor remained. Is he here to make my life better, he thought, or take it away?

Timothy dismounted, leaving his horse to graze, and sat down at the base of an oak tree. He could see the church spire in Tarrytown sticking up over the trees of MacTurley's Woods. Thomas Hastings's Hereford cattle looked like the small, brown polka dots on one of Madeline's aprons.

— —

TIMOTHY'S HEAD DROOPED AND HE FELL ASLEEP, dreaming of his youthful days in Ireland. He found himself running after his brothers. They disappeared into a fog. He ran and ran. Suddenly, he awoke to the loud cry of a cat.

He awoke and looked into the green eyes of a large cougar standing in the tall grass a short distance away. Instinctively, he remained perfectly still. The large cat looked away toward his horse that had recognized the threat. The steed pawed the ground with one of its hooves. It neighed three times.

Slowly, Timothy reached down to his holster. He pulled out his revolver. The cat looked back at him, screeched and reversed its direction, running up the hill and disappearing into the woods. Timothy stood, his hands shaking. He remembered McGregor warning him of the danger of cougars that often came down from Bear Mountain.

Timothy felt the uneasiness of his horse after remounting and riding toward his western border. Horses don't talk, but they sure know what's going on, he said to himself. Timothy re-crossed the creek, gazing at the endless line of barbed wire separating his sheep from McGregor's cattle. It's like a line drawn between two worlds, he thought.

Timothy relied on his dogs and didn't need fences. Nature had claimed most of the pre-Civil War split-rails, overgrown with grasses and shrubs.

He arrived home and dismounted next to the barn. After removing the saddle, he led his horse into the corral and let it loose. He heard

Madeline's voice and turned. "Who do you suppose killed them sheep and Lassie?"

"The Erlocks for certain," Timothy said. "But we have a new threat out there."

"What's that, Timothy?"

"Ah saw a large cougar. It looked meaner than the devil. Ah need to pay Thomas and the McGregors a visit—tell them about the big cat."

— —

MITCH MCGREGOR WATCHED TULLY breaking in a young stallion. His smile disappeared and he slapped himself lightly in the face when the young rider got thrown and landed roughly on the ground. Greb, another of his hands, rushed to the fallen rider's side. "He's fine, boss."

Mitch nodded and glanced at a horse and rider trotting over from the McGearney's. Greb mounted the next yearling. "Hang on—hang on," Mitch whispered.

Grabbing the brim of his hat and thrusting it into the air, he celebrated as Greb trotted the yearling around the corral. The huge grin on his hand's face brought a wide smile to Mitch's face. His large blue eyes narrowed watching the rider approach. Heck, it's my neighbor, Timothy, Mitch said to himself.

Timothy remained in the saddle after halting his horse. "Ah thought we might have a chat, McGregor. Someone killed ten of my sheep and one of my dogs. Have ya seen anyone about, near the creek?"

Mitch grimaced. "Naw, but ah wouldn't put it past those Erlocks."

Timothy nodded and remained in the saddle. He narrowed his soft brown eyes. "Ah saw one of those large cats up near the tree line this mornin'."

Mitch tightened his lips. "It's probably likin' the looks of your sheep. The big cougars don't seem to bother my cattle any—but ah best keep the young stock close to the barn."

"When ye hear massive barks from my Collies, ye might know

that a big cat is near. They've learned to gang up on the threatening intruders. So far ah haven't lost a single woolie to the cat."

Mitch nodded and smiled. "Good."

Timothy turned his head eastward and said. "Ah gotta get home, Mitch, top of the day to ye."

He jammed a spur into his horse's side. The steed neighed loudly and jerked forward. Mitch watched as his neighbor galloped off.

25

J.P. WEATHERBY'S EXPANSIVE REAR-END FELT EVERY BUMP in the road as he eased the reins on his horse, pulling a one-seat buggy. Man all-mighty, he thought, I've been gone from my hotel room for three days and three nights.

His primary mission representing the Pinkerton Detective Agency was to organize a posse to find and capture the James-Younger gang. He succeeded in getting a group of twenty two men together, but they had no luck in finding the gang, There was talk that they had fled north to Minnesota.

Weatherby's eyes fell on the line of bushes and trees that populated the bottoms of Bear Creek. He knew his horse needed food and water. I need the same, he said to himself, plus a warm bed. Within the hour, I'll deliver the buggy and nag back to Toby at the corral.

As the buggy wheels rumbled across the planks of the creek bridge, he noticed the Hastings's buildings. He frowned because the head of that farm was a friend of outlaw Bob Younger. I should've had a talk with that young man, he said to himself. Not too late.

Weatherby glanced at the wide stretch of trees that extended down from the foot hills of the mountain. He marveled at the change in color—green near the road and a dark blue higher up. It seemed to him that most of the conversations he had heard at the Frontier Saloon included MacTurley's Woods.

The massive number of trees in the woods appeared to be moving in his direction as he got closer and closer. Weatherby smiled with pleasure as he smelled the fragrant leaves.

His conveyance approached the stretch of road shaded by tall trees. Weatherby saw three horsemen mingling in a clearing next to a copse of poplars. One of them moved his horse to the side of the road and put up his hand.

"Whoa! Whoa there," Weatherby said, not really wanting to stop. He looked up and down the road, seeing no one else. Since there're three of 'em, I better see what they want.

"Nice buggy ya have there," the white-faced stranger drawled.

The detective smiled in spite of feeling danger as he looked at the pink eyes. "J.P. Weatherby at your service. What can I do for you gents?"

The man with the twisted smile said, "Ya can get off that seat and began walking. I want that buggy."

"He-YAH" Weatherby yelled and laid the whip. The horse responded and broke into a gallop. His escape didn't last long as the other two horsemen angled ahead of him, and one of them grabbed the halter, bringing the buggy to a stop.

"Now, you men best be getting along. Someone is gonna see what yar doin'. The marshal will go after ya," the detective said calmly.

The man with a pale face and pink eyes laughed loudly. His partners did the same.

"No! ya can't—"

During his lengthy career, Weatherby had experienced crises situations. His survival depended on his tactful handling of belligerent people. He thought about the time in Chicago when he felt the cold barrel of a gun pushed into his neck. He said his Hail Mary's, and then prepared to die.

I've had miracles in the past. Lord, I need one right now, he said to himself, feeling the coarseness of the hemp on his wrists. His feet and hands were bound, and a rag, partially pushed into his mouth, had been tied around his head.

He felt every single jostle of the wheels as they rolled along. It's not the first time that I've been bound and gagged, he said to himself.

My capturers have always made a fatal mistake. They assume that I am inadequate because of my overweight appearance. He groped the area behind the seat for a sharp edge.

The scent of sour whiskey guaranteed him that his captors would be of lesser mental capacity. Being fat is an attribute, he thought to himself, smiling in spite of his life threatening situation. It's like insulation in more ways then one.

When the carriage finally came to a stop, there wasn't a bone or muscle in his body that wasn't sore. The sudden tranquility relaxed his mind, allowing thoughts of fantasy. He imagined falling from the arms of his mother into a bottomless pit but then being rescued by a prince on a white horse.

Suddenly, his mind cleared. Daylight had ended. The whiskey that the Erlocks had consumed added to the potential for an escape. He had successfully removed his bindings, and his mind became totally alert. He smiled thinking about his captors. They're a bunch of drunkin' fools. He got up on his knees and remained still, attempting to see or hear his surroundings.

Weatherby slid off the back compartment of the buggy. He saw that the driver had fallen to the ground, his gun still in the holster. Weatherby moved quickly and plucked out the weapon.

A flash of light exploded in his brain. The instant pain from a sharp blow to the back of his head disappeared after he drifted into unconsciousness.

— —

BERTRAN LASSITOR HAD BEEN WATCHING WITH HIS BROTHER BILLY from the top of a hill as the buggy approached, dragged up an extraordinarily rough trail. He saw the pinkish face of Bone Erlock seated, thrashing the horse with a whip over and over again.

As the buggy got closer and closer, he knew that the three brothers had gotten themselves into a drunken state. He saw Grit raise a whiskey bottle to his mouth, some of the liquid running down his chin.

Bertran rubbed the curled, brown whiskers on his face. He had cold penetrating gray eyes and a rugged scar above his left eyebrow, distorting an otherwise pleasant look.

The buggy stopped not far from the Erlock's house. Bone staggered off the seat and fell to the ground. He saw the big man slide off the back end of the buggy and rush over to Bone, grabbing the gun out of its holster.

Bertran pulled out his gun. He walked over quickly and quietly behind the detective and hit him over the head.

— —

"YA CAN'T STAY HERE ANY MORE, BONE," Bertran insisted. "That's a detective you brought with you. If I hadn't been standing over there, you and your brothers would have been nothing but jail trash."

Bone held up a wad of green bills. "Look what ah got."

"We gotta get the woman and kids out of here—and right now," Bertran said.

26

THOMAS HAD RECOVERED FROM HIS HANGOVER. He felt bad but knew that he didn't hurt anyone but himself. He felt even worse realizing that he didn't visit Sarah yesterday. He spent most of the day lying on the divan in the house. Maybe the spirits had me do it, he thought. My system needed a break.

He strapped on his holster and spun the cylinder of his Colt revolver to make sure all slots were filled with bullets. Thomas walked outside and saw Poncho Ortiz standing, holding the reins to his horse. "Mornin', Poncho. How's the family?"

"They are fine, Senor Thomas. Please greet your wife from myself and me wife."

Thomas nodded. He grabbed the reins and mounted. "I'll try not to get drunk on this trip."

Poncho doubled up with laughter. "Si, senor." He laughed some more, slapping himself on the hip, and walked toward the barn.

Thomas turned his stallion onto the Tarrytown Road and headed toward MacTurley's Woods. A buildup of smoke near the top of Bear Mountain caught his attention. That's about where the Erlock's den is, he thought. Maybe I'll get lucky and it burned down. Then he scolded himself—there are women and children living up there.

An object lying in the tall grass next to the road caught his eye. Then he heard the sound of wheels and saw a one-horse carriage headed toward him. Thomas stopped his horse and anxiously watched. As it got closer, he realized a lone woman handled the reins. Rosemary Pikes stopped her carriage.

"Hello, Miss Pikes. Not so sure it's safe to be out here all alone."

"Somethin' I've got to do, Mister Hastings. I'll be all right. Don't worry about me."

Thomas rubbed his chin with his fingers and watched as Rosemary jostled the reins and the carriage moved forward. He dismounted and watched until the carriage could no longer be seen. Then he led his horse toward the tall grass next to the road. Stooping down, he picked up a gray bowler hat with a wide black band above the brim. Ah wonder who this belongs to, he asked himself.

Thomas stared at the wheel tracks in the tall grass. Jaysus, they're headin' up. It's a tough pull up that slope. He walked along his fence line for a short distance, admiring the barbed wire. Thomas saw that the wheel track markings in the grass continued.

The smoke appears to be lessening, he thought. Thomas returned to his horse and fastened the hat to a rope behind the saddle. He remounted and guided his horse back onto the road, setting it into a fast trot along the stand of trees.

Each time Thomas passed the place where he and Sarah had been attacked, he felt more bitterness and anger toward the Erlocks. Thomas set his gray to a gallop and kept the reins loose until he saw the school house and cemetery, just past the corner of the woods.

He saw children playing outside, and slowed his horse to a walk, looking for Tyler Hastings, his nephew. At age eight, the lad had stretched in height recently and stood close to a head higher than some of the other boys.

Thomas moved his horse closer to the group and noticed that Miss Barnard wore a blue bonnet and matching shawl. He waved and said, "Mornin' to ya, Miss Barnard."

She spoke and waved back.

Thomas yelled, "Hey, Tyler! Ya study hard now—hear me?" He didn't wait for a response and rode off.

Thomas pulled up in front of the marshal's office minutes later and went inside.

Ben Buford fingered the hat, running them around the brim. He turned it upside down, estimating the size. "Big size, 'tis," he drawled.

"Hey, Lance, look at this, would ya?" the marshal said.

Lance had been sweeping the inside of one of the jails. He strode over and stared at the hat. "So, what's with the bowler top?"

"Thomas found this by the road at the northwest corner of MacTurley's Woods."

"Hey—they—that looks like the detective's," Lance muttered.

The marshal tightened his chin and looked down into his deputy's eyes. "That ain't all. Thomas saw smoke up in the mountain—somewhere near the Erlock's shack, he thought."

"Them Erlocks may be goin' up in smoke," Lance said.

The marshal scratched his chin. "Thanks, Thomas. Well, Lance, maybe we best ride up there and have a look."

Buford walked out onto the sidewalk with Thomas. "Best regards to Sarah."

"Thanks, Ben—good luck with the Erlocks," Thomas said softly.

"When the day comes—and the Erlocks are in jail, ah'll be cheering just about as much as you." The marshal sighed. "Yup." He put a hand on the door. "Thomas, ah want you to be careful ridin' up and down the Tarrytown Road. When yar wife is ready to go home, let me know. Ah'll send a rider with ya."

Thomas nodded and untied his horse's reins. He walked it toward the doctor's office.

— —

THOMAS CARRIED A VASE OF FLOWERS in a hand held behind his back. The door to Sarah's room was open and he peeked in.

"Thomas, you've come. I was worried about you. You missed yesterday."

He walked over to the bed, kissing his wife on the lips, and swept his arm out front, displaying the flowers.

"Oh, Thomas, you shouldn't have."

She grabbed the vase with both hands and looked up at her husband, smiling wide. Her smile vanished. "Does that mean you did something wrong?"

Thomas laughed. "Ah might as well tell you right now, otherwise you'll hear about it sooner or later."

Sarah frowned. "What is it?"

"Ah—"

Thomas plopped his forefinger into his stomach. "Ah had too much whiskey two nights ago and didn't make it home."

"Didn't make it home? What do you mean?"

"Ah stayed at the hotel—by myself of course."

"You naughty boy." Sarah smiled. "When my pappa did that, mamma wouldn't talk to him for days."

Thomas chuckled. His forehead creased slightly. "Sarah, ah talked to the doctor and ah'll be taking you home soon."

Her face beamed with happiness, then she frowned. "But what if I can't walk, Thomas? What then?"

He forced a smile. "You're alive, Sarah—that's what really matters."

— —

ROSEMARY CROSSED THE BEAR CREEK BRIDGE. She shuddered and shook her head at herself. This is crazy, she thought. Meeting an outlaw in the lawless countryside. You don't know who you'll run into. What if the Erlocks are about? But she thought of his strong hands on her shoulders and warmth of his kisses. She sat up straighter in the seat and urged the horse forward.

She hardly noticed the herd of black cattle, most of the cows staring at her, as she passed by the Haggard farm. If all I see is cattle along this road, I'll feel good, she said to herself. Meeting up with the Erlocks would be the worst thing to happen to me. Rain would be next. Rosemary smiled looking up at the sky and seeing generous patches of blue amongst streaks of gray-blue clouds.

At last she saw the cluster of trees just beyond the McGregor fence. Rosemary had met Bob at that site before. It became their secret spot. She slowed her horse and brought it to a stop. Looking up and down the road, she felt relieved that no one was about. Then she pulled the left rein to leave the road and head toward a narrow opening in the copse of aspen. Her wheel track from the previous visit had almost vanished.

"Whoa," she said softly. The horse stopped and she stepped out of the carriage. Rosemary wore a polonaise walking suit of blue-colored lightweight wool and silk pleat-trimmed skirt. She tied the reins to a tree and padded her clothes with her hands. Rosemary used her mouth to blow the dust off her bonnet that was trimmed with artificial silk violets.

She hummed a tune spreading the blanket on the grass next to two tall trees. Then she returned to the carriage and brought back a basket. Rosemary gently lowered herself to the ground, making sure her skirt wouldn't wrinkle. She felt elated, expecting Mister Younger to show up soon. Then she saw it.

The piece of paper was nailed to a tree just beyond where she sat. Carefully she got to her feet and strode forward. Rosemary grasped the paper and pulled it away.

Dearest Rosemary,

I regret to inform you that I will be unable to meet you as we planned. My older brother and Frank James insisted that I come along with them to Minnesota.

We will be gone for about three weeks. I will inform you as soon as I return. Until then, please be patient. I miss you very much. Your

true and loving friend,
Bob Younger.

Her heart felt like it had fallen into her stomach—the disappointment, so deep. She neatly folded the paper and returned to her blanket. She placed it into the basket.

Quickly, she rolled up the blanket and returned to the carriage. Minutes later, she was back on the Tarrytown Road. Rosemary looked straight ahead as she pushed her horse, almost to the limit. Directly in front of her, she saw a horseman approaching. She felt relieved to see Thomas Hastings again. Rosemary pulled on the reins, stopping her horse, wet with sweat.

"Well, Miss Pikes, glad to see you're safely on your way back to town."

She stared at him, saying nothing.

"Something wrong?"

"Yes, but I don't want to talk about it," she said and flicked the reins.

Thomas followed her until she came abreast of the church, then he turned his horse and headed for home.

27

MASON JOHN HAD BEEN STACKING BOXES in the rear storage room of Mercantile Goods & Services when the marshal entered the store through the street door. He walked to the counter and nodded. "Seth, ah'm looking for that nephew of yars."

"Has he done somethin' wrong, Marshal?" the owner asked, chuckling under his breath.

"Naw, but I would like to borrow him for awhile. Ah hear he's plenty handy with a gun."

"Yup, sure is. He goes out in the woods almost every day and shoots targets. He's gettin' mighty quick on the draw, too."

The marshal scratched his chin. "He'll get paid. Ah need him this afternoon, say about 1:00."

Seth pointed. "He's back there in the storage room. You ask him yarself."

Mason John's heart pounded with excitement overhearing his uncle talk to the marshal. He threw the last of the boxes up on the stack and headed for the door. "You lookin' for me, Marshal?" he said.

"Yup." The marshal nodded. "How would ya like to join me and Mantraux this afternoon for a ride up the mountain?"

Mason John felt so excited that he could hardly muster a word. "S—su—sure, Marshal."

"You'll have to agree to be sworn in as a deputy and wear a badge."

Mason John's soft brown eyes widened. "Yes, sir. When do ya wanna go?"

"Right after eats. See you at my office about 1:00. Have your horse saddled and ready to ride."

— —

PIERRE MANTRAUX SAT AT A REAR, CORNER TABLE of the Frontier Saloon. He glanced at the door after hearing it open and saw the marshal approaching. He continued his solitaire card game, knowing by the expression on the lawman's face that he came in to talk to him.

Pierre kept flipping cards until he heard the boot steps cease. Pierre then looked up, keeping both hands on the table.

"Mantraux, ah need yar help. The Pinkerton man has disappeared. Ah strongly suspect that the Erlocks and Lassitors had somethin' to do with it. Ah'd like to hire ya and take you and young Miller along on a ride up to the Erlock shacks. Thomas Hastings had seen smoke up there earlier this morning."

Pierre looked up at the marshal, his narrow black eyes shaded by the brim of his hat, a long narrow cigar protruding from his lips. "What do ya expect to find up there?"

"I'm afraid that they've done somethin' to Weatherby. His hat was found by the road, and he and his buggy are missing. Thomas claims to have seen wagon tracks along his fence leading up toward the mountain."

Pierre said, "Ah could use a good ride. You can count me in, Marshal. When are ya goin'?"

"Right after ah have some vittles."

"I'll do the same and meet you at your office."

— — -

SHORTLY AFTER 1:00 P.M., MARSHAL BUFORD flanked by his two newly appointed deputies, rode out of town. They turned onto a cleared area next to the Hastings property and headed for Bear Mountain.

Mason John rode third in the column as they began the climb. High above the marshal's hat, he saw sporadic wisps of smoke. He saw the Hastings's buildings in the distance to the west. Mason John looked upon the man dressed in black riding ahead of him as a hero. He had saved Thomas and Sarah Hastings from certain disaster. Just about everyone that came into the store for days after talked about the incident.

They had ridden for close to an hour when the marshal signaled a halt. Just ahead lay a shallow draw with narrow stream of water visible in the bottom. Mason John's eyes followed its course downward. He assumed it drained into Bear Creek after crossing the Hastings's property line.

The marshal led them across the creek and stayed close to the wall of trees making up part of MacTurley's Woods. Mason John smelled the smoke. He knew they were getting close.

He saw widgets of boards that made up the outside walls of a building. A window appeared. The marshal led them past a copse of trees and then he saw the house with its mossy roof and grass growing up the sides of an unpainted rough-surfaced outside wall. That's one of the most unkempt houses that I've ever seen, he thought.

Farther down, he saw the charred remains of a smaller building.

The marshal dismounted and drew his revolver before entering the house. Pierre dismounted also and drew his gun. I'd better do the same, Mason John thought.

The marshal came out moments later. "No one about boys—looks like they flew the coop again. Let's have a look around."

They all walked to the burnt-down building site. "Smells like burnt chicken," Pierre said.

Mason John walked into a small clearing beyond the building. "Marshal, there's a grave over here."

Ben and Pierre hurried to Mason John who pointed at a hump in the soil. "Looks like it's been dug some time ago. It couldn't be the detective," the marshal said.

Pierre reached down and probed the hump in the ground with his gloved fingers. "Yeah, Marshal, yar right."

The marshal pointed eastward. "To the horses, boys—gotta follow those wagon tracks."

They mounted and slowly worked their way along a trail that followed a ledge in the mountain. The leaves of copses of quaking aspen fluttered in the breeze. "Two wagons," Pierre said.

"Yup, Weatherby's buggy and one of their own wagons—from whoever they stole it," the marshal drawled.

They came to a drop-off where the trail narrowed for a stretch, bringing the wheel tracks dangerously close to the edge. The tower of the church in Tarrytown became visible.

Mason John anxiously glanced behind him, worried that the Erlocks would ambush them. He had heard many people at the mercantile talking about they had attacked the Hastings and severely injured the woman. He noticed that Mantraux kept the flap of his jacket open, exposing the handle of his gun.

The marshal signaled a stop. "Boys, this is where the trail forks, the left one, ending up down by the cemetery in Tarrytown."

He nudged his horse and continued on the eastern trail that led upward toward the summit. The trees became sparser and shorter in height as Mason John followed behind Mantraux's horse, feeling excited, but not without apprehension.

When they came to a ridge, Mason John saw the marshal raise

his hand and look back. He smiled and said, "Steady up here, boys, ah want you to see somethin'."

Mason edged his horse forward, coming abreast of Buford and Mantraux. He saw a bulky, red figure stumbling down a slope. "Ben, what the hell is that?" he asked.

The marshal didn't answer right away. Then he turned. "Boys, ah think that we've found Weatherby."

28

THOMAS MOUNTED HIS HORSE, ready for a tour of his Herefords. He rode to his western border and southward along the fence line, then halted his steed to watch a flock of McGearney sheep grazing beyond his barbed wire fence. Two dogs squatted on their hind legs and watched him. He waved at the collies and headed northward toward the creek. After crossing it, he angled toward the Tarrytown Road.

He pulled on his reins seeing a lone rider coming up his roadway. That looks like that lanky Marshal Buford, he thought. Nudging his horse, he galloped toward his house. Dismounting, he tied up his horse and waited for the rider to arrive.

The marshal trotted his horse toward Thomas and dismounted. "Howdy, Thomas. Mind if we talk a bit?"

"Not a bit, Ben. Let's go sit on the porch."

Ben Buford followed Thomas. They sat down.

"Thomas, did ya see the smoke a couple of days ago?"

"Ah sure as heck did. It was quite the plume. Ah sure hope it didn't burn any trees."

"It didn't. Gotta couple of the boys together and rode up there that afternoon. 'Cept for a few patches of brush, the fire contained itself."

"Was it the Erlock's buildings?"

The marshal nodded. He looked into Thomas's eyes. "One of the shacks is gone, the main house still stands, though—if ya can call it one?" He shook his head. "The Erlock boys weren't home."

"Jaysus, ah'm not surprised. They're a slippery lot."

The marshal smiled. "We found Weatherby wanderin' down a trail aimlessly in his underwear."

"In his underwear?"

"Yup, red at that, too."

"It must have been a funny scene, Marshal."

The marshal laughed. "That 'twas."

Thomas had mixed feelings. He felt gladdened that the Erlocks had left, even though the main house remained standing. That meant the family had moved away, the women and children. "Weatherby is a lucky man. They could've killed 'im if they wanted to."

"Yup, ah agree, but apparently they wanted the buggy and the horse more than anything—his money, too."

Thomas didn't respond. He looked off into the distance.

The marshal laughed. "This shouldn't be funny."

He swept his fingers across his mouth. "When ah said underwear, that's all the man had left. He looked like a humpty dumpty coming down that trail—and they got his gold pocket watch, too."

Thomas chuckled. "Maybe we've seen the last of the Pinkertons."

"Don't know, but ah've never seen anyone so damn mad before. The man was out of his wits. Ah wonder if ah shouldn't have thrown him in the clinker for a few days 'til he cooled off. He's liable to go back up that mountain after the Erlocks and Lassitors."

"Lassitors! Were they involved?" Thomas asked.

"Yup, it was actually Bertran Lassitor who knocked out Weatherby; otherwise he would've gotten the draw on the three Erlocks. They all got drunk—the detective would've had the drop on 'em."

Thomas snickered. "Ah shouldn't be laughing, Marshal Buford, but it's the funniest thing that's ever happened around here."

The marshal stood. "Thanks for the coffee, Thomas. Ah gotta ride along. Ah don't want you to go get yar wife without an escort. Do ya understand me?"

"Yup, ah do."

"Pierre Mantraux is gonna be around for a few days. Ah think he would hep you out."

"Where do ya suppose the Erlocks have gone?"

"Ah heard the brother-in-law—Bertran is his name—gotta place in the mountain farther to the east. I would wager they all moved over there."

"Do ya know where 'tis, marshal?"

"Naw, ah don't. Ah reckon we'll just have to watch out for them renegades. If they do show their faces, ah'll throw 'em in jail. We'll get a judge out here, and that'll be the last of the Erlocks and Lassitors."

The marshal stood by his horse. He turned and looked at Thomas. "Say, young man, ya didn't start that fire at the Erlocks by any chance?"

Thomas forced a grin. "Naw, I didn't, Marshal. Ah didn't."

"All right, ah believe ya."

"Ah sure hope so." Thomas stood and watched the marshal mount his horse and ride off. His thoughts drifted to his wife. Ah wonder how it will feel to bring Sarah home if she can't walk, he thought, hating the Erlocks even more.

29

THOMAS TURNED THE BUGGY ONTO THE TARRYTOWN ROAD. He felt extraordinarily excited after hearing from the doctor that Sarah was well enough to go home. The leaves of the patches of sumac along MacTurley's Woods had turned red. Ever since the marshal's visit, he didn't fear the Erlocks as much. They've likely left the country, he thought.

As his buggy rolled into town, he moved to the side of the road to make room for the stagecoach. It had just left the station and the team of six pulled it toward him. He waved at Lafe and Morgan, excited as he watched the spectacular red-painted, four-wheeled conveyance.

Thomas stopped his horse and stared at the departing coach, watching it diminish in size until disappearing from view.

He guided his horse back onto the road and continued toward town. A group of men stood and mingled on the boardwalk in front of the marshal's office. Ah wonder what's goin' on, he thought. Out of curiosity, he moved past the doctor's office and stopped the horses by the men. He saw Mitch McGregor talking to Abel Kingsley.

"What's happened, boys?"

"The marshal got word by telegraph that the James-Younger gang has left the state."

"Northfield, Minnesota," Thomas muttered. "Ah remember Bob telling me they were headin' that way back in August."

"That so, Thomas?" Mitch drawled.

Abel licked his upper lip. "Why would they be goin' there? That's a long way from home."

"'Tis, for certain," Thomas replied. He saw a stranger walking from the Smithy toward the bank.

"Who's that big guy with the huge boots and small bowler hat?" Thomas asked. He smiled watching the man's hat blow off his head. The stranger isn't accustomed to our wind, Thomas said to himself.

"He come on the same stage as Weatherby and Mantraux did," Abel said, rushing out onto the street and recovering the hat, reaching out to hand it to the man.

Abel returned and said, "He came from Sweden. Gotta job with Charley—doesn't know any English—well almost none. 'e does say 'Yah.'"

— —

SARAH HEARD THE WHEELS OF A CARRIAGE outside in front of the doctor's office. She knew Thomas had arrived. Sarah's immediate excitement lasted for only moments. What is he going to say when he sees that I cannot walk at all? Not even one step. The past week, I worked hard...always believing that my legs were going to respond—they did not.

She heard the sound of boots clattering on the boardwalk. The front door opened. She anxiously waited—then counted four soft footsteps approaching the door. Thomas stood in the doorway of her room.

"Sarah, you're dressed like a queen."

"Oh, Thomas, I'm so anxious to get home."

He walked to her chair, leaned over and held her by the shoulders. "Come on up to me, Sarah. Ah'll hep ya."

Sarah eyes filled with tears. "Thomas, I've worked so hard—but, I can't even stand."

She looked up into his blue eyes and saw what she had feared—pity. As if on cue, the doctor's wife came into the room. "Can I help you get Sarah into the buggy, Thomas?"

He looked at the woman and nodded his approval. "Would ya hold the door open, please? Thank you."

Thomas got his arms around Sarah and lifted her tight to his chest. "Sarah, yar goin' home."

— —

THOMAS GUIDED THE TEAM ONTO THE MIDDLE of the Tarrytown road. He glanced behind him and saw Pierre Mantraux following. That's the work of the marshal, he thought, feeling more secure than ever.

His spirits lifted looking at his wife. Thomas absorbed the joy radiating from her eyes. Her legs may be gone, but her heart sure isn't, Thomas said to himself. As they passed by the place in the road where they had been attacked by the Erlocks, he stiffened.

His thoughts flashed back to 1861 and the brutal killing of their neighbors, Mr. and Mrs. Sunnerland, also victims of the Erlocks. He had ridden to the site with his father, sitting behind the saddle. Ah'll never forget the sad look on Lafe Sunnerland face, holding his mother's head in his lap. Thomas shook his head slowly in sadness.

Pierre Mantraux trotted his horse a short distance behind as Thomas watched the clearings at the edge of the woods. He felt a special warmth toward the man who had saved his and Sarah's lives. He slowed the horses as they approached the roadway to his home. He looked back and returned Mantraux's wave as the rider turned his horse around and rode back toward town.

He halted his team next to the house and saw Luke rushing over from the barn. Thomas got off the carriage and walked around to the other side.

Luke lifted his tall-crowned black hat off his head. "Sarah! So good to see ya home. Need any hep, Thomas?"

"Yup, Luke—would ya put the team away?"

"Sure thing, boss."

Thomas glanced at the house. He saw Annabelle, their housekeeper, in the window. His eyes watered observing the glow of happiness on her round face. She disappeared and he knew she would be at the door in moments. Thomas quickly stepped to the other side of the carriage. "There ya go, Sarah."

Thomas planted his boots on the ground and cradled his wife. He staggered slightly, but regained his footing. Sarah put her arms around his neck and kissed him on the neck. Thomas carried her to the house.

"Miss Sarah—you're home at last," Annabelle said, holding the door wide open. "Ah've got the big chair ready for ya, sweetie."

Annabelle fussed with a set of pillows and Thomas set Sarah down in the chair. His wife looked around the room, her eyes dancing with billowing happiness. Thomas felt uneasy, uncertain of what his role was to be. Thank God, ah've got Annabelle, he said to himself.

"Sarah, I'm going out to the corral to see to the horses. I'll be back in before supper."

"You go right ahead, husband. I just wish to sit here and look around. It's so good to be home."

Thomas returned from the corral and stood inside the door. His heart melted watching Sarah's smile. Thomas walked to his wife, stooped down and kissed her on the lips.

Annabelle had set the table for dinner and Thomas carefully pushed Sarah's chair toward it. Ah wish this thing had wheels, he said to himself.

— — -

THOMAS MOUNTED HIS HORSE KING and waved at Sarah. Annabelle had placed her on a chair in front of the window. He felt goose bumps forming watching her lily-white fingers touch the inside of the window glass. Grasping the brim of his hat with two fingers, he pulled on it lightly and bowed. Then he galloped his horse toward the Tarrytown Road.

Thomas slowed his horse to a walk and turned onto the road. Abreast of Abel Kingsley's barn, he glanced up at the rough trail leading up to Bear Mountain. Ah hope that we're rid of the Erlocks for good, he thought. Ah won't miss 'em, that's for sure. MacTurley's Woods loomed ahead.

He rarely passed by the school without thinking about his former friend, Carr Walker. Thomas still had a mental image of Carr's long blond hair flaring in the wind as they ran from school toward town. One of the major shocks in his life came when his friend died in the schoolhouse—shot between the eyes as a result of a skirmish between the Gray Riders and Union Cavalry.

Anxiety built in his stomach watching two horsemen riding toward the mountain between the cemetery and the woods. They turned eastward after reaching the trees. "Damn—could it be them Erlocks again?" he muttered. The riders disappeared beyond a stand of birch trees, not far from some of the residences of Tarrytown on the slope of the mountain.

Ah'd better let some of the boys know, he said to himself. Thomas trotted his horse into Tarrytown and directed it to the mercantile store. He dismounted and headed across the street toward the marshal's office. The marshal's horse nibbled at blades of grass growing next to the boardwalk.

Thomas entered the room. The marshal sat at his desk. He looked up. "Howdy, Thomas. What kin ah do for ya?"

"Ben! Ah'd like to thank ya for sending Mantruax my way when ah drove Sarah home."

The marshal nodded. “Ah told you before that yar not to be alone when Sarah’s ’long.”

Thomas nodded and smiled. “Ah think I just saw two of the Erlocks. They were ridin’ along the tree line eastward toward the houses.”

“Sure ’twas them, Thomas?”

“No, ah’m not. Could ’ave been someone else, suppose.”

“Ah’ll get Lance and Pierre to take a ride over there. How’s Sarah doin’?”

Thomas shook his head. “Well, marshal, she’s in fine spirits, but there’s a tough road ahead.”

The marshal nodded.

Thomas clenched his fists. “Ah’m goin’ over to see Seth. Sarah needs some wheels under that chair of ’ers.”

“Wheelchairs. Ah’ve heard of such a contraption. If anyone can find one for ya, it would be Seth.”

Thomas strode to the other side of the street and entered the mercantile store. He cornered Seth in the backroom. They talked about wheelchairs and Seth brought out a catalog. They spent ten minutes thumbing through the pages. Thomas pressed down a finger and nodded.

He left the store and headed for home.

The Wheelchair

EGYPTIANS, IN ANCIENT TIMES, were known to use wheelchairs. In modern years, the first wheelchair recorded in history belonged to Phillip II of Spain. A drawing in Henry Howard’s Dictionaire de l’ Ameublenment *depicts Phillip in a chair with a quilted back, hinged arms and ratchets to adjust the angle of its back and legs.*

Wheelchairs were modified dramatically as a result of the invention of roller skates in the mid 1820’s by John Joseph Merlin. The Merlin Chair innovation used full-sized wheels, with a smaller outer wheel.

Wicker wheelchairs emerged. They were lighter but couldn’t stand the wear and tear. The wheelchair name was officially coined in the late 19th century when rubber metal-spoke bicycle tires became part of the apparatus.

Herbert A. Everest broke his back in a mining accident in 1919. He utilized the help of his mechanical engineering friend, Harry C. Jennings. They created a lighter weight metal folding chair. The millionth chair was manufactured by Everest & Jennings on November 12, 1973.

30

COLLIN'S STOMACH FELT JITTERY. HE HELD HIS BREATH. His brother, Timothy McGearney, rode his horse up the middle of Main Street. Collin was looking out the window from his new home in the Smith Building. Collin rented a suite with two rooms recently, a big improvement in space and quality from the small room he had been living in at the Grand Hotel.

Timothy's back slumped slightly. The far-away look in his eyes matched the gate of his horse as it slowed to a walk. Ah wonder what he would think if he knew ah was watching him at this moment, Collin thought, taking a deep breath, a tight smile forming on his face. Our meeting time is coming, brother.

Since arriving in Tarrytown, Collin spent hours tossing and turning in his bed at night, planning on how he was going to confront his brother. He had a difficult decision to make: to be a thorn in his brother's side or to reconcile the past and start over—perhaps even help Timothy with his sheep farm.

He left his room and walked the long corridor. Collin took the stairs down and approached the front door. He opened it and paused before stepping onto the boardwalk. Collin saw his brother standing in front of Mama's Kitchen. What's he doin' over there? Collin asked himself. Ah just saw him go into the saloon.

Collin stepped back into the vestibule and waited. His brother stopped and talked to a tall man. Ah think that's one of the Scotsmen from the farm west of Timothy's, he thought. They don't appear to be exactly friendly toward each other right now. Timothy's always had a difficult time getting along with neighbors.

The two men separated and Timothy stomped back into the saloon. The Scotchman threw up his arms and walked into Mama's Kitchen.

Collin took his cue and quickly walked towards Toby's Corral. "Billy, would ya saddle me Nellie?"

He waited out on the boardwalk. Minutes later, Billy led Nellie out onto the street. "Thank ye, Billy," Collin said and mounted.

He headed westward and glanced back toward the saloon. Timothy's horse remained tied to a rail in front.

— —

YELLOW-GREEN FOREST PANSY REDBLOODS grew in clusters along the edge of MacTurley's Woods. Collin admired the plants and trees of Missouri. His home in Ireland didn't have the luxury of massive foliage. The sky offered a tapestry of lazy, thin, gray-white clouds partially blocking the mid-afternoon sun.

At the corner of the woods, he turned his horse onto a trail that led upward and parallel to Hastings's fence. As he had hoped, there were no riders in sight. He saw the tributary of Bear Creek looming ahead. Thickets of weeping cherry trees intermixed with the redbuds. He stopped to admire a stately burr oak tree. As he had done at other times, he crossed the small creek and angled across the fields toward his brother's property.

A herd of Herefords lifted their heads to watch him as they grazed and lazed within a barbed wire fence that paralleled the north edge of the creek. Collin saw the roof line of Thomas's barn from close to a mile away. He saw the corner of the barbed wire fence and he knew his brother's property began just beyond.

Collin kept his horse at a walk, staying on the south side of the tributary. As he approached Bear Creek, he saw flocks of sheep in the distance. They remained within the boundaries of the McGearney property thanks to a fleet of dogs and the pitiful but stoic remains of a pre-Civil War split rail fence.

Collin dismounted and led his horse to a stand of emerging aspen trees. Tying up his horse, he removed his Remington rifle from its scabbard and proceeded to cross the creek on foot. He saw two dogs but knew a dozen more lingered in the area. One of them looked his way but didn't bark or rise from its haunches.

Collin sat on the ground and lit a cigarette. He enjoyed watching the sheep and hoped they would migrate in his direction as they grazed. Collin ran his fingers over his father's belt buckle in his jacket pocket. This time, my brother is going to find a clue—he will get a message.

An hour passed and Collin's mind eased into a gentle sleep. He awoke to a rustling sound behind him.

"Git up! Put yar hands in the air!"

Collin felt stunned. He turned to look. A man wearing a bowler hat stood at the edge of the creek, clutching a carbine with both hands. Collin placed a hand on the ground and pushed himself up. His weapon lay on the ground out of his reach.

The sneer on the man's face looked cold as a bucket of ice. "I've finally caught up with ya, McGearney," the man muttered, taking a step forward and lining up the sights with his right eye.

Collin knew that he had gotten himself into an awful twist. "Aye, but I'm not—not McGearney. Me name is McBride."

The man sneered at him. "Shore you're not. Tell me another one."

Collin saw a pair of coyotes emerging from the creek, a distance behind the cowboy. The two collie dogs got to their feet. They barked at the predators and moved cautiously toward them. Collin saw his adversary roll his eyes toward the dogs, then he turned his head toward the coyotes.

The man raised his rifle and took aim. He fired. Collin reached down to pick up his carbine.

The man quickly turned, his nostrils flared as he looked at Collin and reestablished his aim. "Ah wouldn't do that if ah were you, Mister."

Collin's right hand remained rested on the stock of his carbine. He looked up into the barrel of the cowboy's rifle. Realizing his predicament, he straightened his frame.

"Back off from that rifle, mister."

Loud shots rang out. Collin felt a tug on his left shoulder. The man's bowler hat flew off his head, and his rifle went airborne as he lurched backward and fell to the ground.

Someone, remaining out of sight at the edge of the creek, had fired the two shots. Collin, wild eyed, looked at the two dogs. They maintained their alert position in readiness to defend their flock. The coyotes were nowhere in sight. Collin crouched, his mouth agape. The fallen man groaned. The dogs hunkered down again. Their heads turned, watching his every move.

Collin ran to his horse. "Come on, Maggie—git on with ya!"

As he galloped along the southern edge of the tributary, he felt panicky and confused. "It wasn't me. I didn't shoot 'em. Someone else did."

— —

TIMOTHY MCGEARNEY saw his brother ride off and had no intention of pursuing him. He cautiously walked over to the man lying on the ground. The carbine lay well off to his side. Timothy stood beside the man. He felt nauseated. Somewhere ah've seen this person before, he thought.

Timothy saw the blackish hole, surrounded by spears of blood, in the man's jacket. He knew that the man would not be a threat. He set down his carbine and knelt beside him. "Who are ya?" Timothy asked.

The man groaned. His mouth opened. "McGearney—there's two o' ya."

Timothy took a closer look at the man's face. "My God, it's Kelli Kennedy."

The man's eyes opened. "Timothy," he muttered. "Come closer. I have something important to tell you."

Timothy lowered his head, turning it so one of his ears was only inches from the man's mouth.

"'Twas me who killed Patrick."

Timothy's mouth gaped open. "You!"

"Ye brother had it going with me wife. I couldn't stand it. I had to kill 'im."

Timothy nodded. "Then, it wasn't Conor."

"No...." Kelli's voice tailed off.

Timothy looked up at the sky. He thought about his brother riding away in panic a few minutes ago. He saw Kelli's mouth open slightly, then the head jerked and dropped.

"My God, the man's dead."

— —

PEDRO ORTIZ DREADED THE LONG WAGON RIDE he was soon to take with his family. Thomas Hastings's fall farm work was almost completed. As he had done every year for the past five years, he planned to move his family to a warmer climate near Houston, Texas. Working in a factory didn't appeal to him, but his family needed the money to survive.

He felt well rewarded after a bountiful harvest. Pedro rode one of Thomas's mules to the creek tributary to seek out young strays that sought shade in the bottomlands. He worked the mule westward, continuing on until he reached the fence line.

Two sharp rifle shots split the air. The mule he sat on jerked and turned sharply, almost sending Pedro to the ground. "Dios mio! Nos libramos por los pelos." Good God, that was a close call, he thought.

Elevating his body, he anxiously gazed toward the sound of the gunshots. The air stilled. Minutes later, he heard the sound of horse's hooves. Through breaks in the underbrush, he saw a rider approaching. That's the Irishman who Luke hired, he said to himself. He watched as the horse continued to gallop eastward on the other side of the creek.

It's none of my affair, he said to himself. Satisfied that there weren't any strays in the area, he steered his mule homeward. He stopped to watch Luke and the others breaking horses in the corral. Thomas walked over from the house and perched his leg onto a rail. "Hey, Pedro, find any strays?"

"No, amigo, none."

"Good. Take the rest of the day off. Oh, I heard some gunshots from over there." Thomas pointed.

"Si, senor—so did I."

"Did ya see what 'twas?"

"No, amigo, but I see horseman riding very fast."

"Which way was he headin'?"

Pedro pointed toward the mountain. "That-a-way."

"Did ya see who 'twas?"

"The Irishman, ah think."

"The Irishman! Which one?"

"The one who Luke hired."

Thomas nodded, turned and began walking back towards the house, wondering about the man he had recently hired.

31

THOMAS READ THE LETTER A THIRD TIME, curiously glancing at Sarah, expecting a reaction. He set the letter down on the table and she turned her head toward him. "Well, Sir Thomas, something is up—I can feel it. You have that look."

Thomas chuckled. "Sarah, it says here in the letter that my parents are comin' for a visit. They're arriving by train to Stillman Mills. Grady is gonna get a telegraph on when to pick 'em up. He's gonna drive 'em out here."

Sarah placed a hand on her hair. "Oh, Thomas, that's delightful news. I'll be anxiously looking forward to their visit and—"

"And what?"

"I'll need my hair done."

Thomas smiled. He walked over to her and placed his arms around her shoulders. "Ah'll talk to Annabelle."

Sarah grasped his hand. "Thank you. I appreciate that."

Thomas gave her a squeeze and moved away. "Ah'm ridin' into

town today and Ah'll stop at the telegraph office and see if they've heard anythin' yet."

Sarah looked up from the book she had been reading. "Annabelle said that we're totally out of flour."

Thomas nodded his head. "Ah'll keep that in mind."

Half an hour later, Thomas mounted his stallion and guided him up his roadway.

He looked forward to his parents' visit. He had seen them in Independence back in August. Thomas felt confident that Sarah would benefit from their being here. He did have some misgivings about his mother's first reaction. Emma had a strong tendency to show her feelings, especially if a family situation was involved.

Thomas saw a herd of Abel's Angus cattle from across the Tarrytown Road when he heard the unmistakable sound. "The stagecoach! It's comin'," he exclaimed.

He watched with awe as the wheels bounced on the planks of the bridge. The magnificent scene unfolding before him sent shivers up his spine: the rustling of the harness, the clip-clop of the horses' hooves beating on the ground and the long narrow snake-like whip sailing through the air. A streak of red moved past his roadway. Thomas raised his right arm high into the air after seeing Justin Haggard raise his.

Thomas watched until the stagecoach had reached the edge of MacTurley's Woods before he guided his horse onto the road and set it into a fast trot toward town.

As he expected, the stagecoach parked in front of the stage office. Thomas saw that more than the usual number of people had gathered. Wonder what the news is, he said to himself and prodded the stallion into a gallop.

Thomas rode up to the mercantile store, tied up his horse and stomped across the street. He saw Grady talking to the marshal. "Howdy, Grady—Ben. What's happened?" Thomas asked.

The marshal, looking down at Thomas, his chin shifting from side to side, said, "The Younger and the James boys have robbed the bank in Northfield, Minnesota. Two of 'em got themselves kilt."

Thomas gaped, shocked.

Grady put his arm on his shoulder. "Sorry brother, ah know how close you were to Bob."

Thomas shook his head. "Damn, ah had a bad feeling when ah visited with him last. Do ya know who was killed? Was it any of the Youngers or Jameses? Jaysus, ah hope not."

"Naw, the newspaper mentioned two men who ah have never 'eard of before—Chadwell Stiles and Clell Miller."

He heard a gasp behind him. Turning, he saw Rosemary Pikes, her hand covering her mouth, listening intently to the marshal. "Anything wrong, ma'am?" Thomas asked.

She looked up at Thomas, her eyes watering. "Did you hear the names of the men who were killed?" she asked, one of her hands reaching up and covering her mouth.

"Yup, I did—never heard of 'em before."

"It wasn't Bob Younger who was one of 'em—those who got kilt, I mean?" she asked.

"Nope, 'twasn't," Thomas said.

Thomas looked at Rosemary's face, sympathizing with her concern. She breathed a huge sigh of relief. No one deserves real bad news, he thought. Well, maybe—the Erlocks and Lassitors are an exception. Thomas's thoughts flashed back to the Civil War, when he marched up the slope to the cemetery with his family.

How can I ever forget my best friend, Carr? Thomas wiped a tear from his eye. Then there was Will Walker, Grady's best friend. He stared down at the boardwalk thinking about Jubal and Justin Haggard's parents being buried. Then there was Justin's wife. Jaysus, ah really cried.

Thomas watched the coach slowly being drawn toward the corral by the horses, steaming with perspiration. He thought about visiting the saloon, but decided against it. Instead, he walked his horse across the street toward the mercantile.

He went inside and looked at the counter. He remembered when his sister, Genevieve, worked there during the war. Thomas closed his eyes and saw her standing behind the counter, smiling. Jaysus, she looked so great, he thought.

"Anything we can do for ya?" Mason John asked.

Thomas's head jerked. "Ah yah—ah need some material for Sarah."

Mason John looked down at Thomas, confused. "Oh yeah, yar wife. Ah'll get Mary to hep ya."

Thomas secured his purchases to the back end of the saddle and mounted. He trotted his horse westward, beyond the Smith Building. When he approached the church, he turned away. So much sorrow there, he thought.

The Northfield Bank Robbery

ON SEPTEMBER 7, 1876, JUST BEFORE 2:00 P.M., three riders dressed in white dusters crossed the Cannon River Bridge in Northfield, Minnesota. They were Bob Younger, Frank James and Charlie Pitts. They turned right on Division Street and dismounted in front of the bank.

Cole Younger and Clell Miller rode in side by side, coming from the south. A short distance behind them rode Jesse James, James Younger and Chadwell Stiles. J. S. Allen, owner of the hardware store, was standing on the street when the nine strangers aroused his suspicions.

Mr. Allen approached the strangers in front of the bank and got pushed around. He hurried back toward his store and shouted, "Get your guns, boys. They're robbing the bank."

The three original riders had already entered the bank. Shooting broke out moments later, most of the shots being fired into the air by the robbers, intending to scare away the local citizens.

Henry M. Wheeler had been sitting in front of his father's drug store across the street from the bank. When he saw Mr. Allen getting pushed around, he yelled, "Robbery! Robbery!" He eventually got his hands on a .50-caliber Smith carbine and raced to an upstairs window.

Nicolaus Gustavson, a Swedish immigrant who worked as a blacksmith for William Hagen Wagon Company, was on the street that day. But because he didn't understand English, he didn't take the robbers' heed. As a result he was shot and later died.

The three robbers who were in the bank demanded that someone open the safe. Joseph Lee Haywood, acting cashier, was in the center of the violence. One of the robbers said to him, "Open that safe right now, or I'll blow your head off."

During mass confusion within the bank, Haywood yelled, "Murder! Murder! Murder!" Frank James hit him over the head with his revolver, felling him to the floor.

A. E. Bunker, one of the tellers, made a courageous and dramatic escape, running out the back door. Pitts pursued and shot him through the shoulder.

Pitts returned into the bank. Bob Younger, responding to a call of desperation by his brother, Cole, from outside, left the bank. He was followed by Pitts. Frank James came out last after he had fired a fatal shot into Haywood's head.

Outside, the street became a shooting gallery. Elias Stacy, armed with a shotgun, shot Clell Miller in the face. From an upper window, across the street, Wheeler shot and killed Miller.

Wheeler also shot Bob Younger in the right elbow as the robber came out of the bank. The youngest of the Younger brothers tossed his revolver into his left hand.

G. E. Bates, who owned a store across the street, stuck an empty revolver past the slightly opened door as a decoy to draw fire and confuse the robbers.

Anselm R. Manning, the owner of the hardware store, grabbed a rifle from a window in his store and headed outside, peeking around the corner of the building. One of his shots killed one of the robber's horses. Having great difficulty in reloading, Manning secured a different rifle. He took careful aim and shot and killed Chadwell Stiles.

During Manning's heroics, he played a shooting hide-and-seek game with Bob Younger.

After Bob Younger's horse had been shot, he eventually jumped up behind his brother, Cole.

The robbers left town after four men were fatally shot. A large sum of money was left in a bag, lying on the bank floor.

See References at the end of the book.

32

THE RAYS OF THE SUN LIT UP THE BACK of Marshal Buford's high crown hat as he rode westward past the church. He turned his head back toward town and blinked at the brightness of the morning sun. The light sifted through the trees at the edge of MacTurley's Woods, sending streaks of light across a bed of maroon-colored leaves.

His horse let loose a series of knickering shrieks as a deer emerged from the woods and leaped across the road in front of him. He kicked the horse's flanks and trotted to the corner of the woods at the beginning of the Hastings's property.

"Whoa—whoa—whoa."

His horse dug its front hooves into the sod in the middle of the road and stopped. The marshal glared along the tree line upward toward Bear Mountain. He scowled thinking about the red figure of a man—the detective, floundering his way down the slope of a trail a couple of days ago.

Ah know that ah've seen the last of Weatherby after seeing him get on the stagecoach yesterday, he said to himself. He shook his head. Ah really don't blame him. The poor detective didn't know, but he was in the middle of a unique situation. The James-Younger gang was one thing, but the Erlocks are somethin' else.

That's a fine herd of white faced cattle, the marshal said to himself as he rode by the Hastings's roadway. He continued on over the bridge and turned off onto the McGearney roadway.

The marshal rode over to the barn area and dismounted. Timothy came out of the house and joined him.

"Howdy, Timothy," the marshal drawled.

"Likewise, Ben. Nice mornin', huh?"

"Sure is."

"Timothy, ya know why ah'm here, don't ya?"

The Irishman nodded.

Buford dismounted and looked down at the Irishman. "Do ya know who 'twas who ya shot yesterday?"

"That ah do, Marshal."

The marshal placed a hand on top of a fence post, his head angled forward. "Ya knew the dead man?"

Timothy told the marshal the story about the killing of his brother Patrick in Ireland. "I believed that Conor did it. Conor thought that I did it. Would ya imagine that?"

Timothy took a deep breath. "Marshal, ah shot at a trespasser who held a gun on my brother and could've been a threat to my flock."

"It does look like a justifiable shooting to me, McGearney. The stranger was trespassing and held a gun on your brother."

Timothy's forehead creased, his lower jaw trembled. "Ah didn't mean to kill him—just to scare him off."

The marshal nodded his head. "McGearney, ah need to get together with you and your brother and have you both sign some papers—then, we can put this all behind us."

Timothy nodded. "Ah shall, but ah can't do it now."

The marshal placed a toe into a stirrup and swung up onto the saddle. "Much obliged, McGearney—thanks for tellin' me the truth. Ah'll look up yar brother and arrange for the three of us to get together."

Minutes later, the marshal walked his horse toward the roadway. A horse followed carrying the body of Kelli Kennedy on its back.

— —

THOMAS SAT ON HIS PORCH AND SAW TWO HORSES approaching from the west. The tall man on the lead horse has to be the marshal, he said to himself. The rear horse had a figure draped across its back. They crossed the bridge and headed towards Tarrytown. Thomas had heard about the shooting at the McGearney section of the creek. Someone had been shot and killed. The procession moved past his roadway. Thomas lit a fresh cigar, his curiosity building.

Thomas whiffed the dinner that Annabelle prepared in the kitchen. He brought the brandy glass to his lips and took a long swig. His mind drifted to the other news that he had heard in town yesterday...the bank robbery. Why would the Youngers ride such a long distance? He asked himself. He thought of the possibilities: getting even with someone, maybe the money. Ah wonder where Bob and his brother are now. Thomas had read a section of the news article, and it mentioned that a posse assembled immediately and pursued the bank robbers.

From what he had heard from his neighbor, the Erlocks had nothing to do with the shooting at McGearney's yesterday. He took another sip of brandy, feeling the heat in his cheeks, rage against the Erlocks building. Every time ah look at Sarah trying to move, ah think of those bloody bastards. I can only sit around and do nothing for so long. If they aren't brought in soon, ah'm going to round up some help and go after 'em.

Ah best wait until my family leaves, and until I get that wheelchair for Sarah. It should be here on the next stage.

— —

THOMAS KISSED SARAH ON THE LIPS and left the house. Luke had two horses harnessed to his wagon and tied to the rail out front. He had mixed feelings about getting the chair with wheels. It will help Sarah, but then she may quit trying, he thought.

The anger in his heart grew stronger and stronger as his team approached the Tarrytown Road. He looked down at his two carbines lying in front of the seat. I hope those Erlocks try somethin' today. Ah'll kill 'em all, he said to himself.

Thomas felt pleased with the fortress his hired men had prepared and installed in the wagon. If them Erlocks attack me, Ah'll git in there and pick 'em off one by one.

He passed by the first clearing in MacTurley's Woods where the Erlocks had been known to await their victims. Thomas made certain that the horses rested before getting abreast of the woods. He whipped them into a gallop, glancing anxiously toward the trees. He slowed the team when the bared hill beyond the trees came into view—no trees, only a large cross and grave-markers.

Thomas waved at Deputy Milburn as he guided his team toward the mercantile store. Stepping off the wagon, he tied the reins to a post and entered. He saw Mason John talking to a customer near the counter. Thomas seriously considered the idea of asking the young sharpshooter to ride along when he decided to go after the Erlocks.

He walked by Mason John and nodded a greeting, continuing toward Seth, who busied himself restocking a shelf. "Good morning, Seth. Did the wheels come in?"

Seth looked up. "Mornin', Thomas, yup it did, and ah tell you, it's quite the contraption."

He led Thomas into the back room. "Thar 'tis."

Thomas stared at the chair, wondering at the two large, thin wheels snuggled to the sides. He walked behind it. "Sit, Seth. Let's try it out."

Thomas smiled, pushing the wheelchair with Seth aboard. He pushed it into the main room of the store. He heard laughter coming from all directions and said, "It looks good, Seth. Get me the bill."

After paying for the chair, he wheeled it outside and hoisted it onto the wagon. Life will never be the same, Thomas said to himself and sent his team into a trot westward.

33

THE TRAIN SLOWED AS IT APPROACHED STILLMAN MILLS, wheels screeching and dark smoke billowing from the black stack. Henry Hastings stood in the aisle, pulled up his sagging breeches and said, "This is it, Emma." Staggering slightly when the train car lurched, he began to gather their belongings.

"Genevieve, are ya awake?"

"Yes, Pa," she replied, rubbing her eyes.

Emma glanced out the small window. "If only Grady didn't forget. I don't see him out there."

Henry inhaled and rubbed a knuckle over the tip of his nose. She's been worried all the way from Independence that we were gonna get held up, he said to himself, smiling.

"Oh, don't worry, Emma, he'll be here."

Henry led the way, a large case in one hand, and a smaller one in the other. A corner of the larger case caught on the armrest of a seat. He muttered a curse and jerked it loose.

"You two go first," he said to his wife and daughter.

Emma approached the first step of the portable ladder the conductor placed for the passengers.

"There we go," the conductor said and volunteered a hand to assist Emma down each step.

"Easy does it," the conductor said to Genevieve as she hopped down the steps.

Grady Hastings had been patiently waiting next to his carriage. He was leaning against a support timber. Edging forward, he yelled, "Ma! Pa! Genevieve!"

Rushing forward, he hugged his mother. "Pa, how ya doin'?"

Grady grasped his father's hand and held it tight for a moment. "Yar lookin' good, Pa. Have ya got any cigars left for the trip to Thomas's home?"

"Gotta couple."

Grady pulled his sister tight toward his chest. She gasped for breath. He kissed her on the forehead and released her. "Yar lookin' great, Sis."

"Thanks," Genevieve said.

Henry pointed. "Mebe we can stop at the Seth's place and get some more."

Grady smiled wide. "Sure, Pa."

Grady hoisted his parent's and Genevieve's luggage into a rear compartment. Henry helped Emma up onto the front seat and took one of the rear seats. Genevieve sat next to her father.

Grady waited for a large wagon loaded with stuffed canvas bags to pass by. He directed the team onto the road and flicked the reins to launch a smooth trot. Emma grabbed onto the vertical rod that supported the surrey. Henry had lit a cigar and reached out to flick off an ash. Genevieve covered her nose and mouth.

— —

GRADY ANXIOUSLY EYED THE TERRITORY toward the foothills of Bear Mountain. Even though the Erlock's house was vacant, he considered the possibility of an attack by the three renegades. He knew any such event would be totally devastating to his mother and sister.

Turning his head, he caught a glimpse of his father spinning the cylinder of his revolver and peering through the barrel. A lever- action Remington rifle leaned against the seat next to him.

Grady's confidence grew as the black cross on the left side of the road came into sight. Only two miles out of Tarrytown, he said to himself. He wondered if his father was thinking about the skirmish the Gray Riders had with a Union cavalry unit just outside of town in 1863. Grady didn't feel he needed to ask. He noticed the far away look in his father's eyes.

He looked at his mother. Her hands were clasped together. She leaned forward slightly and met his eyes. "How's Sarah?"

"Ma, Sarah is fine, but...."

"But what, Grady?"

"Ma, the doctor said that she will never walk again."

"No! No! You can't mean that—surely the doctor must be wrong."

"Ah hope 'e is," Grady said.

Emma shook her head. "Bad enough—losing the child."

Grady glanced at two horses running and bucking at the far end of Toby's Corral. The two young stallions kicked up sod that landed on the other side of the split-rail fence. He slowed the team and guided them toward the mercantile store. "Whoa there."

Two cowboys, sitting on a bench out front, looked up. One of them lipped a droopy cigarette. "Howdy, boys," Grady said.

He jumped off, tied up the team and hurried over to the other side of the carriage. "Easy does it, Ma."

— —

HENRY DROPPED DOWN ONTO THE STREET. He stretched his arms high over his head and wiggled his hips. Stepping onto the boardwalk, he cupped his hands and lit a cigar. He inhaled deeply and a blast of smoke emitted from his mouth as he looked up and down Main Street.

The cross-arm of the letter 't' in the sign "Mercantile Goods & Services" had been broken off at an angle. Farther down the street, Frontier Saloon had new swinging doors. The Constable's office across the street was now a U.S. Marshal's office and jail. The building addition next to it housed a telegraph office and stagecoach depot. "Modern times," he muttered.

The undertakers and barbershop haven't changed a bit, he thought. "Ah heard that Digger Phillips is still plantin' people, and Shol Clarity is still cuttin' hair," he said.

Grady opened the door to the mercantile store. "Yup, they sure are, Pa."

Genevieve led the way in, followed by her mother, her father and Grady. Henry watched as his wife began running her fingers along lengths of bright material. Grady looked at him and Genevieve, smiling. "Let's go find Seth."

The two men and Genevieve walked up an aisle toward the counter. "Hey, Seth, look who ah brought ya," Grady said.

"Well, ah'll be hanged—Henry Hastings—and Gen!" Seth Miller exclaimed and hurried out from behind the counter.

He rushed to Genevieve and hugged her tight. "Ya look splendid, young lady."

She smiled widely and blinked her dark brown eyes. Her hair was no longer pulled back in a bun—it hung loosely, bouncing on her shoulders. "Mr. Miller, you're just as busy as ever."

Seth placed brawny fingers on Henry's shoulder as he shook his hand. "How the heck are ya? It's been a long time."

"Ah'm fine. Yes, it has. Yar store looks better than ever."

Seth blinked his eyes and looked across the room. "Hey, Mase! Come on ova 'ere. Ah want ya to meet someone."

"This is my nephew, Mason John. He's going to run this place someday—came all the way from St. Louie, 'e did."

"Howdy, Mason John," Henry said. Moving his cigar from one hand to the other, he shook his hand.

"This is Mrs. Hastings and their daughter, Genevieve."

Mason John shook Emma's hand. He looked at Genevieve, hesitating. He shook her hand, too, holding it longer than the others.

Trains

THE TRANSCONTINENTAL RAILROAD IN AMERICA began as a dream in 1832. Congress approved measures for surveyors to plan routes in 1852. Ten years later, congress formally authorized the building of the railroad.

Union Pacific Railroad began building the track west from Omaha. Central Pacific Railroad built tracks east from Sacramento, California. In 1864 the Pacific Railway Act was modified allowing twenty alternate routes.

The progress in construction of new tracks was severely subdued during the Civil War. When the war ended, rail construction resumed, overcoming hard winters, Indians, hot summers and lack of supplies.

A spike made of gold was driven in the last tie plat to commemorate the joining of the Union Pacific and Central Pacific at Promontory Summit in Utah on May 10, 1869. On June 4, 1876, in celebration of the nation's centennial, the Transcontinental Express left New York and rolled into San Francisco in a record-breaking time of 83 hours and 39 minutes.

34

HENRY, EMMA AND GENEVIEVE exited the mercantile store after visiting with their old friends. They stopped on the boardwalk. Grady followed them out. He waved to their former neighbors and Gray Riders, Abel Kingsley and Justin Haggard sitting on their horses in front of the store.

Justin towered over his friend and neighbor, Abel. The loss of his right leg during the war didn't affect his straight-back posture. Thick, curly black hair squished out from underneath the rim of his hat. Justin smiled, his soft, silver-gray eyes beaming. "Howdy, Mr. Hastings—Mrs. Hastings—Genevieve."

"Justin—Abel—it's so good to see you two again," Emma Hastings said.

Genevieve smiled widely. "Howdy, gentlemen."

Henry and Emma walked toward the horses and reached up their hands to Justin and Abel. Abel dismounted and hugged Genevieve. He assisted her to her seat and curtsied.

Grady placed a hand on Abel's shoulder. "Thanks, boys. Ah'm really glad that you could make it."

Abel Kingsley's deep-set hazel eyes watered slightly. "Ah only wish that we would've been along when the Erlocks hurt my sister." His narrow face had darkened since boyhood days. Abel's light brown hair no longer hung beyond the ears. It was cut shorter. His thin mustache drooped down to his chin.

Grady boosted his mother onto her seat. Henry lit a cigar and sat down in the back. Grady looked back at his two friends and yelled. "Gidi-yap! Gidi-yap!"

Grady felt confident and proud because he had special escorts. He glanced at his mother and wondered if she trusted the escorts. Grady smiled. She sat there with that deep, long, smug look on her face. Her face lit up when she turned her head. The school house's fresh paint gave it a magnificent appearance. Mother's goin' home, he said to himself. "Gidi-yap!"

— —

THE RHYTHMIC SOUND OF PLODDING HOOF BEATS and clattering harnesses splashed at the air along the Tarrytown Road. Grady anxiously inspected the small clearings at the edge of MacTurley's Woods, always on the alert for a renegade attack by the Erlocks. He felt more at ease after Thomas's property came into view.

Grady felt a tap on his shoulder. "Grady, would ya pull up a bit?" his father asked.

"Whoa—whoa."

He directed the team off the road and brought the carriage to a stop. Henry stepped down and stiffly walked toward the three- strand barbed wire fence. He stopped next to the wire. Henry reached out and lightly rubbed his fingers on a barb. Licking the tip of his finger, he turned. "It's sharp."

"Grady, look!" Genevieve exclaimed.

In the distance, to the west, he saw the emerging bulk of a stagecoach. Emma, Genevieve and Grady stared as the conveyance got closer and closer. A distant yelp was the first sound. "That's gotta be Lafe," Grady said.

Genevieve's face brightened. "Lafe?"

"Yup, Lafe's usually got the reins. Sometimes it's his brother, Jesse."

"Oh, that's so exciting. I've never seen a stagecoach before," Genevieve said, her face beaming.

Clouds of dust partially obstructed the red-painted structure. The high-crowned hats of the two men on the high seat bobbed with the bounces of the wheels.

"He-YAH! He-YAH!"

The clattering increased as the coach approached. Henry remained next to the fence. He turned and gawked at the stagecoach. The lead horses appeared to be all eyes and teeth as the coach neared the carriage. "It's Lafe and Jesse!" Grady exclaimed.

He took off his hat and raised it high. "He-YAH!" Lafe yelled, his high-pitched voice barely discernable.

35

THOMAS WATCHED FROM THE FRONT PORCH as the stagecoach passed by the carriage. That had to be my father standing next to the fence, he thought. Sure as hell, he's testing the wire. I bet he doubts that it will stop the cattle.

He turned his head toward the door and yelled, "Sarah, they're coming!"

Thomas rose and opened the door, allowing Sarah to wheel through, her face beaming.

The carriage, followed by two horsemen, turned onto their roadway. Thomas stood on the planking of their front stoop, placing both palms on the railing. "One of the riders is Justin! Hey, the other is yar brother, Abel!"

Sarah raised her arm, a white handkerchief flitting in a mellow breeze. She saw her brother remove his hat and wave. "Oh, Thomas, this is so exciting. I shall never forget it."

Luke strolled over from the corral. He peeked around the corner of the house. "Look like they ah comin'."

The squeaking noises ceased after the carriage halted next to the house. Abel leaped off his horse and rushed to the porch. Leaning over, he kissed and hugged his sister.

"How's it goin', Thomas?"

Thomas stood and shook Abel's hand. "Ah can't complain, Abel. At least we're alive."

Abel shook his head. "We'll git those sons-of-a-bitches. Ya can count on it."

Justin hobbled over. "Hey there, you two. Thomas! Sarah! We brung your parents and sister."

Genevieve stepped onto the porch. She rushed to Sarah and held her tight. "You dear girl, I've been so concerned about you."

Emma walked over and stared at Sarah. "Mother!" Thomas exclaimed. He jumped off and grabbed her. "Ma, ya look great."

She backed away from his tight hug. "What is that?"

"It's known as a wheelchair, Mother."

She frowned. Sarah looked down at her and put out her arms.

Emma stumbled on the first step and grabbed the rail. She cautiously walked up the three steps. Her frown increased as she walked toward Sarah. Emma grasped both of Sarah's hands. She didn't say a word.

Thomas stared down into the dark eyes of his father. "Howdy, Pa. Glad you could make it."

"Son, ah like the feel of the barbed wire—but doesn't it tear up their hides?"

Thomas shook his head. "Not a problem so far."

A caravan approached up Thomas's roadway—two conveyances and two riders. He recognized William Farnsworth holding the reins of the first carriage. The former cavalry leader's niece, Helen, Grady Hastings's wife, sat next to him. Grady's children, Tyler and Clarissa, sat in the back.

The size of the three riders behind the carriage tipped Thomas off as to their identity. He knew they were the McGregors: the tall father Orly, and Mitch, the eldest son.

The second carriage belonged to Jubal Haggard and his wife, Jessica. She was the sister of Helen, Grady's wife. Thomas became overwhelmed with excitement as his neighbors approached. He dashed into the house and returned with two bottles of whiskey.

Jubal and Jessica surrounded Sarah. Jessica leaned over and kissed her on the cheek. Thomas felt moisture building in his eyes.

"Howdy, Thomas," Jubal said.

They shook hands.

"Good to see yar family."

"Thanks for comin'. Ah know for certain that Sarah is so glad to see you two."

"Yar parents and Genevieve look great," Jubal said.

Thomas pointed at the bottle. "Would ya like a shot?"

Jubal licked his lips. "Darn tootin'." He lifted the glass to his lips and drank it all, burping as he handed the empty back.

"Another?"

"Nope, later," Jubal said and wiped his lips with his hand.

Thomas walked over to this father. "Have one, Pa."

"Don't mind if ah do."

Henry hoisted up the glass and drank the entire amount. He brought it back down. "Ah'll have one more, son."

Thomas grinned. "Sure, Pa." He filled the glass and gritted his teeth as his mother frowned.

All the men except for Thomas had gathered in the shadows of the house. They passed the bottle around. Spirals and small clouds of smoke danced in the air above them.

Most of the women sat on porch chairs near Sarah. Genevieve and Emma left the group to prepare eats in the kitchen. The men's voices got louder and louder.

Midnight came and went. One by one, the men lay in the grass and fell asleep, some with blankets, some without. Sarah had returned to the house just before dark. All the women except Emma retired. She sat in a rocker and munched on a piece of meat.

36

TIMOTHY LEANED AGAINST A FENCE POST, frequently shifting his position. He eagerly watched the fields that sloped up toward the mountain. His hired hand had not reported back from the daily inspection of the sheep flocks. Timothy had hired Sparks after losing a dog and several sheep to the Erlocks.

"Where is that lad?" he muttered.

Timothy walked into the barn and saddled his horse. He grabbed his carbine from the rack and opened the breech. It's loaded, he said to himself. Jamming the rifle into a scabbard, he led the horse outside and mounted.

He rode south, past the old dilapidated slave buildings and toward Bear Creek. Timothy dismounted and walked his horse southwestward, parallel to the creek. He eagerly inspected his herds of sheep. Timothy felt relieved that his dogs were in position and the wooly animals appeared undisturbed.

He watched two carriages and several riders moving toward the Tarrytown Road from Thomas Hastings's place. Timothy smiled, thinking about the noises that he and Madeline had heard the previous evening. Thomas must have thrown quite the party, he thought.

The wall of green trees and bushes lining the creek bottom caught his eye. He slowed his horse, approaching the place where Kelli Kennedy died. Dismounting, he felt the crispness of the moist air. Rolls of fog slid down the mountain slope. He retched when he saw the dark red discoloration in the grass. I can't believe that I shot and killed a man, he said to himself.

A barking dog alerted Tim and he turned his head sharply. Timothy saw a rider approaching from the area where the sheep had spent the night. He recognized his hired hand Sparks, and raised an arm.

"Aye, Sparks, how is the flock this fine mornin'?"

"They're good, Timothy. Ah'm headin' back now."

Timothy nodded and got back up on his horse. He watched Sparks ride toward the buildings. Timothy guided his mare across the creek and walked it eastward toward the Hastings's property. Except for the shrill screams of blue jays, the air sounded dead quiet. Slow floating, streaky, white-gray clouds filled the sky.

— —

COLLIN MCBRIDE HADN'T SLEPT WELL. The celebrating over by the house went on well into the night, but he didn't feel any ill will toward the celebration. Collin felt glad that Thomas's family came for a visit. He decided to ride out and look after the herds.

He galloped his horse toward the mountain, slowing when he reached the herds a short distance from the creek. Several cows raised their heads as he rode by. The brief visit by the sun during the sunrise period had ended. It currently remained hidden behind rolling clouds of fog coming down from the mountain.

Collin slowed his horse as he approached Thomas's barbed wire fence that paralleled the north side of the creek. For a nostalgic moment, the surroundings reminded him of Ireland...the haze created by the fog...the dampness...the sounds of birds chirping.

He walked his horse westward, looking for herds of cattle. "Woah," he said and tugged on the reins. Collin stared at the fence. The wire had been cut leaving a gap that the entire herd could pass through. He straightened in the saddle and nervously surveyed the landscape, seeing no one. He had been warned by Thomas that the Erlocks would stop at nothing to cause them grief.

Collin sat firmly on his saddle challenging himself to make a decision: ride hard back to the house and alert Thomas—but the men likely all had hangovers. He didn't feel comfortable disturbing Thomas or his guests. Ah could count the animals but that would take too much time, he said to himself. Collin dismounted and looked for cow tracks.

Luke is having his morning coffee in the bunkhouse, he thought. Should I ride back and tell him? But then, he probably has a hangover, too. Collin decided to mosey around a bit more. He nudged his horse forward, advancing toward the break in the fence. Suddenly, he heard the sound of hoof beats approaching on the other side of the creek. He grabbed his carbine from the scabbard and levered in a shell, feeling his heart beating against the inside wall of his chest.

The noises stopped. Collin heard voices. Only one thought came to his mind—the Erlocks. His stomach jumped when he heard the hooves plodding in the dried leaves of the creek bottom. Collin saw the shadows of horsemen crossing the creek directly in front of the downed barbed wire. Collin pulled back the hammer of his rifle and pointed it at the moving figures. His chest heaved from shortness of breath and a rapidly increasing heart beat. The barrel seemed to have a mind of its own as it wavered.

Three horsemen emerged from the bottom. "It's them bloody Erlocks, I say," he muttered. Collin pointed the barrel over their heads and pulled the trigger. He dismounted quickly and heard pistol shots. The frightening zinging sound of a bullet passing nearby caused him to drop down. A chunk of soil kicked up and landed on his boot. Ah hope Luke hears the shooting, and some of the boys will come runnin', he said to himself, squatting low, looking for a tree or shrub to hide behind.

Collin felt dizzy as he continued to fire his rifle. His visibility had disintegrated. He couldn't see any people, just flares of light and smidgeons of smoke. Collin's eyes danced wildly, attempting to pick out a moving figure. He focused on a thick shrub only a few feet away. Collin shook his head. That's not one of 'em, he said to himself.

He knew that someone from the farm would come riding along soon. If only I can hold out for a few minutes more, he said to himself. The shrub that Collin had seen earlier appeared to move. He got up on his knees and pointed his rifle.

A blast of gunfire froze him. Collin gasped and felt himself driven backward. A bullet had hit his right shoulder, knocking his carbine to the ground. Collin crawled toward his rifle and grabbed it with his left hand. Collin desperately dragged himself toward the creek bottom, looking for a hiding place.

Then he heard a shot coming from farther down the creek to the west. The sounds of bullets zinging around him stopped. Collin saw the outline of a horse approaching from Timothy's farm. He watched in awe as his attackers turned tail and galloped their horses across the creek and out of sight.

— —

TIMOTHY HAD RIDDEN ALONG UNTIL HE REACHED the Hastings's property line. He dismounted and walked his horse across the creek. Timothy reached out and touched the barbs in the wire. He realized that barbed wire would not be the choice of fencing for sheep.

Timothy visualized a different type of fence, one that would be made of wire—no barbs, but crossing patterns of wire that would not tear the wool.

Suddenly, he heard a shot, then more shots. Timothy's instincts drove him back into the saddle. He hesitated for a moment and then rode toward the noise.

Through breaks in the fog, he saw three riders. Timothy saw the flashes of fire coming from the barrels of their pistols. They continued to circle their horses while firing at something or someone down by the creek. Timothy pulled out his carbine. Suddenly, he knew: it's the Erlocks!

He flipped the reins and dragged a spur against his horse's belly, sending it into a gallop. Moments later, Timothy spotted some riders near the creek. He pulled up abruptly and began to fire his carbine. Timothy's feelings of rage mushroomed, thinking about the ten dead sheep he had found earlier. This is my chance, he said to himself, shooting his rifle. He clicked on an empty cylinder and placed it back into the scabbard.

Timothy grabbed his Colt revolver from its holster, determined to drive away the invaders. A wave of adrenaline flowed through his body as the Erlocks retreated and galloped across the creek and out of sight. Then he saw a rider-less horse. He pulled sharply on the reins and looked around.

The loud groan that he heard sent shivers up his spine. He dismounted, cautiously leading his horse toward the creek. Taking one step at a time, he saw the bulky form of a human lying on the ground. Edging closer, he took one last look around, feeling confident that the attackers had gone for good.

Timothy locked his eyes on a face, his legs feeling his breath catching in his throat. "My God! It's Conor! Me brother!" he muttered.

Timothy's thoughts drifted back to Ireland. He saw the fog—the arm reaching high up above and striking his brother Patrick...again and again. His heart and thoughts sank thinking that the arm belonged to Conor. Having learned differently recently motivated him to help his brother.

He raised his arms and flattened his palms against the side of his head. Please Lord, what am ay' to do now? Timothy thought in anguish. He reacted by jerking away Conor's bloody vest and tearing away his shirt.

Timothy saw the ugly wound in the shoulder, blood seeping out. He placed the shred of shirt against the wound and pushed down. Timothy felt encouraged feeling Conor's chest rising and falling. He made a quick sign of the cross with his right hand. At last, the sound of hoof beats coming from the Hastings's farm reached his ears.

Moments later, Pedro Ortiz and Luke knelt down beside him. "Senor Timothy, we hear the shots."

Timothy looked up. "The Erlocks cut your fence. They must have come to rustle cattle, but Conor happened by. They exchanged gunfire and Conor got hit. I heard the shots and came riding over."

"Conor!" Luke exclaimed. "That's not Conor—it's Collin McBride."

Timothy gave Luke a hard look of disdain and curiosity. "This is my brother. I should know his name!"

Luke said, "Ah get it. He's changed his name."

Pedro's face lit up. He jabbered something in Spanish. Licking his lips, he said, "Si, senor, the other day I hear this shot. Minutes later, a man rode by on the south side of the creek—he was in a big hurry. It was this man." He pointed.

Timothy stood. "I'll tell ya straight out, gentlemen, we best get my brother to a doctor, and right now."

He looked down. He looked up. "Luke, would ya ride like the wind and bring back a wagon—plenty of padding in the bottom?"

Luke leaped onto his horse and galloped off.

— —

THOMAS AND GRADY RAN OUT TO THE BARN EAGER to learn what was happening.

"It's Collin—he's been shot!" Luke exclaimed as he dismounted.

"Collin! Shot?" Thomas exclaimed.

"Yup! Gotta get this team hitched up and get out there."

Thomas and Grady helped Luke with the horses. "Thomas, ya

best get King saddled, too," Grady said.

Minutes later, the team, with Grady holding the reins, pulled the wagon toward the creek. Luke had thrown several forkfuls of hay into the wagon box. He then rode on ahead of them to show the way.

Grady pulled on the reins. "Thar 'e is!"

Thomas jumped off the seat. "Jaysus," Thomas said after crouching next to Timothy. "Are ya ready? Let's get 'em up into the wagon."

The men gently lifted Collin off the ground and laid him down on top of the hay. Grady got on the seat and flicked the reins. The team galloped toward the farm as Timothy crouched down beside his brother.

Thomas, Pedro and Luke, on horseback, followed closely behind, with Timothy's horse trailing behind Luke.

"Ah'll get our rifles," Thomas yelled and dismounted next to the house. Grady galloped the team right through the farmyard and onto the roadway.

Henry appeared in the doorway with a cup of coffee in his hand, a puzzled look on his face. "What's goin' on?"

"It's Collin. He's been shot."

Thomas grabbed his carbine and remounted, galloping after the wagon.

"Why, them thieving, cowardly Erlocks. Someone has to put an end to them bastards. They don't deserve being alive," Henry said.

37

TIMOTHY SAT ON A CHAIR CLOSE TO COLLIN'S BED at the doctor's suite and held his head between both hands, attempting to deal with his feelings. Ah know that Conor didn't kill Patrick, but does he know that ah didn't kill him either? he asked himself. Timothy's brother lay still, his head hot with fever. The eyes remained closed.

Timothy hadn't returned to his home since bringing his brother to the doctor. He asked Thomas to ride to his house and inform Madeline. Timothy could not pull himself away from his brother and he spent the night slumped in the chair.

Next morning, Timothy had that rough-hewn look after a sleepless night. He doubled his hands into fists and pushed them down into his lap. Taking a deep breath, he stood. Reaching behind his chair, he grabbed his boots and pulled them on.

Doctor Blake entered. "Your brother doesn't appear to be any worse. Ah'll examine him now."

Timothy cleared his throat. "Ah'm gonna step outside for a bit."

Timothy thanked the doctor and walked outside to a very quiet street. An occasional wagon rolled by. Two riders heading west passed by the Smith Building. He shook his head over and over again. I've got to move around, he said to himself. Ah'm daftly unsettled.

Stomping onto the boardwalk, he felt his heart thump against his throat when he saw a tall rider approaching from the west. "Me heavens above, that's the marshal," he muttered, feeling relieved that it wasn't one of the Erlocks.

Buford angled his horse toward the doctor's office and stopped in front of Timothy. "How's yar brother doin', McGearney?"

"Not good 'tall. He's in a bit of a shemozzle with the fever, and I don't know what to think."

"Sorry to hear that—ah hope he gits better. Well, ah've got to move along. Oh by the way, Thomas sent Luke over to yar place, to keep an eye on things 'till ya get back."

Timothy took a deep breath and nodded, hoping to keep from getting unglued. He thought about Madeline and how he had not talked to her since riding out yesterday. Ah sure hope that Thomas made it over there and talked to her.

He opened the door and peeked back in. The doctor nodded to him as he entered Conor's room. Timothy anxiously watched as the doctor examined his brother.

He stood by the door and waited. "How does it look, doctor?"

The doctor sighed. "Won't be able to tell for a day or so—not until the fever lets up. I'm hopin' it will happen today. The nurse is gonna apply cold packs to his skin."

Timothy stood there, his head hanging down. "Well, Doc, nothin' I can do here now ah guess it's time to get home to the missus. I'll ride back later today."

The doctor turned his head and nodded. Timothy felt despondent as he studied the man's expression. It doesn't look good, he thought.

— —

TIMOTHY'S BRAIN FELT LIKE SCRAMBLED EGGS on a breakfast plate as he mounted his horse at the corral. He looked up at the sun. It had emerged over the tops of the trees of Bear Mountain, working its way through a maze of whitish-blue clouds. Timothy trotted his horse westward, glancing at the door of the doctor's office as he rode by. He padded the stock of his carbine, making sure he hadn't forgotten it at the stable.

I need to start going to church, he thought, observing the spire as he passed. Madeline has mentioned it many times. Perhaps it would help Conor...help me, too.

Timothy set his horse into a gallop after reaching the corner of MacTurley's Woods. The Erlocks could be lurking in any of the small clearings up ahead, he said to himself, startling a red fox that had been lying in the field on the north side of the road.

He slowed his horse after coming abreast of the beginning of Thomas's fence. Most of the Herefords from a small herd near the road watched him as he continued westward. Minutes later, he dismounted in front of his house and dashed in to see Madeline.

— —

TIMOTHY RODE BACK TOWARD TOWN AFTER EATING SUPPER with his wife. He loved Madeline dearly and wished that he didn't have to leave her again, but his brother's condition was serious. Conor could die, he thought. It's important that ah be there.

Timothy hurriedly entered the doctor's office, eager to learn if his brother had made it through the day. There wasn't anyone else in the room when he tip-toed in. "Conor—holy almighty, you're awake."

He looked at the confused look on his brother's face. "Conor, it was me—shot and killed Kennedy. Ya remember that rascal, don't you?"

Conor opened his mouth to speak, but no words came out. "That's fine, Conor. Ya don't need to say anything," Timothy said, placing a hand on his brother's forehead. "My Lord man—the fever has let up."

Timothy smiled and sat down, noticing that his brother's eyes had followed him. He tried real hard not to show the pity that he felt for his brother. "Conor...."

Is now the time? Timothy asked himself, sending glances toward his brother.

He pulled his chair up near the bed. "Conor—" He patted his brother on the hand. "I moved away from home thinking that you—you were the one who murdered Patrick." Timothy noticed deep creases forming in Conor's forehead and looked up at the ceiling.

"The man who I shot and killed on my property the other day was Kelli Kennedy." Timothy swallowed hard. "Just before he died, he confessed that he killed Patrick."

Conor's mouth opened. He tried to talk. Then he coarsely whispered, "Thought it 'twas you who killed Patrick."

Timothy bowed his head and placed his thumb and forefinger across his forehead. "I'll be a son-of-a-gun. All these years, and we both thought the other did the killing." He shook his head. "Conor, would ya like me to call ye Collin?"

Collin nodded.

"Henceforward, you will be Collin to me and Madeline. Soon as you get well, I want you to move to my home."

Tears filled Collin's eyes. He slid a hand over to the side of the bed. Timothy grabbed it in both hands and lifted it to his mouth. He kissed it and smiled. "Ye get better now, Collin, do ya hear me?"

Collin smiled and nodded slowly, his head barely moving. Timothy looked into his brother's eyes, flooding with warmth that he didn't know existed. He stood and walked to the door. Turning, he smiled and waved. Once again, Collin's head moved slightly, following him out the door.

Timothy hurried across the street and entered the saloon. He didn't look back and hoped that his brother would be alright by himself. Pushing the swinging doors open, he strode to the bar.

Brett's stern, pock-marked face fixed on the Irishman. "What'll ya have today?"

"Whiskey, lad—whiskey."

Brett opened a bottle and filled the shot glass which he had just set down.

"Leave the bottle, barkeep."

38

THOMAS FELT SAD as he loaded Genevieve's and his parent's luggage into the carriage. "Up ya go, Mother," he said softly and assisted her onto her seat in the back of the buggy.

He watched his father's yearning eyes make a last sweep of the barn and corral. Knocking off a chunk of ashes from his cigar on the buggy wheel, Henry climbed the step and sat down by Emma.

Thomas flicked the reins and the horses began walking up the roadway. His brother, Grady, and Abel Kingsley had agreed to meet them on the road. When the buggy reached the turn, Thomas saw his expected escorts waiting a short distance away. He pressed the pair into a fast trot. Looking back, he saw his father stretching sideways to see his land for perhaps the last time.

His sister sat stiffly, looking straight ahead. Thomas knew that she felt eager to return to her family in Kansas City. As they approached Grady's roadway, he saw the church steeple pointing upward toward a clear blue sky.

He saw Genevieve staring at the schoolhouse. Thomas figured that her thoughts concentrated on memories of their youth. He respected and enjoyed his family's visit, but wondered why they all needed to suffer so much from the sadness of leaving.

As he had expected, the stagecoach was parked next to the depot, its very long naked, wooden pole tilting downward, its tip sitting on the ground.

He saw four men, including Lafe and Jesse Sunnerland, leading the team of six horses from the corral. Some of the horses strutted and clomped as they took their places in front of the coach. He watched them bring the steeds into alignment and begin to connect their harness to the long pole. Thomas stopped his team abreast of the coach. He remained in position as Grady and Abel removed the luggage and assisted the ladies from their seats.

Lafe Sunnerland stood by the step that he would use to get up into the driver's position. He paused and looked up at Thomas, his face somber. "Thomas, the Younger boys have all gotten captured!"

The news jolted Thomas. He remained seated and looked up at the sky. He narrowed his eyes and faced Lafe. "Are ya sure?"

Lafe nodded.

"Jaysus, Lafe, ah've had enough bad news lately, ah don't need any more."

Thomas's former neighbor didn't say a word, but his lips tightened together. Miss Pikes sat on the bench in front of the marshal's office. She had her face buried in her lap. He felt her pain.

Thomas took a deep breath. "Where did it happen, Lafe?"

"A swamp in Minnesota, near a town by the name of Madelia."

"Ah wonder what's gonna happen to 'em?" Thomas asked.

"If they're lucky, they'll only go to prison. They're lots of people who want 'em to hang."

Thomas directed his team to Toby's Corral. He left them and walked back to the stage depot, saddened by the news. He didn't see any of his family and assumed they had moved into the depot.

He walked over to Rosemary Pikes and laid a hand on her shoulder. "Sorry, Rosemary. Sorry."

She looked up at Thomas, her eyes wet with tears. "I knew it was gonna happen. I just knew."

Thomas tapped her shoulder gently and walked away. He stopped in front of the depot door, taking a seat on a bench and placing his head between his hands.

— —

THOMAS HUGGED HIS SISTER, helped her up the step, and followed her into the coach. The Concord had nine seats available. Henry took the rear seat by a window. Emma sat next to him. Genevieve sat down by the other window. Thomas held his mother's hand.

"Take care of yourself and Sarah," she said. "She will walk again, ya know."

Thomas gripped his mother's hand tighter. He looked into her eyes. "Do ya really—really think so?"

"I know so," his mother said and released her hand.

He shook his father's hand but avoided eye contact. He knew that his father really didn't like living in Independence and would rather be here on the farm. Thomas paused at the door to allow other passengers to enter the coach. They all moved into the front section. Nodding, Thomas stepped out of the coach and closed the door.

Lafe and Jesse had finished loading the passenger's luggage onto the top of the roof. Morgan sat up on the seat holding the reins. Thomas saw Lafe nod at Justin Haggard, who, along with Jesse McGregor, had agreed to escort the stagecoach to Stillman Mills. Thomas knew that his mother dreaded the thought of riding the coach and had to convince her that with Justin and Jesse going along, she and the others had nothing to fear.

Thomas had looked forward to his family's visit. Now that it was over, he felt an emptiness in his stomach as Lafe climbed up into the driver's seat. Morgan had moved over to take his riding-shotgun position. Thomas saw Jesse and Justin mount their horses and line up behind the stage.

"He-YAH! He-YAH!" The team of six bolted forward, jerking the stagecoach wheels into action. Thomas stood by his brother and watched as the bulk of wood and metal rolled onto the middle of the road. He felt a large part of his life drifting away as the coach faded into the distance.

The Posse

THE SURVIVING SIX BANK ROBBERS RODE toward Dundas, three miles south of Northfield. Jesse James and Jim Younger both nursed gunshot wounds on their way out of town. They stole one horse at Dundas before crossing the Cannon River Bridge, heading west.

Pursuit by two men, Jack Hayes and Dwight Davis from Northfield, began in about ten minutes after the gang raced out of town. Among one of the many mistakes that the robbers had made was not to cut the telegraph wire. News of the robbery and the direction the robbers were moving spread quickly.

Two hours and eleven miles after leaving Northfield, the bandits arrived in Millersburg. Amazingly, their behavior was unruly, attracting attention, strengthening and multiplying their pursuers. They continued on the Old Dodd Road, through Morristown, and into LeSueur County.

The size of the posse grew to over one thousand men. General E.M. Pope, a Civil War hero living in Mankato, assumed early charge.

Periods of heavy rainfall for the next two weeks hindered the different elements of the massive posse. Groups of men came from many of the area towns, including Janesville, Winona, Owatonna, Waseca, Eagle Lake, St. Paul, Minneapolis, St. Peter and others. The Northwestern Telegraph Company volunteered their services free of charge.

Five days after the robbery, the outlaws had covered a distance of less than fifty miles. Many of their pursuers had abandoned their efforts, but others would join. The noose around the robbers began to tighten in a wooded area near Mankato.

On September 14th, the robbers were getting desperate. Both Bob Younger and his brother James were severely wounded. A mutual decision was made: The Youngers and Pitts would remain; Jesse and Frank James would split, hopefully drawing the posse away.

Their plan worked. The Younger boys and Pitts sought cover in a

Welsh settlement for the next few days as the majority of the posse members pursued the Jameses toward Dakota Territory. Eventually the remaining robbers were forced from their hiding and they led their pursuers into a swamp seven miles north of Medelia.

In the thicket of the swamp, Charles Pitts said to Cole, "We are entirely surrounded. We had better surrender."

Cole Younger replied, "Charlie, this is where Cole Younger dies."

"All right, captain. I can die just as game as you can. Let's get it done," Pitts replied.

Minutes later, Pitts was fired upon. His body became riddled with bullets and he did die. The three Younger brothers continued their effort to escape. Heavy shooting took place, coming from both sides. James got hit in the mouth with a rifle ball, knocking out all the teeth on the left side of his lower jaw. He fell unconscious,. Cole got shot in the head, the bullet lodging above his right eye. He, too, became unconscious.

Bob Younger yelled, "I surrender. They're all down but me!"

Frank and Jesse James had escaped the posse, riding into Dakota Territory and eventually returning to Missouri.

See References in the back of the book.

39

COSETTE BARNARD THOUGHT ABOUT HER FIRST MONTH as a teacher in Tarrytown. She felt pleased with the progress. Most of the children appeared anxious to learn. The community had accepted her and she felt comfortable living in an apartment in the Smith Building.

Like all the other women in town, she feared the Erlocks. Every school day, she got Deputy Milburn to escort her to and from the schoolhouse. Thus far, she hadn't been approached by the outlaws.

Today, Friday, she planned on having dinner at Mamma's Kitchen as she had done regularly each week since moving to Tarrytown.

Yesterday's news of the capture of the Younger brothers didn't make her feel any safer. Though she knew they would never cause her any harm...not so with the Erlocks. She had heard all about Thomas Hastings's wife Sarah and the loss of her child and use of her legs.

Then she saw Collin McBride carried into the doctor's office. Cosette had warm feelings for the Irishman. He had been a proper gentleman when they visited on Main Street and in the restaurant. I will go see him after school is out today, she thought.

She dressed in a tight Basque jacket and skirt with a wraparound overskirt, all blue wool. She tied her hair back with a lace kerchief. After a final glance in the mirror, Cosette left her apartment and walked down the steps onto the boardwalk. She glanced to her left, pleased at seeing Deputy Milburn's saddled horse tied to the post in front of the marshal's office.

Cosette angled across the street and began to make her way toward the school. She anxiously glanced back and saw that the deputy was mounted and would soon be at her side.

"Mornin', Miss Barnard," the deputy said after coming abreast.

"Thank you, deputy. I appreciate this," Cosette said as she had done every school day previous.

The deputy set his horse to a trot, arriving next to the school ahead of her. Milburn dismounted and waited for the school teacher to arrive. He removed his hat and watched her enter the school.

— —

SHORTLY AFTER 4:00 P.M., COSETTE ESCORTED the last of the children out the door. She saw the deputy walking his horse toward them. Cosette's respect for the marshal's office deepened as she watched parents safely pick up their children.

She reentered the school, got her things together, and locked the door. Cosette saw two riders approaching on the road near the corner of the woods. She knew they weren't the Erlocks by the manner in which they rode their horses. It's the Hastings brothers, she said to herself, feeling good.

Cosette saw the deputy approaching on his horse from the east and she began walking toward the road. She stepped along quickly, feeling very confident with so many potential escorts. Cosette smiled wide as she waved to the two riders. Thomas diverted off the road, riding over to the school teacher. "Good afternoon, Miss Barnard."

"Hello, Thomas. How's Sarah?"

Thomas lowered his head. He forced a smile. "Sarah is good."

Cosette nodded. "I am praying for her. I want you to know that."

Thomas's lips tightened, his eyes narrowed. "Thank you." She saw him direct his horse back to the road to join his brother.

— —

THOMAS MUTTERED, "Some fella around here is going to be mighty lucky. She's a beautiful woman." He swung back onto the road and joined Grady. They decided to have a men's evening out and spend some time at the saloon and supper at Mamma's Kitchen.

"Hey, Grady, ah need to stop at Seth's for a bit. Ah'll meet you at the saloon shortly."

Grady nodded and Thomas rode on toward the mercantile as Grady tied his horse to the post in front of the saloon.

Thomas entered the store. He saw Marshal Buford talking to Mason John Miller near the back room. Thomas felt excited, seeing the aroused look on Mason John's face. They're going after the Erlocks, he said to himself. I should be going with 'em, he thought, but the marshal won't let me.

Thomas walked to the counter and brought out a paper from his pocket. He talked to the clerk, occasionally looking down at the piece of paper. The clerk nodded several times and grabbed the list.

He watched the marshal leave the store hurriedly, reinforcing his view that a major attempt to capture the Erlocks was imminent.

40

COSETTE BARNARD PAUSED ON THE BOARDWALK in front of the Smith Building, grabbing the handle of the door. She promised herself that she would visit Collin McBride today. She changed her direction and walked quickly toward the doctor's office.

She opened the door and entered the waiting room. Cosette looked around, seeing no one. She saw two doors in the room, one of them closed, the other partially open. Stepping quietly, she approached the open one. Pushing it farther, she peeked inside. Collin lay on a bed, his eyes closed.

Cosette entered the room and walked over to the patient. She cringed, noticing the paleness of his skin, and placed a hand over her face. What has happened to the handsome man whom I met on the stagecoach? she asked herself. Her eyes widened when his dark brown eyes opened.

They stared at each other for what seemed to her forever. Suddenly, he smiled widely, a pinkish color spreading over his cheeks. "I just had to come over and see how you were, Mr. McBride," she said, her voice wavering.

Collin opened his mouth partially, desperately trying to talk. He closed his mouth and jammed his elbows down against the bed, raising himself up. He tried again, this time finding words. "I am so happy—to see you—Miss Barnard."

Cosette heard a sound behind her. She turned. The doctor walked in, his face glowing with amazement. "Collin! I heard you speak!"

Collin's face beamed with delight. Cosette reached out her fingers and laid them against the back of his hand. Turning her head, she said, "Doctor, this man is going to recover. Do you see that color in his cheeks?"

"I certainly do, ma'am. You've done in a few minutes what no one else has been able to do in days—get him to talk."

Collin's lower jaw began to shake. He brought up a hand to support it. Then he said, "Miss Barnard is much prettier than you are—that's why."

Both the doctor and Cosette laughed loudly. She heard someone else come in the room. Looking back, she saw Rosemary Pikes. "Good evening, Rosemary," she said.

Rosemary clapped her hands lightly together. "I do declare. My man has come alive."

The doctor went out into the waiting room and returned with chairs. "You people visit for a bit—only a few minutes, please. The patient needs plenty of rest. Too much visiting could do him harm right now."

Half an hour later, Cosette returned to her apartment, feeling very happy with her visit.

— —

MARSHAL BUFORD SAT BEHIND HIS DESK reading the Jefferson City newspaper's report of the capture of the bank robbers. He had never met the Youngers nor the Jameses, so he didn't share the same feelings as others in Tarrytown. As far as he was concerned, they broke the law over and over again and had to be punished.

He realized that the Younger boys had friends in the area and he needed to remain neutral. The marshal's thoughts focused on the Erlocks and the heinous crimes that they had committed in his territory since he took on the job: making a cripple of Sarah Hastings, killing her unborn child, shooting Collin McBride and the attempt to rustle some of Hastings's cattle.

The marshal pulled on the brim of his hat and walked out onto the boardwalk, needing air. He felt encouraged that Mason John had agreed to accompany him the next morning. Buford had several thoughts in mind: track the Erlocks down, bring 'em into jail, and get a judge from Stillman Mills in for a trial.

He walked over to the saloon and entered, stopping next to the door, drawing glances from patrons. He saw Grady and Thomas Hastings sitting on stools at the bar. Pierre Mantraux sat by himself at a table in the rear. "Howdy, boys," the marshal said to the Hastings brothers as he strode toward the back of the room.

Buford didn't stop to talk to them, suspecting that they would want to ride along when he pursued the Erlocks. Pierre didn't look up as the marshal sat down on a chair at the table. "Mantraux, ah need yar help again."

Pierre looked up, continuing to play his cards. "When?"

"Tommora' mornin'"

Pierre lowered his head, continuing to deal and shuffle. "One day or more?"

"Best be prepared for more."

"I'll be ready at dawn."

The marshal stood and walked toward the door.

Grady Hastings watched him leave. "Looks like the marshal is up to something."

"Yup, I know. I saw him talkin' to Mason John over at the mercantile," Thomas said.

— —

MASON JOHN MILLER TOOK OFF HIS APRON after the marshal had explained his plan. Wisps of excitement crawled up and down his stomach wall. He looked back at his uncle. "Uncle Seth, I'll be back to help ya close."

He walked briskly out of the store and headed across the street for the corral, carrying a carbine and a gun belt containing two Colt .44 revolvers. Mason John needed to make certain that his black stallion would be saddled and ready in the morning. He talked to Toby.

Mason John hurried outside. He saw Thomas Hastings enter the saloon and felt the need for a thirst quenching mug of beer. Ah shucks, ah best keep my promise and help Seth close. Mason John crossed the street and reentered the mercantile.

— —

THOMAS LICKED HIS LIPS AND SET the mug back on the counter. "I'll have another, Brett," he said.

"Ah hear that Collin McBride is doin' a lot better," Grady said.

"Yup, sure is. Ah'll be glad when he's up and around. We miss him out at the farm. He's gotten real good at tendin' to the Herefords—good with the lasso, too."

The saloon door opened and Hjalmar Johannssen stood in the doorway. Grady looked at the burly figure and said, "Come on in, Jal—have a drink with us."

The immigrant stepped forward and paused. He smiled widely. "Yah," he said and stomped over, the bottom of his wide-soled boots dragging on the floor.

Thomas and Grady shook his hand. Brett handed him a full mug. The Swede lifted it, jiggled it a little, smiled and drank until it was empty.

The front door opened again. Mason John Miller walked inside. He headed directly over to the three men. "Hey, Mason, ah hear ya got somethin' goin' with the marshal," Grady drawled.

Mason nodded. "It's hard to keep a secret 'round 'ere."

Thomas handed him a full mug. "Drink up, Mason."

Mason John licked his lips. "Might tasty. Hey, Jal, ya best be careful with these dudes."

"Yah."

41

MORNING CAME. Cosette, still in her nightcap and gown, walked to the window and looked out. She saw a band of light forming over the ridge of Bear Mountain. It's the beginning of a beautiful day,

Collin, she said to herself, recollecting the pleasant thoughts of yesterday's visit.

She hoped that soon the handsome Irishman would spend part of his days sitting on the bench on the boardwalk. The loud neigh of a horse interrupted the stillness of the morning. She remained at the window and saw a horse and rider come into view.

Other horsemen appeared, all moving westward. She recognized the lead rider as that of Marshal Ben Buford. His tall stature dwarfed the gray gelding that he rode. A very large, holstered gun showed through the swept back area of a white duster. The brown stock of a carbine protruded from a leather scabbard.

Following the marshal, a white horse bore a rider totally dressed in black, a black duster hanging down almost to the level of his stirrup. A narrow, thin mustache curved slightly downward toward a narrow, pointed chin. The man sat straight in the saddle, his face straight ahead.

The largest of the three horses, a black stallion remained two to three strides back. She recognized Mason John Miller, the strapping young man who sat across from her on the stagecoach. He wore a white, high-crowned hat that made him appear taller then the other two, his duster the same color as the marshal's.

All of the riders had a bulky roll of blankets fastened to the wide strap between two saddle bags.

The three riders angled to the south side of the road and moved into the grassy area next to the school house. The horses lurched upward, taking the riders past the cemetery, and toward the mountain.

Cosette watched until they disappeared into the shadows of the foothills.

— —

MASON JOHN'S EYES SQUINTED catching the first rays of the morning sun. He knew they would succeed in finding the Erlocks instead of an underwear-clad detective. He chuckled thinking about the pudgy man stumbling his way down the trail.

Near the schoolhouse he saw a bald eagle dip its wings and land next to a rabbit carcass between the building and woods. His black stallion twisted its neck in defiance when he spurred it to catch up to the marshal and Mantraux.

They rode into the shadows of the trees following the well-used trail that began just beyond the cemetery. The horse's hooves clattered occasionally, striking the rounded rock projections. The mixture of cimmaron ash and burr oaks with an occasional black walnut tree dominated the landscape as they climbed. The height of the trees lessened as they continued.

They passed by a cluster of white spruce and arrived at the beginning of the east-west trail. The marshal dismounted and looked for tracks. "Do you see anything fresh?" Mason John asked.

The marshal nodded. "Yup, mostly deer tracks." He looked up. "We'll head east, boys."

Buford remounted and prodded his horse into a walk eastward.

Mason John jerked on the reins, holding his steed back, allowing Mantraux to go next. Hunger pangs began to play his empty stomach as the marshal continued to lead them up the trail.

Suddenly, the marshal raised a hand. He dismounted and squatted down by the trail. He pointed. "Someone's ridden here within the past couple of days." The marshal stood and scanned the surroundings for a time.

Buford squinted at Mason John and smiled. "Ya gettin' hungry, young man."

"I'm always hungry," Mason John said.

The marshal laughed. "We'll make a stop farther up. I remember a clearing some distance ahead. The view is better."

— —

MASON JOHN MILLER'S STOMACH sounded like rolling thunder in July when the marshal finally signaled a halt. He looked out over the valley, barely able to see the spire of the church in Tarrytown. The marshal had dismounted and unbuckled his saddle bag, bringing out a package.

"Here boys, compliments of Belle Streeter," the marshal drawled, smiling for the first time since they left.

Mason John's mouth gaped open. He turned to look at Pierre who narrowed his eyes, smiled and nodded. Mason John walked over to the marshal and grabbed a pre-cooked turkey leg. Buford handed him part of a loaf of bread. "Find yourself a place to sit, Mason John. Ah've got another of those drumsticks, if ya see fit." The marshal laughed.

He looked around. Spotting a tree at the edge of the clearing, he sat down at the base, keeping his back to the summit of the mountain so he could view the valley below.

After eating, they mounted and the marshal led them up the trail that continued eastward, at times leading to new heights of the mountain. The shadows from the trees behind them became longer and longer as the marshal drew them deeper and deeper into the mountain.

Mason John accepted his fate because he trusted the marshal. The success of their mission remained his number one priority. He shuddered hearing the roll of thunder coming from behind him. It wasn't dark yet, but the sun had set. The marshal signaled a halt. He dismounted near a small clearing, next to a rugged, rock-lined drainage bed coming down from the peak.

Pierre created a ring of small rocks. He had gathered dry pieces of wood and started a fire. Mason John felt sleepy after eating chunks of beef steak that Mantraux had baked over the flames.

The threatening clouds to the west held back long enough to allow them to finish dinner. Mason John spread out his bedding near a leaning oak tree. He looked up and saw the marshal approach, a folded tarp in his hand. "Put this over yar blankets, Mason John. It'll keep ya dry."

In minutes, sheets of rain began falling from the heavens. Mason John heard and felt the pounding on the canvas that the marshal had generously provided. He shivered and closed his eyes, feeling uncomfortable. And this, too, shall pass, he said to himself.

— —

THE CLANGING OF METAL COFFEE CUPS awakened Mason John the next morning. He opened an eye and saw rolling fog hanging over the upper two-thirds of the mountain. The marshal and Pierre sat on logs next to a wood fire. Mason John saw the flames reflect on a metal cup as the marshal lifted it toward his lips.

Mason John emerged from the confines of his blankets and tarp. He rubbed his eyes and smelled the coffee, reminding him of his uncle's store. Mason John shook off the water droplets from the surface of the canvas and grabbed a cup.

After a bread and bacon breakfast, the men saddled their horses, no words spoken. Mason John mounted and inhaled the crisp fresh air. He studied the gleam in the marshal's eyes, a hint that today they would meet up with the Erlocks.

They rode in silence for half the morning. He noticed that the marshal had slowed their pace. Suddenly, the law officer raised his hand, turned and placed a finger to his mouth. Quietly, the marshal dismounted, signaling for the others to do the same.

Mason John watched the marshal draw his revolver and slowly spin the cylinder. Mason John did the same with both his revolvers and looked at Pierre Mantraux, whose eyes had narrowed to black slits.

They followed the marshal on foot, eventually coming to a clearing. Mason John's mouth gaped open seeing the three Erlocks sitting around a dying fire, passing a bottle around.

"Hold it right there!" the marshal exclaimed, pointing his gun.

Mason John saw a flash of metal as one of the Erlocks turned his body. A gun blasted and he dropped to his knees. His right hand warmed as he pulled the trigger over and over again, spraying the Erlock with bullets. Mason released his empty gun after it clicked and reached across his body to his other holster, glancing at the marshal who also had dropped to one knee.

He saw Mantraux, who appeared beyond the marshal, holding two smoking revolvers. The acrid smell of gun powder filled the air. One of the Erlocks shrieked and coughed loudly. Mason John was about to pull the trigger again but he hesitated, seeing the pale-faced Erlock raise his hands in the air.

"Anybody hurt?" the marshal said anxiously, turning his head to face each of his deputies.

"Ah'm good. How about you, Mason?" Mantraux said.

"Good here!" Mason John yelled. He watched as the marshal used the toe of his boot to nudge each of the Erlocks who lay on the ground.

Mantraux advanced toward the standing Erlock, keeping the barrel of his guns pointed forward.

The marshal placed his revolver back into his holster. "Mason John, would ya get that coil of rope from my saddle?"

Suddenly, one of the downed Erlocks moved, his arm extended with a gun clenched in his hand. Both of Mantraux's revolvers exploded. The Erlock gasped and plopped back down to the ground, his gun flying out of his fingers.

Mason John inhaled deeply, his heart beating rapidly. He ran back toward the horses. Moments later, he returned with a coil of rope and handed it to the marshal. He watched the officer roughly jerk the pink-eyed Erlock by the shoulders, turning him around.

"Ya keep yar hands still, Bone, if ya know what's good for ya," the marshal said and wrapped the rope around the outlaw's wrists.

42

THOMAS STEPPED OUT THE DOOR OF HIS HOUSE. The severe thunderstorm lasted most of the night and Annabelle correctly sensed the need for a later-than-usual breakfast. He felt good because Sarah had recently shrugged off the tension that tormented her since the attack on Tarrytown Road.

He spent most of the morning with Luke breaking in foals to pull a wagon or carriage. Wiping perspiration from above his brow, he looked at Luke. "I'm going in the house for some eats."

Thomas removed his leather chaps and gloves, leaving them on a bench near the barn. The oak trees in a thicket on the west side of his house looked more orange than yesterday, he noticed as he approached.

Thomas walked in the door and hung up his hat. Turning, his mouth gaped open—Sarah stood next to the table. He had never ever seen her smile so wide. Thomas cautiously made a step forward, feeling sparks of excitement radiating throughout his body. He thought about their wedding day. This is bigger, he said to himself.

The only sound in the room came from Annabelle humming in the kitchen. Thomas's mouth remained partially opened. Then Sarah took a step toward him.

Thomas pounded a fist into his palm and felt his breath catching in his throat. "Sarah!" he exclaimed. "What happened? Am I dreaming?"

Annabelle came into the room, her round face smiling from ear to ear. Thomas cautiously walked toward his wife. He reached out his hand. She grabbed it. "Thomas, I can walk. I've been practicing for a week now, intending to surprise you."

"Surprise is right!" Thomas blurted, moving closer and holding Sarah in his arms, tears building quickly in both eyes. He closed them both and thought of his mother...she said it, he said to himself. She said that Sarah would walk again. How did she know?

— —

LUKE HITCHED THE TEAM TO THE CARRIAGE and rolled it up in front of the house on a late Saturday morning. He stepped back, tied the reins to a post and waited.

Minutes later, the door opened. He stared in awe, seeing Sarah, helped by Thomas, walk down the three steps. "Well, ah'll be danged," he said, smiling wide.

Thomas had never sat up straighter nor felt better as he walked the team up the roadway. He often glanced at his wife who sat on the seat next to him, smiling all the time. He didn't fear the Erlocks today, knowing that the marshal and his posse likely kept them occupied.

Nevertheless, when he reached the corner of MacTurley's Woods, he set his team to a gallop. As they passed over the site where they had been attacked, Thomas glanced at Sarah. She looked straight ahead and continued to smile.

Thomas slowed the team after coming abreast of the schoolhouse. Today is Saturday, he thought. There won't be anyone there. He saw someone sitting on a bench in front of the Smith Building. "Sarah, look, it's Collin McBride!"

He guided the team close to the north boardwalk and pulled on the reins. He raised up an arm. "Collin, look who I've got up here."

Collin's thick, bushy eyebrows appeared to cover half his forehead as he smiled. He stood and ambled over to the carriage. "Sarah, aye, 'tis you." He reached up a hand. She grabbed it and got up on her feet.

Collin's mouth gaped open.

"I'm glad to see that you are better, Collin," Sarah said, the crease of her smile reaching from ear to ear.

"That I am," he said, his eyes filling with moisture.

"Hey, Collin, when can I expect you out at the farm again?" Thomas asked, his face beaming.

"Soon, me man. Aye best get back in now. It's a little chilly out here."

Thomas stopped in front of the hotel and tied up the horses. He reached up and grabbed Sarah around the waist, assisting her down to the ground. He held only her hand as she deftly stepped onto the boardwalk. Thomas grinned watching Milburn across the street. The deputy stood in a crouched position, his arms dangling.

Thomas opened the door to Mama's Kitchen and led Sarah through. Belle Streeter hurried over. "Sarah! I can't believe it—you're—you're walking!"

She led them to a table, Thomas cautiously guiding Sarah along. He pulled out a chair for Sarah and sat down next to her, taking his hat off.

The door opened and everyone turned. Abel Kingsley let out a whoop. "Ah can't believe it! Is it really you, Sarah?"

He squeezed the shoulders of his sister tightly. "Thomas, it's a miracle."

— —

THOMAS PROUDLY ESCORTED HIS WIFE onto the boardwalk after eating. "I bet you can make it to the mercantile," he said, guiding her in that direction. They reached the edge of the building when he heard a yell from a man, part of a group standing on the boardwalk in front of the mercantile store.

"The marshal is comin'! They're back!"

Thomas saw a short column of riders approaching from the east. "Here, Sarah, best have a seat." He helped her to a bench. Thomas remained standing and continued to watch. Deputy Milburn walked out onto the boardwalk, joining a rapidly increasing number of spectators.

"It's the marshal all right," he heard someone say.

Thomas counted six horses, four of them mounted, two bareback. As they got closer and closer, now abreast of the corral, he placed a hand on Sarah's shoulder. "They got the son-of-a...."

Sarah turned her head.

"The marshal caught 'em. That's Bone Erlock himself. See those ugly pink eyes."

Sarah sat quietly, her mouth partially open.

Thomas looked down at this wife. Then back at the outlaw. He caught the pink eyes surveying every inch of Sarah's body. Thomas placed an arm around his wife's shoulder. "He can't hurt us anymore look at his hands. They're tied together."

Pierre Mantraux sat straight in the saddle, showing no expression. A long rope extended back from the horn of his saddle...back to a rider-less horse...well, not quite—a body draped across the back of the horse, directly behind the saddle. Mason John's saddle also connected to a rider-less horse, another body draped over its back.

The marshal led the procession to the rail in front of his office. He dismounted and pointed toward the undertaker's. Some of the men removed the bodies and carried them away. The marshal grabbed the outlaw and yanked him off the saddle. The Erlock swung his elbows viciously at the marshal's stomach. Buford grabbed his prisoner by the throat and shook him violently.

A large crowd had gathered around the new arrivals, making it difficult for Thomas to see what was going on. He looked down at Sarah and saw tears, knowing that their celebration over her walking had temporarily ended. We lost a child because of the brutal Erlocks, he said to himself, grabbing her hand. She held on tightly. Thomas didn't trust himself if he joined the crowd that had gathered around Bone Erlock. Ah'm afraid ah would shoot him...right there. He sat down, knowing that he needed to remain with his wife.

43

MARSHAL BEN BUFORD SPENT PART OF HIS DAY at the telegraph office on the Monday following the capture of the Erlocks. He needed a trial judge, a prosecuting attorney, and a defense attorney. Tarrytown had never had an official legal trial in its existence.

The marshal met with the mayor and a decision was made. The school house had been selected as the site because the meeting room next to his office was too small. "It shouldn't take more than a day—two at the most," the mayor said.

Buford knew that he needed to have the trial as soon as possible, because some of the local residents had been talking loosely at the saloon. A few whiskeys too many, and words such as 'lynch the bastard' began to surface. He didn't know just how far they would go. On most days, Buford spent his nights at his apartment in the Smith Building.

He doubted his supervisors would agree to an around-the-clock surveillance at the jail. It wouldn't take much coaxing for a few drunken, loose heads at the saloon to form a mob. Every single day since he had jailed Erlock, he made the rounds of the saloon before retiring.

Only one night did he have any reason for concern. Several strangers spent the evening in the saloon that day. The marshal gladly watched them ride out of town after the saloon closed.

The next day, after the prisoner had been fed his evening meal, Buford looked at the clock on the wall. The time had arrived to lock his office. His deputy had left for his home an hour ago. He walked to the door, stepped outside and saw several horses tied to the hitching posts in front of the saloon.

He turned the key in the lock and dropped it into his pocket. Two riders approached from the east. He stood in front of his office and watched them pass, one of them tipping his hat. They pulled up in front of the saloon and dismounted. After they entered, Buford walked across the street to the mercantile.

Seth's head bobbed up and down as he swept the floor near the back of the room. He looked up and said, "Evenin', Marshal."

"Seth. Mason John gone yet?"

"Yup, about an hour ago. I'll be locking up shortly."

The marshal nodded. "See ya tomorrow," he said and walked toward the door and left.

He hesitated on the boardwalk. More horses were tied to the rail since he entered the mercantile. Fourteen total, he said to himself, standing next to the door, counting. The setting sun looked spectacular—a giant red ball dipping down into a bank of gray-blue clouds in the west.

He took a few steps and paused, watching the sun temporarily break through, gradually lighting up the surface of the Tarrytown Road. He saw the school teacher walk out the door of Mamma's Kitchen and hasten across the street toward the Smith Building. Buford waited until she got safely inside, then walked through the door and into the saloon.

Most of the loud voices and laughter appeared to be coming from the cowboys sitting at a table in the rear. He saw Rosemary Pikes head that way, carrying a tray of whiskey bottles. Buford made his way over to the bar. "Good evenin', Marshal," Brett the bartender said.

The marshal nodded. "Ya got a bunch of live ones in here, I see."

Brett nodded. "No trouble so far."

"Have ye seen Mantraux around?"

"Nope, hasn't been in here all evenin'."

Buford frowned. He turned and walked toward the door, pausing and looking back toward the back of the room. He shrugged his shoulders and walked out the door.

— —

SHORTLY AFTER 11:00 P.M., THE MARSHAL LAID DOWN on his bed. He left his clothes on, his gun belt hanging on a chair next to the door. He fell asleep within minutes.

A gunshot woke him up shortly after midnight. Rubbing his eyes, he stood and walked over to the window. He saw several cowboys milling around their horses, one of them mounted and waving a pistol. The cowboy fired again into the sky.

Buford walked to his door, strapped on his gun belt and put on his hat. He stomped down the stairs and walked out the door, pausing on the boardwalk and saw the cowboys had mounted.

He instinctively walked rapidly toward his office. "Hey, Marshal," he heard. "We're gonna hang the Erlock. Would ya open the door?"

Buford didn't reply. He unlocked the door to his office and jail house and entered. Locking the door behind him, he edged over to the window. Some of the cowboys had walked across the street. One of them carried a rope. "Marshal, we want 'em. It'll save you a lot of bother. Them Erlock ain't worth it."

The marshal unlocked the door and stepped outside, holding a shotgun across his chest. "Yar gonna have to get by me, cowboy. Give it up and go home. The law will take care of Erlock."

"Ah come on, Marshal. Ya know he's guilty as hell."

"Try me, cowboy!"

"Break it up, boys!"

Buford turned toward the voice. He saw Pierre Mantraux standing in the street, his right hand fingers inches away from his gun. Then he saw Mason John walking from across the street, carrying a shotgun.

The talkative cowboy said, "Let's go, boys. We'll get Erlock another time."

The belligerent cowboys mounted and rode out of town toward

Stillman Mills.

44

THE TRIAL FOR BONE ERLOCK WAS SCHEDULED for Friday, October tenth. School children had all been dismissed at the close on Wednesday. The next morning, on Thursday, the marshal had organized a group of men to convert the school into a temporary court room.

Thomas Hastings, his brother Grady, Abel Kingsley, Jubal Haggard, Mitch and James McGregor, Mason John Miller, and Timothy McGearney began work after breakfast, rearranging the benches inside and hauling all the chairs stored in the mayor's quarters. They unloaded a wagon partially full of wooden posts. The marshal insisted that the hitching rails be expanded to accommodate a large number of horses.

At 4:00 p.m., the marshal rode up. He tied his horse to a rail and entered the school room.

"Boys, ya've done a good job. The judge will be pleased. Ah think the mayor owes ya all a drink. Ah'll see you all at the saloon."

Thomas and some of the others let out a whoop, and they almost fell over each other getting out the door. Mayor Blaise Harrington was waiting for them when they arrived. He had Brett set up shot glasses in front of each stool at the bar.

Abel Kingsley barged into the room first, followed by Thomas Hastings. They wasted no time in downing a shot of whiskey.

The mayor held up his hands after all the men had entered. "Because you all did such a good job, have another. It's on the house."

— —

THOMAS AND ABEL HAD THEIR ARMS around each other's

shoulders as they left the saloon and walked onto the boardwalk. "There comes the first one," Thomas said.

The classic sounds of a moving stagecoach had reached his ears. They hurried across the street, angling for the depot. Lafe Sunnerland, sitting next to Morgan Taylor, pulled on the reins. The smell of horse's steamy hides reached Thomas's nostrils as the horses came to a stop.

Morgan quickly descended from the seat and hastened to the door. He grasped the handle and swung it open. Judge Lewis Ringer of Lexington set foot on Tarrytown soil for the first time. The marshal and mayor moved forward, shaking the visitor's hand and welcoming him.

The judge used his large fingers to brush the dust off his long, dark-gray frock coat and matching waistcoat. Adjusting his purple-checked silk cravat, he took off his top hat and placed it against his chest. Running a hand through his graying, thinning hair, he looked around. "I gather this is Tarrytown."

The marshal nodded and pointed. "Ya've had a long ride. Some of the boys over there will help get yar luggage over to the hotel."

Thomas and Abel stepped forward, reaching up and each grasping a suitcase handed down by Lafe Sunnerland. The judge followed them across the street.

The second passenger to step down wore a gray bowler hat and a tweed suit, the jacket opened at the midriff. The marshal stepped forward. "Welcome to Tarrytown."

The round faced, much shorter man extended his hand. "My name is Landon Polk. I'm here to see that my client gets a fair trial. When can I see 'em, Marshal?"

"Anytime you wish. Perhaps you want someone to get you settled into the hotel first?"

The short man nodded and pointed at the top of the coach. Lafe lowered a large briefcase.

"Marshal, I'll be back within the hour."

Other passengers, all male, got off the stage. They represented various newspapers throughout the area, the farthest one being from St. Louis. After all the luggage had been removed, Morgan grabbed the bridle of one of the lead horses, and led them toward the corral.

Thomas and Abel had returned from the hotel. "There comes the second one," Thomas said.

Jesse Sunnerland and Justin Haggard waved as they pulled an identical-looking stagecoach up in front of the depot. A tall, lean-looking man with a narrow black, handle bar mustache exited first. He carried a black leather case. From a distance, Thomas overhead someone use the word 'prosecutor.'

Abel said, "His name is Alex Hines."

Thomas watched while several more men got off. I bet they're more newspaper people, he said to himself.

— —

BY 9:30 THE NEXT MORNING, half of the benches and chairs in the court room had been filled. Grady Hastings, Jubal and Justin Haggard, Lafe and Jesse Sunnerland, Mitch and James McGregor and Baskhall and Elkanah Jackson had all taken seats in the rear row, against the back wall.

The twelve male members of the jury sat in chairs lined up in two rows against the east wall.

Noisy talk in the room weakened when Cosette Barnard, Rosemary Pikes and Lady Constance, the only women in the room, sat down on chairs near the front. It ceased completely when the Marshal Ben Buford and Deputy Milburn came through the door. They led the prisoner, his wrists bound together, toward the front.

Bone Erlock attempted to jerk away and at times refused to take steps. The officers dragged the prisoner along, finally depositing the Erlock on a chair behind the defense table where Counsel Landon Polk waited.

Timothy McGearney and his wife Madeline slowly came up the aisle. They were followed by Collin McBride, his right arm in a sling. They found three chairs, three rows back, near the prosecutors table. The man behind the table, alongside Bone Erlock, sat stiffly with a stony face.

The judge, led by an assistant came in next. The aide quickly walked to the front and turned. "All please rise. The Honorable Justice

Lewis Ringer presiding."

The judge took a seat behind the desk and rapped his gavel. "Please sit down. Are both sides present?"

The defense attorney rose. "Yes, your honor."

"And you, sir?" the judge looked at the prosecutor.

"All here, except for our star witness. She should be along shortly."

"Very well," the judge said, and then the door opened.

The room became totally silent as Thomas guided Sarah up the aisle, followed by her brother, Abel Kingsley. They stopped next to the first row behind the prosecutor table. Abel led his sister into the aisle, followed by Thomas, and they sat down.

The judge pointed his finger. "Mr. Erlock, would you please stand?"

Bone Erlock stood. He curled his lower lip and narrowed his pink eyes, looking around the room. His crooked jaw stopped moving and he glared at Sarah Hastings. His attorney got to his feet and nudged his client, pointing his finger at the judge.

The judge cleared his throat. "Bone Erlock, you are charged with murdering the unborn child of Sarah Hastings—and—and causing her physical harm."

Judge Ringer stared at the accused. "How do you plead?"

Mr. Polk said, "Not guilty, your honor."

"Very well," The judge said. "You may begin, Mr. Hines," the judge added, pointing.

45

PROSECUTOR ALEX HINES STOOD. He walked out from behind the table, his long, thin legs moving gracefully. He stood as tall as Abraham Lincoln, differing from the former president by his small barrel-shaped chest. His long fingers brushed aside a plait of black hair that hung over his left cheek and then tidied his neatly trimmed, partially gray beard.

Hines spoke in low tones for ten minutes, explaining to the jury the horrors that the defendant had wrought upon this community. Toward the end of his opening statement, he walked over and stood in front of Bone Erlock.

He pointed his finger and raised his voice, "This man caused the death of Thomas and Sarah Hastings's child. The testimony you will hear from my witnesses will prove me right—the accused along with his brothers deliberately with intent to harm—provoked the carriage to overturn.

"Then! Then—while this man and his brothers were in the process of rustling the Hastings's cattle, he shot and nearly killed Collin McBride."

He took a step towards Collin and placed a hand on his shoulder. The prosecutor paused and walked over to the jury. "Yup, stealing cattle—that's somethin' they've done a lot of these past few years. Gentlemen of the jury, stealing is one thing."

Hines paused and eyed each one of the jury members. "Killin' an almost-born healthy child is infinitely more serious."

The prosecutor walked slowly and stopped directly in front of Bone Erlock. He pointed at the defendant. "Then to shoot and leave a man to die on the ground." Hines turned toward the jury. "That wretched human being deserves to die for his crimes!"

Hines took a seat.

The defense attorney stood. He cleared his throat. He glanced at the judge, then the jury. "My client did no such thing, and I shall show that the witnesses cannot prove any of these laughable insinuations. The real killer is sitting over there behind my client. It's the marshal and his deputies who shot and killed my client's brothers. Think about it."

The attorney's face turned red. "Yes, the marshal—the deputy—they attacked the Erlock boys on an assumption—an assumption of guilt. Why—Bone told me—he told me that he would've gladly come in if the marshal had asked him."

Several loud mumbles rumbled from the audience and the judge banged his gavel on the bench.

— —

"MR. HINES, WOULD YOU CALL YOUR FIRST WITNESS?" the judge asked.

"The state calls Doctor Blake to the stand."

The doctor explained the serious condition of Sarah Hastings when she was brought in after the attack by the Erlocks. Mr. Polk got the judge to strike that statement, arguing that it hadn't been proven that it was the Erlocks who attacked the carriage.

The prosecutor and defense attorney got into a heated argument over whether an unborn child is a human being. The judge sat with his fists pushing down on the bench. He allowed both men to argue all they wanted. After an arduous cross-examination, the doctor wiped his forehead with a towel before finally being dismissed.

Thomas Hastings got called next. Alex Hines asked him who the men were who had attacked and caused his wife injury. "It was the three Erlocks." He pointed. "Led by that man sitting over there—the one with the pink eyes. I shall never forget his face on that day—NEVER!"

Landon Polk walked right up to Thomas. "Pink eyes, you say? I don't think that the Erlocks attacked your carriage. I believe that the horses got away from you, and the accident was your fault."

Thomas stood, his face reddened. "You'd better get out of town and fast when this is over!"

The judge smacked his gavel heavily on the bench. "Mr. Hastings, I'll have none of that."

Polk smirked at Thomas. He walked back toward his seat and turned. "No more questions, Judge. That man doesn't know what he's talkin' about," he muttered loudly enough for the jury members to hear.

Collin McBride got called to the witness chair next. He pointed at Bone Erlock. "He's the one who shot me after cutting the fence."

The defense attorney talked only about the fence. "Did you see someone cut the fence, McBride?"

"No, but...."

"No more questions, your honor."

The judge ordered a noon recess.

— —

"MR. HINES, WOULD YOU CALL YOUR NEXT WITNESS?"

The prosecutor stood. He turned his head slightly. "I call Sarah Hastings."

Thomas stood and grabbed his wife's arm to assist her to her feet. He guided her into the aisle and then forward, expecting to help her to the witness chair. She gently pushed him away and continued walking on her own, the shuffling noise of her deliberate, small steps, the only sound in the room.

Several people gasped when she almost fell, catching her balance, causing Thomas to step forward. She turned toward him and held up a palm. He watched until she reached the chair and sat down.

The prosecutor tip-toed over to the witness and asked her several questions in a soft, kind-hearted voice. Sarah's voice quavered at times, but she spoke slowly and clearly with some of the jurors leaning forward in their seats.

Mr. Hines walked over and stood next to her. He looked out over the crowd. "Mrs. Hastings, do you see the man who did this awful thing—causing your carriage to tip—to hurt you—causing the loss of your unborn child? Do you see him in this courtroom?"

Thomas looked at his wife's eyes. Jaysus, they look just like ice, he thought. He heard several gasps coming from people around him as she stood and pointed. "That's him! The white one!"

Mr. Hines walked over and stood next to Bone Erlock. "Do you mean this man, ma'am?"

Sarah stood and took two steps. "Yes! I DO!"

The judge said, "Mr. Hines, would you escort Mrs. Hastings back to the witness chair? If you are finished, then Mr. Polk may have some questions."

Sarah turned to look at the judge. "Your honor, I don't want to talk to Mr. Polk."

The judge finally succeeded in convincing Sarah Hastings that she had to answer the defense attorney's questions. Teary eyed, she finally agreed, but refused to return to the stand, instead remaining in her chair between Thomas and Abel.

After one of the questions, Thomas stood and pushed the attorney away. Marshal Buford quickly intervened by grabbing Thomas by the arm. "Take it easy, Hastings—take it easy. Now sit down—"

Polk finished his first summation and took a seat. The judge looked at the wall clock. "You have ten minutes, Hines."

The prosecutor reiterated his earlier points, often walking back and in the aisle between where Sarah and Thomas and the jury men sat as he talked.

Landon Polk insisted that the Erlocks just happened to be riding by and Thomas Hastings was at fault. At close to 3:00 p.m. he said, "I'm finished, your honor."

The judge asked the marshal to remove the prisoner before anyone else left the courtroom. Buford grabbed Erlock by the shoulder and steered him toward the door. Deputy Milburn had patiently been waiting outside with horse and wagon. The marshal quickly assisted the prisoner into the box.

The rest of the attendees filed through the door and spread out in the school yard. Thomas led Sarah to their carriage and helped her into her seat. "We may as well wait here, Sarah," he said.

Abel Kingsley had followed them out and took a seat next to his sister. "This shouldn't take too long. It's an easy decision for the jurors. Hines did a great job."

Most of the other people remained in the school yard also. In half an hour, two men came out the door. One of them mounted a horse and rode toward town. The other raised an arm. "You can all come back in now. The jury has reached a verdict."

The people stood back and waited for Thomas and Sarah to enter ahead of them.

"We'll get the bast..., Sarah!" someone yelled.

After everyone sat, a shuffling sound at the door caused heads to turn. Marshal Buford literally dragged Bone Erlock up the aisle. He grunted as he flung the prisoner onto his chair. "Tie him to the back, Lance."

The judge entered and took his chair behind the desk. He ran the long fingers of his hand over his thinning hair. His eyes looked up at the jury over his metal-rimmed glasses. "Have you reached a verdict?"

"Yes, we have."

"Guilty or not guilty?"

"Guilty!"

46

THOMAS SAT STIFFLY EVEN THOUGH THE VERDICT satisfied him totally. He grabbed Sarah's hand and looked at her face. Her glassed-over eyes stared straight ahead at the jury foreman who had returned to his seat. Her lips quivered. "No one can give us back the life of our child," she muttered softly.

The judge rapped his gavel sharply to stifle the noise caused by Grady and the boys stirring in the back row. The marshal stood, draping his right hand over his low slung holster. He looked at Mason John. "Go stand by the door."

The judge rapped his gavel again. "Mr. Erlock, would you please stand?"

Bone Erlock glared at Thomas and Sarah Hastings. She placed a hand over her face and turned away.

"Mr. Erlock, are ya gonna stand or will I have to ask the marshal to git you up?"

Landon Polk tried grabbing Bone's arm, but the defendant jerked away. The marshal stepped toward them and glared. Bone Erlock stood.

Judge Ringer read from a paper lying on his desk. "Mr. Erlock, the heinous crimes which you have committed don't give me much choice. I order U.S. Marshal Buford to return you to jail. Then, as soon as convenient, you are to be hung until dead!"

Thomas stood in the aisle and watched his brother and the others leave. The school house began to empty, but the marshal and Mason

John remained near the prisoner, both anxiously looking around.

Sarah squirmed in her chair, her head lowered and cupped between her hands. "Take me home, Thomas. I don't want to be in the same room with an Erlock anymore, not for one second."

Thomas grabbed Sarah's hand. They begin walking toward the door, followed by her brother.

"Abel, would ya hold it up for a moment?" the marshal said.

Abel turned his head.

"Would ya tell Lafe and Jesse to get the stage ready. The judge wants to leave soon as possible."

Abel nodded and stomped up the aisle and out the door.

— —

THOMAS HELPED SARAH DOWN THE STEPS and to their carriage. "It's over with at last," she said, accepting his hand and stepping up into the seat.

He reached over and touched her on the shoulder. "We have to forget about the past and concentrate on our future. God will deal with Erlock.

Thomas untied the reins and got up into the carriage. He glanced toward the town as he approached the Tarrytown Road. I bet Erlock is back in his cell, he thought. His days are numbered, and then we can have peace around here again. Jaysus, it's been a long time. Actually, since I was thirteen years old.

The sun passed the darkening slope of Bear Mountain as it worked its way toward the place where it would set, just to the left of Tarrytown Road. Thomas felt a strange elation. Why, he thought, we can start over again. The doctor never did say that Sarah couldn't have any more children.

Thomas raised an arm and snapped the whip.

47

"LANCE, YOU KEEP AN EYE ON THINGS. Ah'll be back in two days," the marshal said to his deputy, Lance Milburn, on a sunny late September morning.

"Don't worry, Matt. Bone ain't goin' anywhere. Ah'm gonna watch him like a hawk."

The marshal mounted his horse. "Just remember, if you need any help, you've got Mason John over there." He pointed.

"Now git on with ya—ah'll be fine," the deputy said, scratching his whiskers.

He stood on the boardwalk and watched the marshal boot his horse, setting it to a walk up the middle of Main Street toward Harrisonville. "Time for a cup of coffee," Lance muttered and plodded across the street toward Mama's Kitchen.

"Hey, Belle, ah'll have some of yar breakfast fixin's," Lance said, smiling.

— —

THOMAS KISSED SARAH ON THE LIPS and walked down the steps toward his horse. He mounted and turned his head. "Take care of her, Annabelle," Thomas yelled. He waved and trotted his horse toward the road. He looked forward to meeting with some of the boys at the saloon. They had planned to do this some time ago, but decided to wait until the trial ended.

He arrived at the Tarrytown road and looked westward, expecting to see Mitch McGregor and the two Haggard brothers. He walked his horse slowly toward town, looking back occasionally. Maybe they got there ahead of me, he thought and spurred his horse into a light gallop. He stiffened and remained silent passing the place on the road where the Erlocks had attacked him and Sarah.

The pink-eyed bastard is gonna hang, he said to himself. Then we can relax. I've never passed by this place without thinking of them Erlocks. He glanced back and saw the rim of the sun fade into the dark blue landscape...no Mitch or Justin yet.

Thomas rode by the schoolhouse. He thought about his early days as a student. The new teacher is a good looker, he said to himself. Some young fella 'round these parts is gonna find himself a fine bride. Thomas halted his horse in front of the saloon, tying it to a rail next to Abel Kingsley's horse.

Thomas saw Lance Milburn come out the door of the marshal's office and stand on the boardwalk. Over in front of the stage depot, Hjalmar Johannssen held a flame up to a gas lamp. Then the Swede headed toward the deputy and the next lamp. It's time for a whiskey, Thomas thought, entering the saloon.

"Hey, Thomas, over 'ere," Abel Kinsley yelled and waved.

Thomas smiled wide and joined the boys at the bar. He said hello to Abe Kingsley, Justin Haggard and Mitch McGregor. "Brett, a whisky for my friend," Abel added.

"Hey, boys, let's grab a table," Justin said.

Thomas picked up his glass and followed. He paused and smiled at Rosemary Pikes who had walked over from the other side of the room. She wore a pleat-trimmed, dark-blue, silk skirt and a wine-colored short-sleeve blouse. "Can I get you boys anything?" she asked.

— —

HJALMAR JOHANNSSEN'S FACE GLOWED WITH PRIDE as he lit the first lamp in front of the telegraph and stagecoach office. He had accepted the job of lighting and putting out the Main Street lamps from the mayor. Hjalmar stood back and watched as the first lamp reached full brightness. Stomping down the boardwalk, he reached the second lamp in front of the undertakers. He saw Thomas

Hastings enter the saloon.

After lighting the third lamp next to the Smith Building, he headed across the street and lit the hotel lamp. The bank lamp became his next target and lastly lit the lamp in front of the mercantile store to glow. Hjalmar returned to the smithy. He had a hand on the door knob and a foot inside when he saw two riders approaching from the east.

A third horse, saddled but rider-less, followed. Hjalmar closed the door and watched through a window. The riders dismounted. He saw them tie up their horses to a rail and walk onto the boardwalk. Hjalmar reopened the door slightly and saw them stay close to the buildings and stop in front of the marshal's office. The two men disappeared. They must have gone inside, he thought.

Hjalmar hurried across the street and made his way toward the several horses tied to the rails in front of the saloon. He glanced at the marshal's office and saw no one, just the dim glow of a light through the window.

— —

THOMAS SAT DOWN AT A TABLE with his friends, Abel, Mitch and Justin. They jostled each other, getting louder with each drink. Thomas saw the door open and Hjalmar enter. He sensed something wrong watching the big Swede stomp across the floor toward their table. The big man's eyes opened real wide, glowing with excitement.

All eyes were focused on the Swede. He planted his boots and exclaimed, "Horses!" He held up three fingers. "Riders!" He held up two fingers. "Erlock—yah—"

Thomas shoved his chair back, knocking it over onto the wooden floor. He rushed to the door and pushed it open. The Swede caught up to him and pointed over Thomas's shoulder at three horses tied up in front of the smithy. "Yah! Three!"

Thomas turned and yelled. "Get yar guns, boys, they're breakin' out Bone Erlock!"

Brett, the bartender, rushed to the end of the bar and began handing out the gun belts. Abel got his and Thomas's and ran to the door.

Thomas grabbed his and moved outside, buckling it on. Mitch and Justin followed close behind, Justin taking long strides with his crutch.

Thomas turned toward Justin. "You stay here and guard the horses. Get the carbine out of my scabbard and use it if ya have to. We'll run over and take their horses."

The men ran across the street. Thomas untied one of the horses and led it toward the livery. Mitch and Abel followed with the other two. They took the horses through the door and tied them up in stalls. Thomas headed back toward the door and stopped short. Shots erupted behind him. Sounds like my carbine, he thought.

Thomas opened the door part-way and saw three men running toward him, shooting back toward the saloon as they ran. He heard a slug hit the outside wall of the livery. Thomas saw another flash in the saloon's direction. Justin had crouched to partially conceal himself behind a post. He fired at the outlaws. "Let's bolt the door and head out back!" Thomas yelled.

Mitch led the men past all the stalls to the big open door in the rear. "Jaysus, there they go!" he exclaimed and grabbed his pistol.

Thomas saw men running along the outside of the split rail fence, heading toward the far end where several horses had gathered near a pile of hay. Thomas put up a hand. "Mitch, you stay here. Abel and I will go up the sides—we can't let them take any of those horses.

48

BERTRAN LASSITOR STOPPED WALKING when he reached the window of the marshal's office. He put up a hand to stop his brother. Bartran peeked in and said, "Come on, Turk, the deputy's havin' a snooze."

He pulled out his gun and burst through the door. Deputy Milburn leaped off the easy chair, reaching for his holster.

"Ah wouldn't try that if I were ya," Bertran said. "Turk, get his gun."

"Yar not goin' to get away with this," The deputy said.

"The key to the cell—now!"

"I ain't gonna give it to ya. Yah'll have to kill me first."

Bertran threw a coil of rope at turk. Tie him up—hands behind his back first—then put him on that wooden chair over there," he pointed.

Turk roughly jerked the deputy's arms backwards and looped a rope around his wrists, tying a hard knot. He pushed the deputy toward the wooden chair and set him down, then he tied the waist and back of the chair together.

Bartran walked over to Milburn. He pushed the barrel of his revolver into his chest. "The key!"

The deputy shook his head.

"Turk, give me yar knife."

Bartran pushed the blade against the deputy's neck. "The key! Where is it?"

Milburn twisted his neck, desperately trying to move away from the blade. He felt his own warm blood seeping down his neck. "All right, it's in the bottom drawer—left side of the desk."

Bartran jerked the drawer open and threw out some papers. "Got it."

He walked down the short corridor, stopped in front of one of the cells and said, "Come on out, Bone, yar free."

Bartran walked over to the deputy and grabbed his gun off the floor. He swung and hit the lawman on the side of the head. "Thar, that should keep ya quiet, ya little weasel."

He handed the gun to Bone and led the way onto the boardwalk. Bartran loped toward where they had left the horses. He stopped dead in his tracks. "What the? The horses, they're gone!"

"Come on let's get those across the street," he said and began crossing.

A rifle blast sounded and Bertran jumped and dashed behind a post, cursing. A bullet zinged past. "Come on, boys, let's make a run for it—the corral. We'll get some horses there."

The three men ran past the smithy and headed for the door to Toby's livery. Bertran pulled on the handle—it didn't budge. He kicked the door, cursing some more. "Follow me!" he yelled and ran around the corner, following the outside wall of the smithy, heading northward toward the fence.

Bertran, followed closely by Bone Erlock, stopped at the northwest corner of the building. He stared at the big back door of the livery building. "Come on, the door's guarded. There's some horses out back." He pointed and they ran toward the far end of the corral. Part of the way there, they crossed the fence and moved inside.

"There they go, Abel," Thomas said. "You go up that side, along the outside of the rails. I'll take this side." He pointed.

Thomas hurried to the split-rail fence and crossed. He cautiously strode toward the far end, the dusk making it difficult to see. He heard voices and pulled out his revolver. Moving slowly, he could make out a pile of hay and someone moving. He pointed his gun upward and pulled the trigger. The horses panicked and ran toward the closed end of the corral. Thomas heard Bone Erlock curse loudly.

Just as Thomas had hoped, they fired back, and the horses galloped right by them, back toward the livery. They don't have a chance now, he thought. They're on foot to stay.

"Abel—Abel!" he exclaimed.

There was no response.

He took a couple more steps and heard the zing of a bullet pass by close to his head. Ducking down, Thomas saw the outline of a figure of a man along the fence. It's one of them, he said to himself. Aiming carefully, he pulled the trigger. The man screamed and fell.

Thomas heard Abel fire two shots and then another man yelped. Two down, Thomas thought.

Splinters of wood smacked him in the face and he hit the dirt. Then Thomas saw the man who he had felled earlier. "It's one of the Lassitors," he whispered. The outlaw carried a pistol and staggered closer. Thomas raised his gun. He held his breath and pulled the trigger. "Click."

He pulled it again—same result. "Oh Jaysus, ah'm in big trouble now," he whispered again. His legs felt like fence posts and they didn't move as he wanted to run back toward the buildings. He saw the pistol shake in his trembling hands. "Ah'm never going to see

Sarah again."

Suddenly, from behind him, he heard a boom—followed by a zing. Then another zing. The Lassitor's pistol dropped out of his hand. He staggered, clutched his chest and fell to the ground. Thomas turned. Mason John stood a short distance behind him, smoke coming from his rifle barrel.

Thomas took a deep breath. "Jaysus, Mason John—you've saved me." He rubbed a palm across his chest. Thomas yelled across the corral, "Hey, Abel, are ya there?"

"Hell yeah, ah got one of the Lassitors."

Thomas reloaded his revolver. "Only one left—it's the Erlock—Bone."

He looked at Mason John. "You stay here and cover me. He's behind that pile of hay and he's all mine."

Mason John opened his mouth as if to speak.

Thomas raised a finger. "All mine."

Mason John nodded and held up his rifle.

Thomas crouched as he moved slowly along the outside of the fence. He kept his eyes on the pile. Stopping to listen, he stared into the shadowy darkness. Suddenly, a figure ran from the hay pile toward the far corner of the corral. Thomas placed his revolver back in its holster and pursued. He approached the corner, thinking the Erlock had run out into the field. Suddenly, Thomas felt someone crunch him in the waist. He lost his balance and fell. Thomas felt pain and smelled whiskey. He bounced up quickly and saw the pink eyes. "Erlock," he muttered.

Bone Erlock swung at Thomas's head but Thomas ducked and the blow missed. Thomas ripped his adversary under the jaw with his fist, driving him back. Erlock grinned and lifted his chin, pointing toward it. Thomas faked a right. Erlock moved back a step. Thomas lunged at him, driving him to the ground.

Thomas landed on Erlock's chest but his momentum carried him past. They both rose to their feet. Thomas thought about Sarah. He visualized the sadness in her face when she first heard the news of losing their unborn child. Then he saw her smiling in the wheelchair. Rage flooded his mind.

He faked a left. Erlock ducked. Thomas planted both his heels into soft soil. He flexed his knees and took a deep breath. Thomas drove his fist upward into Bone Erlock's jaw. Thomas heard a loud snapping sound and felt pain in his hand. Flexing his fingers, he knew that he had broken Erlock's jaw bone.

Bone Erlock sneered and stayed on his feet. The outlaw reached down to his boot and pulled out a knife. Thomas froze in his tracks and backed up a step, holding his breath. His mind went blank. Then without thinking, he lowered his right hand and felt for his holster. His mind came alive. He grabbed the handle of his gun and jerked it out.

Thomas saw the pink in Erlock's eyes. He held the Colt in both hands and pulled back the hammer. Suddenly, Erlock came at him. Thomas squeezed the trigger. The gunshot rang out. Bone took another step and stopped. The outlaw placed a hand over his chest, an ugly smile forming on his face. Bone raised the knife, readying it for a throw. Thomas fired again. He saw a sudden change in the man's eyes—pink turned to white. Thomas shot at the outlaw one more time. Bone Erlock's eyes went blank and he fell to the ground.

Thomas heard running footsteps. He turned his head and saw Mason John and Abel running toward him. Thomas kept the barrel of his gun pointed at the fallen Erlock. He heard the earth crunching as his two friends stopped.

Abel bent over, trying to catch his breath. He coughed. "You got the bastard!"

Mason John knelt down beside the fallen Erlock. He looked up. "This one won't be botherin' anyone no more."

Thomas placed his gun back into the holster and lowered his head into his hands.

Abel placed a hand on Thomas's shoulder. "It's over, boys. The last of the Erlocks has bit the dust."

Thomas looked up at the blackened sky. "Sarah, we're free at last."

BOOK THREE

TEN YEARS LATER: 1885

1

THOMAS HASTINGS DIRECTED HIS TEAM toward Tarrytown on a warm day in June of 1885. His son, Matt, sitting next to him, scanned the sky, looking for Keeya, his hawk. He placed a hand up over his face, shielding his eyes from the mid-morning sun.

The one room school house that he attended appeared after they passed by the corner of MacTurley's Woods. Matt had celebrated his ninth birthday on April 15, shortly before graduating from the third grade. Matt watched the sky above the tree line, hoping to see the hawk.

He pointed. "There it is, Pa!" Matt exclaimed, his high-pitched voice hadn't yet reached the age of change.

His mother, sitting next to him, smiled and patted him on the shoulder. "My rabbit, Hops, didn't care for your hawk very much when I went to school there. He had to watch out for his life every single day."

Thomas pulled on the reins, slowing the team. "My pa used to laugh at me when ah called Keeya mine."

"You gave him to me, remember?" Matt said, his head turning upward.

Thomas laughed and flicked the reins, rolling the wagon past the schoolhouse. "Yar right, son, it's yar hawk—don't let anyone tell you any different."

"All right, boys, now you've got the hawk problem solved," Sarah said, laughing.

— —

THE HASTINGS FAMILY HAD GONE THROUGH major changes during the past ten years. Henry Hastings passed away in Lexington, Missouri in 1882. Thomas's brother, Grady, followed his father to the grave one year later, dying of a cancer.

Helen sold the land that her father had left to her, and moved to St. Louis with her son, Tyler, age eighteen, and daughter, Clarissa, age sixteen. Tyler had a keen interest in railroads and committed himself to becoming an engineer. As a young boy, he had often spent time at their northern property line, watching the trains rumble by.

Emma, Thomas's mother, continued to live with Genevieve and her husband in a house in the outskirts of Kansas City. Thomas knew that his recent decision to sell his farm, cattle and horses bothered his mother immensely. Since Grady had passed away, Thomas had lost his heart for farming. He had studied other options during his lifetime a great deal, and finally accepted a provisional position with the Union Stock Yards in St. Paul, Minnesota.

He felt pleased that Collin McBride married the former school teacher, Cosette Barnard. Then they agreed to buy his farm. The couple had been living in a small house up the slope of Bear Mountain near Tarrytown. Timothy McGearney, Collin's brother, who owned the farm next to him, encouraged Thomas to make the move.

Thomas realized that for the past few years Timothy had coveted the Hastings's land. His neighbor intended to expand his wool operation. Thomas witnessed large wagons, owned by a shipping company in St. Louis, passing by with ever-increasing frequency. They hauled the baled wool eastward toward the railroad station in Stillman Mills.

Thomas's biggest concern focused on his wife, Sarah, and how she would adjust to the move. Her parents had both died in the past ten years, and she had only one relative left, her brother. Abel had married in the late 1870s, but his wife had died during childbirth. Abel continued to live alone, tending to his Angus cattle along with his partners, Baskhall and Elkanah Jackson.

Thomas reached over and touched Sarah on the shoulders. She turned her head and smiled. They had decided to take the wagon into town—she needed to go shopping. Thomas brought the horses to a stop in front of the Mercantile Goods & Services store. He stepped off the seat. His son had already done so and stood in front of the window looking at merchandise. Thomas walked around the rear of the wagon to the other side and reached up for Sarah's hand.

"You know, Thomas, every time that I make a step, I am thankful to the Lord." She stood on the boardwalk and looked around, her face beaming with pleasure.

He nodded, a wide smile forming on his face. "I sure miss Seth, though."

"How long has it been since Mr. Miller died?" Sarah asked.

"Three years. I used to feel so sorry for him, watching him snuggled under his blanket, sitting on a bench in front of the store for two summers."

"Now where did that young fella go?" Thomas looked around. He yelled, "Come on, Matt, let's get in there and talk to Mason John."

Matt led the way into the store. He walked right over to Mason John, who had taken complete control when his uncle fell ill—something involving lost blood supply to one side of his body and part of his brain.

"How are you there, young man?" Mason John asked, tapping Matt on top of his hat.

"Mr. Miller, I've come to pick up the books that you ordered for me."

Mason John placed a hand on his forehead. "Oh, yes. Ah remember now. They're in a box in the back room."

Thomas and Matt followed the owner through a back door leaving Sarah to browse the materials near the front window. She made some selections and waited with them at the counter.

Thomas paid for their purchases and then loaded the box and other supplies into the wagon. Thomas helped Sarah onto her seat and led the team on foot, turning them westward.

He glanced at the weathered boards of the hangman's scaffolding that filled some of the space between the smithy and the telegraph office. The never-used facility was built to hang Bone Erlock ten years ago, just before the attempted escape and the shootout at Toby's corral.

Thomas thought about the spectacular trial of the last remaining Erlock, Bone. The jury convicted the outlaw of killing his and Sarah's unborn child. The judge had sentenced the outlaw to die by hanging. It took the men only one day to build the scaffolding. Thomas's thoughts painfully fixed on the past, when the community lived in continual danger because of the threatening Erlocks.

He remembered pulling the trigger and killing the last of them at Toby's Corral.

— —

MATT BURIED HIS FACE INTO THE OPEN PAGES of a book on their way back to the farm.

Thomas thought about how disappointed he and the rest of the community felt when Marshal Buford left town on the stagecoach, never to return. A few days later, while Thomas worked on his fence near the Tarrytown Road, he saw Pierre Mantraux riding west, a huge roll tied behind his saddle.

Thomas knew that he would never see him again, either, and that he and his wife Sarah owed him their lives. He stood and watched the black-clothed rider until he rode over the bridge and disappeared from sight.

Thomas's wagon rolled along next to his barbed wire fence. Some of the Herefords watched with their usual disinterest. Now that his father and Grady were both gone, he didn't feel guilty about leaving the farm.

He saddened, realizing that he would miss the two Haggard boys. Jubal continued to farm and his brother rode shotgun for the Wells

Fargo Stagecoach Line. Justin belonged to a stagecoach driving team, including another former Gray Rider, Lafe Sunnerland.

Lafe's brother Jesse, who used to work for Wells Fargo as a stagecoach driver, had met a woman in Topeka, Kansas. They got married and Jesse moved away from Tarrytown to work for his wife's father, a banker.

He turned the team onto his roadway, feeling sad, knowing that he wouldn't be doing that much longer.

2

COLLIN MCBRIDE GOT UP ON HIS WAGON SEAT. He had mixed feelings regarding his neighbors leaving. I'll sure miss 'em, he thought, but bringing me bride here to live will be pure heaven. I'll have me own place—and right next to me brother, Timothy.

His head dropped down after glancing at Thomas and Sarah who had just exited their house for the last time. Collin remembered how he felt when he left his land in Ireland. I wonder if it's the same for everyone, he thought.

Thomas led Sarah to the wagon. He looked toward the barn and yelled, "Matt, it's time to go!"

Collin watched the lad run toward him and the wagon. He got there ahead of his parents, scooted up the steps and into the box, sitting down quickly on a stool. Collin knew that Matt looked forward to the adventure that comes with moving to a new land. He had talked to the lad many times in the past, the youngster telling him what he had learned about Minnesota.

For her journey, Sarah wore a silk skirt underneath a polonaise walking suit of wine-colored, light-weight wool. After Thomas boosted her up the step, she straightened her bonnet, trimmed with artificial silk violets.

Thomas took his seat and looked back. "Are ya ready, Matt?'

"Yes, Pa."

"There comes yar brother," Thomas said to his wife.

A lone rider walked his horse slowly toward them on the Tarrytown Road. Thomas flicked the reins and the wheels began to roll. That's gotta be Abel, he thought.

Thomas's brother-in-law sat straight in the saddle, a glum look on his face as he waited for the carriage. Thomas felt guilty taking his sister away and wished that Abel would find himself a woman.

Collin set the team into a trot and headed toward Tarrytown. Abel followed. Thomas turned his head and stared at the house where he had been raised. He raised a hand slightly toward the Herefords inside the fence. At least the cows won't know the difference, he thought.

The tree tops of the mountain formed a wavy line from west to east. Endless gray clouds stretched beyond the horizon. 'Tis a fitting day for us to leave, Thomas thought.

He thought about his father and how he would have been shocked and disappointed. He'd have a fit if he were alive, Thomas thought, smiling. Pa used to say: '*This farm will stay in the family forever.*' Grady would have understood the move. He always knew that farming was never going to be my thing.

Thomas shuddered thinking about his mother. She'll have the fits, he said to himself. If Emma sat in this wagon right now, she wouldn't admit that she knew us. Genevieve couldn't give a squat whether we moved or not. She never liked the farm.

The wagon approached the corner of MacTurley's Woods. Thomas turned his head for one last look. He noticed that Matt did the same thing. "Are you going to miss the farm?" Thomas asked his son.

"No, but I'll miss Keeya."

Thomas smiled and looked at the tree tops. He felt Sarah's frame stiffen as the schoolhouse came into view. The trial of Bone Erlock had occurred in that building nearly ten years ago, but Sarah had never set foot in the building again. That may be why she is so cooperative with our moving away, he thought.

Looking ahead, he saw a reddish-looking coach parked on Main Street. It's waitin' for us, Thomas said to himself, raising his resolve to successfully move his family.

Collin's horses pulled the wagon up to the boardwalk just behind the stagecoach. "Whoa," he said softly.

Matt jumped off first and stood next to the coach, looking up at Justin Haggard who busied himself arranging baggage on top.

"Well, Sarah, we're here," Thomas said and stepped down. He escorted her to a bench in front of the stage depot and assisted Collin in carrying the luggage from the wagon to the coach.

"Well there little fella, 're ya leavin' us for a spell," Lafe Sunnerland said to Matt, wiping his lips with his gloves after a wad of spit hit the surface of the street.

"I'm going to St. Paul. You know where that is?" Matt asked.

Lafe shook his head. "Naw, ah don't, but I heard that it ain't too far from where the Youngers got caught."

Thomas and Collin finished carrying their bags, setting them down next to the coach. The smell of manure and damp leather permeated the air as Lafe stepped up onto his seat. Justin finished placing the luggage and he sat next to Lafe, adjusting his breeches and shirt into a comfortable position. He laid his white duster on the seat next to him, looking up at the overcast sky.

Justin removed a revolver, and spun the cylinders. After placing it back into the holster, he went through the same procedure with a second and a third. Justin pulled out his carbine and sprung open the action. Satisfied, he closed it and placed it back into the scabbard.

Abel Kingsley stood next to his sister at the stagecoach door. He grabbed her tight, tears filling his eyes. "Ah'll come visit next summer," he said, his voice trailing off.

"You take good care of yourself, brother. Do ya hear?'

Abel nodded, gave his sister one last squeeze and helped her up onto the step. Matt, who had already taken a seat by the window put his book down and helped his mother into the middle seat.

Thomas shook hands with Collin McBride and Mason John Miller. "Stay out of trouble, fellas," he said and quickly stepped into the coach.

The depot agent came out the door. He held a clipboard in his hand. The agent wore a blue-shaded, brim-banded hat pulled down over his eyes. He raised the brim and looked up at the sky, then at the two drivers. "You boys better have your rain dusters along."

Lafe pulled his up off the seat and lifted it. The agent smiled, waved and went back inside.

"He-YAH!"

3

THOMAS SAT BY THE WINDOW AND WATCHED the mercantile store get smaller and smaller as the stagecoach rolled out of town. No one spoke a word as the coach picked up speed and sound of harness and buckles filled the air.

He reached over and touched Sarah's hand. She looked up at him and smiled. "We're going to have a good life in Minnesota, husband. Matt will attend the University. He will become educated."

Thomas squeezed her hand and looked out the window. He saw the giant black cross that marked the gravesites of those that died during the Battle of Tarrytown. He had heard the tale so many times that he had a strong visual image of it. Over forty of the Riders lined up on the east side of town. His brother Grady had raised his saber and ordered the charge against an approaching Union Cavalry unit.

Each time he had heard someone tell the story, Grady's victory charge got more exaggerated—a lop-sided battle. Thomas smiled, thinking about the saloon and the stories he had heard. "Grady and his men drove them Bluecoats clear up and over the mountain," Deputy Milburn had said.

Thomas chuckled remembering one man at the saloon who raised up his arms as high as he could, a glass of whiskey in each. *Ah saw that flash of light come off that saber and thought it came from the heavens. We was ridin' with the spirits.*

Thomas knew better. He believed the version he had heard from Lieutenant Farnsworth. The Union officer had said that if Quantrill hadn't showed up when he did, Tarrytown would have fallen to the

Union. Beyond the cross, on top of a small hill, he saw another cross—a very small one. That's where the Erlock's and Lassitor's were buried—Boot Hill, they called it.

He reached in his pocket and pulled out a paper. He re-read the letter which he had gotten from the Union Stockyards of St. Paul. They had offered him a promising position of employment, one of the reasons why they headed north.

— —

THE COACH SLOWED AS IT ENTERED STILLMAN MILLS. Matt looked out the window. "The train ain't here yet, Mother."

Don't worry, son, it will be here soon enough," Sarah said.

The coach finally came to a stop at the train depot. Lafe had come down and helped Sarah and Matt out. "It should be along soon," he said.

Lafe grabbed Thomas's hand and said, "Ah'll miss ya hangin' around, Thomas." Lafe gave Thomas's midsection a big squeeze. "Ya'll be back some day, ya just wait and see."

Matt and Sarah had gone inside the depot and Thomas felt waves of mixed feelings flow through his body, color moving into his cheeks. He looked up and saw Justin holding a piece of luggage over the edge. Lafe pushed him aside gently, grabbed it, and set it down. Thomas sat down on the bench and watched his dear friends unload the rest of the luggage from on top.

Two strangers entered the coach. Thomas knew the time to leave approached watching Justin and Lafe climb up to their seats, readying for departure.

Thomas saw Lafe stand and raise a hand up high, signaling the depot agent. They're about ready to roll, he said to himself, watching Lafe sit back down.

"He-YAH!"

Thomas lit a cigar and saw the back end of the stagecoach as it rolled eastward. He stood in one spot and watched until the bobbing heads disappeared from his view. He took a deep drag from his cigar, feeling an emptiness building in his stomach.

Just then, he heard the shrieking whistle of a train horn. He felt someone touch his arm. Turning, he saw Sarah. "Thomas, why don't you come in and wait with us?"

"I'm watching Lafe and Justin leave."

"But I don't see them any longer. They're gone."

Thomas rubbed two fingers across his eyes, dropping his hand to his chest. "Justin and Lafe will never be gone. They will always be here."

4

MATT SAT NEXT TO HIS MOTHER. He heard, "All ye board!"

He felt a jerk, then several more. The depot building that he saw out the window began to move. "Mother, how come the building is movin' and we're not?"

Sarah laughed and reached out her hand. "We're the ones who are moving. Here, give me your hand and close your eyes."

She placed his hand against the seat. "Feel that, the seat is moving and so are we."

Matt grinned from ear to ear. He sat down and pressed his nose against the window glass. "The buildings are movin' faster than ever," he said, smiling and scratching his forehead.

"Sit down, Matt, you're making me nervous," Sarah said and closed her eyes.

The train clattered along, heading for Kansas City. Matt watched the countryside. He saw the steeple of a church. "Is that Tarrytown church?"

"Yes, it is," she said and yawned.

Matt narrowed his eyes and he thought about the funeral, the only one he had ever been at. It happened about two years ago. He remembered sitting in the back of the carriage when arriving at the church. His father and mother did not talk. No one did.

His father kept him from falling, by grabbing his arm up when he tripped on the carpet in the middle of the aisle. He sat squeezed between his parents listening to a tall, funny looking man talk and talk....

When the funny man finally sat down, six big men stomped to the front of the church where a large wooden box lay on the floor. Three of them got on each side and they picked it up. They began carrying it to the door. He couldn't see a thing as he followed behind it.

Outside, the pallbearers loaded the box in a wagon. A man wearing a black suit and a white shirt got up on the seat and the wagon begin rolling up the slope toward the cemetery. A short distance in front of the wagon, a man with only one leg, using a crutch, led a rider-less horse by the bridal.

"Pa, there's no one riding the horse. Why?"

Matt made a few more steps before his father answered. "Matt, your uncle Grady is on that horse. You just don't see 'im."

Matt frowned and looked up at his father's face. His mouth opened as if to speak, but he didn't say anything, seeing his father place a finger to his lips.

Matt's mind drifted to an evening at his home some years ago. He had gone up to bed. His father and a group of men, visiting their home drank whiskey and talked about old times. He lay on his bed, soaking in the words that he had heard from down below. Grady's low murmur painted a picture as if he had been there himself. Matt could see Grady Hastings spread out his men along the eastern border of Tarrytown to defend against a Union cavalry coming up the road. "Sabers!" his uncle had yelled. "Charge!"

Matt visualized his uncles, Grady and Abel, sabers waving in the air, charging the enemy.

The wagon arrived at the cemetery. Matt didn't think they were ever going to get to the top. The pallbearers removed the massive box and set it down by a deep hole. Matt saw a square stone planted in the ground nearby. He tried reading the words: *Will Walker...Battle....*

Then the preacher man opened a big black book and read for a time. Matt remembered his last words. "Grady Hastings, we commit you to join your Maker."

— —

SARAH AWOKE AND LOOKED OUT THE WINDOW. She saw many buildings, some of them large. This must be Kansas City, she thought, watching a large volume of smoke emitting from massive smokestacks. She glanced at her son and felt glad that he had fallen asleep, his face sunk into a pillow next to a book.

She thought about the happy look on Cosette McBride's face as she and Collin toured their house. It would soon be theirs. She will be totally happy and I am happy for her, Sarah said to herself.

Sarah thought about their wedding of so many years ago. Even though the air outside felt bitterly cold, it felt warm in the church that day. Cosette wore a striking bridal dress of white satin draped with brussels lace and trimmed with orange blossoms.

The two McGearney brothers—one of them had changed his name—dressed almost alike, she thought. Collin's tailcoat appeared a bit longer, and a little darker brown. Their satin lapels looked identical.

The train began to slow. She saw Matt stirring. Her husband's head remained in the corner, his eyes closed and mouth partially open. She felt the first jerk and Thomas's eyes opened. Matt got off his seat and stared out the window. "Look! We're in a big city."

— —

THOMAS FELT GOOD AFTER HE SUCCESSFULLY TRANSFERRED his family and their luggage to the Hannibal & St. Joseph Railroad Company train. As it left the station, he picked up a bulletin and read about the huge railroad bridge that had been built across the Missouri River.

Suddenly, the train slowed and he knew they were about to cross it. "Matt, look at the river. We're going to cross over a huge bridge. It has six super piers, sunk to bedrock. Would you believe that it took

1,500,000 feet of lumber to build it?" Thomas looked at his wife, grinning. "And you, young lady, might be interested to know that it took 16,000 cubic feet of concrete."

Sarah laughed and placed a hand over her mouth. She glanced at her son, who looked thoroughly confused. "You've really impressed your son."

Sarah tapped Matt on top of the head. "I don't care how many materials it took to build it. I'm only interested in getting safely across—right, Matt?"

The youngster nodded.

The train increased its speed after crossing the bridge. "Where are we headed now, Pa?" Matt asked.

"Next stop, according to my map, is Union Station in St. Joseph. Then after that we don't stop until we get into Iowa."

"Iowa, what's that?"

"It's one of our states, mostly a huge flat piece of land between Missouri and Minnesota. Sioux City, it says here—then we are going to transfer again, this time to the Chicago, Central & Pacific Railroad."

Sarah clasped her hands and placed them over her head. "Do you realize, Thomas, that neither of us have ever crossed the Missouri border?"

— —

THE HASTINGS FAMILY SPENT TEN HOURS WAITING for a train in Sioux City, Iowa. They boarded shortly after 6:00 a.m. Thomas frowned, glancing at his pocket watch. He carefully placed it back into his vest pocket, treasuring his father's gift.

He felt confident he would succeed at the stockyard job. He could offer considerable insight into the formation of the new stockyards on a 260-acre track alongside the Mississippi River, three miles south of Saint Paul. Hadn't he worked with cattle since he was a small boy?

Thomas looked forward to meeting Alpheus B. Stickney, president of the Chicago Great Western Railroad, and one of the chief organizers. Thomas had been informed that English investors, the

Robert H. Benson and Company of London, had agreed to buy two million dollars in mortgage bonds to provide the capital to build the facility.

Matt sipped from a glass of milk sitting next to a window in the diner. Thomas envied his son, his whole life ahead of him...education in the makings.

"Look buffalo!" Matt exclaimed.

A herd of at least one hundred animals browsed prairie grass in a shallow draw. The land sloped down to a creek lined with shrubs and small trees. A white-uniformed African-American waiter stood next to the table. "You'll see many more of those big brutes as you head north, young man."

Hours later, they had crossed the Iowa border. "Thomas, look, we're in Minnesota," Sarah said.

"How the devil did you know that?"

"I saw a sign back there a ways," she said, pointing.

The train slowed for a town. Thomas looked at his map. "This must be Albert Lea," he muttered, looking out the window and seeing a railroad man pick up a stick with a wire loop on the end.

5

"WE'RE HERE AT LAST," THOMAS ANNOUNCED as the locomotive screeched and came to a jerky stop in the early afternoon hours of a June day in Minnesota. The sign outside next to a small wooden building read: *Saint Paul Union Pacific Depot*.

Thomas made certain that all their bags had been stacked by the door before stepping down onto the platform. He helped Sarah down first, and watched his son get down on his own. The blue sky above played host to only one visitor—the sun.

"Well, Matt, how does it feel to step onto Minnesota soil for the first time?" Thomas asked.

Matt stomped his foot. "Solid."

Thomas slapped at his cheek, feeling the sting of an insect. "Uh-oh," he said. "I've heard about Minnesota mosquitoes. This is a big one." Thomas swept the carcass off his palm with his hand.

"Pa, there's our name."

A horse hitched to a wagon stood nearby nibbling at tufts of grass. The man up on the bench seat held up a sign: *Hastings*. Thomas felt that the money had been well spent, hiring a firm to provide a driver and wagon. They would be delivered to their new home without delay. He felt nervous regarding the furniture and furnishings that had been shipped days in advance, and he hoped, especially for Sarah's sake, that they would be in place in their new house.

"No, don't touch a thing, Sarah," Thomas said. "Matt and I will get it loaded."

Thomas helped Sarah into the seat next to the driver, and he and Matt sat on luggage pieces in the box. The driver snapped a whip and they rolled southward, back in the direction from which the train had come.

The wagon climbed a slope that Thomas thought was at least a mile in distance. The space between houses became less and the quality of the buildings improved dramatically. His spirits rose when the wagon came to a stop in front of a wooden, two-story house with two bay windows on the ground floor.

Thomas climbed down from the wagon and walked around quickly to assist Sarah. He helped her down and held on her hand, walking her two steps toward the front door. "This is our new home, folks. Let's get our things out of the box, Matt."

"I can do that, sir," the driver said.

Thomas nodded and walked toward the house. Matt had already run to the front of the structure and peeked into a window. "What do you think, Sarah?" Thomas asked.

"It's—it's beautiful," she said.

Thomas forced a smile, feeling that his reputation was on the line, buying a house that they had never seen before.

Thomas wrapped his arm around Sarah's waist. They walked up the front steps. He held on tight and forced her to wait with him as they stood and looked at their new house. He cherished the moment and didn't feel hurried to enter.

"Let's go in, Pa," Matt said, placing his hand on the door knob.

"You're more anxious then opening Christmas presents, Matthew," Sarah said.

Thomas smiled and removed his arm from Sarah's waist. He stepped forward, dangling a ring of keys from his fingers. "All right, Matt, you go in first." Thomas turned the key and pushed the door open.

Matt dashed inside, leaving his parents standing at the door. He ran up a curved stairway, the dark wooden steps matching a banister with vertical spokes. That's quite a change from climbing a ladder going to my bedroom back in Missouri, Thomas thought.

— —

MATT SAW HIS NEW BED FOR THE FIRST TIME. He skipped to a window and looked out. A huge valley spread in front of him, blanketed with many trees. In the bottom, a blue streak of water wound through the trees and bushes like a snake.

He wondered why they called it the Mississippi. Matt had read about the river in school, and he knew that a state had the same name. Hmm, Missouri state and Missouri River...Minnesota state and Mississippi River...Matt thought that he needed to ask his father why the Mississippi River ran through St. Paul, Minnesota.

Matt skipped back down the stairs. His mother opened and closed cabinet drawers in the kitchen. My mother is one excited lady, he thought.

His father came in the front door carrying luggage. Matt rushed forward. "I'll help ya, Pa."

Matt ran outside, grabbed two of the smaller pieces, and lugged them through the doorway. His mother stood in the center of the room, her face beaming. "I found my room, Mother," he said.

"Do you like it?"

"Sure do. The window has a great view."

6

THOMAS FINISHED UPGRADING THE HARNESS AND SADDLE in the common stable behind his house. The long, low wooden structure served eight homes. Within the first couple of weeks, since his family had arrived, he purchased two horses, one to pull a new carriage and another for saddle.

He had a difficult time adjusting to the city after living in the country all his life. The attraction to Minnesota which he treasured the most was the 11,000 lakes he had read about. He had learned that Minnesota became a state in 1858, shortly before the Civil War.

Thomas also concerned himself about his son's education. He had promised himself that they would buy a home within a reasonable distance of an institution of higher learning. The University of Minnesota, which was within driving range of his carriage, opened its doors in 1869.

The next day, he would ride his horse and visit the grounds where the Union Stockyards were being built. He had an appointment to meet a Dan Brown who had hired him. Thomas concerned himself with Sarah. He hoped that she would find new friends.

Thomas felt encouraged on the previous day entering their house and meeting Marie Buntrock, their next door neighbor. Sarah and she hit it off real good, he thought.

– –

THOMAS RODE HIS HORSE SOUTHWARD, following the directions in a mailing that he had brought with him from Missouri.

Rolling hills dominated the countryside, much like in Missouri.

He passed by the last of a thinning row of residential houses. Up ahead, he saw the makings of a building and stacks of wooden posts and rails.

He rode up to a shanty that was built with wood and looked like a box. Thomas dismounted. A tall man wearing a wide-brimmed, black hat came out through a creaky door. "You must be Thomas Hastings. I've been anxiously awaiting your arrival."

Thomas shook the man's hand. "That I am, and I am here to meet a Dan Brown."

"Welcome to St. Paul—well, actually South Saint Paul. I'm dreamin' that a city will be built around the stockyards that we are buildin'."

Thomas visualized miles of corrals filled with cattle. "What type of work are you going to start me with?" he asked.

"You, Mr. Hastings, are going to be in charge of hiring the men who will work here. Since you've been a cattle raiser for many years and have had experience with employees, you should fit the job nicely."

Thomas smiled. "Ah can do the job, sir."

"Come on inside and I'll show you your desk and where you will be conducting your interviews."

The room had only one window and through it he saw the roadway that he had used to get there. The stack of papers on a desk attracted his attention. "Is that where I work?" he asked.

"You've got it right, Hastings. By the way, are you aware that the first governor of Minnesota was a gentleman by the name of Henry Hastings?"

Thomas forced a smile. "That was my father's name."

7

FIVE PROSPEROUS YEARS for Hastings at the stockyards had passed. During the year of 1890, Thomas got a new office in a brand-new central building at the St. Paul Union Stockyards. He used his gray mare to ride back and forth to and from work Monday through Friday.

Sarah busied herself daily with community social activities, her most prominent one being a volunteer at the local hospital. She had learned a great deal about Minnesota: State bird—the Loon; State flower—Lady's Slipper; and the State tree—the Red Pine.

Sarah had also demonstrated an interest in Women's Suffrage. After listening to a speech one day, she became deeply concerned about her rights as a woman. We do so much work and cannot legally vote, she thought. How ridiculous is that?

Matt attended the university, studying commerce and geography. He had an intense interest in local history, learning that Fort Anthony, a bastion for fur traders and such, was founded in 1820. In later years, the name had been changed to Fort Snelling.

As early as 1870, 440,000 people lived in Minnesota. They were mainly of German, Irish and English extraction, migrating from Europe to engage in farming the rich Minnesota soil.

Matt had read in the local newspaper that large numbers of people of different nationalities were currently immigrating to Minnesota. They mostly came from Norway, Sweden and Finland.

He learned that flour mills and lumbering had become prominent industries in Minnesota, leading to exportation of the by-products to the entire world.

Matt saw the name of John S. Pillsbury in the newspapers frequently. He must be one of the leading businessmen in the community.

— —

MATT HASTINGS GRADUATED FROM THE University of Minnesota in 1895. At the end of the ceremony, he accepted a warm hug from his mother and a soft handshake from his father. Matt felt concerned. His father's face showed pain. Matt heard forced breathing and a gasp.

His father's health had become Matt's biggest concern recently. Thomas had developed heart problems and was forced to resign from the Union Stockyards in 1896. Matt's mother remained in good health, busy as ever with her hospital and suffrage work.

Matt went to work for Pillsbury immediately after graduation, accepting a position in the bookkeeping department. During the first few months of employment, Matt took advantage of the St. Paul Railway system, riding it to and from work every day.

One drizzly April morning, the coach stopped in front of the Pillsbury building. He stepped out and opened his umbrella. A young woman behind him slipped on the step and crashed into his back almost knocking him down. He turned.

"So sorry, sir," she said.

"I'm Matt Hastings. Are you all right?"

"Oh, my ankle, I think it might be broken."

Matt held onto her waist and helped her through the front door of Pillsbury. He assisted her to a bench by the wall. "Oh, thank you so much. I'm Ann Polski."

— —

MATT HASTINGS AND ANN POLSKI WERE MARRIED in a quaint church, six blocks in distance from the Mississippi River, on July 13, 1896. One of his best friends whom he had met at the university was the best man. Ann's first cousin from Minneapolis filled in as her maid of honor.

The reception was held in a plush hotel, downtown St. Paul. Sarah had successfully convinced her brother Abel that he should attend. She felt enormous happiness and gratification when he agreed to come.

Thomas gave the toast during the meal. He directed his glass toward his brother-in-law. "I want you all to meet one of the bravest men who ever fought for the Confederacy—Abel Kinsley."

Thomas got a mixed reaction from the crowd but knew that he said the right thing. Grady would have been proud of me, he thought.

Sarah felt pleased that her husband had hired a carriage to transport them to the wedding, reception and back home again. She felt a chill in the air, but warmed when Thomas placed an arm around her shoulder during the ride back to their home.

The partial moon had begun its descent. "Thomas, do you realize that it's past 2:00 a.m.?"

He chuckled. "Yup, we sure danced up a storm, didn't we?"

"Oh, Thomas, that was so much fun. Ann certainly has a splendid family."

The clop-clop of the horse's hooves echoed against the wooded slopes of the Mississippi valley.

Thomas pulled his arm away. "Do you mind, Sarah? I need a smoke."

"Of course not," she said and gave his hand a squeeze.

Thomas lit his cigar. "Sarah, I have something to tell you and this could be the perfect time."

Sarah turned to look at her husband, a worried look on her face. "What is it?"

"I bought some land north of here in the lake country. I've always been a country boy and the day will come when I will want to be one again."

"Thomas, that sounds so exciting."

8

THOMAS PEERED AROUND THE CURTAINS of their front window. His son assisted Ann down from the coach. Thomas and Sarah hadn't seen them since their wedding day. "They're here," he said, looking back into the room.

Sarah hastened to join him at the front door. Thomas placed an arm around her shoulder, turned the knob and gave it a pull. The women hugged. The men shook hands. Jubilant hellos followed. Later, Thomas and his son sipped a brandy in the den. The women visited in the drawing room.

"Matt, Your mother and I have made a decision. We are going to move again."

"Move! But, you have it so good here."

"Yup, we do, but it's not my life style."

"Where are you moving?"

"I've bought some property up north in the lake country, near a small town called New Dresden."

Matt shook his head, frowning deeply." We'll miss you," he said weakly.

— —

MATT STOOD NEXT TO THE CONESTOGA WAGON. His mother and father sat up in their seats, awaiting the signal to move forward. He and several of his friends from Pillsbury had assisted his parents in packing their belongings. They spent hours loading them into the wagon. Matt wished that Ann could have come but she had a work conflict. The wagon is as full as it can get, he thought.

He had mixed feelings about the move—glad for his father who looked forward to a new life, but not so glad for his mother, who would likely experience huge burdens.

Matt heard a yell up ahead and suddenly his legs felt as stiff as fence posts. Matt knew that the wheels would soon turn. He stepped up next to his mother and wrapped his arms around her. He placed his lips on her cheek. Matt felt weak when she muttered softly, "Goodbye, son. I love you and will miss you."

Moisture built in his eyes as he remained snuggled next to his mother. Matt finally let go, grasped his mother's hands for a moment, and stepped down. The wagon in front of them began to roll. Matt quickly walked around to the other side. He reached up and grabbed his father's hand. "Good luck, Pa. I'll come out and see you two after you're settled."

Thomas nodded and tightened his grip on Matt's hand. Releasing quickly, he turned his head and saw all the wagons moving. He flicked the reins and the wagon lurched and rolled forward.

Matt watched for what seemed like hours before the last wagon disappeared from sight. Is this the end of something or is it the beginning? he asked himself. Matt slowly walked back toward his horse and buggy.

Book Four
The Hastings family: 1897

1

FRANK WAS BORN in the year 1897 to Matt and Ann Hastings. His sister, Ann, came the very next year. Following her, another sister, Helen arrived. Thomas's birth occurred on the first day of April, 1900.

In 1904, just after Joseph, his fifth child was born. Matt got word at work one day that his father, Thomas, had passed away. He sat behind his desk at Pillsbury for an hour, thinking strictly about his life in the past and his fondest experiences with his father. Matt thought about his mother, Sarah, all alone.

Matt turned the crank and started his 1904 Ford automobile. He got behind the wheel, put on his goggles and pushed a lever, sending the four-wheeled two-seater forward. He smiled all the way home, enjoying the wide-eyed glances he received from bystanders.

Matt felt tormented after breaking the sad news to Ann. He poured himself a whiskey and carried it into his study. He lit a cigar and thought about his mother. I should be there, he thought. I should be there helping her.

"What's wrong?" Ann asked after dinner.

"We have to move north. All of us have to move north."

Ann nodded and smiled. "I knew the day was coming, Matt."

She stood and walked over to her husband. She put an arm around his shoulder. "It was only a matter of time."

— —

The History of the American Automobile

BROTHERS, FRANK AND CHARLES DURYEA BUILT the first American gasoline powered automobile. They did not succeed in making it usable for general use.

Henry Ford built an engine in 1893 that ran. It resulted in the creation of his first automobile in 1896. He called it a Quadracycle and sold it for four hundred dollars. In 1899, Henry formed the Detroit Automobile Company but did not offer an auto for sale until 1903.

Ransom Eli Olds began production of his first petrol powered car in 1899. He had established the Olds Motor Vehicle Company of Detroit. His company sold 600 units in 1901, and as many as 5,000 units in 1904, becoming the first mass producer of gasoline powered automobiles in America.

The Rolls Royce Silver Ghost was built in 1906. The engine had six cylinders, and car remained in production until 1925.

The eight cylinder Cadillac roadster found its way to Winfield, Kansas. It was specially built for a doctor and had all the modern appliances of that time.

Driving an early American car required special clothing, including duster coats, goggles, hat and gloves. It also required abnormal skills, one of them being the ability to change a tire, as they were notoriously unreliable.

— —

BY THE YEAR 1916, THE RUMBLINGS OF WAR HAD SPREAD through Europe like creeper vines in Virginia. President Woodrow Wilson of the United States felt the pressure from his European Allies to intervene with the German Kaiser's attempt to conquer parts of the continent.

The headlines in the newspapers throughout the country blared in big ink: *War is Imminent!*

Frank Hastings had just celebrated his 17th birthday when the mailman delivered an envelope addressed to him. He read that he had been drafted into the United States Army and was ordered to report to a training camp in St. Paul.

Frank had four brothers and sisters, all younger than he. Thomas was too young for the draft, and he attended a one-room school house with his older sisters, Mary and Helen. Joseph had reached the age of five, too young to attend school yet.

Frank kept his face pressed against the passenger train window, watching his family, standing and waving on the platform. He slid his cheek to the far upper corner, keeping his family in view for as long as he could. The last family person he saw was his grandmother sitting stoically in her wheelchair.

The image of Grandma Sarah stuck in his brain as the train rumbled on. “She’s the grandest lady in the world,” he muttered, listening to the incessant clatter of the wheels.

REFERENCES

THE STAGE COACH INFORMATION WAS DERIVED from the Internet site of Linecamp.com.

The Telegraph section is based on an article written by Franklin L. Pope in 1872, but revived and posted on the Internet by J. Casale.

The credit for the information about barbed wire goes to the website: barbwiremuseum.com.

All of the information in the Northfield Bank Robbery section was borrowed from the wonderful historical book by John J. Koblas, *Faithful Unto Death*.

All of the information in the Posse section was borrowed from John J. Koblas's, *Faithful Unto Death*.

EPILOGUE

EXPLOSION AFTER EXPLOSION got on the nerves of Frank Hastings. I don't know if I can stand this any longer, he said to himself, peering over the edge, seeing only smoke and the broken branches of trees. He had spent almost an entire week in the same trench in France.

He looked up at the sky and saw a break in the clouds. It had been drizzling for three straight days. Frank avoided the murky, muddy bottom by digging out a seat into the dirt wall. The smell of earth had penetrated his nostrils at first but he had gotten accustomed to it.

Frank thought of home and his family most of the time but the hours dragged on. The nights are the worst, he thought. Some of the guys sleep on the ground above the trench, ignoring the potential danger. I did too if the wind wasn't unbearable. This has got to end. I cannot go on living like this.

$16.95 EACH
(plus $3.95 shipping & handling for first book, add $2.00 for each additional book ordered.
Shipping and Handling costs for larger quantites available upon request.

PLEASE INDICATE NUMBER OF COPIES YOU WISH TO ORDER

______	BLUE DARKNESS	______	GRAY RIDER
______	THE TOWERS	______	SLEEP SIX
______	DANGER IN THE KEYS	______	GRAY RIDERS II
______	NIGHT OUT IN FARGO	______	ICE LORD
______	PURGATORY CURVE	______	RIO GRANDE IDENTITY

Bill my: ❏ VISA ❏ MasterCard Expires __________

Card # ____

Signature ____

Daytime Phone Number ______________________________

For credit card orders call 1-888-568-6329

OR SEND THIS ORDER FORM TO:
J&M Printing • PO Box 248 • Gwinner, ND 58040-0248

I am enclosing $____________ ❏ Check ❏ Money Order
Payable in US funds. No cash accepted.

SHIP TO:

Name ____

Mailing Address ________________________________

City ____

State/Zip ____________________________________

Orders by check allow longer delivery time. Money order and credit card orders will be shipped within 48 hours. This offer is subject to change without notice.

THE HASTINGS SERIES

Blue Darkness
(First in a Series of Hastings Books)
This tale of warm relationships and chilling murders takes place in the lake country of central Minnesota. Normal activities in the small town of New Dresen are disrupted when local resident, ex-CIA agent Maynard Cushing, is murdered. His killer, Robert Ranforth also an ex-CIA agent, had been living anonymously in the community for several years. Stalked and attached at his country home, Tom Hastings employs tools and people to mount a defense and help solve crimes.
Written by Ernest Francis Schanilec (276 pgs.)
ISBN: 1-931916-21-7
$16.95 each in a 6x9" paperback.

The Towers
(Second in a Series of Hastings Books)
Tom Hastings' move to Minneapolis was precipitated by the trauma associated with the murder of one of his neighbors. After renting a high-rise apartment in a building known as The Towers, he's met new friends and retained his relationship with a close friend, Julie, from St. Paul. Hastings is a resident for less than a year when a young lady is found murdered next to a railroad track, a couple of blocks from The Towers. The murderer shares the same elevators, lower-level garage and other areas in the highrise as does Hastings. The building manager and other residents, along with Hastings are caught up in dramatic events that build to a crisis while the local police are baffled. Who is the killer?
Written by Ernest Francis Schanilec. (268 pgs.)
ISBN: 1-931916-23-3
$16.95 each in a 6x9" paperback.

Danger In The Keys
(Third in a Series of Hastings Books)
Tom Hastings is looking forward to a month's vacation in Florida. While driving through Tennessee, he witnesses an automobile leaving the road and plunging down a steep slope. The driver,

a young woman, survives the accident. Tom is totally unaware that the young woman was being chased because she had chanced coming into possession of a valuable gem, which had been heisted from a Saudi Arabian prince. After arriving in Key Marie Island in Florida, Tom meets many interesting people, however, some of them are on the island because of the Guni gem, and they will stop at nothing in order to gain possession. Desperate people and their greedy ambitions interrupt Tom's goal of a peaceful vacation.
Written by Ernest Francis Schanilec. (210 pgs.) ISBN: 1-931916-28-4
$16.95 each in a 6x9" paperback.

Purgatory Curve
(Fourth in a Series of Hastings Books)
A loud horn penetrated the silence in New Dresden, Minnesota. Tom Hastings stepped onto the Main Street sidewalk and heard a freight train coming and watched in horror as it crushed a pickup truck that was stalled on the railroad tracks. Moments before the crash, he saw someone jump from the cab. An elderly farmer's body was later recovered from the mangled vehicle. Tom was interviewed by the sheriff the next day and was upset that his story about what he saw wasn't believed. The tragic death of the farmer was surrounded with controversy and mysterious people, including a nephew who taunted Tom after the accident. Or, was it an accident?
Written by Ernest Francis Schanilec. (210 pgs.) ISBN: 1-931916-29-2
$16.95 each in a 6x9" paperback.

Gray Riders
(Fifth in a Series of Hastings Books)
This is a flashback to Schanilec's Hastings Series mystery novels where Tom Hastings is the main character. Tom's great-grandfather, Thomas, lives on a farm with his family in western Missouri in 1861. The local citizenry react to the Union calvary by organizing and forming an armed group of horsemen who become known as the Gray Riders. The Riders not only defend their families and properties, but also ride with the Confederate Missouri Guard. They participate in three major battles. Written by Ernest Francis Schanilec. (266 pgs.) ISBN: 1-931916-38-1
$16.95 each in a 6x9" paperback.

Sleep Six (Sixth in a Series of Hastings Books)
Revenge made Birdie Hec quit her job in Kansas City and move to New Dresden, Minnesota. A discovery after her mother's funeral had rekindled her memory of an abuse incident that had happened when she was six years old. An envelope containing six photographs, four of them with names, revealed some of her mother's abusers. Birdie moved into an apartment complex in New Dresden, using an anonymous name. She befriended three other women, who were all about the same age. While socializing with her new friends, Birdie scouted her potential victims. She plotted the demise of the four men whom she had definitely recognized...
Written by Ernest Francis Schanilec (250 pgs.)
ISBN: 1-931916-40-3
$16.95 each in a 6x9" paperback.

Night Out In Fargo
(Seventh in a Series of Hastings Books)
Tom Hastings property is within view of the senator's lake complex, and once again he is pulled into the world of greed and hard-striking criminals.Hastings is confused, not only because of the suspenseful activities at the senator's complex but also the strange hissing sound in the cornfield next to his property. Armed guards block him from investigating the mystery at the abandoned farmstead. Why are they there, and what are they hiding? Written by Ernest Schanilec.
ISBN: 1-931916-44-6 (280 pages)
$16.95 each in a 6x9" paperback.

Gray Riders II
(Eighth in a Series of Hastings Books)
The Gray Riders are in the saddle again, battling the Union in Western Missouri and protecting the folks of Tarrytown from ruthless jayhawkers. But their biggest threat comes from within - when an albino mountain man named Bone Erloch sets his sights on Sarah, Tom Hasting's pregnant wife. Gray Riders II brings back Grady, Justin Haggard, and all of his saddle mates. There is no shortage of new arrivals to spice up life in Tarrytown. So saddle up, it's time for a wild ride.

Written by Ernest Schanilec. ISBN: 978-1-931914-50-5 (276 pages)
$16.95 each in a 6x9" paperback.

Ice Lord
(Ninth in a Series of Hastings Books)
Tom finds himself up against a killer who haunts the fishing houses on Border's Lake. Tom spots the first burning house from his back deck, and is forever sucked into a world of vengeance and greed where it will take all his wiles to stay on top of thieving thugs, wisecracking bullies, two women who want his love, and a solemn murderer who believes he is carrying out God's will. The January ice will never feel so chilly again.
Written by Ernest Schanilec.
ISBN: 978-1-931916-56-1 (264 pages)
$16.95 each in a 6x9" paperback.

Rio Grande Identity
(Tenth in a Series of Hastings Books)
It sounds too good to be true. Ten percent return on your investment, guaranteed. Or so claims Rio Grand Development Corporation, a Texas firm that has Texas retirees lining up to plunk down their hard earned savings. Tom Hastings and his friend Samantha are at the head of the line with check books open, just as excited as the others. But then the questions arise. Why is a mysterious car parked outside their apartment in the evenings? Why does the neighbor's apartment burn down right after they give Tom a mysterious package for safe keeping? Why does the firm's director have to enter Texas crossing the Rio Grande on a creaky rowboat in the dead of the night?
Written by Ernest Schanilec.
ISBN: 978-1-931916-66-0 (288 pages)
$16.95 each in a 6x9" paperback.